GHOSTS:
Surviving the
Zombie Apocalypse

SHAWN CHESSER

CONTENTS

ACKNOWLEDGMENTS

For Maureen, Raven, and Caden ... I couldn't have done this without all of your support. Thanks to all of our Military, LE and first responders for your service. To the people in the U.K. who have been in touch, thanks for reading! Lieutenant Colonel Michael Offe, thanks for your service as well as your friendship. Larry Eckels, thank you for helping me with some of the military technical stuff in Ghosts. Any missing facts or errors are solely my fault. Beta readers, you rock, and you know who you are. Thanks George Romero for introducing me to zombies. Steve H., thanks for listening. All of my friends and fellows at S@N and Monday Old St. David's, thanks as well. Lastly, thanks to Bill W. and Dr. Bob ... you helped make this possible. I am going to sign up for another 24.

Special thanks to John O'Brien, Mark Tufo, Joe McKinney, Craig DiLouie, Armand Rosamilia, Heath Stallcup, James Cook, Saul Tanpepper, Eric A. Shelman, and David P. Forsyth. I truly appreciate your continued friendship and always invaluable advice. Thanks to Jason Swarr and Straight 8 Custom Photography for the awesome cover. Once again, extra special thanks to Monique Happy for her work editing "Ghosts." Mo, as always, you came through like a champ! Working with you has been a dream come true and nothing but a pleasure. If I have accidentally left anyone out ... I am truly sorry.

***

Edited by Monique Happy Editorial Services
www.moniquehappy.com

Prologue

Trying to become one with the massive Douglas fir, Raven squatted and pressed her back hard against its gnarled trunk. With the unpleasant sensation of coarse bark grating her skin through the thin tee shirt she'd thrown on during her hasty retreat from the compound, she strained mightily in the dark to hear anything over her heartbeat and labored breathing.

Finally, after a few seconds spent listening and probing the dark with her eyes for any signs of movement from the direction of the footpath leading to the grass-covered clearing, she heard twigs cracking and the hollow thuds of plodding, unsteady footsteps.

Then, seemingly from all around, she heard the ubiquitous rasps—like dried cornstalks rustling in a stiff breeze—of determined first turns on the hunt.

Stay here, her mom had hissed a beat prior to melting into the night, clad only in white panties and bra, minus the usual stubby carbine which was still in two pieces, an integral part having been dropped and lost in the deep grass hours earlier. In its place, clutched in Brook's fist as she left to become the hunter, was the black pistol she had dragged hastily from the holster still belted to the pair of pants she'd been forced to leave without.

Goose flesh welled up on Raven's forearms and rippled down her sides. She felt the rapid-fire *thump, thump, thump* of her heart threatening to leap from her ribcage. Her ears burned hot and her body heaved with each drawn breath.

Focusing on the moonlight-dappled game trail a dozen feet to her fore, she pulled her knees to her chest, held her breath, and strained to hear the sounds of the living: hard breathing, whispered words, a volley of gunfire; anything but the screams of the dying to let her know she was not alone.

But the latter came first. A shrill keening wail that set the hairs on her arms on end. It ceased after just a few seconds, but the echo careening through the forest lasted nearly as long as the shiver-inducing real thing.

Let Sasha have your rifle, her dad had said before leaving the Army base in Colorado. *We'll get you another after we get to the Eden compound*, Mom had said. *Famous last words* thought the twelve-year-old, her barely clothed body throwing an involuntary shiver. *Lot of good it did her*, thought Raven, fairly certain that the death knell had belonged to Sasha.

She couldn't fathom how things had gone so wrong so quick. One second she was asleep, warm under the covers, and the next she was being yanked from her bed in the dark by a pair of frantically grabbing hands. Then the light snapped on and her mom was ushering her out and grabbing the weapon. Strangely, as she sat nestled against the tree trunk, she couldn't remember her mom saying a word, merely pointing to what was happening outside.

Gunshots in the dark snapped Raven back to the situation at hand. *Three shots*, she thought. *Sounds of the living*. But the gunfire that she'd wished for had only summoned more dead from the surrounding woods. Oblivious of the trail, they crashed through the underbrush moaning, hissing, their numb bodies snapping off low hanging branches, the sharp reports making Raven jump.

Then her mom returned, two blurs of white cotton demarcating the tanned skin, black mane flowing in her wake. The pistol was thrust out in front with orange licks of flame lancing from the muzzle, the sharp reports quickly swallowed up by the nearby foliage.

The hollow thuds of infected bodies hitting the forest floor were suddenly interrupted by a creak of metal on metal that carried on the night air from the compound. Looking that way, Raven picked up indistinct male voices, giving her a modicum of hope. But the scene that she saw when she shifted her gaze back to her mom crushed it instantly. Took the air from her lungs. Gasping, she saw

2

her mom being yanked to the ground. Claw-like hands were twisted into her hair and more were reaching from the gloom, the dirt- and blood-crusted nails carving a jagged road map on her smooth skin.

The pistol bucked twice then suddenly went silent as a dozen shadowy forms piled on. Even in the dark Raven could see that her mom was doomed. Caught between the overwhelming urge to run into the fray unarmed or bolt and save her own life, discretion won out and she chose the latter.

With the metallic tang of freshly spilt blood hitting her nose, Raven witnessed the woman who had brought her into the world fighting for her life. Lashing out. Blows landed on decayed flesh to no effect. The struggle lasted for a second or two until finally, mouth locked into a silent O, all of the fight left Brook's petite form. As the dead rent flesh from her blanching extremities, her heart continued beating, sending blood sluicing from a gaping neck wound. It pooled around her head, black like a crow's wing, then shiny runners broke free and ran downslope, crisscrossing the dirt path in front of Raven's curled toes.

Terrified, she stood to run and was instantly tripped up on a knotty root angling away from the trunk. Eyes still fixed on her escape route, she went down like a base runner stealing second, face first, arms outstretched to cushion her fall.

While still airborne two things happened simultaneously. She screamed, shrill and high-pitched with a lot of lung behind it. Then, as quickly as it erupted from her chest, the soul-wrenching sound was cut off by what seemed like a kid's entire sandbox worth of dirt, pebbles, and pine needles, as gravity brought her back to earth face first.

Through her side vision she saw the monsters' heads turn in unison. With steaming entrails in their greedy clutches, they rose together and began a slow trudge in her direction.

Her second scream snapped her awake and, judging from the distinct smell of pitted metal and slight dampness permeating the air, she knew instantly that she was safe and secure in her new subterranean home.

In the next instant she was awash with gratitude and realized the hand clamped over her mouth stifling the scream belonged to someone with her best interests at heart. There were no dead piling on top of her prone form. No gnashing teeth rending meat from her bones. No wiry fingers scooping her innards out in preparation of a feast. Just a warm body with a familiar scent who whispered six soothing words: *"It was just a bad dream."*

The hand withdrew and Raven rasped, "Huh, uh. That was a full on *nightmare*, Mom."

There was a moment of silence.

"And in it *you* died."

"But I'm here now. Alive and well," said Brook in the dark. She kissed Raven on the forehead then added, "Shhh. Do you hear that?"

But before Raven could reply, two closely placed clicks echoed off the ceiling. Then the stark white radiance from the single sixty-watt bulb blinded her. Squinting, she shook her head. Answered, "No. What am I supposed to be hearing?"

"I guess it's more of a feeling right now. Get dressed," Brook requested. "And make it quick."

Nothing about this sounded good to Raven considering that the still lingering nightmare had commenced similarly. Fully convinced she was awake and had not been thrown back into the horrific scenario conjured up by her subconscious, she lowered herself from the bunk. As she pulled on a tee and a pair of jeans, her head tilted a degree to the side and, eyes still narrowed, she queried Brook: "When do I get my gun back?"

With one arm poked halfway through a sleeve and the other probing for an opening, Brook paused and looked at Raven one-eyed through the shirt's stretched out neck. "Why?" she asked before forcing her head completely through.

"I'd feel more comfortable. That's all." Raven looked away and finished dressing, lacing up a pair of boots left behind by the family that used to call this end of the compound home.

Brook said, "I'm sure we'll find something from the quarry that fits Sasha better. Then you'll get yours back."

Raven smiled then started the overhead bulb swaying, which sent the shadows against the wall undulating in random directions.

There were footsteps on the wood flooring outside and then a beat of silence which was followed by a light rap on the metal door.

Taking the two pieces of her disassembled rifle in hand, Brook rose and said, "Who is it?"

"Chief," came the sonorous reply.

Seeing that Raven was fully dressed, she opened the door and found herself eye-to-eye with the stocky Native American who went by Chief. Not a rank or noble distinction. He had made that clear when they first met. Just a nickname some of the inmates with like ancestry had attached to him during a long stint in a correctional facility in California. And though he was *Jake*—a derogatory name given the correctional officers in charge of the Native Americans' wing in the prison—no matter how hard he tried to distance himself from the nickname it was always there. With a nod, Brook said, "What's up, Chief?"

"There's a chopper inbound," he said slowly, in a soft voice that reminded Brook of how mall Santas talked to kids—only Chief's words were wholly believable. No underlying hint of subterfuge whatsoever. At that moment she decided the man held honor in high regard. Kind of reminded her of a much older version of her husband, Cade. Two decades older—at least. "I felt its vibration in my bones," she said. "Spent a lot of time around them lately."

Before Chief could respond, Raven squealed, "Daddy!" and bolted past both of them, the nightmare completely forgotten.

Grinning at the display of youthful enthusiasm, Chief said, "We better catch up with her."

Agreeing with a nod, Brook set her disassembled carbine aside and scooped up her gun belt with the compact Glock 19 snugged in its holster. Under Chief's watchful eye she drew the semi-automatic and aimed it at the floor. Checked the magazine, rammed it home, and cracked the slide to confirm that one was *in the pipe* as Cade was wont to say. "Good to go." She holstered the pistol, belted the drop-down rig around her waist, and secured the holster to her right thigh.

As Brook stepped into the corridor, the sound of rotor blades hammering the night air reached her ears. Louder still, footsteps and excited voices—male and female—bounced around the confined corridors.

She squeezed through the foyer and, storming out of the compound, instantly ran into the cool blast of rotor wash and found herself blinded by the brilliant white landing lights of the inbound DHS Black Hawk. Instinctively raising a hand to ward off flying debris and squinting hard against the blinding light, she pulled Raven close and watched the trio of younger survivors, in various stages of undress, form up next to her.

"They're back," Wilson shouted excitedly over the buffeting winds pushing ahead of the flaring chopper.

Raven craned towards her mom and hollered, "Is Daddy in there?"

"I'm sure he is," replied Brook. She thought: *He better be*, then glanced at her watch, which read 0125, and wondered what she'd be doing at this hour back in Portland if the Omega virus hadn't torn her small family's world asunder. Probably, she conceded, *shushing* a bunch of pre-teen girls who didn't understand the *sleep* component of *sleepover*. Far better than standing here, gut churning, hoping to see her husband emerge from the settling bird whole and unscathed, both physically and mentally. And seeing as how her trained eye told her that some of the other survivors here at the compound were exhibiting obvious signs of PTSD, one of her biggest fears was Cade coming home broken after one of these missions. Succumbing to depression and shutting everyone out. Or, the opposite, growing angry and lashing out at the world or loved ones, or—God forbid—both.

As the helicopter touched down it bounced minimally and rolled forward a couple of feet before the turbine whine dropped from a Banshee-like wail and the rotors began slowing noticeably. Clearly, thought Brook, the pilot, whom she barely knew, was still grappling with the finer points of flying the big noisy machine. Stomach in knots, she saw the helicopter's side door slide open and a slim woman whom she'd never seen before jump to the ground, crouch low, and hustle away from the spinning rotors.

Her anticipation mounting, Brook shifted her gaze back to the chopper and saw Daymon jump from the cabin, crossbow in one hand, and a stubby black shotgun in the other. Close behind him, two more camouflage-clad forms exited the craft. The first, brandishing a black carbine, she recognized as the former soldier named Lev. The second form was silhouetted against the airframe by the landing lights. She stared hard at the wavering form and concluded the build was all wrong. Whoever it was looked to be about Cade's height, but twenty or thirty pounds heavier. Then the man took a few steps forward, head bowed under the whirring rotors, and was illuminated fully by the glare of the landing lights. It wasn't Cade. Of that Brook was positive. She shook her head side-to-side as the completely bald and goateed stranger strode through the shin-high grass, following tentatively in Lev's footsteps.

Brook felt a tugging on her shirt and looked down at Raven and read worry in her eyes.

"Where's Dad?" she asked, her words choked and raspy.

Before Brook could answer, Raven's face blanched and a coughing fit ensued.

Casting furtive glances towards the Black Hawk, Brook gently patted Raven's back until the convulsions ceased. "You going to be OK?"

Nodding, Raven wiped a thin rope of drool from her lip. Then dried the back of her hand on the front of her shirt. "Probably just allergies," she insisted. To which Brook felt inclined to agree seeing as how Utah was probably host to a thousand different types of pollen.

A minute after the engine noise lessened, the Black Hawk's rotor blades became discernable as four separate spokes and began to droop noticeably. Finally the turbine whine died out completely, leaving the clearing in a crushing vacuum of silence.

Raven coughed again, a phlegm-addled fit that caused Sasha to venture over from her brother's side. She offered Raven a tissue then sniffed the air. "Smell that? she said. "Smells like smoke."

Raven's coughing bout subsided. She said, "It stinks like Schriever to me. Dad says it's from the JP something or other burning."

Sasha turned away. Stuck her nose in the air and said, "That's not just fumes from the helicopter." She completed the circle, sniffing the air as Wilson and Taryn looked on. "No way. That's wood burning ... somewhere. We better tell an adult."

"You're almost an adult," proffered Raven. "Said so yourself."

Shaking her red mane, Sasha stalked off towards the resident firefighter for confirmation.

Tugging Raven along by the hand, Brook took a few tentative steps towards the chopper and craned her head as the cockpit door facing her hinged open. A black boot emerged and planted on the grass.

Chest swelling, Brook walked her gaze up the tucked and bloused black pants leg and then over the like-colored load-bearing vest. A tick later a helmet broke the plane and she saw the short beard and ready smile underneath the smoked visor and was one hundred percent certain that the man in black was indeed her Cade.

Reuniting with him was always the same. She withheld all celebration until she had *eyes on target*—another of Cade's sayings. The call that had come in earlier indicating that he and his team were en route carried no water at all. It only told Brook that he hadn't died before the chopper was wheels up. There was no way for her to know if he'd been bitten or taken a bullet on the ground and died mid-flight. She'd been around the teams long enough to know that chickens weren't meant to be counted until they were back in the coop, so to speak. So up until now she had remained stoic and reserved for Raven's sake. But the instant she saw Cade's face, all of that went out the window and she let go of Raven's hand and sprinted into his arms with tears, hot and salty, flowing freely down her face.

***

Leaving the bulk of his gear in the chopper, Cade took the rugged Panasonic laptop and his M4 and walked with his ladies toward the compound entrance. There would be ample time tomorrow to go over the mission and debrief with Lev, Duncan, and to a lesser degree Daymon, whom Duncan had nothing but praise for, yet Cade wasn't completely sold on. Cade supposed spending more time with the dreadlocked firefighter might eventually bring him around to Duncan's way of thinking, but until his gut changed its tune, all of his training and life's lessons told him to take a kid gloves approach to their already strained relationship. That he hadn't let Daymon come along on the snatch and grab mission to Robert Christian's mansion in Jackson Hole was probably not completely forgotten, and figured into the man's sometimes surly demeanor. Time would tell.

For now, family and a good night's sleep called. The former needed much attention first. The latter, however, though as exhausted and road weary as he was, would never be attainable so long as the dead walked the earth.

Chapter 1
Outbreak - Day 40
Winters's Compound near Eden Utah

Three weeks had passed since justice was meted out inside the charnel house on the shores of Payette Lake in central Idaho. After returning to the compound aboard the DHS Black Hawk piloted by Vietnam veteran Duncan Winters, and with the night sky north showing an unnatural radioactive glow, Cade Grayson and his cobbled-together team were welcomed home like World War Two returnees—minus the tickertape parade, of course.

Jamie, who by all accounts should have had the hardest time readjusting after her short yet intense time as Ian Bishop's hostage, literally hit the ground running from the Black Hawk as if nothing had happened. And as far as the people who had been there were concerned, nothing had.

So with nothing to do but struggle forward putting one foot in front of the other, the small group of survivors circled their wagons, determined to honor Duncan's brother Logan in death by fortifying the compound as he would have wanted it—a task he was working towards the day he and Gus and Jordan were murdered at the abandoned mining quarry east of the Eden compound.

***

A handful of miles west of the compound, Daymon placed the chainsaw on the State Route 39 blacktop, removed his worn leather gloves and with both hands ruffled his newly formed beard, a move that sent tiny chips of pine and dogwood launching into the air.

He removed the sun-heated metal hardhat and trapped it between his elbow and ribcage. Ran his free hand through the picket of short wiry dreadlocks and found the credit-card-sized patch of scar tissue where the dead had relieved him of a handful of his tightly braided locks. He had wanted nothing to do with it when Heidi mentioned cutting the dreads. He'd been wearing his hair that way—more out of convenience and ease of care than any kind of statement—since his late teens. But in order to suture the ghastly wound he'd suffered, literally, at the hands of the dead, and to prevent the twisted locks from being torn from his scalp again, Heidi convinced him to let her cut the tangle of dreadlocks down to three-inch nubs and allow Brook to clean and suture the wound. In hindsight, Daymon thought, as he worried the area of semi-numb and fully hardened skin, he should have fought harder to keep them as they were.

Now, three weeks later, with the wound fully healed and two dozen rubber bands securing the *baby dreads*, he looked at his shadow on the gray asphalt and pondered the new nickname the ballbuster-in-chief, Duncan, had given him. *Sea Urchin* had stuck for the first week. Week two saw it shortened to just *Urchin* or *Urch* if Duncan had a few belts of whiskey in him. And the harder he lobbied the crusty Vietnam veteran to drop the moniker that made him bristle like the namesake sea creature, the more glee Duncan derived from uttering it. In fact, some of the other survivors had taken to calling him Urch. Behind his back at first. Then over the last couple of days, starting with Phillip of all people, he was being called Urch, often and unashamedly to his face.

Daymon stared hard at the shadow tentacles and decided that they did in fact seem to have a life of their own when he moved his head suddenly. Snorting in disgust, he tossed his helmet to the road where it clattered and spun before coming to rest upside down near the shoulder.

"Keep it down, *Urch*," cackled Duncan. "Or the rotters might find saws of their own and start cutting through yer barrier."

The buzz of the chainsaw was far more appealing to the dead than a simple clatter of metal on asphalt. Of this Daymon was certain. In fact, fifty yards to the west, over the interwoven tangle of trees blocking the two-lane, he could see the blackened and hairless

11

heads of the dead lolling side-to-side as they jostled for position. And though he couldn't see the condition of even the tallest rotter's body from sternum on down, in his mind he imagined their crispy naked bodies pressing futilely against the tons and tons of fallen timber. Only if he stood up tall, on his toes, could he make out the darting whites of their eyes seemingly hovering in space above pickets of stark white teeth—an illusion created when their lips and eyelids and all the other dangly fleshy bits cooked off when the nearby town of Eden burned down around them.

Daymon tilted his head back, closed his mouth, and drew in a deep breath through his nose. *No smoke*. Also gone was the awful stench of burning flesh that had sullied the air for a full week after the conflagration burned itself out.

He sat on the tailgate with the saw on his lap and started running a file over its dulled teeth. Lost in the monotony of the task, his thoughts wandered back over the events of the past three weeks.

He would never forget the first days back from the mission north. Exhuming Jordan's body and reburying her next to Gus and Logan and the others had also dug up dead and buried emotions. He spent the next two weeks in a funk thinking about his mom and all of his new ghosts while he and the other men went about stripping the quarry of anything useful, all the while breathing in the gray haze hanging low in the valley. And equally imprinted in his memory over those two weeks were the stunning red sunsets—byproducts of the unhealthy particulate-laden air.

Listening to the rasps of metal on metal competing with the dry rasps of the dead, Duncan rooted in a cargo pocket and extracted a battered flask emblazoned with the yellow and black image belonging to the First Air Cav, Airmobile, his old Army Aviation unit. With a practiced swipe of the thumb, he spun the cap off then tilted his head back and took a long pull, fully aware that he was being watched.

"Whatsa matter, Urch? I need to ask your permission before bellying up to the bar?" He shot Daymon a sidelong glare and added, "Don't worry. I'll be sober when we take the bird up."

Looking away, Daymon answered quietly, "No worries. That's your thing. I was just thinking about my Moms ..." He went quiet. Then, obviously deep in retrospective thought, he looked down and resumed his monotonous task. Slow even strokes. One, two, three. Then on to the next jagged gap down the line.

Duncan adjusted his glasses, stared incredulously at Daymon, and asked, "You ... had two moms?"

"No," answered Daymon, his brow furrowed. "It's not Ebonics speak. I just liked to call her *Moms*. Always have. That's all."

"She didn't make it?"

From the far end of the makeshift barrier, as if offering an emotional-filled yet wordless answer to the question, one of the newer turns milling there emitted a guttural, mournful moan.

Goose flesh rising on his arms, Daymon cast a glance towards the sound and said, "She was too close to Salt Lake. I tried, but—" He went silent and attacked the chain. The muscles on his forearms rippled as his grip tightened on the gnarled tool and the pace quickened. Then the file jumped from the channel and a raspberry-sized plug of flesh was left behind on one of the newly sharpened teeth. "Motherfucker!" Daymon hissed. Wishing he'd been wearing his gloves, he tossed the file to the ground, balled his hand into a fist, and watched the blood run around his wrist and hit the asphalt with soft little patters.

"Let me see that," drawled Duncan.

Tentatively, Daymon uncurled his fist. He flexed his hand, shrugged, and shot an *I'm OK* look Duncan's way.

Having none of the *tough guy* routine, Duncan sauntered over, took hold of Daymon's hand and, without warning, doused the wound with a liberal torrent of sour mash whiskey.

Flinching, Daymon said, "Thanks for the warning. Wanna kick me in the nuts too?"

"Just put your gloves on and we'll have Brook take a look at it later."

"Nurse Ratched?"

Both men broke out in laughter.

The dead joined in with scratchy cat calls and moans of their own.

Still smiling, Duncan said, "How'd such an easygoing fella get hooked up with a ball-breaker like her?"

"She's easy on the eyes."

"Heck yeah," said Duncan agreeably. "Coming *and* going."

Somewhere down the draw off to their left a pair of crows struck up a conversation. The cawing and chortling rose to a crescendo that lasted only a handful of seconds.

Daymon flipped the birds the bird then went on, "*Lift with your knees*, I heard her tellin' him. *Put some Neosporin on that cut*, she told Wilson. *Check the safety on that thing*, she told *me* the other day."

"You've gotta admit she fixed you up after your fight with the razor wire back at Schriever."

Daymon nodded in agreement.

"And she sutured your noggin up pretty good. Don't see as how Cade could do himself much better than that."

Chuckling, Daymon said, "I concur."

"And you had it coming, you know," Duncan said. "Can't go walking around with your piece hot and ready to go."

"I'm sorry. Hell, this thing is new to me," Daymon said, patting the Sig Sauer. He snatched the file off the road and laid it on the tailgate. Grabbed the gas can and swished its contents around. And, as if a light bulb just went off in his head, turned slowly and fixed his gaze on Duncan. "You told her? You were the one who narked me out?"

"Don't be sore. I'm just more observant with my new eyes."

"Next time tell me yourself ... spare me the embarrassment."

Duncan waggled the flask near his ear. Put it to his lips and drank the contents in one pull.

Daymon sighed audibly. He said, "I've got enough fuel to drop another dozen trees." He nodded at the pickup. "Then *I'm* driving us back. Agreed?"

"Understood." Duncan moved forward, alert for any of the newly discovered *semi-aware* creatures that may have crawled through the tangled warren of trunks and branches. "Clear," he said, eyes shifting, constantly scanning the forest on both sides of the roadway.

Without a word, Daymon yanked the Stihl to life and, like he was back to fighting wildfires, went to work on a nearby medium-sized fir.

Chapter 2

For the first time in a long time day-to-day living had settled into a normal rhythm for most everyone calling the Eden compound home. And since Jordan, Logan, and Gus were murdered at the quarry, the Grim Reaper had been conspicuously absent.

Heidi, unfortunately, was one of the few exceptions to this new normal. And though she hadn't actually met the Reaper, she was, however, slowly dying inside. Haunting memories of the terror-filled weeks as Robert Christian's concubine left her reluctant to leave the perceived safety of the subterranean compound. That she had watched a video clip of the man's execution by hanging made no difference. She claimed she could still smell his aftershave weeks after being dragged from his bed and dumped and left for dead beside the Teton Pass road. And though she never spoke of the horrors she'd endured at the 'House' on the hill in Jackson Hole, their effects on her fragile psyche were glaringly evident. Since she was constantly battling one anxiety or another, she didn't eat regularly and it showed. By her own account her weight had dropped to the fudged number she'd declared on her first driver's license fifteen years ago. Sleep was something that only came for her in the early morning, and though there was a total absence of natural light inside the compound she only got three to four restless hours and spent the rest of her time trying to connect with the outside world via the high-powered ham radio.

So she took a big gulp of tepid coffee, adjusted the headphones down to their smallest setting, and placed them over her head, leaving one ear uncovered. Before powering up the ham radio she glanced at the trio of wall-mounted flat panels recently installed by a middle-aged man named Jimmy Foley, the Eden compound's newest arrival. On the center screen both lanes and a hundred feet of the nearby east-west running state route were rendered in full color. Though the surveillance equipment taken from the quarry compound was state-of-the-art and beamed the video wirelessly from the cameras mounted in various locations about the property, the cameras themselves had a couple of weaknesses. The first being how the lens lent a gentle funhouse-mirror-like bend to the curving road near the gate. The second glitch was less annoying but still troublesome. Even though the feed was in HD it was virtually impossible even with optimum lighting to see who was driving the Police Tahoe straddling the centerline, let alone, to any degree of certainty, discern how many occupants were inside the vehicle. However, Heidi could tell who the two men standing near the vehicle were. On the left was Phillip, achingly thin and a hair under six feet. He held an AR-15 comfortably at low ready and was shifting his weight gently, foot to foot. Though she could hear nothing but the low rumble of the idling engine it was apparent that Phillip was talking to former Jackson Hole Chief of Police, Charlie Jenkins. So she picked up the Motorola two-way radio, checked the channel, and thumbed the talk button. "You hear me, Charlie?" After a moment of dead air she saw a flurry of movement in the gloom inside the police cruiser. Then her radio hissed and Charlie's voice came through loud and clear.

"Charlie here. What's up, darlin'?"

Heidi choked up momentarily. She imagined herself in the former police chief's shoes. Just the thought of traveling the roads east to the Woodruff junction, which based on eyewitness accounts was clogged with vehicles and teeming with dead, made her chest go tight. Venturing there in a group amounted to a huge risk. Going there solo, by her estimation, was little more than a death sentence. But Charlie was through feeling useless, he'd told her as much. And the last time she'd tried to talk him out of the foolish odyssey of his, he insisted he wasn't just chasing ghosts. He was hell bent on finding his daughter—or dying, whichever came first.

16

On the monitor she saw Phillip's head swivel around and his eyes seemed to lock with hers. Then a shiver wracked her body and she was back in the security pod, physically and mentally. Feeling the anxiety attack ebbing slightly, she took a deep breath, exhaled slowly and again keyed the talk button. "You sure you won't reconsider, Charlie? Just stay through fall and winter? Maybe those things—"

Cutting her off, Charlie craned out the cruiser's window and, looking in the direction of the black plastic dome housing the security camera, said matter-of-factly, "The rotters are here to stay, Heidi. And as far as the cold killing them ... Brook said the scientists at the Air Force base already tried and failed."

Heidi bit her lip, hard. She glanced at the Dollar Store shower mirror taped to a shelf just above eye level. The nearly bald woman staring back through eyes shot with tiny blood red capillaries made her shudder. She was practically bald by choice. She'd cut her hair weeks ago in solidarity with Daymon. But unlike his coerced trim job, she'd gone overboard and sheared her once long blonde locks down to stubble. And as she kept her hair short with a pair of electric clippers, the ensuing weeks spent underground lightened her already pale skin to the point where she looked like a concentration camp victim or, from a distance and in the right lighting, one of the living dead.

Her eyes darted to the trio of satellite phones sitting silent on the shelf near the mirror. For the third time in an hour a quick once-over confirmed they were powered on and plugged in, charging. Not wanting to risk another missed call, she picked up each phone individually and confirmed all of their ringers were turned on.

"You still there?" came Charlie's voice, sounding distant in the confined space.

Snapping out of her funk, Heidi keyed to talk and said, "You be careful out there, Charlie. I guess I just wanted to thank you for saving my life and reuniting me with Daymon." Up on the monitor she saw Charlie stick his hand out the window and wave. Then Phillip stepped back and the Tahoe started a slow roll east down the state route. As the engine rumble and soft hiss of tires faded away, Charlie said, "To serve and protect." That he was chasing ghosts and had a better chance of being struck by lightning than finding his daughter alive wasn't lost on Heidi as she wiped away a stray tear and watched the Tahoe crest the rise and disappear altogether.

Chapter 3

Weeks had gone by since Air Force Major Freda Nash had indulged in a drink. In fact, since the hell of a bender she went on after learning of the loss of her good friend, Delta Force Commander Mike Desantos, she'd all but sworn off the stuff. But the satisfied feeling of victory was diminishing. Softening around the edges. True, the nukes stolen from Minot Air Force Base were now back in the custody of the United States Air Force. And as a byproduct of that successful mission, thanks to a tip from Cade "Wyatt" Grayson—one of her *boys*—the perpetrators threatening the survival of the United States had been, to a man, eradicated. But that was then and this was now. Due to circumstances beyond her control a monumental decision had to be made. And the monkey wrench thrown into her machine was the temporary stand-down orders President Valerie Clay had recently dropped onto her and newly promoted General Cornelius Shrill's collective laps.

She kicked off her shoes and pushed her chair away from her desk. She had purposefully turned off all but the *red phone*—the direct land line connecting Schriever with the new White House deep inside Cheyenne Mountain, the old NORAD facility twenty miles to the southwest. Sequestered in her cramped little office over the last six hours mulling over the pros and cons of actually following through with her foolhardy plan had left her hungry, angry, tired, and lonely. But not necessarily in that order. Mostly she was lonely and had been since Z-Day plus one. The last three hundred and sixty some odd minutes, every second of which saw her locked in a battle of self will, had done nothing to ease the feeling of emptiness. Instead it had brought her to the doorstep of a conclusion to the detriment of her mind, body, and spirit. She was fighting a monumental headache that had her neck muscles corded and looking like twisted cables beneath the skin.

"Hell, Freda," she said to herself. "I think it's five o'clock somewhere. Prime time to self-medicate." A little liquid pain killer, she reasoned, wasn't far from whatever tranquilizer her own doctor would have prescribed—had he not perished along with the thousands upon thousands of other Colorado Springs residents. She rose and retrieved the tequila bottle from its hiding place. Closing the filing cabinet, she cast her gaze on the photo of her and her daughter Nadia. It was the first day of college and the USC freshman was on the receiving end of a kiss from her doting mom. Nash closed her eyes and relived the moment. There had been a breeze from the east, possibly the stirrings of a Santa Ana. It had been spring, but since it was dry and eighty degrees Freda had been uncomfortable in her uniform. It didn't show in the picture on the wall. Both women wore smiles. Nash's a little tight, like her smartly ironed and rarely worn dress blues. And Nadia's was toothy and wide, the prospect of autonomy and boys no doubt the culprit.

Nash placed the bottle, a squat rocks glass and a pair of shot glasses on her desk blotter.

She retrieved a tripod from next to the filing cabinet, extended the legs, and powered on the attached video camera. Placed it a few feet from her desk and checked that the autofocus was engaged.

"Fuck it." She twisted the cap and crinkled her nose. If this tequila was made from agave somebody had wiped their ass with it first. It definitely was not Patron. And it certainly smelled like ass.

Three fingers went neat into the rocks glass. She didn't bother lining shots up for the fallen. Since Z-Day there were just too many for her to acknowledge. So she poured another two count into her glass in honor of Mike "Cowboy" Desantos.

She engaged in a staring contest with the golden-hued liquid. Just as she was about to nod off the AC unit grumbled to life and the unexpected blast of cooled air had her wide awake and the tasks awaiting completion were once again front and center in her mind.

On her desk, sitting amid stacks of unfiled paperwork inches high, was her Panasonic laptop. Frozen on the screen was the compilation of satellite video footage she'd been watching on and off over the last six hours.

She looked at her watch. It was nearing noon and she realized she hadn't eaten since yesterday—whatever day that had been.

"Fuck it," she said again. "Use 'em or lose 'em." Simultaneously she set the video to moving on the laptop and downed half of the triple shot.

Chapter 4

Brook spread the white sheet out on the ground before her. Conveniently, the grass had been crushed down days before by Daymon, Lev, and Duncan. There were several spokes running off perpendicular from the landing-pad-sized circle and capped off, like antenna on a cartoon alien, by smaller car-sized circles of their own. Seven hours spent on a failed practical joke. She shook her head remembering the look on Cade's face when he first saw the manufactured crop circles. The first words from his mouth would stick with her forever. He gazed at the trio of survivors responsible, locked eyes with Duncan and said: *Why in the hell didn't they take you with them?* To which the funk they'd all been in from having to exhume and move Jordan's corpse to the makeshift cemetery on the hill was immediately lifted as laughter filled the clearing and the tears of joy flowed.

Still smiling from the memory, Brook cast a cursory glance over the two-foot wall of grass, located Raven on her bike in the distance, and only then did she proceed to break down her stubby Colt carbine.

She arranged the parts carefully, trying her best not to lose any of the small pieces as she'd done in the past.

But slow movements and due diligence weren't enough, and once again a small spring, integral to the operation of the bolt carrier group, squirted from her grasp and skittered a couple of feet before normal friction brought it to a complete halt, in plain sight—black on white—on the corner of the sheet.

"Fuck you, Murphy," she said quietly, policing up the part. She placed it close to her and wet a scrap of tee shirt with Hoppes #9 and proceeded to clean and oil all of the applicable components. There was no instruction taking place. All of the younger survivors, Raven included, could now just about breakdown and reassemble any of the firearms in the group's arsenal, in the dark. So she worked quickly and, using an old toothbrush on the bigger items, scoured them free of cordite residue and small particles of dirt and whatever else had found its way into the weapon's internals.

Ten minutes later she had finished the necessary maintenance, and while she put the M4 back together her attention was divided between Raven, who was making lazy laps of the clearing, a shirtless Cade, who was stretching pre-run, and Sasha, Taryn, and Wilson, who were in a far corner near the tree line taking turns with Daymon's crossbow, firing it time and again at the upper half of a store mannequin they'd brought back from the quarry compound. Though Cade's newly honed upper body was easy on her eyes, the latter scene held the most appeal. For every time the arrow hit its mark, the flesh-colored upper torso, which was perched atop a long metal pole jammed into the ground, would shake and shimmy like a drunk at a club doing the 'white guy' dance. And much to Brook's amusement, by the time the shooter crossed the open ground to retrieve their arrows—hits and misses alike—the target, as if beckoning the shooter onto the dance floor, would invariably still be moving at a metronomic pace somewhere between a Sashay and a half-assed Charleston. That the creepy armless department store fixture had been hidden in a footlocker along with its stand and anatomically correct lower half complete with shapely legs and a taut gravity defying rear end made Brook wonder not only who had stashed it away there in the first place, but why. The most logical conclusion was someone planned on making their own clothes sometime down the road. But the most unsettling, she conceded after a little deeper introspection, was that whomever had taken pains to squirrel it away in a box and then place that box in a footlocker and in turn hide the footlocker in a dark corner of the buried Conex container had to be a little embarrassed by its mere presence, and most likely had planned on using it in place of human companionship down the road when the need arose.

She threw a shudder thinking about being all alone in the world with only the dead and her thoughts keeping her company. Like Charlton Heston in the '70s movie Omega Man, she knew she'd be talking to herself first. Then, before long, maybe an imaginary friend or two would come into play. In the blink of an eye the nightmarish scenario played out in her head. And unlike Heston in the film and the person whose mannequin was taking a beating, shot through with scores of pinpricks of light to the point of becoming nearly see through, she had a feeling had she lost Cade and Raven she'd jump right past the mannequin stand in for company and instead suck on the Glock and end it all. That would shoot her chances of going to Heaven all to hell if her long-held beliefs rang true. But anything—even Hell or purgatory for that matter—would be preferable to living out her remaining days without her family.

Just as Brook was securing the carbine's upper receiver to its lower half, a shrill scream pierced the air. She lunged for a loaded magazine, slapped it home and was on her feet just in time to see Cade running an arm's length behind Raven's juddering mountain bike and playfully batting at her windblown pigtails.

The scream dissipated to nothing. Then, carried on the light breeze, Brook heard giggling and Raven hollering, "Stop it, Daddy. No fair. You're faster than me."

For a moment, the walking dead be damned, time stood still for Brook and most everything was alright in her world—or at least in this little corner of Utah she and her family now considered home.

A contented smile on her face, Brook set the carbine aside and went to work emptying the three polymer magazines, thumbing all of the rounds into a jangling pile in front of her crossed legs. After wiping an errant bead of sweat off on her white tank, she shook them one by one, rattling any loose dirt free and then blew sharply into each one before finally finger testing the spring's movement. Finally satisfied her rifle was *squared away*, as Cade would say, she began the time consuming process of loading the trio of magazines with the ninety loose cartridges.

Chapter 5

Glenda Gladson looked at herself in the mirror. Eyes the color of jade peered back. Her face had gone gaunt since the event, a good thing considering her plan. And though she didn't have a scale in the house—like every female Gladson who came before her she abhorred the things, especially the new *unfudgeable* digital models— she knew by her reflection, and the way her hips and ankles no longer hurt upon waking, that she'd probably dropped a good forty or fifty pounds since daily forays to the marina for an ice cream cone became a luxury of the past. Scattered atop the white oak vanity and collecting in a small pile around her bare feet were wispy curls of her gray-streaked auburn hair.

Fighting weight, she thought to herself, wincing as another lock lost out to her scissors and drifted feather-like to the hardwood floor. She figured she was now under a buck fifty sopping wet and all it had taken to get there was an extinction-level event followed by her town being besieged by both the dead and a group of local have-nots turned lawless hedonists.

Thankfully almost a month back a squad of soldiers in black helicopters had arrived unannounced and decimated the undesirables. The attack lasted less than ten minutes, and by the time she'd fetched the binoculars to watch the action up on the hill the helicopters were taking off again. But the Gods still weren't done challenging her and Louie. And apparently it wasn't their time either when the conflagration that first cleansed Eden jumped to Huntsville, driven by a hot summer wind, and burned ninety percent of the town but not nearly enough of the walking dead.

Eventually the fire burned out leaving the old Queen Anne and a couple of other older homes standing on the hill looking west over a sea of charred timbers and poured concrete foundations, last testaments to the town founded in 1860.

With all of the homes she was planning on raiding for supplies gone and her stores of food and water dwindling rapidly, she came to the conclusion she better get now while she still possessed enough energy to move and forage. "Yep, old girl," she mused aloud, still looking at herself in the mirror. "You're down to the same svelte chassis you flaunted sophomore year at Yale." She cocked her head and smiled, flashing her straight white teeth. "Look out Skull and Bones boys, here comes Glenda."

More hair lost the battle to sharpened surgical-grade steel as a dry rasp emanated from the room beyond.

"It's going to be alright real soon, Louie. No more hungering for my flesh every time I walk by." She opened a clamshell-shaped compact and dabbed the cotton ball in circular motions in the bluish-tinted compound inside. "God knows if I put your current condition out of my mind I start to tingle in all the right places. Hell, Bub, it's been a decade or more since you've shown me this much attention. *You* hit fifty and your old libido switch got thrown into the *not now honey* position."

The makeup went on smooth, casting her already pasty white skin with a deathly pallor. Paying extra attention to the area around her eyes, she created faux-shadows from her crow's feet to the bridge of her nose. Wiped a liberal amount on both cheeks, creating the perception that they were sunken even more than they actually were.

"Perfect," she exclaimed gleefully after a quick up close look in the compact's miniature mirror. Snapping it shut, she craned towards the open French doors behind her, rose, and walked stiffly through them and onto the second story veranda to survey the streets below. The odor of burnt flesh so prevalent following the great fires was gone. However, the sickly sweet pong of carrion had replaced it tenfold. But Glenda had grown accustomed to it. And acclimatizing herself to the eye-watering stench was part of her plan and one of the reasons she'd kept Louie around even after it was abundantly clear that help—let alone a cure for the so-called *Omega* virus—was never coming.

Thinking about how she came to this point in time, she walked back inside and sat down at the vanity. Unbeknownst to her, the *normalcy bias* that she and Louie had fallen victim to early on had saved their lives. In fact, when all of their neighbors were descending on the sole IGA store in downtown Huntsville to stock up, the false belief that everything was going to be back to normal—"As soon as the authorities intervene," insisted Louie—kept them at home on the hill and had ultimately saved them from the roving groups of infected that appeared seemingly out of nowhere the first day of the outbreak.

But it wasn't until later that she'd figured out where all of the walking corpses had come from. The close proximity to Ogden and the natural conduit that was 39 was the main contributor to Huntsville's downfall. First the waves of cars and SUVs full of families, some bringing along their infected, began showing up. Then the soldiers arrived on their heels and inexplicably sealed off the main roads in and out. But by then the damage had been done. The genie was out of the proverbial bottle and there was no putting it back in. So with the numbers of dead quickly multiplying, Glenda had crushed her rose-colored glasses and went with Louie on the foraging run that had sustained her to this point. And when they returned she had convinced the usually reserved Louie to forget about wood putty and repainting the damage and get off his ass and help her board up the windows and doors on the lower floor.

That move had saved their lives for the second time in as many days.

But two weeks ago Louie seemed to lose it. Started showing signs of dementia. Muttering about going to church. Resenting Glenda because of all of the Sunday drives he was missing out on.

Nothing she'd been through in her life up to that point could have prepared her for the one-two punch coming next. In the dead of night, with the flesh-eaters roaming freely outside, Louie had locked her in their room and went on a stroll to the garage to start the car—"To keep the battery charged," he'd said later. But all he'd accomplished during the foray was getting bit and somehow finding his way from the garage back to the house alone and confused and bleeding. How Louie escaped the dead was still a mystery to Glenda. And why none of them had followed him inside afterward she'd never know. Because by that point Louie couldn't name the sitting President, let alone what can of food they'd last shared for dinner.

Glenda had patched him up and hoped for the best. But the latter wasn't in the cards. Such a small wound, she'd thought at the time. Louie lasted six hours. Once he ceased fighting Omega and died for the first time it took Glenda thirty seconds to tie him to the deathbed and begin planning her escape.

Louie's turn was horrific. He fought against his restraints and snapped at her. In that moment when he crossed the plane from her slack-faced peaceful Louie to hungering-for-human-flesh Louie she decided that he was going to help her survive the dead one last time.

Glenda blinked away tears and stared at the photo of her sons. Pete and Oliver. Both good boys. When the outbreak started Peter was at his house in Salt Lake City with his small family. Last Glenda heard from him he was venturing out to the Lowes for supplies so he and his wife and their two young kids could ride the *event* out *until help arrived*. Oliver, the youngest at thirty, the odd bird in the family, had been habitually out of work and was allegedly hiking the Pacific Crest Trail, and for all she knew, was still alive— somewhere. Carefully, Glenda took the framed photo and laid it face down. She did the same with the most recent school pictures of her grandkids. The photo in which she and Louis were in their thirty-year-anniversary pose received the same treatment, leaving them destined to stare at the vanity top together—forever. Then she retrieved the letter she'd composed earlier and left it on the overturned frames, in plain sight, where it would be easily found.

With hot tears still rolling down her cheeks, she rose and walked slowly to the railing and gazed at the downtown core which amounted to nothing more than a handful of sign poles and a picket of soot-covered light standards rising above steadfast cement foundations also darkened by the incredible heat of the passing flames. Save for a few pleasure boats anchored in place and hiding who knew what behind darkened portholes, the reservoir, pristine and glasslike under the noon sun, was a scene deserving of a full-page spread in a travel magazine.

Admiring the tattered pink bathrobe concealing the layers of magazines she'd diligently duct taped to her arms and legs, Glenda shuffled the length of the porch, performed a wooden-looking pirouette at the far end and then limped back, careful to keep her hikers from squeaking on the wood decking underfoot. And as she transited the twenty feet in plain view of the dozen corpses patrolling the street below, a cursory glance from them was all the gimpy stroll garnered. *Perfect*, she thought. *Time to the ice the cake.*

***

This was the phase of the plan Glenda hadn't given much thought to. So she stood in the middle of her kitchen, eyes moving over the counters until her gaze settled on the set of knives there.

Too messy.

She opened drawers and pawed through the specialty cooking gadgets that rarely saw the light of day. Hefted the metal mallet she'd used now and again to pound cheap cuts of meat palatable.

Too noisy.

She considered risking a trip to the garage but, fearing an outcome like her husband's, quickly dismissed that idea.

Rifling through a little-used drawer she spotted two possibilities. But seeing as how she had no idea how deep inside the cranium the area of Louie's brain the CDC scientist on television said she needed to destroy was located, she quickly ruled out the pewter-hued pick that worked so well at rending walnut meat from the shell. Ditto on the sharpened spike that hadn't chipped ice since the Reagan era when she'd found a daily drink necessary to quell the notion that the cowboy President was trying his hardest to get every man, woman, and child in the United States incinerated in a nuclear exchange with the old U.S.S.R.

She slammed the drawer, muttered an expletive that would have made a merchant marine blush, and exited the kitchen. Passed through the little-used formal dining room and, after throwing the lock, slid the pocket door open with force sufficient to bang it into the back of its housing. A blast of stale air hit her in the face as she crossed the threshold. Then, making a beeline for the sewing table taking up space in the converted butler's pantry, she looked at the carpet and realized that she was walking with her normal gait and another salty outburst left her lips. Followed instantly by: "*Get with the program, Glenda*," bellowed loud enough to cause Louie's reanimated corpse to answer back from upstairs with a goose-flesh-inducing moan. "Who asked ya?" she countered as her gaze fell on precisely what she'd come looking for.

Chapter 6

By the third lap Cade found his second wind. Legs pumping furiously, he followed in his own footsteps counterclockwise around the clearing, creating a nicely beaten-down path through the knee-high grass. Freed from the husk, seed filled the air forming a turbid comet-like tail in his wake.

Four more laps, he thought as he cut the corner behind the *Kids,* who had retired the half torso and were taking turns firing arrows into a four by eight foot rectangle of plywood. In a way he was pretty impressed because these daily practice sessions had started immediately after, and seemed a direct result of, unsolicited advice he'd offered up days ago. *Instead of sitting around and rehashing days gone by,* he remembered saying to Sasha, Wilson, and Taryn, who had been doing just that in-between the doled out daily chores, *you oughta start honing new skills that will see you through the days yet to come.* True, it was the same kind of *woo woo* shit Mike Desantos was apt to say to one of his Green Berets trainees on a rudderless tangent. And since Cade had learned most everything he knew about survival from Greg Beeson and then later from Desantos himself—the fact that he'd just spouted some *woo woo* shit didn't surprise him one bit.

He saw Taryn take a deep breath and exhale as he passed silently a half-dozen yards behind her. Then he craned his head ever so slightly and saw her lean in and release the arrow and registered the direct bull's eye in his side vision as he passed underneath the static Black Hawk's drooping rotor blades.

The young people were turning the corner. That was for sure. Wilson, Taryn, and even Sasha had fired their weapons in self-defense and emerged unscathed. A little shaken, one and all, but safe all the same.

Brook, on the other hand, was slow in coming to grips with her part in countering the ambush set for them outside of Green River, Utah. That she'd killed at least three men in the process was hard for the nurse in her to accept. Her job had always been to nurture and care for other humans—Raven especially. And now that she was on the other side of the equation she had begun to question her own morality.

Cade deviated from the tamped-down trail and leaped powerfully, clearing the blanket and Brook, blowing a kiss in her direction before spinning around on his fully healed left ankle and powering off towards the far end of the clearing where the brown stripe of unimproved airstrip gave way to thick forest, the edges of the leaves on the deciduous trees already turning muted shades of yellow, orange, and red.

Scooping up the loose shells she'd dropped when Cade had startled her, and picturing the shit-eating grin no doubt spreading wide on his face, Brook, fueled by justifiable anger, hollered after him, "You little shit, Cade Grayson. I almost peed myself." As she watched him near the end of the clearing without breaking stride, there was a whooshing to her right and Raven screamed along the trail on her metal steed, pigtails flowing freely behind her.

Barely a second later a furry brindle-colored missile, following the same tangent as Cade, cut the airspace above Brook and scattered the rest of the rounds destined for the half-filled magazine still clutched in her hand.

"Damn it Max! You too?" Momentarily exasperated, and slightly amused, Brook dropped the magazine and plopped onto her back on the blanket amongst the tinkling brass and stared up at the handful of fluffy white clouds scudding overhead.

Cruising by the *motor pool*, Cade eyed the dozen or so vehicles parked under the double canopy. Yin and Yang—the immense flat black F-650 and once shiny white Ford Raptor—sat quietly side by side, gassed up, grills facing the clearing and ready to go at a

32

moment's notice. Duncan's repatriated Humvee sat nearby within a cluster of American and import trucks and SUVs, its turret-mounted .50 caliber Ma Deuce aimed menacingly across the clearing at the tunnel in the forest where the feeder road from nearby SR-39 emerged.

As Raven passed Cade on a parallel path of her own making she registered as a purple and chrome blur in his side vision. Her breathing, however, sounded distinctly and loudly over the swishing grass and clicking of the bike's freewheel. It was the new normal. A soft wheezing that Brook had written off as late summer-early fall allergies, usually remedied by a half-dose of one of the adult strength Benadryls the late Logan had thoughtfully stockpiled. But this sounded different to him. A kind of *snap* and *crackle*. Kind of like Rice Krispies minus the *pop*.

He made a mental note to have Brook utilize the stethoscope—another prep of Logan's—and listen to Bird's chest.

The final four laps, roughly a mile and a half, Cade guessed, went by in a blur without so much as a twinge from the ankle he'd nearly broken in a helicopter crash a little less than a month ago. In a way he wished for a little residual pain. A sharp stab now and again. A dull ache, maybe. Hell, anything to serve as a subtle reminder of the friends who hadn't survived the jarring impact with the Dakota soil and the subsequent race from the crash site, hundreds of walking dead closing in on all quarters.

Sweating profusely in the noon-time sun, Cade plopped down next to Brook. Chest heaving, he rolled over onto his side and stared up at her. He was going to mention Raven's labored breathing when the hairs on his arms stood to attention. He sat bolt upright and remained stock still as beaded sweat made the slow journey over his furrowed brow, meandered down the bridge of his nose and hung there, seemingly frozen.

Brook rolled her shoulders forward and mouthed, "What?" Simultaneously her nose crinkled and she reached for her carbine. In one fluid motion she slapped a magazine in the well and racked back the charging handle. Off went the safety as both her olfactory sense and Cade's whispered words dumped a tsunami of adrenaline into her bloodstream.

Chapter 7

In normal times and under normal conditions a number ten knitting needle is good for little beyond its designed purpose. Outside of knitting colorful throws and scarfs and silly lopsided cubes only uglier than the pastel-hued Kleenex boxes they covered, scratching an itch deep inside a plaster cast was the only other use Glenda had found for one of the ten-inch anodized items.

But times had ceased being normal and conditions had deteriorated so fast and severely that she was no longer an atheist and now believed wholeheartedly that she was living in the oft talked about *end times*. So, needle in hand, she left the repurposed butler's pantry, closing the pocket door behind her, softly, the action matching her mood. Resignation mounting, she went back into character, dragged her toes across the carpeted floor, and, contrary to how she'd been walking for close to sixty years, consciously distributed her weight as unevenly as possible and shambled to the base of the stairs, which, to avoid a fall and possibly a broken a hip, she scaled normally.

Resuming the uncomfortable routine, she hobbled down the upstairs hall, entered the master bedroom, and then stood beside the king bed, wavering silently, mouth agape.

Reacting to her presence, the trussed and decaying creature that used to be Louie turned its head slowly but remained placid, its dead eyes moving up and down, in sync with her swaying motion.

She smiled. *Aced the test, Glenda.*

The monster in her bed reacted instantly to the display of emotion by letting out a rasp and straining mightily against the makeshift four-point restraints. Eyes moistening, Glenda cast her gaze at the pantyhose tied to her undead husband's stick-thin wrists and ankles. And once she determined they were holding fast and there was no danger of the blood-slickened bonds sliding off, she bent at the waist and whispered into the creature's ear, which, after having been chewed off in the zombie attack, was little more than a shiny crescent-shaped scrap of cartilage abutting a pus-encrusted dime-sized orifice. "You were right, honey. There is a God."

Glenda let her forearm hover an inch above undead Louie's snapping teeth and tattered bits of flesh—all that remained of the once million dollar smile. "Honey," she said. The creature went still and regarded her momentarily, as if a snippet of memory had been jogged. Then, with the awful sound of vertebra cracking and popping, it lunged and found purchase on Glenda's terry cloth robe, clamping down firmly midway between her wrist and elbow.

Instead of recoiling, which Glenda's inner voice screamed at her to do, she put one leg on the bed and her entire upper body on the zombie's sternum. Hearing what she presumed was a rib or two breaking under the trifecta of gravity, her weight, and the latter two crushing against the corpse's futile thrashing, she lodged her forearm in deeper and pressed its head hard into the pillow. "I'll see you on the other side," she said quietly as the number ten needle met a little resistance at first, then slid cleanly, behind a considerable amount of applied muscle, into one of her undead husband's baby blues.

Newton's Law made two things happen near simultaneously. First the eyeball imploded, releasing a copious amount of foul-smelling black fluid from within the thing's cranium. Then, as the needle perforated the frontal lobe and continued on deeper and hit bone, all fight left the bucking corpse and Glenda rent her arm from its slackening maw. Finally, as if the act itself wasn't morbid enough, seemingly in slow motion, the pasty eye socket filled to brimming and overflowed. Still clutching the needle, Glenda felt the cold blood wetting her clenched fist and watched it cascade down the corpse's cheek and form an uneven black halo on the sheet around its head.

Slowly, with the finality of the act still settling in, Glenda slid from the cold corpse, released her grip on the needle, and wiped her bloodied hand on her robe.

Trembling slightly and dreading what was to come next, she whispered, "I'm sorry," and trudged towards the vanity to fetch the scissors.

Chapter 8

Head moving *on a swivel* as Desantos had drilled into him years earlier, Cade rose to standing, turned a half circle and locked his gaze at the break in the trees just left of the gravel feeder road. Quietly and slowly he said, "We've got company."

Nose crinkled against the sickly sweet stink of decaying meat, Brook replied, "I smell 'em. And they're *real* close."

Grabbing Raven's wrist before she could wheel away, Cade plucked her off her bike and handed her off to Brook. Turning back, he yelled across the clearing at the Kids. "Wilson, where's Chief?"

Hollering back, Wilson answered, "Chief Jenkins *just* left for Salt Lake."

"*No*," Cade bellowed, shaking his head. "*Chief.*"

"Oh ... *Chief.* He and Lev are hunting ... left at dawn," replied Wilson, dropping the crossbow in the grass.

Realizing that he and the Kids were the only ones available to counter however many Zs had breached the wire, Cade called for Wilson, Taryn and, rather reluctantly, Sasha to join him. At once a black pistol appeared in Wilson's fist and the twenty-year-old former fast food manager was on the move with Sasha, his fourteen-year old sister, and Taryn, the raven haired nineteen-year-old survivor from Grand Junction, Colorado, following in his footsteps.

Silently, his cropped ears fixed facing upwind, Max threaded his way through the grass, passed between the trunks of two massive fir trees, and melted into the woods like a wolf on the hunt.

With a pained look settling on his face, Cade scooped up his carbine, which was on the sheet and next in line to be cleaned and oiled. He addressed Wilson, who had swiftly closed to within a dozen yards. "Duncan and Daymon ... where are they?"

Skidding to a halt and breathing hard, Wilson shook his head, saying, "They're out working on the roadblock."

Cade held Wilson's gaze for a second, came to a decision, then looked to Taryn. "You two come with me." He grabbed Brook's elbow. Drew her near and whispered, "You have a radio?"

Brook nodded.

"Good," Cade said. "Get inside with Rave and Sasha and keep them close by." He stared at the redhead and said, "You good with that?"

Nodding, Sasha fingered her rifle nervously and then walked her gaze over the impenetrable gloom at the clearing's edge.

Again Cade said, "Good." Shifting his attention back to Brook, he added, "I'm taking these two with me. We'll check the inner perimeter first." He kissed Raven on the head, Brook on the mouth and, looking into his wife's big brown eyes, said, "If we don't return, I *do not* want you to come looking for us. Do not leave the compound unless your survival is at stake."

Understanding the implication behind the statement yet remaining stoic in the face of the possibility of losing Cade to a little bite or another breather's bullet, Brook corralled her carbine and herded the girls towards the compound entrance. She craned over her shoulder and saw Cade striding towards the tree line, clean-shaven and bare from the waist up, the *INFIDEL* tattoo between his shoulder blades rippling with menace. Then, catching her off guard, her man's deep voice emanated from the two-way radio buried in her thigh pocket and she listened as he relayed his intentions to Seth and Heidi and anyone else who was listening.

Chapter 9

Heidi started when the two-way radio came to life with a shrill electronic warble. Fearing that her old friend Charlie Jenkins had run up against a horde of undead and was in trouble less than ten minutes into his journey to Salt Lake City, she snatched the chiming handset from the shelf just as another voice emanated from its small speaker. Instead of a plea for help coming from Jenkins, the words of one of the compound's newest members, delivered crisply and in a businesslike manner, dropped a more ominous and danger filled sit-rep (situation report) onto her lap. Simultaneously the words *Zombies inside the wire* filled the air and resonated loudly in her mind. A nanosecond later the first tendrils of fear caressed her spine, cold and feathery. "Copy that," she replied. "How many? And where?" Releasing the *Talk* button she stared ahead at the sat-phones plugged in and charging, their little lights pulsing independently of one another, like a trio of hearts beating to totally different rhythms.

On the other end, Cade said nothing.

Thumbing the *Talk* button again, she first asked if anyone else could hear her, then pressed Cade for more information. There was nothing but dead air for a few long seconds before she heard Lev's voice, tinny and distant. "What's going on?" he asked.

"We have *zombies* inside the wire."

"Where?" asked Lev.

"No idea," replied Heidi. "Cade just reported it and then went silent."

Lev said, "Try him again."

"Copy that," replied Heidi. "Cade. You there?"

Nothing.

"Come in, Cade. You have anything new for me?"

Still nothing.

Breaking the silence, Lev said, "Me and Chief are a mile east of the compound. Bagged a mule deer but we'll leave it and beat feet to the clearing. Be listening in for updates. Over and out."

"Good copy," said Heidi, ending the call. She looked up at the container roof and sighed loudly. Lev asking for information that she couldn't provide had left her feeling hog tied. Cade not answering her repeated calls was beginning to piss her off. Giving him the benefit of the doubt, she waited another full minute and when she'd not heard a peep from him, nor anyone else, she set the Motorola aside, swiveled her chair towards the partitioned flat screen and spewed a string of expletives under her breath. Still wondering why Phillip—who was never at a loss for words—hadn't responded yet, she settled her gaze on the upper right panel showing the area near the concealed gate where she had just watched him seeing Jenkins off. The Tahoe's bulk was no longer filling up the screen and the thin forty-something was also out of frame, no doubt still hiking back up to his hide overlooking the road. In the lower left rectangular partition, the camera trained on the clearing picked up only the gentle wave-like movement of an early fall zephyr coursing through the sun-splashed grass. And sitting there, small and silent and inert in the background, was the gold and navy blue DHS Black Hawk. The other panel showed the smattering of gore-streaked pick-up trucks and SUVs sitting in the *motor pool*, but no rotters. Heidi returned her gaze full circle and studied the front gate feed again. *Where are you, Phillip*, she thought. And just as she was about to pick up the radio and try to raise him it crackled to life, he said, "Phil here. Jenkins is gone and the gate, fence, and road are clear of rotters."

"Roger that," said Cade.

Bastard, thought Heidi. She kept her eyes glued to the monitor and didn't bother acknowledging either of the men. *What's the use?* Shaking her head, she shoved the Motorola across the desktop and it shot off the edge and clattered to the floor.

A beat later Brook and Raven appeared in Heidi's side vision, moving left to right behind her, a hint of carrion-tinged air trailing them. In passing, Brook asked, "Did you call everyone back to the compound?"

As if she'd just been asked the stupidest question in the history of the world, Heidi smirked and answered with a nod. *See how you like the silent treatment,* she thought to herself as she watched two-thirds of the Grayson family disappear around the corner.

***

With the strange one sided interaction with Heidi on her mind, Brook burst through the door to the Graysons' spartanly appointed quarters and, with a brisk tug of the dangling string, clicked the single light bulb to life. Under the gently swaying cone of diffuse yellow light she maneuvered Raven to the nearest low slung bunk and, after getting the girl's full attention, ordered her to remain in the compound until either her or Cade or one of the other survivors came for her. Told her in no uncertain terms to stay away from the front entrance and if a problem arose she was to get out via the emergency escape tunnel hidden behind a false wall fronted by a phalanx of plastic five-gallon buckets in back of the dry storage area. Then Brook had Raven repeat, verbatim, what she'd just said and made doubly sure the diminutive twelve-year-old was clear on how to get to their family's pre-arranged rendezvous site.

Once she'd repeated every detail to her mom's satisfaction, Raven cocked her head and thrust out her arms.

Satisfied that her girl was in a right frame of mind, Brook wrapped her up in a tight embrace. Held her for a ten count then rounded up the lightweight Ruger 10/22, confirmed that the safety was engaged, and placed the rifle across her daughter's slender knees. Finally, flashing a tight smile and with her own stubby carbine in hand, Brook strode purposefully out the door, closing it firmly behind her.

With the possible finality of their parting driven home by the metallic clang echoing in her wake, Brook passed ghost-like behind a preoccupied Heidi, transited the T and, just as her eyes began to mist, entered the darkened entry foyer. A pained smile tugging the corners of her mouth, Brook thought glumly, *Mission accomplished.* In light of the circumstances, which up to now she had been treating as a worst case scenario, that she'd successfully adhered to her own self-imposed edict to *not* cry in front of Raven was monumental to say the least. To remain stoic, and, childhood and lost innocence be damned, begin forging the girl into the weapon she must be in order to survive her tween years was her and Cade's unspoken common goal. So tears, they had concluded, must be shed away from the impressionable girl. Teaching her it was acceptable to wear her emotions on her sleeve, Cade had said during a private moment, was tacitly setting her up for failure. Unknowingly conditioning her ever so slightly that one day in the future emotion might win out over practicality thus giving her a reason to give up in the face of adversity. Hard as it had been for Brook to implement the doctrine herself, ever since Cade's mission north to retrieve President Valerie Clay's stolen nukes she had, so far, successfully kept a week's long streak intact.

But the prospect of losing the newfound normalcy this little slice of heaven nestled in the glacier-carved valley in rural Utah now provided was too much for Brook to bear.

So with hot tears painting silver rivulets down both cheeks, she choked back a sob, closed the outer door and locked it with the supposedly zombie-proof mechanism Chief had devised, and pressed the Motorola to her lips.

***

Shattering the still, like some kind of military Klaxon in the confined space, one of the Thuraya sat-phones screamed for attention. Heidi plucked the offending device off the shelf, glanced at the display and let it finish ringing. *He's not answering*, she thought to herself as the LCD screen went dark. Then she replaced the phone on the shelf and said under her breath, "And I sure as hell ain't nobody's secretary."

As if in response, taken more like an accusatory retort in her troubled mind, the sat-phone emitted a soft beep and the green LED transitioned from the usual heartbeat-like rhythm to a more urgent attention-getting strobe.

Chapter 10

For Glenda, making the initial incision went much better than performing the coup de grace. In fact, Louie's eye had proven harder to puncture than the skin above his navel and, hard as it was for Glenda to fathom, due to gravity and three weeks in a supine position there was very little blood. Just like she'd done hundreds of times when wrapping presents for her kids and grandkids, she opened the scissors a few degrees and inserted the lower blade just under the pallid dermis and let the upper blade remain outside the body. With a little forward pressure the sharp edge rode just underneath the skin and, like cutting a sheet of wrapping paper, she opened Louie up from navel to sternum. The sucking sound she was expecting didn't happen. There was little of what decades of watching horror flicks had conditioned her to expect. A writhing mass of milky guts didn't burst forth, showering her with bile. The full scope of what she was trying to do didn't hit her fully until she snipped through the atrophied muscles and sinew and got her first glimpse of her beloved's inert internal organs.

Grimacing from the stench that even three weeks cooped up with the living corpse had failed to prepare her for, she reached a gloved hand inside the puckered opening, rooted in the cavity, and came out with a slimy rope of intestine. Not stopping there, she punctured the thin membrane and slathered a handful of its rotten contents over the entire front of her bathrobe. On the verge of retching, she cut free a three-foot length with the scissors and whipped it over each shoulder a couple of times, adding a matching coating of blackish sludge to the back of her robe. And as she did so she imagined that to a casual observer, her actions could have easily been mistaken for self-flagellation.

"I'm sorry, Louie," she said during a silent lull between wet slaps. "It's the only way." She looked away from his unmoving corpse and settled her gaze on the cherry wood bureau. There on its flat top, stuck fast in colorful pools of hardened candle wax, was her entire perfume bottle collection. Mixed in among the candle nubs and onion-dome-like bottles were at least a dozen photographs of the couple, both alive, enjoying happier times.

On the wall next to the bureau was an old full length dressing mirror in a dark wood frame. The thin film of polished metal was cracking and fading around the edges, but Glenda still got a good look at her own self staring back—and it hardly resembled the Glenda of forty days ago. After the initial sudden start, she dropped the intestine to the floor and walked slowly towards the mirror, eyes locked with those staring back. She cast her eyes down and spun a slow circle, taking in the awful sight of the detritus splashed bathrobe. *Perfect.*

Chapter 11

Five minutes after entering the trees Cade located the source of the stench. Using pre-arranged hand signals he motioned Wilson and Taryn over. Then, with knife-edged branches dragging against his exposed skin, he led them through the undergrowth and just as they stepped into a clearing where two beaten game trails converged, there came a distinct and instantly recognizable noise, like brittle leaves skittering across concrete.

"Zs," mouthed Cade, nodding in the direction of the sound. Having them follow he stepped quietly from the bushes and padded down the foot-wide strip of beaten earth. When he stopped and Wilson and Taryn formed up, the latter mouthed, "How many?"

Quietly, Cade said, "Seven.".

Taryn pressed close and in a stage whisper asked, "So how'd they get over the fence?"

"On the backs of the others, I'd be willing to bet," answered Cade before dragging a finger across his neck, universal semaphore implying he was done with the Q and A session. In the next instant a low rumbling guttural sound came from the direction of the rasps, rising above them for a second before dissipating and then starting anew. Cade stopped abruptly and pressed tight against a towering fir, using the substantial girth of its trunk for cover.

Doing the same behind a pair of smaller trunked deciduous trees, nearly skeletal, their ochre and yellow insect-ravaged leaves thick underfoot, Taryn and Wilson simultaneously brought their Beretta pistols to bear on the interlopers.

The source of the out-of-place noise, just short of the interwoven barbed wire barrier, teeth bared and hackles up, Max stood his ground, warily eyeing the wavering corpses.

Crouched down and reaching between the tightly strung barbed wire, an obvious first turn, its skin pale and taut over an emaciated frame, pawed at the growling animal.

"Good boy, Max," said Cade, imparting an unnatural, almost cheery tone to his voice that conflicted with the strange sight.

Looking on, Taryn couldn't help but smile. It was as if Max had led them all to a pond full of mallards, not a clutch of festering zombies, half of them impaled on the randomly placed sharpened stakes that, at Daymon's insistence, had been added to the newly erected fence.

In unison the creature's vacuous eyes swung up from Max who must have just beaten Cade and the Kids there. Then the seven pair of jaundiced orbs fixated unblinkingly on Cade as he stepped from cover. Throwing a shudder, the usually unflappable former Delta operator noted the laser-like intensity in them and how, seemingly in the reptile part of their brain, he was already in their clutches, the marrow being sucked slowly from his bones. He set the M4 aside and drew his black Gerber from its sheath. In his side vision he saw Taryn and Wilson holstering their pistols.

In the next moment Wilson produced a six-inch Kershaw lock blade and fanned out left, while Taryn, who'd acted a little bit quicker, approached the jostling Zs dead on, Cold Steel blade held on a flat plane, outstretched at eye level with what, at this stage in the zombie apocalypse, she considered a rare find. Because, like her, thought Taryn, to have lasted this long, the newly turned female must have been a gritty survivor in her past life. Late teens or early twenties, she guessed, before taking into account the nearly dozen piercings ringing both ears plus the thousands of dollars and hundreds of hours of elaborate ink work which—though Taryn was loathe to admit—easily trumped hers in quality and surface coverage. A tick later, after processing all of the clues in front of her, Taryn concluded that the floral sleeve tattoos, fully colored and vibrant on the alabaster skin, was way too much chair time for someone just north of eighteen to have endured.

Crawling green stems adorned with like-colored thorns and lipstick red pedals rippled atop the dead woman's pallid arms, which were thrust through the fence in a feeble attempt to get ahold of Taryn's tight fitting camo top. Just out of range of the Z's kneading fingers, Taryn watched its eyes follow the squared-off tip of her black tanto-shaped blade, then, rather comically, cross just before she rammed it home. As the thing's arms went limp Taryn pushed off of her back foot with enough force to send the tatted Z toppling backwards. And as it hinged over there was a ripping sound and Taryn saw, stuck fast to the rusty barbs, the white roundel and black fabric scraps of a vintage Ramones tee shirt.

The rasps suddenly increased and Wilson returned his attention from Taryn's first kill to the pair in front of him. Cadaver number one was draped over the fence—pushed there by the other or acting on its own accord, Wilson didn't care to know. He wanted the things dead and gone and the only way that was going to happen was up close and personal. Shirt hiked up and covering his nose, he made it to the fence at about the same instant rotter number two was ramping up the first one's back.

Like a fish breaking the surface the rotter powered over the other, twisted its upper torso and hinged sideways onto the uppermost barbed wire strand, the added weight stretching it downward. After a clumsy pirouette that seemed to play out in slow motion the male cadaver pitched forward and struck the ground face first with a hollow thud. Needles bounced and leaves were disturbed by the impact, but Wilson ignored the writhing wreck and, like some kind of fencing move he'd seen on the Summer Olympics, lunged forward, burying the shiny blade to the handle in the first rotter's bald pate. He heard the grate of honed steel against bone then a wet squelch as the corpse went slack against the wire.

Similar sounds were coming from Wilson's right flank but he had no time to check Taryn's progress, and knowing that Captain America was on her right and had probably already filleted his fair share of zombies without breaking a sweat, there was no need.

So he yanked his Kershaw free and, sidestepping the resulting blood spurt and patter of wet gray matter, hauled back and sent one of his steel-toed boots hurtling forward in a shallow arc on a collision course with the prone Z's exposed temple. A split second before impact a thought crossed his mind. Either he was about to land a bone crunching death blow or he would miss entirely and look like Charlie Brown duped yet again by his nemesis.

Thankfully, but with unintended consequence, the former came to fruition. Upon impact a live wire shiver coursed up Wilson's tibia and fibula, shot through his femur—the biggest bone in the human body—and like they were components of a desk top kinetic sculpture, set his testicles crashing violently against each other. The resulting nausea doubled him over and, as he watched the semi-aware rotter go limp and crash to the forest floor, horizontal, its skull a miasma of tattered flesh and crushed bone, he caught sight of his lover making quick economical thrusts with her black blade.

***

Max's barking caught Brook's attention and by the time she had crossed the clearing he was waiting for her, stubby tail twitching, a knowing tilt to his head. After yawning widely the multi-colored Shepherd spun a one-eighty and padded into the forest, undoubtedly taking her to Cade.

***

A short while later, after performing some bushwhacking of her own, she heard the distinct sound of a first turn carrying over the top of muffled voices. She snugged her carbine to her shoulder, slowed her pace, and made every effort to slip through the brush ninja-quiet. She'd only traveled a few more paces towards the commotion when the voices became recognizable. And a few short steps after that the beaten game trail spilled into the tiny clearing near the inner perimeter fence, where she saw Cade, Taryn, and Wilson milling about a scene of utter carnage.

She greeted the trio and surveyed the aftermath. To her left was a middle-aged male rotter that had inexplicably gotten over the fence and now lay face down, its skull wildly misshapen and leaking black blood and viscous spinal fluid. Hanging on the fence nearby was another male first turn, scrambled brains oozed from a small slit in the center of its bald head. Blood had pooled shiny and black on the leaves near its feet and, adding to the spreading puddle, slender, saliva-like strands dripped from its open maw. On the opposite side of the loosely strung wire fence were five more corpses. Three lay on the ground, arms and legs askew, each with a gaping hole where an eye had been. Pathetically, the other two Zs which were the source of the dry rasps were stuck fast on sharpened stakes jutting from the ground. They hissed and reached for Max as they marched in place, their bare feet digging shallow furrows into the dirt.

Looking at Cade who was sitting a dozen feet away, back propped against a tree, Brook said, "You going to finish the job?"

"Let's wait a minute and see if they have any undead friends roving around between the wire. Then we'll cross over and take care of these two and see how they got here."

Rocking her head side-to-side as if to say *Six of one, half a dozen of another*, Brook made her way past Taryn and Wilson who, so engrossed in each other, had barely noticed her arrival. She sat down hard on the ground next to Cade and nodded at the pair of wire-scaling Zs. "Those two your doing?" she asked.

"No. They're Wilson's kills," said Cade. He finished cleaning his blade and slid it in its sheath. Then, squinting against a bar of light infiltrating the forest canopy, he looked up at Brook and added softly, "I put down the naked woman there." He paused for a second, felt Brook's eyes boring into him, and also claimed as his the undead little girl crumpled in the dirt near the naked corpse. He threw a shiver at the sight of her. The one-eyed stare, alabaster skin and dainty hands and feet made her look more like one of Raven's old American Girl dolls than a twice-dead toddler.

Looking at Wilson but nodding towards the other corpses, Brook said, "See how Cade did his? Nice and clean. That's what you've got to work on next. Because now we're going to have to bury the gore and churn the blood into the dirt since it's inside the wire."

Coming to the redhead's defense, Cade said, "He did fine, Brook. And so did Taryn. She dropped hers before I finished with the mom there."

Brook said nothing.

Taking that as his cue, Cade said, "I think that's all of them. Come on, Wilson ... let's get these ones disposed of." Pushing off the tree, Cade rose to standing and checked his pants and boots. Then he examined his arms and chest for blood or minuscule scraps of detritus that might have gone airborne and landed on him. After running his fingers through his hair he asked Brook to inspect his back.

Taking swipes at the wood chips and moss accumulated between his shoulder blades, Brook went to her tip toes and whispered in his ear, "Just a little bark. That's all. You're good as new ... *Infidel.*" Then, oblivious to the group of young people now gawking at them, Brook grabbed one of Cade's muscled shoulders, spun him around to face her and went up on her tiptoes. The kiss, taking him by surprise, was one for the books. *Greta Garbo, eat your heart out*, she thought, her tongue probing his mouth, both hands cupping his face. But, sadly, it was over before it got real good. She pulled away and delivered the look that he knew all too well. Those smoldering brown eyes had just issued him a rain check to be redeemed later for a private rendezvous. And since the new world hadn't changed Brook's libido one bit, Cade was confident that he'd be cashing in his chit before the day was done. Finally, with more than a little color spreading to his cheeks, he looked over at Taryn and Wilson and said, "Move along here. Nothing to see."

***

Back at the compound, inside the security container, Heidi was losing her battle against a rising tide of guilt. Though she'd grown fairly thick skin as a result of her longtime bartending job, after the outbreak the things she'd endured at Robert Christian's mansion in Jackson Hole had broken her down completely and changed her perception of people in general. Now, reluctant to open up to anyone but Daymon and bound by an unrealistic fear of the outside, she eschewed any prolonged human interaction and had come to embrace fully the subterranean safety of the compound. And as a result, due to the lack of daylight and whatever vitamin it normally provided, she was moody and quick to anger. And that anger, recently unleashed by the perceived snub brought on by Cade's no-nonsense attitude over the radio, had hijacked all rational thought for a short while and was now just beginning to ebb. Unable or unwilling to admit she had been wrong in ignoring the incoming call, she thought up a creative way of absolving herself of the transgression. A little white lie wouldn't hurt anybody, she reasoned as she thumbed the radio and tried to hail Daymon or Duncan or whoever happened to pick up first.

After three tries Duncan's familiar drawl came back at her. That there was a little bit of a slur to his words went over Heidi's head and, forgoing a hello or any type of small talk, she instead immediately—with little warmth or inflection in her voice—asked to speak to Daymon.

Coming across to Heidi like Cade had earlier, Duncan said nothing. He held the radio up and paced a few steps left of Daymon and waved the Motorola back and forth, trying to get the dreadlocked man's attention.

The warbling whine of a hardworking chainsaw somewhere in the background sounded in Heidi's ear for a handful of seconds. Suddenly there was silence and she heard static and the rustling noise indicative of the phone changing hands. Finally Daymon said, "What's up, hon?"

Heidi asked Daymon to switch over to a channel where they could expect a degree of privacy.

Daymon took off a glove and manipulated the rubberized keys until he found the channel and sub-channel Heidi requested he go to. "What's up?" he asked.

The words came out of Heidi's mouth rushed and at times unintelligible as she rehashed the events leading up to the moment the satellite phone registered the incoming call.

Shaking his head, Daymon said nothing for a short while. Then he said, "I think you're reading into it too much. He's all business. And so is Duncan when he's not half in the bag drunk."

"But ..."

Daymon keyed the talk button, cutting her off. He said, "Drop it. You're projecting. I'll be back when I'm finished here and we can talk it through."

"Whatever," she said.

Daymon turned the volume back up to max and glanced at Duncan, who had been feigning disinterest, rather poorly.

"Everything OK?"

"Same old same old," answered Daymon. He switched the radio back to the previous channel. Sat down hard on the Chevy's tailgate and cracked a water.

Smiling, Duncan took a seat next to Daymon on the dusty tailgate. He pulled out his flask and said, "Would misery like company?"

Back in the compound, Heidi slapped a palm on the plywood desk. "Men are such assholes," she said, switching the two-way back to the agreed upon community channel, 10-1. Then, alone in the dimly lit container with only her conscience and a crushing silence, reluctantly, she pressed the talk button and asked for Cade.

**

Radio in hand, and about to deliver a sit-rep back to the compound, Cade smiled when the unit vibrated for a second time in as many minutes. Hearing Heidi asking for him, he said, "Great minds," and depressed the *Talk* button. "I was just about to call you. Everything is OK," he said. Then he went on and described the encounter at the inner fence and added that someone would be returning to the compound shortly to get a couple of shovels. He released the Talk button and heard a click, presumably Heidi, followed by the soft hiss telling him the channel was open. Finally Heidi spoke up. "I'm sorry, Cade. Everything is *not* going to be OK. A call came in on your phone a little while ago and I ... I kind of *sat* on it."

"Why?" asked Cade, disbelief evident in his voice. "And who was it?"

Eyes bugging from her head, Brook mouthed, "What the hell?"

Putting a hand up, Cade shook his head and repeated the questions.

"Because everybody ignores me," replied Heidi. "And I'm getting sick of it."

"I don't ignore you," said Daymon, breaking in over the conversation. "But what you did was wrong so answer the man's questions."

There was a brief silence.

Taryn's eyes were locked on the radio clutched in Cade's hand and, reacting to the exchange, her brows arched and her mouth formed a silent O which she quickly covered with one hand.

"Spit it out, Heidi," railed Brook into her own radio.

Inside the comms container Heidi retrieved the sat-phone from the shelf. She hit a random key and, once its screen lit up, thumbed the *Talk* button on the two-way and read aloud the eleven numbers.

Brook was leaning against a tree and staring at her radio and listening to the numbers being read off. Once Heidi was finished and the radio was silent, Brook's face went slack, her arms went to her sides, and she pushed off the tree. Scooping up her carbine, she let loose with a couple of choice curse words and stalked off the way she'd come, with Taryn following closely and trying to talk her out of *killing the messenger.*

"Repeat the number, please," said Cade as he watched the women disappear down the game trail leading back to the clearing a quarter mile distant. Listening closely, he stared at the Motorola in his fist, and once he'd heard all eleven digits his head started to bob and he whispered, "Nash?"

***

A few minutes after Heidi's pseudo come-to-Jesus moment, Cade heard distant engine noise and then the two-way radio started warbling. He answered the incoming call and when he learned that Duncan and Daymon were returning for the day he asked that they stop at the inner ring of fence. A tick later, preceded by the same growling engine, the nearby sound of gravel popping under tires reached Cade's ears. Then there was a slight brake squeal and the engine shut off. Next came two, near simultaneous, resonant clangs. Cade listened to the sounds of the men breaking brush along the fence line, and so that nobody would be mistaken for rotters, guided them in the final twenty yards over the radio.

***

Moving the bodies through the brush to the feeder road took time and considerable effort, even with Duncan and Daymon pitching in. During the process Cade let it be known that the number of the call he'd missed belonged to Major Freda Nash, who he presumed was still running the show back at Schriever Air Force Base.

Hearing this, Daymon abruptly dropped his half of the corpse he and Duncan were lugging, turned and, with his hands on his hips, asked Cade, "What do you think she wants?"

Punctuated with a grunt as he and Wilson heaved the male rotter with the crushed head onto the road, Cade replied, "I've got no idea, Daymon. But knowing Nash ... she's not calling to invite me to the Officer's Ball."

"Well, well, Mister Glass Half Empty," slurred Duncan. He let go of the corpse's bloodied bare feet he'd been holding onto. "Did you think maybe she's calling to tell you the scientists you shanghaied from Outer Mongolia have perfected the dear departed doctor's antiserum?"

Shaking his head, Cade said, "Doubtful."

"That *would* be a game changer," countered Wilson.

Cade didn't answer to that. Guessing the reason for Nash's cold call was the last item on his agenda. Instead he said, "Why don't you go and stay with Sasha and Taryn. When you get there send Seth back with another pickup so we can get these things to the pit and bury them. And have him bring me a shirt."

Wilson perked up. He asked, "I'll bring you a shirt if I can operate the excavator."

"Sheeit, Wilson," drawled Duncan. "Ole ham-fisted Daymon here pilots that Black Hawk better than you work that booger green piece of digging machinery."

"To answer your question, Wilson," Cade said. "No. Can't risk having that thing break on us. Plus ... I have zero desire to go poking around Woodruff or anywhere else looking for parts."

Wilson nodded and took off toward the compound.

Daymon shot his reluctant *flight instructor* an icy glare, brought his hands together at neck-level and pantomimed strangling him.

Swaying noticeably, Duncan fumbled in his pockets for his flask. He spun the cap, took a long draw and grimaced from the burn. Then, apparently having already forgotten his barbed comment, gazed confusedly at Daymon.

Hands by his sides now, Daymon said, "It's not like riding a freaking bike. Not even close. So forgive me if I can't land the thing yet."

"Can't hover it worth a damn either," muttered Duncan. "You know how many hours I logged watching and learning before I even got to touch a stick?"

"No ... but I have a feeling you're about to tell us."

"Daymon, my boy ..." Duncan paused and took another belt of Jack Daniels. Wiped his mouth on a sleeve and went on, "a month of Sundays. That's how many."

"That's days, *not* hours," said Daymon, lips curling to a smile. "And you're drunk."

The radio in Daymon's pocket suddenly blared and Seth said he and Wilson were a minute out.

Thumbing the Talk button, Daymon said, "We aren't going anywhere. And neither are the rotters."

"Copy that," replied Seth.

As the Dodge Ram Dually approached on the narrow road, underbrush and branches slapped and scratched at its bulbous rear fenders, making the sheet metal sing. After squeezing the rig through the opening between a pair of hewn timber posts that didn't look wide enough for the full-sized pick-up, Seth, who was alone, stopped it perfectly with the open tailgate right beside the stinking mound of twice-dead cadavers.

***

Five minutes later the seven corpses were stacked in the box bed like cordwood, their scuffed shoes and twisted and stubbed toes resting on the tailgate.

After shrugging on the tee shirt, Cade slapped the wheel well and moved aside and watched Seth back the truck in a mirror image of the way he'd arrived. A dozen yards down the feeder he found a wide spot in the road, made a three-point-turn, crushing ferns and assorted ground-hugging flora, and sped back towards the compound.

Carbine in hand, Cade looked at Duncan and Daymon and said, "Let's go. Time to open Pandora's box."

Chapter 12

Leaving the two men at the forest's edge near the motor pool Cade hustled across the clearing and ducked into the compound. After letting his eyes adjust to the low light, he noticed Heidi seated a dozen yards away, the glare from the flat panel monitor bathing her face with an eerie blue light.

That she was still at her post led Cade to believe that his wife had wisely taken the high road—a good thing for everyone involved. A confrontation with Brook, who was becoming more hardened to their new world with each passing day, would have been grossly one-sided, and served only to further alienate the already skittish woman from the group, sending her scrabbling and scratching, like a hermit crab, ever deeper into the comfort of the shell the subterranean compound had become to her.

Partially closing the recently oiled door behind him, Cade stood statue-like in the gloom of the foyer and watched the woman going about her work. Though he spent only a minute evaluating her, for the most part she seemed to still be in command of all her faculties. Every few seconds she would ignore the short wave radio, look up and pay close attention to the out-of-sight monitor to her left. And when she did Cade noticed her eyes move by degrees, as if following a grid-like search pattern. He saw the blue glow reflected in them intensify when she paused and leaned in, no doubt scrutinizing each individual partition on the screen.

The new system, which was far superior to the archaic linked game trail cameras it replaced, provided full video coverage of State

Route 39, a long straight stretch of the nearby gravel feeder road, all four corners of the vast grass-covered clearing, as well as the vehicles, aircraft, and dirt airstrip cutting between them. Throw in the camera's rudimentary night vision capabilities, and the round-the-clock need for a warm body manning the over watch near the hidden entrance seemed a bit redundant.

But as this incident had just made crystal clear to Cade, having a level-headed person—not someone running high on emotion—monitoring the live feeds which were the compound's first line of defense and tantamount to everyone's survival had to be priority one going forward. Heidi's first mistake—forgetting to turn on the ringers and missing his call before they'd all been reunited—could be forgiven. No blood, no foul. But ignoring an incoming call because of a personality conflict was, in his book, abject failure and grossly negligent. However, as inept as the action was, and since the compound still ran on a kind of group conscience which required a vote for all major decisions, he too would be following Brook's lead and taking the high road. So he made a mental note to meet with Duncan, who, since Logan's murder, had become the de facto leader of the group, and recommend that she be given something to do to keep her busy and from underfoot. One where failure couldn't get anyone killed. And if she refused the overture and it came to a vote to oust her, then, and only then, would he bring the issue up with Daymon—who saw her involvement in the day-to-day operations of the compound as the only thing keeping her somewhat sane.

Clearing his throat, Cade cracked the door open behind him a few inches and then made a show of closing it. Ducking through the passage, carbine trained at the floor, he waited for Heidi to make the first move.

She said nothing.

So he walked through the wall of brooding silence, hearing only his mom's voice in his head urging him to not say anything unless it was good. And at the moment he couldn't think of anything in that column worthy of him stopping and being cordial so he kept on going, mouth shut, lips pursed into a thin white line.

After a quick right turn he stood outside of the Grayson quarters. The door was dogged shut and with no sound coming from the other side of the three by six plate of steel he decided that better safe than sorry applied here. So he rapped softly, his knuckles producing a sonorous gonging tone that echoed in the cramped corridor. Far from any kind of a Zen-like state, he stepped back and waited.

A half beat later there was a rasp as the inside bolt was drawn. Then the door hinged inward and Raven's tanned face, barely noticeable in the corridor's low light, peered out at him.

"Who goes there," she asked, erupting in giggles.

Feeling twelve feet tall while looking down at his daughter, Cade placed the backs of both hands on his forehead, twisted his fingers to represent antlers, and answered in a silly voice, "I'm the Knight who says '*Ni*.'" Usually the first to laugh at one of her dad's random juvenile outbursts, Raven instead pursed her lips and said nothing. *Injury,* thought Cade. Then, after suffering the added indignity of being on the receiving end of a long blank stare from his twelve-year-old, which he chalked up as the *insult* component of the one-two sucker-punch that had just shaken his usually impenetrable *daddy aura,* he hung his head and inched past her. If he had a tail, he conceded inwardly, it would be firmly tucked between his legs.

Sat-phone in hand and shaking her head at her husband's dated attempt at humor, Brook patted the bunk, beckoning him to join her.

Cade didn't budge.

Craning her neck to see around him, Brook said, "Raven. I need you to go and visit with the Kids for a while."

"Take your rifle," said Cade, grabbing the Ruger from its spot behind the door and handing it over.

"Muzzle down. And keep the safety on," added Brook, nodding.

Flashing them both a look that said, *I got this,* Raven grasped her rifle by its walnut stock, checked the safety, and, after seeing that it was indeed engaged, slung it over her shoulder with the slender black barrel aimed at the wood floor.

Remaining standing, Cade uttered their new family mantra. "Stay frosty," he said while bugging his eyes at her with one brow cocked awkwardly.

58

The antics produced the result he'd sought earlier and Raven closed the door like she'd opened it, wracked by a case of the giggles.

Once the dainty footfalls receded into the distance, Cade pulled up a folding chair, straddled it backward, and looked at his better half over steepled fingers.

After a few moments of uneasy quiet, Brook *blinked* first. "What?" she blurted, shrugging, her arms outstretched.

Cade said nothing. Just matched her stare, unblinking.

"She was wrong holding back that information."

"Agreed," said Cade, dropping his chin, gaze settling on the floor near his boots. "But attacking her over the radio? Two wrongs do not make a right. Don't forget ... Raven's learning everything that she'll be taking forward, right now, by watching you ... me, and all of those we choose to surround ourselves with. She doesn't have the luxury of learning from her mistakes like we did. There is no more trial and error. Best case scenario ... error equals a quick and final death. Worst case ... she'll get bit and suffer a stint in purgatory before someone grants her final rest. So we've got to be extra careful the messages we send and what and how we say things when she's within earshot, however explosive or subtle those may be."

Now Brook remained silent, lips pursed, a solid set to her jaw.

"Just for the record. I'm glad you didn't go off on our forgetful friend."

The silent treatment continued.

Straightening up, Cade placed his hands on his knees and asked, "Did you?"

"Of course not. She's still breathing, isn't she."

"Good point. What's on the phone?" he asked, gesturing at the slim black device that didn't appear quite so small clutched in her tiny hand. "Is it a text or voice message?"

"It's a voice message. Three guesses who it is. The first two don't count."

Goose flesh breaking out on his ribs and running up his spine, he said, "I have a good idea already just going by the number itself. It's Nash ... isn't it?"

Narrowing her gaze, Brook nodded and mouthed, "Bingo."

"What'd she want?"

Swallowing hard, Brook passed the phone over.

"Well?"

"I have no idea," she said. *But I have a feeling it means you'll be leaving us again*, is what she was thinking.

Thumbing in the unlock code to the metaphorical Pandora's Box, Cade asked, "You listened to it, right?"

Nodding, Brook said, "Nash wants you to set up the laptop and the accompanying dish and follow the same procedure as before ... whatever *that* means." Then for the third time in as many minutes she went silent. Biting her lower lip, she looked at the floor. After a few seconds she swept her eyes up to meet Cade's and added quietly, "Apparently in order to find out what she wants you're going to have to peel some layers from the onion. And if you do it in my vicinity Mister Grayson, I'm liable to break down and start crying."

"Looks like you already have been," he said, going to his knees.

"Guilty as charged," she said, watching him extricate the rigid Pelican case from under the bunk.

"I noticed back at the clearing. Didn't want to call attention to it in front of the Kids."

"I didn't cry in front of Raven."

"Must have been tough."

"Don't keep her waiting any longer, Cade Grayson." Brook inched towards the end of the bunk and wrapped both arms around the support. Rested her cheek on the cool metal there. "Now I'll do a little praying that she isn't trying to steal you from me again."

"No one is *stealing* me away from you. It's duty to country and the future I want our daughter to enjoy that keeps making my mouth say yes. Even when I want to stay with you really, really bad." He went silent for a moment.

For the second time Brook lost it. She looked up at him through teary eyes and said, "Please go by and tell Raven to stay with the Kids for a while longer. So I can compose myself."

Cade rose to his feet and hefted the Pelican container in one hand. He nodded an affirmative and kissed Brook atop her head. Said, "I'm sure everything will work out for the best. For all parties involved." He pulled the rugged laptop from his rucksack and left without another word.

Brook waited until she could no longer hear Cade's footfalls. She glared at the ceiling and growled, "Stay the hell away from my family, Murphy."

Chapter 13

"Hold it. Right there ..." said Jimmy Foley, who was standing on the top rung of a teetering twenty-foot ladder, biting his lip in concentration, his upper body contorted into a shape rarely found outside of a yoga studio. Fighting gravity and his forty-one-year-old joints that were clearly not used to this kind of manual labor, he strained mightily at full extension and finally succeeded in threading the nut onto the galvanized bolt.

"Third times the charm," said Tran, smiling and looking up at Foley. "Glad that's the last one. I was getting tired of holding this ladder and having to find all of your fumbles."

Sweat dripping off the tip of his nose, Foley looked down and said sharply, "Give me a break, Tran. I'm an IT guy, *not* a building superintendent. If I had my druthers, I'd take troubleshooting and rebuilding a roached office network over this kind of work ... *any day*."

"Yeah, but once this array is up and running we will only have to rely on the generator when it's *really* needed. That means fewer gas runs. And without the constant mechanical noise all of those rotting demons out there will leave us alone. Duncan promised as much."

Foley said nothing. He descended a few rungs, took the socket wrench from Tran, and looked closely for the first time in at least a week at the slight Asian man's face. Save for the puffiness in Tran's left ear (*cauliflower* was what he'd heard Brook call it), the rest of the swelling had left his face entirely. The deep scratches on his cheek and neck had healed, leaving behind a roadmap of white scars. When Foley had first met Tran three weeks ago his eyes were still mostly swollen shut from a beating suffered at the hands of Bishop's henchmen. And a week ago the whites were still bloodshot and jaundiced. Now they were nearly wide open and harbored a knowing twinkle. A spark, is what first came to Foley's mind. Embarrassed at the realization he'd been staring, Foley grabbed the tool and climbed back up the ladder. He called down, "How tight do the bolts have to be?"

"Duncan said a quarter turn past real tight," answered Tran, still bracing the ladder two-handed.

"Figures," muttered Foley, his bald pate an angry shade of red. "That guy wouldn't know specific if it bit him on the butt."

"Says the scatterbrained IT guy," quipped Tran, suppressing a chuckle.

***

Ten minutes later the unlikely duo stood back to admire their handiwork. There were eight gleaming black three by five-foot rectangles bolted securely in two rows. The solar array, thought to produce roughly two and a half kilowatts per hour, sat atop a jury-rigged metal frame that resembled scaffolding put together by a team of blind men. The entire setup, liberated from the quarry compound, would provide enough juice during the day to power the lights and closed circuit system while charging the reserve batteries sufficiently to last throughout the night. A given during the summer when the sun was prominent in a cloudless sky most of the day—an entirely different proposition during the late fall and winter months when the sun could stay away for weeks on end.

But that was not this IT guy's department. Besides, thought Foley as his foot touched the soft earthen forest floor, *by the time the clouds roll in permanently, Daymon will have finished blocking the road at points both east and west and using the high output generator taken from the quarry will be a non-issue.*

"I'm done up here. What do you say we take a break and get us a beer?" Foley said.

Shaking his head, Tran sighed and said, "I *still* don't drink. My religion frowns upon it."

"Doesn't hurt to ask. I just hate to drink alone." Foley pocketed the wrench and asked, "So the Dalai Lama doesn't ever hoist a cold one?"

In an unusual display of humor, Tran quipped, "Not anymore."

"I meant *didn't,* past tense ... before everything went to shit and all of this became necessary," Foley said, gesturing toward the giant wood and metal housing that, despite its cobbled-together nature, somehow remained standing.

"Help me with the ladder," Tran said, ignoring the question. "Only the easy part remains."

"Yep," agreed Foley. "Wiring up the invertor. *That* this IT guy can handle."

Chapter 14

Eager, yet reluctant, to see what surprise Nash had in store, Cade strode purposefully across the clearing, the dried grass swishing against his smartly bloused MultiCam pants. The sun was warm on his face and the breeze present earlier had tapered off. Tilting his head back as he walked, he drew in a deep breath through his nose. *Nothing.* The carrion stench present earlier had gone along with the bodies. From somewhere west of him, deep into the property and well away from the State Route, he heard the soft chug of the excavator working hard digging a grave for them. He imagined Seth at the controls, with nobody to talk to, the engine noise drowning out his thoughts.

"All in the name of survival," he said to himself, halting near the phony crop circle. After depositing the heavy gear box on the matted-down grass, he knelt and popped the latches. The inside was mostly thick black foam with each component of the small satellite dish snugged into its own form-fitting compartment.

He extricated the parts for the stand first and quickly assembled them. The dish went together rather easily and when he placed it on the stand the whole thing came up to just above his kneecap.

The low whine of a straining gearbox got his attention. Looking west towards the noise he saw a Chevy pick-up driven by Daymon, branches scraping its side and whipping the air as it emerge from the tree line. From the passenger seat, Duncan waved a greeting as the rig nosed in near the other vehicles.

Cade waved back then shifted his focus to the task at hand. Using the compass feature on his Suunto, he found due south and fixed his gaze on one gnarled tree in particular, a victim of a past lightning strike, and rotated the dish until its center post was aimed at the blue sky about twenty degrees above its pointy top.

The rest of the setup took but a few seconds. However, booting up the laptop and getting it to recognize the connected dish was a test in patience, of which Cade had vast stores.

Still waiting, he looked up and saw Lev and Chief trudge from the forest to the east. Each man had a black rifle slung over one shoulder, and perched on the other was a hewn length of lodge pole pine supporting a field dressed deer carcass. With each step the buck's head jerked and lolled, the four-point rack carving a meandering path through the knee-high grass.

Waving a greeting to them both, Cade heard and felt his stomach growl. Clearly, he thought, the reptile part of his brain was now aware of the prospect of fresh meat. And in his mind's eye he could already see the fire-braised flesh and hear the white noise of the venison sizzling on the spit.

Shielding the laptop screen with one hand, Cade squinted against the sun, waiting to see the pixelated wheel stop spinning and the cartoonish clasped hands replace it showing him the Panasonic was ready to receive the coded transmission from the satellite orbiting somewhere high above him. Through technology he didn't entirely understand, nor care to, a message from Nash containing what might be a life-altering proposition began downloading onto the laptop.

A short while later an audible chime told him the download was complete, but the glare from the sun prevented him from seeing the file name let alone read it, so he disconnected the cable and hinged the screen closed. Leaving the dish and cables on the grass, he rose and set off to find a patch of shade.

Nearing the motor pool, Cade noticed Duncan puttering around under the open hood of his newly acquired Dodge Ram. When he got within earshot he couldn't help but throw a quip at the master of all quipsters. "What ... Jiffy Lube closed?"

After pushing off of the truck's fender, Duncan sauntered over and squared up with Cade. "What's with the toys?" he asked, nodding towards the crushed grass where only the top of the gray dish was visible. "Trying to pick up DirecTV? Cause if you are, I hate to break it to ya ... there ain't no more Sunday Ticket."

"Breaks my heart," said Cade, which happened to be a lie. Save for his beloved Portland Trailblazers—the only game in town—he could take or leave professional sports. College games, he conceded after a second's thought, he would most definitely miss. The large scale choreography between the cheerleaders and marching bands were a sight to see in person. Yet one more thing stolen from Raven's future by Omega.

"Not a big sports fan?"

"Not so much."

Nodding at the laptop, Duncan asked, "What's with the computer?"

Ignoring the question, but thinking ahead, Cade asked, "The Black Hawk ... how much fuel is she holding?"

"She's sittin' almost half full."

"Perfect," replied Cade. "That's more than enough to get us to Morgan."

Duncan nudged his oversized orange-framed glasses back to their proper resting place. "Whatever's on the computer is need to know. I get it."

"I don't even know what's on it," Cade said. He passed in front of Duncan's truck and climbed inside the F-650 sitting beside it and locked the door to ward off any and all distractions for the near future.

Cracking open the computer, he said aloud, "Alright, Freda, this better be what I think it is."

***

And it had been—sort of. In the file labeled *FUBAR* he discovered more than thirty minutes worth of footage shot mostly from very high altitude and, since jet fuel was in very short supply last he'd heard, Cade assumed it was captured by the sensitive optics aboard one of Nash's Keyhole satellites. Every city the bird passed over—of which there were many during the compilation's run time—had one thing in common: all of the freeways and arterials leading away from their downtown cores, where skyscrapers cast their shadows, commerce took place, and thousands upon thousands of people lived cheek to jowl, were choked with static vehicles. No matter the size of the city, he saw rivers of multicolored sheet metal, the sun glittering off glass and chrome. People's worldly possessions: colorful jumbles of furniture and art and suitcases heaped high in the beds of pickups or lashed atop passenger cars. And judging by the roving herds, those same unfortunate people, who had either sheltered in place initially or were trying to escape the outbreak via those vehicles, now roamed the jams and concrete jungles in search of living prey.

New York was exceptionally bad. From altitude the streets were mostly taxi cab yellow with a smattering of other colors breaking up the solid hue here and there. And when Manhattan Island slid by and the optics zoomed in Cade got a closer look and saw that a gridlock of biblical proportions had taken place when panicked residents fled the security of their three thousand dollar a square foot digs for the already overrun safe zones authorized by the DHS and set up and run by massively overwhelmed FEMA workers.

Strangely, the streets of downtown Chicago were mostly free of vehicles. However, there were roadblocks made of stacked sandbags all up and down the famous Magnificent Mile from the Chicago River to Oak Street. All were now unmanned, but clearly whoever had been there had retreated in a hurry, leaving behind heavy machine guns, ammo boxes, and dozens of their fallen, chewed on bodies in MultiCam fatigues, and all, Cade presumed, head shot in order to keep them from reanimating and joining the burgeoning ranks of the walking dead.

Throughout the grim documentary, Nash narrated in a voice bereft of emotion, calling out each city by name followed by the estimated casualties suffered there, which were nothing short of staggering.

After twenty minutes of this, when Cade had seen more of the destruction wrought by this Extinction Level Event than he cared to, Nash's voice abruptly changed and a measure of empathy crept in as she said: *Cade, your hometown is next. I'm pleased to announce that it has fared better than most,* and then sure enough, Portland, Oregon, the Rose City, known for its bridges and quirky citizenry, got its sixty seconds of fame. And though the brief flyby was shorter than most Super Bowl commercials, the information he gleaned from it was priceless. The once vibrant city, home to nearly one million, now resembled the pictures he'd seen of Detroit before the Omega outbreak.

The main difference between Portland and the previous two dozen cities was the flotilla of watercraft anchored dead center in the slow-moving river. There were small pleasure craft with Bimini tops deployed. A few dozen gleaming yachts, likely in the forty- to fifty-foot range, strained against their anchor chains in what used to be the shipping channel. The RiverPlace Marina on the west side of the Willamette River was deserted, the empty slips now useless pickets of rust streaked I-beams resembling mechanical fingers reaching from the depths. Up on the west bank rows of million dollar condominiums seemed battened down against the dead, their windows darkened and uninviting.

In stark contrast, on the opposite bank of the Willamette River nearly all of the recently renovated warehouses constructed of old growth timber around the turn of the last century had completely burned to the ground, taking with them dozens of restaurants and bars and coffee shops. South of the scorched concrete pads and blackened rubble, sitting in the shadow of the Marquam Bridge where Interstate 5 crossed the river, Cade recognized the block-long Oregon Museum of Science and Industry building—one of Raven's favorite places.

Remarkably, the dome over the IMAX theater was intact. As was OMSI's forty-foot-tall pyramid that sat atop a huge cube-shaped entry, both constructed from hundreds of panes of tinted glass secured to a vast metal framework. Looking closer, he realized there were very few dead wandering the walk near the seawall and the parking lots bordering on the north and west were mostly deserted. All in all, OMSI looked to be untouched. Nothing good to loot in a museum, he concluded. Then, recalling a news article that mentioned how the place had been built around a decommissioned steam plant with a sprawling upper level complete with multiple exits and dozens of rooms, he realized it would make for a good compound. Furthermore, with a couple of boats moored next to the static submarine on display, emergency egress could be accomplished from land or sea.

Movement at the far edge of the clearing disrupted his train of thought. Pausing the image, he shifted his gaze just as Jamie stepped from the tree line and into the sun. He watched her walking slowly in his general direction, a long rifle slung over one shoulder, a pistol riding low on her right hip.

Her black hair, worn short since she'd returned from her kidnapping ordeal, gleamed like patent leather. Lev, who was sweet on the girl—and not very good at hiding it—had mistakenly taken to calling it a pixie cut.

But Cade thought nothing of the sort. This new close-cropped do was all Demi Moore a la *G.I. Jane*. High speed, low drag, and ready for war. And that's what this woman had waged on the dead since coming back. She lived to man the overwatch. Said she appreciated the solitude it provided.

Lev had no chance, Cade thought as he watched her stalk through the clearing. Jamie was never going to forgive herself for Jordan's death. And she sure as hell wasn't getting over losing Logan any time soon. The former he knew from the brief conversation he'd had with her aboard the Black Hawk three weeks ago. A revelation he didn't intend on sharing with anyone. The latter, however, was common knowledge since her and Logan's budding relationship had been cut short by an act of brutality that blindsided everybody.

The wicked-looking tomahawk strapped to her hip beat a steady silent cadence on her thigh as she strode by seemingly unaware she was being watched.

Cade shifted his gaze back to the laptop and started the image moving again, while a dozen feet in front of the F-650's massive front end Jamie's playful one-fingered salute skimmed above the grill just like a shark's dorsal.

Inside the cab, oblivious to the fact that he'd been made by Jamie, Cade stared at the screen. He saw the satellite trace a laser-straight trajectory over Portland and noticed the lens pan slowly aft; he felt a spark of emotion as he recognized his inner east side neighborhood hugging the natural contour of the land and rising gradually away from the river.

Once again he paused the playback and zoomed in on the image with repeated taps of the + key until single family homes leapt out at him. Instantly he recognized Creston Park by the grove of firs that grew noticeably taller than anything else in his old neighborhood. In the center of the park he saw the sun-splashed waters of the pool of the same name where Raven had just completed swimming lessons, earning herself a bump up from Seal to Polar Bear—an achievement she couldn't stop talking about until that fateful Saturday when he'd dropped her and Brook off at the airport. A little triumph over her fear of water she hadn't said one word about since.

While savoring the pleasant mental image of Raven's wide smile as she thrust the certificate excitedly in his face, he traced a finger diagonally right from the pool until he located the alley running east/west behind the house he'd been forced to abandon what seemed like a lifetime ago.

He stopped his finger moving and let it hover over the middle of the dirt track near the fence he'd hoisted his mountain bike over at the onset of this madness forty-some-odd days ago. And to his amazement, right of his finger, still standing—multi-pitched roof and all—was the craftsman-style home he'd grown up in. The same home where thirteen years prior he had carried Brook as a new bride across the threshold. And the same place they'd brought a newborn Raven home to barely a year later.

Suddenly finding himself facing emotions he'd been stuffing for far too long, he started to close the laptop's lid, but stopped short when he heard Nash mention the Omega Antiserum. *Nash being Nash*, he thought. Show him something she knew would tug at his heartstrings. Get him on his heels and then lower the boom.

Stifling his feelings, he hinged open the lid and saw Nash staring him in the face. Judging by the desk, barely visible under reams of paper, and the plaques on the wall behind it, she'd recorded the video in her office. He watched and listened with rapt attention as she talked about the scientists' many failures in replicating Fuentes' antiserum. Her gaze wandered all over as she described how they'd lost dozens of Omega-infected soldiers and airmen even after administering the antiserum. Then there was a long pause as she stared straight into the video camera. *Collecting her thoughts for the sales pitch*, thought Cade. He imagined the lifeless lens staring back at her and the mesmerizing red light, blinking incessantly, reminding her time was mankind's enemy.

After the pause she began listing the successes—of which there were far fewer than failures. No matter how quickly the antiserum was administered, Slow Burns—victims who had suffered superficial bites away from major blood-delivering arteries—seemed to fare better than the quick bleeds. Another variable factored into a victim's chance of survival, Cade noted, was the person's sex and body size. For some reason, no matter their age, males responded to treatment better than females. And people who used to shop at Big and Tall stores—male and female—also had better odds at survival. Through it all Nash rattled off numbers and percentages, most of which Cade didn't pay close attention to. There was one word that he'd been waiting to hear but never did. And it troubled him greatly. Twenty minutes worth of footage meant to show him how far things had deteriorated across the nation. Then sixty sentiment-filled seconds to show him what used to be and presumably, one day, could be again. All followed by the lengthy rundown on the Omega Antiserum during which the word *perfected* never passed her lips.

But she wasn't finished. Scooting closer to the camera, Nash looked over each shoulder. Satisfied she was alone, she let spill the real reason she was contacting him.

During her spiel the main word that leapt out at him was *volunteer*, yet, inexplicably, his mind subconsciously inserted the word *expendable*. As quick as that thought came it was gone and he was in her shoes and feeling her pain. Rapid-fire, Cade weighed the risk versus reward of the mission against one another in his mind. Then, after a millisecond of sharing in the pain, and with the scale tipping toward reward, he was decided and already rifling through the center console for pen and paper. And as the recording finished playing he filled a piece of paper emblazoned with the Denver Nuggets' logo with rendezvous times and GPS coordinates and other pertinent details. Finally, when Nash had finished speaking and she pitched forward and rose to approach the camera, Cade noticed that her brow and upper lip were dappled with small shimmering beads of sweat. And further darkening her navy blue uniform top, two half-moons had spread under both arms.

Once the video quit running, Cade closed the laptop and, cradling it under his arm, popped the door and climbed to the ground. With Duncan dead in his sights he waded through the grass and said, "Forget the truck. Get the bird ready."

From under the hood, his upper body shrouded in shadow, Duncan said, "When are we launching?"

"First light."

"When are we coming back."

"Undetermined," replied Cade.

Duncan bowed his head and stepped down off the front bumper. He wiped his hands on his shirt and said, "What about Brook?"

Cade said nothing.

Duncan watched the former Delta Operator, carrying the laptop in one hand, carbine in the other, as he strode toward the satellite dish in the center of his crop circle. "Why don't you go inside and hook the laptop to Logan's antenna?"

"Doesn't work that way," Cade called back over his shoulder.

Duncan shrugged and removed the oil dipstick from the engine.

With the afternoon sun warm on his neck, Cade knelt and coupled the computer with the dish. He booted up the Panasonic and started the uplink sequence. When it was complete he logged his response to Nash's overture and, before he could second guess himself, quickly hit *Enter.*

With Duncan's words still resonating, Cade broke the dish down and snugged each component into its proper slot and secured the case. *What about Brook?* Mulling over those three words, he lugged the equipment across the clearing and took everything inside the compound with him.

Across the clearing, Daymon emerged from the trees carrying two scrawny squirrels by their tails, the carbon fiber crossbow slung across his back. He approached Duncan and tossed his kills to the ground. "What'd Cade have to say?" he asked.

Duncan said nothing. He regarded the rodents, then arched a brow accusingly and looked a question at the dreadlocked man.

"For the effin dog, numbnuts," said Daymon, tucking a stray dread behind his ear. He shook his head and fixed his gaze on Duncan. "*Really?* You thought I was going to *eat* those tree rats?"

Duncan shrugged. He hinged back under the hood, the shadow hiding the shit-eating grin spreading on his face.

Muttering, Daymon scooped up the carcasses, adjusted his bow and, walking slowly, started off in the direction of the compound entrance following the same beaten path in the grass Cade had taken.

Chapter 15

Nash had been staring at the computer screen for so long that her eyes were itching and dry. There was a dull ache between her shoulder blades—the least of her maladies. Every dozen seconds a lightning bolt of pain would strike behind her eyes, the beginnings of a migraine headache that if left unchecked would grow into a debilitating monster.

Ignoring the half-full bottles of over-the-counter painkillers lined up on her desk blotter she instead rose and crabbed around the desk and hauled open the squeaky top drawer of her government-issued filing cabinet. On tiptoes, she found her last bottle by feel and fished it out.

Pausing by the wall containing photos and framed pieces of paper proclaiming her many achievements, she plucked one off the wall and stared hard at the 8x10 glossy trapped under glass. *Better days*, she mused. *All gone by*. She etched the image into her memory and replaced it on the wall.

Back at her desk, she cracked the seal and spun the cap off the bottle of Don something or other—the good tequila she'd finished weeks ago. The bottle of so-so Anejo tequila she'd just finished sat on her blotter. Wondering if the cloud of depression would lift long enough for her to mount an expedition to procure some more, she tossed the empty into the wastebasket with the others. Then she poured herself a shot and hefted it towards the wall and the photos there. "To you." Crinkling her nose, she downed the clear liquid and refilled her glass.

The message from Cade was still front and center on the laptop screen, the news there simultaneously good and bad.

A few keystrokes later and the reply was gone. A couple more quick taps by Nash and up popped an ominous-looking home page with the words *National Security Agency* front and center. Below the red letters were a whole slew of warnings pertaining to things like need-to-know and detailing how high a security clearance one had to possess to proceed any further. Save for President Clay and a handful of others sheltered in place around the CONUS, anyone with a pay grade and security clearance high enough to allow them access to the NSA servers housing the top-secret PRISM data collection program were still missing and presumed dead.

Bite my pay grade, thought Nash as she once again did something that before the collapse was totally unthinkable to someone without the proper security clearance. Feeling a shudder of anticipation ripple up her spine, she keyed in the password given to her by the President and in seconds was in and navigating her way to the servers that contained metadata concerning virtually every electronic communique made before, during, and after the Omega virus swept the globe. Fifteen hundred miles away in a climate-controlled glass building in Fort Meade, Maryland, the sixteen-character password was received and verified by a Cray XT5h supercomputer nicknamed the *Black Widow.* There was no perceptible lag between keying in the President's only daughter's name and a series of numbers and letters and the screen's change from dire warning to a host of different avenues leading to a slew of highly classified information. Nash moved the cursor and selected a link with an innocuous header reading Data Stores. A fraction of a second later she was granted access to a separate firewalled server bank containing an ungodly amount of metadata surreptitiously collected from Google, Facebook, YouTube, Microsoft, AOL, Skype, Apple, and every major cell provider in the world. That the facility was still up and running didn't surprise Nash one *bit.* She smiled at the pun. A *bit* was a minuscule amount of memory compared to the nearly limitless storage available there and elsewhere around the world. But Meade was still up and running and that's all that mattered to Nash. Before the outbreak it was reported widely via FOIA (Freedom of

Information Act) requests that funds had been allocated and released to build a 150-kilowatt-power-generating substation on the premises in Maryland as well as a vast NSA-run data storage facility at Camp Williams in rural Utah. And knowing the secretive nature of the DoD and NSA and all of the other alphabet agencies as well as she did, Nash believed the construction of the substation had been finished and was up and running well before the funds were even requested. The latter probably coming as a big case of CYA after armies of government bean counters were unleashed in order to account for every last red cent immediately following the worldwide banking crisis that started in 2007 and peaked in 2008. And since Nash had firsthand knowledge that Camp Williams had fallen to the dead just days after the first cases were reported, the data center slated to be constructed there was a moot point even if ground had been broken and construction had started unbeknownst to the congressional gatekeepers overseeing it, or the American taxpayers funding it.

She scrolled past the date now called Z-Day by those who'd survived it and saw the numbers of captured communications fall off exponentially from tens of millions of intercepts a day down into the hundreds of thousands. Then just a week after that awful Saturday when the dead began to walk, the collecting of private data all but ceased including all outgoing calls and data usage from the particular number she was searching.

Freezing the scrolling list of phone numbers three days prior to the current date, which was the last time she'd accessed the servers, she cued up the first capture on the list. At 12:34 AM Eastern time someone tried calling out from a device bearing a West Virginia area code. Probably a prepper with a solar charger for their phone who happened to be lucky enough to have holed up close to one of the few cell towers with its own solar backup system.

Finished hypothesizing, she scrolled slowly through the list, keeping a vigilant watch for a certain area code. There were only a couple of hits before she got to the current day's date. *Nothing new.* And she wasn't really surprised. For over the past week since she'd first started snooping around the NSA's servers she'd conjured up a hundred different scenarios why the number she was hoping to see wasn't still active, none of them positive.

After downing the tequila, Nash slammed the Panasonic shut and leaned back in her chair, eyes fixed on the photo, fingers drumming a slow funeral dirge against the armrests.

***

Thirty minutes later, the phone Nash had taken to calling the *bad phone* jangled. Picking up between the first and second ring, she cradled the fire-engine-red handset between her neck and shoulder, stated her name, and then listened as the President spoke.

***

Five minutes later, President Valerie Clay wrapped up her call and told Nash to relay words of praise from her to the 50th Space Wing—the seasoned group of airmen at Schriever whose job it was to keep the nation's few remaining satellites aloft and continually beaming images of a world fully in its death throes back to Schriever.

Nash hung up the *bad phone* which had once again lived up to its newly bestowed moniker, snatched up the sleek black handset and dialed the Satellite Operations Center.

A young female airman named Jensen, one of Nash's brightest, answered at once. She listened to the instructions while copying them word for word into a logbook.

The entire exchange lasted just a few seconds; however, the implications, if what President Valerie Clay's last remaining intelligence asset had asserted was true, would be felt for quite some time and possibly open up a whole new front in the war in which the nation's very survival was at stake.

Nash said a silent prayer as she replaced the black handset. She consulted her watch. *Forty-five minutes.* That was how long she had to wait to see if, for the second time in an hour, she would be doing another thing, totally separate, yet also unthinkable to her before Z-Day—rooting for the dead.

Chapter 16

The finality of the deed wasn't lost on Glenda as she slipped a pair of Louie's 2X sweatpants over her own pair of Levi's. Holding the bathrobe open, she looked in the mirror and noticed the sharp ridges where the magazines she'd taped there bulged underneath. Like a Saturday Night Live caricature of a hard core bodybuilder, her thighs and calves appeared enormous. *Perfect*. Resisting the urge to stare in the mirror, clap her hands, and say, *I want to pump you up*, she instead slipped back on the worn Hi-Tec hikers that hadn't seen action since last year's trip to Yellowstone. As she cinched the leather and nylon items tight the movement caused a thick strand of sinew to work loose from the robe and fall across the top of her hands with a wet *splat*.

Gloves, she thought to herself.

She found the fingerless leather driving numbers, one of many accessories to Louie's mid-life crisis, in the closet stowed inside the *authentic* Aberford tweed driving hat which was placed strategically on the shelf above the camel hair coat he usually donned for their many weekend countryside drives. She smiled, remembering him in the ensemble. So proud. Yet so goofy-looking. A Scotsman in English aristocratic guise. An article in a car magazine kicked off the obsession and in a weeks' time a restored one-owner Austin-Healy Sprite was taking up space in their garage, as well as her mind. But she loved Louie so she learned to love that car. And the getup. And the faux English accent he'd surprised many a gas attendant with— even the ones who knew him.

She stopped by the bed and ran her fingers through his matted hair. Scooped a pair of number tens and a second pair of the smaller number eight needles from the bedside table. The metal was cool and reassuring against the skin of her left inner forearm as she slipped all four underneath the National Enquirer taped there.

"Bye, honey," she whispered. With two fingers extended in a V she closed his eyes. Cupped his cheek with her palm and let it linger. "See you on the other side."

Worrying the chain and gold crucifix around her neck, Glenda took the stairs down one at a time. Stiff-legged. Robot-like. The turn at the landing was a little challenging. A slow pivot was all it took to get her facing in the right direction. There would be no running with this improvised suit of armor. That much was clear.

Once in the kitchen, Glenda peeked through the boarded-over window and saw nothing dead in the backyard. So she pulled up a chair and prepared her final meal in the only home she'd known. And though she was awash in the stink of death, a dozen saltine crackers and half a bottle of mustard was necessary to mask the fishy flavor and odor so she could choke down her next to last can of sardines.

She stuffed the half-sleeve of crackers and remaining tin of sardines in one of the robe's pockets. In the other she slipped a manual can opener and a medium-sized kitchen knife wrapped tightly in a dish towel. The former she brought in case she found a place to stay the night that hadn't already been thoroughly looted. Nothing worse than having an itch you can't scratch, she figured. The latter she brought as a decoy in case she ran into brigands like the ones who used to prowl Huntsville. Give up the knife, and the knitting needles might go unnoticed. Fifty/fifty chance of that one working, she conceded. She looked around the kitchen and decided that she had no more strategizing left in her. *Time to get the show on the road, old broad,* she thought to herself.

'*Go on living,*' is what Louie Gladson told her shortly before drawing his last breath. '*Keep it simple,*' were his final words. Words that jogged Glenda's memory, spurring her into action. She transited the kitchen and dining room and hooked a right at the arched entry to the living room and wobbled over to her chair, which was smaller than Louie's but as a consolation had a side pocket from which she retrieved a blue book, dog-eared and bristling with sticky notes. It went into the robe's other pocket and she retraced her steps. In the kitchen she took another look between the horizontal boards and saw the coast was clear. So she plucked the claw hammer from the floor and pried a couple of boards loose and, with a tear tracing her cheek, threw open the deadbolt.

***

The Austin's battery didn't have a spark. That had been confirmed three weeks after the dead took over the streets in downtown Huntsville. And was also the reason Louie was dead. She presumed his demented mind must have convinced him it was OK to try and start the thing and go for a midnight drive.

Shaking her head, Glenda eyed the Austin with equal measures disdain and disgust. Why not a reliable pickup? Or a Ford Taurus like every other couple their age over in Logan and Salt Lake City? He might still be alive. If not lost and tooling the countryside without a clue to whom he was or where he was going. At least he died *trying* to do something he loved, she thought warmly.

Seeing a lull in undead activity in the general vicinity, Glenda got into character and quietly hinged the back door inward.

Negotiating the steps was a pain in the neck. She had to take them one at a time in order. Once on the concrete walk she slowly panned a one-eighty from left to right. Left was clear. Just beds of water-starved dirt full of long dead flowers. Harkening in fall, the leaves on the lone oak in the back yard were starting to get tinges of yellow at their edges.

The garage was dead ahead, its door wide open, a useless low-slung car with a dead battery staring right at her. With two massive headlights atop its fenders, the burgundy roadster looked wide eyed, like it'd been caught doing something red handed—or more appropriately, thought Glenda, like she had looked the day she realized the shit really had hit the fan, a permanent state of shock parked on her face.

A bit theatrically, she stumbled off the lowest step and angled for the gate while consciously adding a stagger to her gait. The moment she rounded the southeast corner of her home the sound of

81

bare flesh on flagstone reached her ears. A dozen yards downhill, visible just over the scraggly low shrubs bordering the dogleg-shaped driveway, a female zombie ambled down the sidewalk, eyes fixed ahead, mouth set in a permanent sneer.

A lump formed in Glenda's throat, but she didn't let the fear overwhelm her. *Be them,* her new mantra, cycled through her head.

Ignoring the dead thing, Glenda passed under the kitchen window and two dozen laborious steps beyond it the dining room plate glass slid by in her side vision. Finally she reached the front steps, her first real test, and descended them with zombie-like precision, tottering and stiff-legging every other stair until meeting the sidewalk with a spine-jarring final misstep.

Once again she panned her head slowly to the left, unblinking eyes locked forward, conscious to keep her features free of all emotion. *Be them.*

The sneering monster stopped on the slight incline, its head turned stiffly, and fixed its guileless gaze on her. Head cocked, jaw moving slow and clumsy, like a cow working a plug of cud, it seemed to be sizing her up just as the last vibration coursed through her shin and exited out the bottom of her Hi-Tec. The scrutiny lasted all of two or three seconds—a lifetime for Glenda considering the consequences if the monster saw through any part of her elaborate facade.

Fixing her own vacant stare on a patch of tall weeds across the street, she about-faced left and ambled past the driveway and the zombie wavering there.

When she was but a handful of feet from the first turn it emitted a low rumbling growl, and in her peripheral Glenda saw the thing's putrefied legs from the knees down start to move. The road-worn bare feet with toes scraped down to bloody nubs made a slow shuffle to the left that emboldened Glenda to steal a quick little glance. She saw the back of its head, hair all matted and home to twigs and bugs. A fist-sized piece of flesh had been rent from the lower back area and there were purple ringed bite marks all up and down the left arm, which started swinging rhythmically as the creature put one putrefying foot in front of the other and ambled away in search of prey.

***

Ten minutes later, after another half-dozen benign encounters on her block with flesh-eaters, two of whom she recognized as former neighbors, Glenda turned left and, feeling the sun warm on her face and shoulders and hearing no obvious sounds of pursuit, relaxed and allowed her head to loll and jerk with each choreographed footstep. Leaving several fire-razed blocks of her old neighborhood and scores more walking dead behind her, she proceeded east at a glacial pace towards the car-choked gray stripe of SR-39 shimmering in the distance.

Chapter 17

Cade entered the compound and paused in the perpetual gloom of the foyer. Waited ten seconds. Fifteen. Then from down the corridor came a greeting from Seth.

"Collecting my thoughts," replied Cade, stalking from the shadow and through the T. He stopped and craned his head left, listening for his daughter's infectious laugh. Hearing nothing, he approached Seth, whose hair and beard were in some kind of a race to claim as much open territory on his normally clean shaven face as possible. In the three weeks since Logan's murder Seth had let himself go in the grooming department. His dark brown bangs now covered his eyes like a funeral veil and an inky black beard encroached like wild brambles from all points east, west, and south. And barely visible, protruding from the ragged thicket at each corner of his mouth, the mere sight of which made Cade want to smile, were two spikes of twisted whiskers forming a kind of *stealth* handlebar mustache—obviously cultivated in memory of his lost friend.

"They're all still in there," called Seth. "Heard them playing some music a little bit ago."

"Music?"

"One of them has an iPod or something. Could have sworn I heard Blue Oyster Cult."

"Godzilla?"

"No, better. *Reaper.*"

Ducking his head, Cade entered the communications bunker. "Excuse me," he said, reaching in front of Seth. He plugged the power cord and external antenna lead into the Thuraya satellite phone and arranged it on the shelf next to the others. Checked the pair of long range multi-channel CBs taken from the quarry. Saw they were fully charged.

Without prompting, Seth assured Cade he'd keep a close eye on the sat-phones.

"Figured as much," answered Cade. "Where's Heidi?"

"Daymon asked me to take over. They went thataway," he said, hitching a thumb towards the back half of the compound. "And that's all I know."

"I feel more comfortable with you here as it is. Any luck getting anyone to talk to you on the shortwave?"

"Thanks. And no," replied Seth, absentmindedly twisting one bar of his mustache. He put a finger on the monitor. Specifying the panel showing the entrance, he said, "Both gates are closed and, except for Phillip, everyone's inside the wire." Then his eyes gave away the smile under his beard as he added, "Chief bagged a deer. We're having *venison* tonight."

Busy staring at the monitor where a large group of Zs were shuffling west to east, returning after encountering the fallen trees, Cade said, "I'm already on seconds ... in my head."

Seth chuckled. "See you out there tonight for thirds?"

"Probably, Seth," answered Cade, eyes never leaving the threats on the road.

A peal of laughter echoed from the left. *Definitely Raven*, thought Cade.

Then, twice as loud, angry-sounding voices sprang from the opposite direction. A man and a woman. No doubt about that. Not screaming or hollering, though. Just an intense conversation filled with lots of emotion, none of it his business.

Cade nodded to Seth then set a course away from the adult voices, opting for a tack taking him toward the laughter.

He loitered outside the thin steel door for a second, listening.

Inside, Raven and the Kids were discussing the age at which one had to stop watching SpongeBob SquarePants in order to avoid being lumped into the nerd category.

Someone piped up saying there's nothing wrong with being a *nerd*. Name calling is a form of *bullying*.

Knuckles about to deliver a knock, Cade let his hand hover over the door and smiled because Raven was the one sticking up for others. And there had been real conviction in her response. *We're doing something right*, crossed his mind as he rapped sharply.

All talk ceased.

Cade figured he could hear a pin drop in the corridor.

He knocked again. This time announcing himself.

The door hinged open and Raven was there, smiling, in her ears tiny white buds each trailing a thin wire. "I thought I asked you to give that thing back to Taryn."

"You did," said Raven, much too loudly on account of the music emanating from the tiny speakers.

Cade frowned and shushed her.

She added, "And I did. Just listening to a group called the Clash. Combat Rock, it says here."

Pulling a bud from Raven's ear and speaking loud enough to be heard inside the Kids' quarters, Cade said, "Taryn's got good taste in music."

From beyond the door Taryn said, "Thank you."

"Tell her you want to borrow it again."

Screwing her face up in response to the request running contrary to the previous order issued by her dad, Raven shrugged, looked over her shoulder and asked to borrow the iPhone and pair of speakers Taryn had scavenged from the quarry.

"Phone only," whispered Cade.

"Forget the speakers," Raven called out.

Taryn appeared at the door. "What do *you* need it for, Raven?" And though the question was directed verbally at the petite twelve-year-old, Taryn's dark eyes bored into Cade's.

"For the music," proffered Raven.

Crossing her arms, the tattoos gracing them forming an intricate road map of precise line work, Taryn said, "The battery is almost toast."

Nodding and holding Taryn's steely gaze, Cade replied, "*She* will bring it back shortly. Can *she* have the solar charger also?"

Taryn said nothing. Disappeared back inside.

The tension not fully registering, Raven looked up and mouthed, "The charger? Are we going somewhere?" But before Cade could answer, the door opened wider and Sasha was there, hands on hips. A tick later Wilson appeared, towering over her and shooting a questioning look directly at Cade.

Sighing, Cade began to explain himself but was cut short as Taryn reappeared, handed him the shiny black accessory, and said, "I don't *need* to know. Keep it for as long as *you* want, Raven."

Cade made no reply. He took the charger, turned Raven around by the elbow, and ushered her back the way he'd come, but instead of going to their quarters Cade had them turn right at the T junction. A few seconds later they were topside plopped down in the center of the crop circle. Shortly after that the solar panel was arranged just so and the iPhone was connected and drawing a charge.

Chapter 18

Glenda dug down deep and put one foot in front of the other. She limped forward half a step, paused, and then dragged the opposite foot, making certain to scuff the Hi-Tec's toecap on the follow through before finishing off with another faux half-limp. And though she was laboring under the afternoon sun while wearing two layers over which was draped the detritus covered bathrobe, her entire body was wracked by waves of goose bumps and a cold unending sweat that drenched her from head to toe.

Ignoring the constant chafe and trying her best to keep from shivering, she forged ahead, faithful that the makeup job and stench emanating from the robe would fool the dead long enough for her to get away from Huntsville.

With that little voice in her head urging her to give in to the gnawing fear and run growing louder and louder with each passing second she slowly overtook a few horribly burned foot-draggers and entered a throng of two dozen or so tottering cadavers without garnering so much as a sidelong glance from the entire rotten collection.

Be the dead, she thought, watching their heads bobbing in her side vision.

Limp. Drag. Limp.

Remain in character, Glenda. Do not look them in the eye.

Limp. Drag. Limp.

Be the dead.

Limp. Drag. Limp.

With the sun off her right shoulder, Glenda walked among them while maintaining her *undead* gait with metronomic precision. Suddenly, less than a mile from the State Route as a crow flies, the undead, intrigued by, presumably, some long dead person's abandoned wash flapping and popping on a nearby clothesline, peeled off in unison towards the short paved drive leading up to the property.

The abrupt change of direction startled Glenda, catching her entirely by surprise and for a split second she came out of character to avoid being hockey checked by a scraggly male Z that had been, prior to the sudden about-face, near the head of the procession. As Glenda took one of its clammy bare shoulders straightaway to the mouth, she was knocked aside and one of her upper canines tore a half-moon-shaped gash the size of a quarter just right of its ridged clavicle.

As the oblivious walker staggered a few inches off track, never once taking its eyes from the rustling wash that had piqued its interest, Glenda emitted a soft, barely audible gasp.

Barely audible, that is, to all but the thing she nearly took a bite out of.

Reacting to the new sound, the Z stopped mid-stride, staggered like a drunk at closing time, and slowly swiveled its head left, all interest in keeping up with the rest of the group gone out the window.

Sensing the scrutiny, Glenda focused on the road a yard in front of her toes and picked up her pace.

Limp. Drag. Limp.

But her mantra, *be the dead*, suddenly changed to: *Lead the bastard away.*

And that's what she did. With the shadows of the first turn's outstretched arms falling on the pavement near her feet, she vectored right and away from the short drive leading to the small single-story residence and the clothesline full of intrigue. As the rest of the dead fell behind, the sound of her lone pursuer's bare feet striking hot pavement stayed with her. Maintaining an arm's length lead, she limped along in character like this for thirty yards or so, the next southbound side street her immediate objective.

With the monster still in tow, she made the turn and ambled a block south. Then with the National Guard roadblock where there had been so much honking and gunfire that first weekend of the outbreak in sight, she hooked a slow tottering left and led the hissing abomination east.

Nearing a long line of battered vehicles that had somehow ended up listing in the left-hand ditch, grill to bumper, in one big pileup, she consciously slowed and bent her left arm and, in one fluid motion, withdrew one number ten knitting needle. Timing her move based on the footfalls behind her, Glenda waited for a slap and when she guessed the thing was in mid-stride, spun around slowly counterclockwise, bringing her left arm horizontal as if offering it to the hungry creature. The thing took the bait. Its eyes bugged and it hissed and parted its maw, where on display were two yellowed rows of cracked and splintered teeth with twisted scraps of gristle and dermis lodged in them here and there. The stench emanating from deep inside its gullet was worse than anything Glenda had ever encountered. Worse even than the reek she'd endured hosing down the rendering plant floor in Kansas that hot summer in '74.

But she didn't budge. Instead, six inches from receiving what could be a life-ending bite, she waggled her arm, focused only on the jaundiced white of the abomination's right eye.

Two things happened at once: The first turn grasped her forearm in a two-handed grip, pinching the skin and flesh there and drew her in. Then its eyes went wide and Glenda felt an incredible bone-crushing pressure as it got a good mouthful of pink terry cloth overlaying the National Enquirer's final issue.

Though the thirty-something male stood a few inches taller than Glenda, the knitting needle provided her a ten-inch advantage in reach. And when she plunged the pointed end into its eye, the pop and sucking sound and flood of viscous fluid that coated her hand took her back to Louie's bedside, instantly reminding her how much this thing called Omega had stolen from her. A twist of the wrist turned the writhing Z into a hundred and sixty pounds of dead weight with its jaw locked tight and ten wrinkled and bloody digits still holding fast.

Taking Glenda down with it, the first turn fell in a vertical heap. Mid-fall she twisted her body to the right and landed face first, the jarring impact blurring her vision and embedding grains of blacktop into her cheek and brow.

Shaking the stars away, Glenda craned her head and looked down the length of her body, between the Hi-Tec's scuffed toes, towards the distant driveway. *Nothing.* She was still alone ... *for now.* So she went to work, frantically trying to free herself. First she tore her arm from its bite with back and forth twisting motions until its head lolled away leaving a number of teeth firmly snagged in the triple layers of fabric, duct tape, and paper. The bony hands, however, were ice cold and locked to her robe in a death grip that took a lot of prying with her fingers and the blood-slickened needle to make let go.

On the lookout for approaching feet, Glenda pushed the corpse from her, rolled to her stomach, and cast her gaze towards the right lane. There she saw nothing but a number of trucks and SUVs and cars loaded down with all of the trappings of folks hoping to relocate far away from the heavily populated cities west of Huntsville. There were no crawling half-corpses, nor could she see shuffling feet cutting the light filtering in between the roadway and the undercarriages. Looking higher, through the grimy auto glass, she noticed nothing moving near the shoulder and ditch on the far side of the inert vehicles.

Satisfied the breached roadblock was free of dead, Glenda cleaned the needle on her robe and put it in its place next to the gossip rag and her forearm. Then she rose shakily and, without looking over her shoulder, continued on her way, eastbound, attacking the two dozen miles to Woodruff one clumsy step at a time.

Chapter 19

While the iPhone charged, Cade sat cross-legged, working his Gerber back and forth in slow and deliberate passes against a whetstone.

Nearby, Tran and Duncan prepared the fire pit for the evening's feast, stacking seasoned firewood taken from Logan's stash beside the spit erected over the two-foot-deep hole. The deer carcass hanging from a tree nearby would easily feed the group, but with no way to keep the remaining meat from spoiling it would need to be turned into venison jerky. A task that even taking into account their rustic accommodations, Tran, their resident chef, had nearly perfected. Though there were enough beans, rice, MREs, and freeze-dried food packets stockpiled in the dry storage to see them through the winter and well into the next year, the group conscience was to first live off the land when possible and only eat the stores as a last resort. With Chief and Daymon bagging a deer or boar every few days and Tran foraging for edible plants, the group had been eating like royalty the past three weeks.

Trying to make small talk, something which he was no good at, Cade looked up from his task and asked, "What are tonight's accompaniments?"

"Deer, deer and ... more deer," replied Duncan.

"And wild spinach," said Tran, gesturing at a mound of greens resembling partially eaten oak leaves.

"What are the roots there?" asked Cade as Raven whizzed by on the mountain bike, her breathing unusually ragged and audible over the clicking of the freewheel.

"Cattail root. Grind them into a paste ... like potato."

"For a former Green Beanie you sure aren't very perceptive when it comes to what you eat," quipped Duncan.

"I broke bread with Pashtun and lived to tell the tale," Cade said, smiling. "Therefore, I have no reason to ever worry about what crosses my lips."

Knees popping loudly, Duncan rose, regarded Cade with a serious stare and said, "That bad?"

Cade nodded. Said, "Rotted goat and whatever else was in the stew didn't agree with me. I had the shits for a week. And crapping in the Hindu Kush has its own particular set of challenges." He wiped the oil off the whetstone and pocketed it. Cleaned the Gerber with the kerchief he'd used on the stone and slid the black dagger into the scabbard on his hip.

Raven ripped by again with Max in hot pursuit, the Shepherd's rear paws kicking up rooster tails of dark earth.

"Help us with the deer, would ya?" asked Duncan.

After looking at the iPhone which now showed a full charge, Cade unplugged it from the charger, stood up silently, and followed the two men.

***

Once the deer was trussed and hanging over the fire pit, Cade searched out a quiet place where he could keep an eye on Raven and fiddle with the phone.

He picked a tall fir near the Black Hawk and sat with his back to the trunk. Hitched his sleeves to his elbows then thumbed the phone on and watched the display refresh. On the phone, the background—or wallpaper as he'd heard techy people call it—was a picture of Taryn and an older man. Cade swiped the apps to the left until only one row remained and he could see the important elements of the picture. In it he saw that Taryn's hair was much shorter than it was now. She wore a wide smile and was leaning against a man whose hair was closely cropped, graying on the sidewalls but still dark on top. Standing half a head taller than Taryn, the forty-something was

93

smiling as well, the darkly tanned skin pinching on his forehead and around his dark brown eyes. Behind the pair was a low-to-the-ground roadster of some sort. Short windshield. No top. Dotted with primer spots and sitting on steel wheels painted black, the ride was more Rat-Rod than some well-to-do Baby Boomer's trailer queen. It was a daily driver and a work in progress. That was for sure. And it was also obvious to Cade that Taryn was the older man's little girl. There was no doubt about it. His arm was draped around her shoulder and he appeared to be drawing her in close when the photo was snapped. Cade shivered. He felt like a voyeur looking at one of Taryn's *ghosts*— someone she'd never see again and whose ultimate end would most likely forever remain a mystery. Then something far away in the background drew his attention. Behind Taryn and her dad and the roadster, visible above the rooflines of the half-dozen single-story dwellings ringing the cul-de-sac, he recognized the same red rock cliff band Ari had rocketed the Ghost Hawk up the face of over a month ago. *Grand Junction,* Cade thought as he started flicking backward through multiple screens chock full of colorful icons.

He stopped swiping at the screen when he saw the application shortcut emblazoned with a pixelated gray cog. He tapped the icon and navigated inside the device's general settings and located the slider for Airplane Mode and swiped it off. He pressed the Home button and locked his gaze on the upper left corner and saw that the tiny symbolic jet was now replaced by the words *No Service.* Two words he'd hoped to see. Hit with the realization that his experiment was over before it had even started, he thumbed the Home key and watched the red cliffs and hot rod and smiling faces fade to black.

When Raven passed by next, Cade called her over and, once she jammed to a stop, handed her the iPhone and charger. Seeing the sheen of sweat on her lip and a fiery red tint to her cheeks, and hearing the same barely perceptible wheeze, he furrowed his brow and asked, "You feeling OK?"

Though her appearance spoke differently, she nodded and said, "I'm OK. Just hot and thirsty."

"Then please take these to Taryn and thank her for me. And while you're inside have your mom listen to those lungs."

Rolling her eyes, a move perfected only in the last year or so, she bunched the phone and solar panel in one hand and pedaled away.

Cade called out, "Drink some water, why don't you ... and get something to snack on while you're at it."

Once the girl and dog were out of earshot, Duncan slapped his knee and let out one of his trademark cackles. "You don't need to worry about rotters getting inside the wire."

Cade looked at the deer and the fire Tran had just lit underneath it. He consulted his Suunto and then humored Duncan with a look and a shrug that said *please elaborate*.

After taking a small sip from his flask, Duncan shook his head and said with an alcohol-warped drawl, "You know, you've got a real firecracker there."

"Just like her mom," proffered Cade.

"What I wouldn't give to find a firecracker like Brook," said Duncan, his voice trailing off as he stared at the sputtering fire. There was an uncomfortable silence. Cade looked over at Tran who simply shrugged. Then, apparently realizing how creepy his statement had sounded, Duncan stammered, "No ... no ... no ... I meant a firecracker *like* her ... but with a decade or two more mileage on her chassis."

Cade smiled at the *mileage on her chassis* part of his statement. Then he beckoned Duncan over and whispered in his ear, "Number one ... make sure Brook doesn't hear you compare a woman's body to a pick-up. Number two ... you ought to think about laying off the *Jack*. We launch at first light—" He looked at the Suunto and quickly did the math—"fourteen hours, give or take. We need to refuel first at Morgan then we fly southeast to our objective."

"Objective?"

"All I have is a waypoint in the desert."

"What then?"

"We wait."

Arms outstretched, Duncan bobbed his head like one of those dolls.

Recognizing the universal gesture meaning *tell me more*, and having already decided to wait until the morning when they were in the air, Cade simply shook his head no.

"Fuck it," said Duncan, spinning the cap off the flask, the lid clinking as he tilted back and drained the last of the bourbon. He held the pose and let the final few drops hit his tongue before spinning the cap back on and stowing the flask away in a pocket.

Cade mouthed, "No more tonight. I need you sharp because there's rumored to be a pot of gold waiting for all of us at the end of this mission."

Intrigued by the sound of things, Duncan said, "No problem. I'll be good to go at zero-seven-hundred."

You better, thought Cade as he stalked off towards the compound. A half-dozen yards away he slung his carbine and spun around and walked backwards. "Oh seven hundred," he bellowed. "Hundred bucks says you're late."

And when he turned back around, a knowing grin spread on his face due to those last five words, which were calculated and uttered as a direct challenge meant to activate Duncan's compulsively competitive nature. Craps or blackjack. Baccarat or Texas Hold 'Em. Horses or dogs. Just so long as the *action* was there, the method of delivery didn't matter to a self-professed compulsive gambler like Duncan. And though the former Vietnam-era aviator was wise to it or not, Cade had just surreptitiously provided that action.

And he didn't feel a shred of remorse for doing so.

Chapter 20

From the viewing angle, which left everything on the screen rounded on top and pinched at the edges, Nash knew that the satellite which had captured the days-old footage she was viewing had been locked in a bad orbit at the edge of its effective range. Still, she took note of the warship's spacing, paying close attention to the dozen or so vessels coming in over the horizon. The largest on the right she'd been told by one of her analysts was the *Liaoning*, China's newest aircraft carrier, which had been rushed into commission even before sea trials were completed. Surrounding her were half a dozen support ships, big and boxy and riding closely alongside. Spread out farther, both left and right, were the picket ships, a frigate and a couple of corvettes, plus the standout near the carrier, a stealthy Guangzhou-class destroyer of the same name whose sole role was to provide anti-sub as well as anti-air protection for the carrier.

Already privy to the outcome of the carrier group, she fast-forwarded and found the satellite footage shot over the Eastern Seaboard and paused it at a predetermined time stamp and counted the vessels. The destroyer was there, plowing ahead in calm-looking seas, a jagged white V spreading out from its bow. Next to it on the right was a single Chinese missile frigate, the *Hunong*, and on its right was the unmistakable black rounded hull of a very long Russian Borei-class submarine, the *Yuri Dolgorukiy*. That it was riding the surface with impunity so close to Norfolk was very troubling. More so was the company it was keeping.

Nash forwarded the hours-old footage until she recognized the Chesapeake Bay. The sub was nowhere to be seen as it had submerged shortly after it was spotted next to the other two surface ships; however, it appeared to Nash and was already confirmed through new imaging that the frigate and destroyer were entering the bay apparently intent on making a landing on U.S. soil. She watched the two vessels moving at a cautious pace until they were just offshore from Naval Station Norfolk where, presumably, they were trying to draw some kind of response. Which Nash knew wouldn't be coming. The ships still at dock were ghost ships, their crews either dead or among the ranks of the undead.

Nash pinned her hair up and donned a navy blue ball cap emblazoned with the Air Force insignia and continued watching as the destroyer launched a gray helicopter from its fantail. Adjusting her hat, she plucked the phone from the cradle and punched the autodial button to the Tactical Operations Center. When Jensen answered, Nash asked that the live feed from the satellite in orbit high over Norfolk be placed on the largest monitor front and center. She replaced the handset and closed the laptop. Stowed the nearly full bottle of tequila and glassware and closed the filing cabinet drawer on the way to the door.

Stepping into the carpeted hall, she thought to herself, *Let's see how our interloping commie friends fare against their welcoming party..*

Chapter 21

Shortly after leaving the roadblock and the dozen hollow-eyed immolated corpses behind, Glenda started to acquire rotten traveling partners. Obviously thinking—*or not*—that she, the gray-haired corpse, was onto something, tramping ahead with her newly perfected *undead* limp, the motley crew arrived in dribs and drabs.

The first joined when Glenda was coming to the end of a long, flat, and forgiving stretch of SR-39 flanked by fencing and fallow fields. Dragging a greasy mess of entrails, the upper half of a corpse scrabbled from the ditch and onto the roadway, fixed her with a milky gaze, and started clawing its way east. Then, just fifty yards further where the grade steepened, the second Z, an emaciated and pustule-covered forty-something male, had emerged suddenly from behind an early model Chevy van sitting on four flats. With one bony hand planted on the van's wildly painted side, the thing stood stock still, regarding Glenda hungrily through clouded eyes.

Be the dead.

The mantra worked up until the moment Glenda was within a yard of the undead male and then, suddenly, as if she'd tripped a photo-electric-eye in a fun-park haunted house, the putrid horror lunged into her path. The bathrobe absorbed the impact and before she knew it she and the emaciated corpse were limping lockstep shoulder to shoulder. Almost touching. Dangerously close. So close in fact that Van Man, as she decided to call him, cast a shadow eclipsing Glenda's and in her left ear she could hear clearly the constant clicking of teeth and rasps and moans triggered by the wind rippling the tall grass growing up alongside the road.

Be the dead.

***

Sometime later, on the lee side of the long uphill climb Glenda had dreaded since leaving Huntsville, the half-man crawler fell from sight and was replaced by zombies number two through five.

The quartet had been standing statue-like and, from a distance, they initially struck her as plasticized cadavers posed in mourning over one of their own. Like escapees from the Body Works exhibit that traveled the country from museum to museum before the Omega virus brought the very things of someone's macabre imagination to life.

The unmoving zombies each occupied a point of the compass forming a near perfect box around a long dead corpse that had already given up every last scrap of meat to the undead weeks ago—and the hard-to-get-to morsels, presumably, to the carrion birds and maggots since. Unlike the dead ogling it, the thing on the ground was but a hollow shell. Clumps of gray hair littered the pavement around its eyeless skull. Strips of fabric stiff with dried black fluids clung to the few remaining scraps of brittle, sun-baked dermis.

Of the group standing about the corpse, three were smaller and decayed to the point where making a determination to sex was impossible. The fourth, though stooped, was taller and definitely female judging by the flaccid breasts still constrained by remnants of a threadbare underwire bra.

As Glenda limped by with Van Man shadowing her closely, she wondered, *Why the vigil? Were they a family once? Was the taller one their mother? Mombie?* Stifling a chuckle, she fixed her gaze on a spot on the ground and plodded ahead.

Drawing up alongside the ghastly scene, Glenda saw the inert figures in her side vision and was about to thank God she wasn't on their radars when, inexplicably, and in unison, the four *first turns* made a sound like brittle fallen leaves skittering ahead of a sudden gust of wind. A tick later the one she'd deemed *Mombie* performed a clumsy, three-part shuffling turn to her right and, with the smaller Zs glued to her hip, fell in behind Van Man.

Instantly Glenda broke out in a cold sweat and along with it the nagging fear that as a result her makeup would smear and run.

But it didn't. Repeating the mantra calmed her down again. And the very real possibility of the flesh being ripped from her bones did not come to fruition.

They scaled the uphill grade. A gaggle of unlikely road dogs staggering in a loose little knot. Nearing the hill's apex, the sun at their backs threw shadows long and giant-like before disappearing on the opposite, downhill side, which Glenda tackled without pause.

Even as her knees and ankles screamed out in pain during the arduous journey down the steep grade, she retained her poise.

Be the dead.

Halfway down the steep grade, moving only her eyes, Glenda looked up and saw that the Shell station where Louie liked to trot out his fake accent and preferred to have the Austin Healey serviced had caught fire and burned. Having suffered the same fate, a handful of cars, totally unrecognizable as to make or model, were settled on warped rims nearby. All that remained of the now windowless store and attached garage were four soot-covered cinderblock walls and a rollup door, its steel panels black with soot and wavy and still in the closed position. Clearly compromised by the high heat, the once laser-straight metal roof braces now sagged considerably in the center. And though it was still nearly a mile away, untouched yet illuminated by the waning sun, the red and yellow vacuum-formed sign rising up from one corner of the lot called to her like a beacon.

The last dozen yards before the road again turned flat and smooth were especially killer, the deceleration taking a toll on her fifty-seven-year-old knees. Once she was out of the hill's shadow and saw her own ever lengthening, she knew that dusk was imminent and with it an almost instantaneous drop of ten degrees or more in temperature. Fifty-five degrees she could handle. But at this elevation the temperature was likely to drop to the mid to low forties well before midnight.

A bathrobe and some magazines over two layers of clothing made mostly from cotton wouldn't be sufficient in the open to keep her warm against the elements. And once her teeth began chattering, she knew without a doubt she'd be the next meal for Van Man, Mombie, and her brood. So she began planning her great escape. And the gas station, though a shell of its former self, might be just what she needed.

***

Glenda figured the last arduous mile took her at least thirty minutes to cover. Finally nearing the Shell station which occupied an acre or two on the north side of 39, something moving a hundred yards beyond the ditch, on the south side of the State Route, caught her eye.

Amid the tall grass, she saw hunched backs. A tattered red plaid shirt and a pale white neck and shoulders contrasting sharply underneath. A dozen paces later her viewing angle changed and she realized what she was seeing was a trio of zombies feeding on a deer carcass. And what struck her at that moment was how involved they were whatever they focused on. In this case there was nothing more important than tearing and rending jagged strips of flesh and sinew and jamming it all two-handed into their mouths. The amount of blood sluicing down the chin and wetting the shirt of the creature facing in Glenda's direction sent a sharp jolt down her spine. Then suddenly, perhaps smelling the fresh kill or just excited by the incessant movement, Glenda's entire entourage stagger-stepped right and their hair-raising rasps commenced.

In response to the sound, one right after the other, the feeding Zs rose up. Shorter to tallest. Left to right. Female, male, male. Their ages indeterminable due to their thoroughly blood-spattered faces.

With the Shell sign in her left side vision, no longer sun-splashed but still beckoning her, Glenda made a slow pivot in that direction.

In her right side peripheral she saw Mombie pause and cast a matronly—in Glenda's mind at least—gaze over her shoulder across the two-lane.

Be the dead.

By the time the first shards of glass crunched under the soles of Glenda's hikers, *Mombie* was out of sight, no doubt following in the footsteps of what most likely, in life, had been her offspring.

Chapter 22

Jamie materialized out of nowhere and stopped Cade in his tracks just outside the compound entrance. "Can I ask a favor of you?"

He looked the young woman up and down from head to toe. Not in a creepy leering old guy kind of way. But more of a quick tactical observation. A surreptitious once-over to try and determine her motives before going any further.

Her short dark hair was slicked back and, telegraphing the seriousness of the forthcoming question, her neck muscles were corded and the tanned skin around her ice blue eyes was taut. And as if her proposal had already been denied, she'd already adopted a defensive, arms crossed posture.

There was a black carbine slung over her shoulder; holstered on one hip was a .40 caliber semiautomatic pistol. Tight against her thigh, in a makeshift scabbard held in place by a leather thong, was a two-foot-long tomahawk she claimed to have found in a rundown log cabin twenty miles north of the compound.

That she'd disappeared, rambling the countryside alone for a week following the events at Bishop's lake house, came as no surprise to Cade. Everyone was dealing with the recent losses in their own way. In fact, the chain of events leading up to her rescue were so hard to talk about for some of those involved that those who hadn't been had taken to referring to those three days in August as simply '*the incident.*' A phrase that, mercifully, didn't immediately conjure up images of Logan and Gus's bullet-riddled bodies. Nor did it dredge up awful sights and smells in the minds of the men who had exhumed Jordan's maggot-infested body from the shallow grave at the quarry and reburied it up on the knoll with the others.

Breaking the uneasy silence, Cade said, "Depends on the favor."

Cutting to the chase, Jamie blurted, "I want to go with you and Duncan. I don't care where ... I just want to get away from here."

"Thought you took care of the wanderlust and cleared your mind on your week-long walkabout," said Cade. He leaned against the entry. Crossed his arms and added, "I think you're romanticizing what I do."

"I'm bored to death."

"Careful what you wish for."

There was a silence. Ten seconds. Fifteen.

"I miss Logan. I think about him all the time."

Cade felt the handle rattle from inside and pushed off from the door. A tick later Chief exited, looked the two over and walked on without a word.

"Is Chief going?"

Cade shook his head. Said, "No."

"Lev?"

Cade nodded. Said, "Yes."

"Daymon?"

Again Cade nodded to the affirmative.

"Your wife or Taryn?" asked Jamie. "Are they going?"

For another ten seconds Cade said nothing. A shadow passed over the clearing and the air chilled suddenly as a bank of thunderheads blocked out the sun. He moved his head side-to-side. Said, "No. Brook won't let Raven leave her side. She's kind of a *mama bear* in that regard. And Wilson ... he *needs* Taryn. She wears the pants in that one there. I wouldn't do that to the kid."

"So you're telling me with a straight face that not one woman is going along on this outing."

Cade looked her in the eye. "Only you," he said. "But you need to listen close and follow my every move. Can you agree to that?"

Uncrossing her arms, Jamie smiled. In fact it was the first time he'd seen her pearly whites since she'd nudged Bishop out of the helicopter and into the waiting arms of the dead.

"Thank you," she said. "I won't slow you down."

Cade opened the door. Voices filtered past him. Young. Happy. So full of hope. He stepped part of the way inside and then turned back. "I know," he said. "We leave at first light. Bring the tomahawk."

Cade stopped in the security room to greet Seth. The twenty-something was finally looking better now that the horrors of the *incident* were beginning to fade. And though he'd let his hair and beard grow unchecked since, his gray eyes were full of life and he carried himself with confidence. "Back in the saddle?" asked Cade.

Nodding, Seth said, "Feels good to be back at the helm. How's Heidi?"

Absentmindedly poking a finger at the single bulb dangling near his head, Cade said, "Since all of the shrinks in the world probably became Z food on day one, I think some R and R to get her mind off of things would be a good start. Especially seeing how ever since the *incident* her obsession with hailing the survivors on Logan's list has gotten out of hand."

Seth looked away from the closed circuit monitor, nodded, and then returned his gaze there for a moment.

Cade went on, "Though I'm no shrink ... short of drug therapy, I think forcing her into some kind of routine topside would be ideal. The daylight and fresh air would do wonders for her. I'm sure of that. Might even reset her internal clock so she can get some regular rack time." Cade bobbed his head around the gently oscillating light bulb like a sparring fighter, grew tired of that and grabbed the coffee pot and filled a Styrofoam cup.

"Quiet up at the road," proffered Seth.

There was a short silence as Cade stared at the monitor while mulling over the looming talk with Brook. Finally, ignoring the small talk about rotters at the road, he finished his thought and said, "Nothing any of us can do to help Heidi. Her and Daymon ... they're going to have to work through it themselves." He drank the coffee down an inch. Arched an eyebrow and hoisted the cup as if offering the younger man a toast. "Good brew."

Seth shot Cade a thumbs up then leaned back in the rolling chair and returned his attention to the goings on topside.

Chapter 23

There was a knock on the door and Brook heard Cade announce himself. So she rose and crossed the container, feeling the plywood cold against her feet through her well-worn socks. She let him in and took his carbine and placed it by the door. Retraced her steps and sat on the bunk in the same warm spot she'd just vacated. She smoothed the sheet next to her and patted the mattress, beckoning him to sit.

Instead Cade pulled over a folding chair, spun it around and sat facing her. He had already adopted the familiar pre-mission hard set to his jaw. His body crackled with an unseen energy and in his dark eyes Brook saw a steely determination that told her he was already committed. Then, pressing his chest against the seatback, he relaxed and removed his cap. Over the next thirty minutes he laid all the cards out on the table. Revealed every little detail he was privy to.

When he was finished there was a brooding silence. The shadows in the room seemed to crowd in on them.

Seeing in Brook's brown eyes the ongoing wrestling match, Cade moved over and claimed the smooth spot on the bunk. He held her and said, "It'll work out. It always does."

"Why does Nash have such a hold on you?"

"I just put you and me in her shoes. Then I figured Raven into the equation ..."

Like the drop in barometric pressure ahead of a looming thunder storm, for three weeks Brook had felt this one building. She knew he'd be drawn back in to the teams sooner or later. That he'd already accepted before consulting her hurt a little but came as no surprise. Even the zombie apocalypse had failed to tame the only child in him. Nor temper the unbridled patriotism residing in his heart.

She had listened closely, noting the details, especially the long distance between the compound and his objective. But what troubled Brook most was the high population center he'd likely be getting to know up close and personal during the impromptu mission.

But he hadn't finished with that. There had been good news and he'd saved it for last. And what he told her stole her breath away. It was definitely, as he'd put it, *a game changer* that made his departure that much easier to swallow. It was the kind of news that all of them needed right now, but she couldn't share. But when she finally could, the revelation would serve to trump the low current tingle of despair omnipresent since the dead inherited the earth.

As if the bombshell he'd just dropped in the tiny room had all of the importance of picking out new furniture, Cade rose, arched a brow, and said, "The venison should be done by now."

"Go by the Kids' quarters and send Raven back here. I want to break it to her first. So she can digest it. Maybe she'll wind down some between now and lights out."

"Will do." Cade hinged at the waist and kissed Brook on the mouth, gently.

She drew him in and reciprocated. Then her tongue entered his mouth and she wrapped her arms around his neck and pressed harder. There was a thinly veiled desperation on her end. Abruptly she leaned back and her eyes locked with his and she delivered the look he knew all too well. It said: *You come back to me, Cade Grayson.*

"I will," he answered intuitively. Drawing away, he added confidently, "No doubt about it."

After dragging the back of her hand across her lips, Brook placed a finger on his lips. She traced a lazy circle on his cheek and holding his gaze, said, "We *will* resume this later ... right where we left off."

Cade fetched his carbine from its spot near the door, nodded and smiled a wicked smile that said: *I'm game.* Without another word he was out the door.

Before the door latch clicked she was on her back and staring up at the bottom of the pale yellow mattress and the black springs cutting crisscross patterns into it.

Bad cop time, she thought. Going through her mind was how much to tell Raven.

Chapter 24

Glenda peered through the empty door pane. There were no dead snooping around inside the burned-out convenience store. She ducked under the push bar and all alone walked the aisles of twisted shelving, being careful to avoid disturbing the imploded cans littering the floor.

Besides the now windowless and hollow hulks of a half-dozen reach-in coolers, the only other recognizable item in the fifty by fifty square was the waist-high counter to her left. On that counter was a misshapen block of plastic that she presumed to be the last worldly remains of the cash register. A skeletal framework rose above the molten mess; every last pack of cigarettes once nestled in the warped slots there were gone—previously looted or burned in the fire. She spun a slow circle. Everything was black. Soot-covered. She gazed out the southern facing openings that once held massive sheets of plate glass. Across the road, Van Man, Mombie, her kids, and the other zombies were hunched over and barely visible, no doubt still plunging their hands and faces in and out of the big buck's chest cavity.

Looking up between the sagging roof joists, Glenda sized up the forming clouds and decided what was left of the roof would provide scant cover if it rained.

And so, treading lightly, she shuffled to the door leading to the garage and was happy to find it unlocked. She went up on her toes and looked into the square of glass embedded in its center and saw nothing but her own reflection staring back from the mirror-like black portal. So she withdrew a pair of the knitting needles and, with one clutched firmly in each hand, dipped her shoulder and nudged the sooty door open.

There was no squeal or squeak of bound hinges as she had expected. Instead, as if some byproduct from the fire had found its way into the moving parts, the steel door swung inward quiet as a passing shadow.

Steeling herself for an attack, she peered in. One eye first. The needle held high and following her gaze.

Like the soot-covered window, it was pitch black inside and strangely enough the garage's interior smelled nothing like the rest of the building. Apparently the combination of the steel door and cement wall between the convenience store and garage had acted as a kind of fire break.

Standing on the threshold, Glenda looked up and saw dark clouds moving in fast overhead. *Rain,* she thought. Then she peered back into the gloom and thought: *Better than a case of pneumonia.*

Suddenly, further validating that decision, she heard a low moan that snapped the hairs on the back of her neck to attention. It had come from behind her. Thankfully, from someplace outside of the building. So, bracing herself with one hand gripping the jamb, she leaned back over the threshold and craned her head right ever so slowly.

Standing outside, its distended gut pressing against the locked double doors she'd just ducked through, and clutching the horizontal push rail two-handed, was what looked like a walking piece of charcoal with curls of burnt dermis ringing the sunken empty sockets where its eyes used to reside. The abomination continued with the dry peal and started shaking the loose doors, the resulting rattle sounding like a passing freight train.

With a cold pang of panic fluttering in her stomach, Glenda gaped at the thing, wondering how in the hell it was able to make the sound if its insides looked anything like its outside. Then she noticed movement over the moaning briquette's shoulder. A hundred yards away, on the other side of SR-39, seven heads popped up and, like a troop of demonic prairie dogs, seven blood-streaked faces swiveled around and stared right at her. Then the seven emaciated forms rose together, slowly, and began a steady march in her direction.

After watching the animated corpses negotiate the ditch and step onto the eastbound lane, Glenda imagined—no, prayed for—a kind-eyed cowboy to come along in an eighteen wheeler and throw their pale forms airborne before running them over and grinding their cold rancid flesh into a fine paste. Then, as her split-second fantasy unfolded, she heard an imaginary pneumatic hiss and a crunching of gears as the phantom rig circled back around to save her.

But that was far from happening. She was still alone and in real trouble. The nerve-racking noise stopped abruptly as Kingsford let go of the door, hinged slowly at the waist, and then fell face first onto the carpet of glass shards littering the store entry no doubt usually graced with some kind of a Welcome mat.

But you're not welcome *here*, she thought. And while the crispy zombie got to its knees, groping the air with stubs for fingers, she saw that the others were nearing the State Route's dashed centerline.

Glenda thought: *Lesser of two evils.* Then she acted, stepping blindly into the gloom. Heart racing, she closed and locked the door and spun back around with the two knitting needles held in front of her horizontally. Crouched on the low stair, coiled and full of tension, she imagined that she looked like a bull anticipating the toreador's next move.

At first the garage's interior was as dark as the inside of a casket, the silence absolute. Glenda remained still, listening, and when nothing came for her she lowered the needles. A few more seconds passed and her eyes adjusted and she saw she was in a large rectangular room with a cement floor and a pair of car lifts located centrally and spaced a few feet apart. On the wall to her left was a row of work benches, their tops cluttered with tools and rags and cans containing all kinds of automotive lubricants.

The trio of horizontal windows on the roller door to her right were papered over. And dollars to doughnuts, if Glenda were a betting woman her money would be on the paper having been placed there after the outbreak.

As she scanned the room for a comfortable place to rest and wait out the zombies, the distinct crackle and pop of glass resonated through the door at her back.

A few more seconds passed and her vision improved and she saw the bulky shadow on the far side of the garage for what it was: an old pick-up truck with wide bulbous fenders and a low box bed jutting out back.

Perfect.

Glenda put the needles away and crossed the garage. She weaved around an inert tire balance machine and some part-worn tires and then stepped over the nearest lift's grounded H-shaped support.

Behind her the door started rattling in its frame. Though not as loud as the outside door, the result was the same. Her stomach clenched and the hairs on her arms reached for the sky.

She wiped a porthole in the grimy smoke-clouded side glass with the sleeve of her equally grimy robe. Peered in and saw there were no keys, let alone an ignition to stick them in. There was no steering wheel or column. Nor seat or seat rails. These were all terms she knew second hand from reading the entries in the joint checkbook as Louie poured dollar after precious dollar into his precious Healey. And like the British roadster had once been, this truck was a work in progress.

There was a loud *bang* as something heavy impacted the rollup door. Glenda started, and when she stepped back from the truck, she noticed razor-thin slivers of daylight on both sides of the door near where the rollers rode up in the channels where there had been none before.

Bang. Bang.

In her mind, she pictured her entire entourage—Van Man, Mombie and her three cubs, plus the deer hunters—slamming against the door, inadvertently creating soot angels on the horizontal panels.

Then she had a thought. The banging continued and she hustled around front of the truck. It felt so good to move normally. *Out of character.* To just be Glenda for a moment. She reached the door and crouched and found exactly what she was looking for.

Threw the flat security bolt into the notch cut into the right side channel.

Bang. Bang. Bang.

Seemingly, all of the monsters were now attacking the door. And hearing the racket increasing in volume and tempo, there was a possibility even more had arrived. As she threw the left bolt into place, the panel near her head buckled inward an inch or so letting in a wide bar of light and then a beat later four pasty white fingers were probing the entry.

Glenda sat down hard with her back to the east wall and the tiny breach full of fingers to her immediate left. She pulled out one needle, straightened her legs, and waited.

***

After three or four minutes, tiny rivulets of coagulated blood ran down the inside of the door and the slender fingers were shredded and ringed with lacerations deep to the bone. Suddenly the four digits withdrew and the light was back, painting the gray floor with a splash of gold.

Five seconds later, eclipsing the sun, a milky eye appeared at the opening.

Perfect.

Glenda hovered the point of the needle an inch from the roving eye and, behind a sharp blow, drove its ten-inch shaft deep into the thing's brain.

Over the course of three hours she repeated the process six times until the slivers of light around the door disappeared and she was so tired she found it impossible to keep her own eyes open. Under the watchful eye of the dead, she fell asleep sitting upright and still clutching the blood-slickened needle.

Chapter 25

After consuming a meal consisting of nuts and greens gathered and prepared into a dry salad by Tran and a couple of strips each of perfectly roasted venison, the Graysons climbed into the Ford F-650, closed the doors, and under the soft glow of the dome light held a lengthy family meeting.

When all was said and done Raven had taken the news better than expected, accepting that her dad was going away for a day or two with aplomb not usually found in most modern day twelve-year-olds.

But these were no longer modern times. In fact, Cade thought as he hugged and kissed Raven atop her head, if he and others like him didn't continue pitching in and doing their part, no matter the risk, he was certain her future would be filled more with misery befitting the dark ages than the Jetsons-like conveniences all of them had gotten used to before the fall.

Seeing her dad's eyes misting, Raven loosened her hold around Brook's neck, scooted across the back bench seat and, from behind, covertly wiped a stray tear from the corner of her father's eye. "You'll be OK, Dad." She paused for a second, seemingly having forgotten what she was about to say.

Cade looked at Brook next to him then studied Raven's face in the rearview mirror. Saw mostly her mom's eyes and dark brown hair and defined features there and noted the innocence still contained in the big browns.

A half beat later Raven said, "Stay frosty, Dad. I'll take care of Max and Mom while you're away."

Cade shifted his gaze to the center console, took Brook's hand in his, and locked eyes with Raven in the mirror. Held them for a beat and said in a low voice, "I know you will, sweetie."

There was a long silence and through his side vision Cade saw a pained half-smile forming on Brook's face.

Then, as if the light at the end of the tunnel was anything but the speeding train the grownups saw it as, Raven vaulted forward, balanced her small frame plank-like on the front seatbacks, and asked if she could stay the night with the Kids in their quarters.

Remembering Brook's words verbatim—*we will continue later where we left off*—Cade squeezed her hand and, using the oldest trick in the parenting book, passed the buck. "It's up to your mom," he said with one brow cocked.

Before the word *mom* had crossed Cade's lips, Brook caused Raven to start by blurting, "Yes, it's OK by me."

Smiling, Cade gazed at the gold and red embers in the distant fire pit and saw the seated bodies around it moving slow and purposeful, fed and fully sated for the time being. He counted eight and even from this distance recognized Daymon, who was facing away, by his spiky top dreads. Shifting his gaze clockwise around the fire, Cade saw Heidi, her equally spiky blonde hair glowing warmly. Next to Heidi was Lev and Jamie, heads tilted back, mouths forming silent O's, faces lit up by soft light and laughter. Chief, Tran, and Jimmy were leaned in close, their features also reflecting the fire's radiance. Cade imagined the hushed small talk and occasional outbursts of Jack Daniels-fueled banter coming from Duncan, who was animated and rocking forward on his camp chair. *Comfortably numb* is what the man proclaimed himself to be these days. Cade made a mental note to do a quick recon on the man's state of inebriation before turning in for the night. Then he wondered how Charlie Jenkins's ghost hunt was coming along. Supposing he'd never find out the answer to that question, he looked at Brook and Raven and fumbled for his two-way radio. Looked up at Brook and said, "Checking in with Seth and Phillip. That's all." Worried the party around the fire pit would draw in more dead, he raised Phillip first.

Pretty quiet at the road, the older man said. Then he checked in with Seth and received nearly the same reply. All quiet on the western front, so to speak. Finally he noted the hour on his Suunto and flicked off the dome light. He said, "Zero six hundred is going to come awfully early." He watched Duncan toss a stick of wood on the embers, then list sideways in the camp chair and barely catch himself before keeling over fully. Cade thought: *More so for some of us than others.*

Savoring the moment under a brilliant star-filled night sky, Cade walked slowly, shoulder to shoulder with Brook and Raven, towards the compound. Halfway across the clearing, near the dirt airstrip, he abruptly peeled away from them and, wraith-like, stalked the periphery of the fire pit just outside of the flickering light spill, taking everything in like a snapshot before finally veering back and reuniting with them at the entrance.

Ignoring a pair of funny looks directed his way, Cade led Brook and Raven through the door. Once inside, the wood smoke clinging to their hair and clothes was instantly overpowered by two very familiar odors. First he picked up the scent of damp earth that reminded him of an unfinished basement. Then came the underlying industrial smell of painted steel fighting a losing battle against the tenacious effects of moisture.

At the T he led them left and stopped in front of the Kids' quarters. Dead center on the door, someone, Taryn he guessed, had taped a sheet of copy paper with the words *Welcome to the Mickey Mouse Club* scrawled in red ink. And a tell to her dry sense of humor, like the sign was drawn up by a first grader, every third or so letter was purposefully turned around.

"We're here, Annette," said Cade with a grin.

Raven about-faced and shot her mom a quizzical look. "Who is *Annette?*"

"Annette Funicello. She was a Mouseketeer ... *way* before your time, sweetie."

"Hell ... way before *our* time, honey," added Cade.

There was an outburst of laughter from behind the door.

"Playing Ouija," said Raven. "They've been contacting dead comedians."

"Are they being *appropriate?*" asked Brook, a serious look parked on her face.

Letting Brook play Bad Cop, Cade eased back against the wall, content just watching.

"I haven't heard of *any* of them."

Good, thought Brook, delivering a rapid-fire knock to the door.

The door cracked open and Sasha filled up the opening. Upon seeing Raven, she said, "Is it OK?"

Raven nodded.

In a sing-song voice Sasha called over her shoulder, "Sleepover," pulled Raven inside and slammed the door, leaving the adults alone in the hallway.

"M-O-U-S-E," said Cade, grabbing Brook by the hand. "I'll be Cubby. You're Annette."

Following Cade through the catacombs, she felt her cheeks flush as the first stirrings of want started down below.

Chapter 26

The banging resumed without warning, the resonant rattle of the rollup door's many moving parts jolting Glenda right out of one nightmare and into another. In her dream the dozen charred and eyeless corpses from the Huntsville roadblock had arisen and begun chasing her. Led by the crispy blind creature that was most certainly still waiting for her inside the convenience store, the obsidian black monsters followed in lockstep precision like the soldiers she presumed they once were. And belting out some crude military cadence, whose only concern was ripping the flesh from her bones, they had cornered her here and were succeeding in breaking down the door just before her eyes snapped open.

Not far from the truth, she thought as she scooted sideways on the cool floor, putting some distance between herself and the bulging garage door.

Then there was another tremendous crash prompting her to stand up and crab around in the dark until she banged her knee against the smooth curvature of the pick-up truck's right front fender.

Trying to stifle a few curse words while concentrating on not kicking any more of the spare parts scattered about the floor, Glenda felt her way in the dark to the passenger door. Thumbed it open, climbed in, and clicked it shut at her back. Kneeling where the passenger seat would be, she reached over and felt the unforgiving hump of the transmission tunnel rising vertically several inches above the floor pan. Tuning out the continuous racket, she rested her upper body where the driver would normally sit and, with the tunnel displacing several ribs and the rubber soles of her hikers flat against the passenger's side door, fell back into a deep sleep.

Chapter 27

Dressing in the dark, Cade donned black combat fatigues. He shrugged on his MultiCam plate carrier and cinched the cummerbund tight. Slipped on the leather hand-me-down boots given to him by his former mentor and current commander of FOB Bastion, Army Special Forces Major Greg Beeson. Velcroed his knee and elbow pads into place and secured a half-dozen fully loaded FDE (Flat Dark Earth) colored magazines for the M4 in the vertical pouches on his chest.

He strapped the Glock 17 to his outside right leg in its black drop-leg holster and left the Glock 19 behind for Raven to practice with. The Gerber went on his belt next to his left hip. Lastly, he rose and grabbed his M4 from its place by the jamb and snagged his tactical helmet—the NVGs already attached—from a metal hook by the door.

In the pitch black he peered in the direction where he imagined Brook's sleeping form would be. Drawing in a deep breath of damp air still laced with her scent, he blew a kiss and eased out into the equally dark hallway.

He closed the door firmly and flicked on his Mini Mag-Lite and, leading with the stark white beam, negotiated the warren to Daymon's door and knocked lightly while still on the move. He made his way to Duncan's door and rapped sharply. Paused for a tick and then delivered another staccato volley to no result.

So he moved on through the security area, greeted Seth, and retrieved the satellite phone and a two-way radio from the shelf.

Poured himself a cup of coffee and made sure Seth was clear that whoever was monitoring the CC television feeds also needed to be on high alert for incoming calls on the other Thuraya sat-phones. Cade shook Seth's hand and squeezed past the chair facing the bank of electronics. At the inner T he hooked left and found himself in front of the quarters Lev, Jamie, and Chief shared. No need to knock. The door hung open and the interior was dark. Figuring Chief was already manning the over watch for the morning shift and the others were topside and chomping at the bit for some action, Cade closed the door and headed back the way he'd come. He couldn't blame them for wanting to get a head start. After spending three weeks prepping the compound for winter and working on beefing up the outer fortifications, he wanted out of *Dodge* as well.

Once outside, Cade held the white foam cup in a two-handed grip, savoring its warmth against his palms. He could see steam wafting up from the cup and roiling clouds when he exhaled. He figured the temps had dropped into the high thirties. Holding the cup under his nose, he inhaled the coffee's heady aroma and walked his gaze across the clearing.

The sky overhead was still a dark shade of purple and scattered stars winked like diamonds on a swatch of velvet. To the east the sun was just starting to take the edge off of night, the cusp of darkness there a tie-dye of violet shot through with orange and yellow. In the inky gloom of the forest canopy the birds were just getting started, their halfhearted warbles floating above the clearing.

To Cade's right the fire from the previous night was still smoking. Thin gray tendrils curled up and then drifted south before getting lost in the early morning fog hanging low around the clearing's edge.

A hundred yards left of the fire pit was the Department of Homeland Security Black Hawk, its navy and gold fuselage glazed with morning dew. Cade noticed that someone had already removed the camouflage netting which was now in a heap on the ground near the helo's nose. A dozen feet to the right, Duncan was crouched beside the helicopter's port side wheel, no doubt checking it for proper pressure or torquing down some nut or bolt there. Apparently finished, Duncan rose and with some sort of tool in hand, walked swaybacked around the helo's nose and gingerly took a knee near the starboard side landing gear. *So far, so good*, thought Cade as he started off towards the chopper. Save the obvious effects of age combined with sleeping on a wafer-thin mattress, from afar the aviator appeared *good to go*.

Cade sipped his coffee and started a slow walk through the dew laden grass. Fifteen feet from the chopper the port side door slid open abruptly. Inside, armed with carbines, and looking like they were ready to go to war, he saw Daymon, Lev, and Jamie sitting on the bench seats. Obviously, the three had consulted with each other beforehand. They were dressed identically: MultiCam fatigues, MOLLE gear and plate carriers, plus tan surplus boots liberated from the quarry. Rounding off their ensembles, each had a white foam cup of coffee identical to the one Cade was holding.

Reacting to the rattle clatter sound of the door opening, Duncan reappeared around the nose.

Cade halted, looked at the *Camo Triplets*, and said, "Larry, Mo, and Curly got their morning Joe." Then, ignoring the daggers being stared his way, pivoted left and tongue-in-cheek addressed Duncan. "And how are you? Bright eyed and bushy tailed this morning?"

"Never better," Duncan lied. In fact, he'd never felt worse. After Logan's death he'd surpassed every previously established bottom and was convinced he was rapidly closing with the eternal flames of hell. That he hadn't slept more than four hours in a stretch since late July only added to his misery.

"Could of fooled me," said Cade. "I've seen tree sloths with more giddy up than you, Dunc."

"I'm flying you to an undisclosed location ... not running a marathon. The bird is ready as she's gonna be," he drawled. "Gimme your cup of Joe and I'll be *good to go*."

The last three words made Cade smile. But that smile was fleeting. His face and eyes hardened and all business-like he questioned the aviator about the Black Hawk's air worthiness.

"She ain't a Huey, that's for sure," conceded Duncan. "Duct tape and chewing gum isn't going to keep her flying. According to the manual she needed a PMS check twenty flight hours ago."

Daymon snorted and looked away. Which led to Lev losing it and doubling over, his belly laugh echoing in the cabin.

Even Cade cracked a smile.

Shaking his head, Duncan said, "Juveniles." He craned his neck and looked at Jamie. "You gonna stand for that crap?"

Jamie said nothing.

Considering the things the young woman had seen and done lately, Duncan wasn't at all surprised that she'd ignored the acronym. Speaking slowly for the benefit of the wiseacres, he said, "Preventative ... maintenance ... services." Then he rounded the Black Hawk's curved nose, calling back to Cade, "Helmet up and strap in, Wyatt."

Ignoring Duncan's use of his nickname, Cade donned his helmet and pointed Daymon to the port side seat. Said, "No time like the present."

"Urch's not ready," called Duncan, a trace of anger in his voice.

"Who said he's flying?" shot Cade. "You planning on having an in-flight medical emergency ... Old Man?"

Making no reply, Duncan strapped himself into the right seat and donned his flight helmet.

Daymon poked his head between the seats and, defending his honor, said matter-of-factly, "You already pointed out the important gauges and taught me how to plug in the waypoints. I used to bounce around in the bitch seat aboard a little King Air calling fire retardant air drops ... *remember?*" Then, silently chastising himself for not following through and hacking off *all* of his dreads, Daymon tucked the side hangers behind his ears and snugged on a flight helmet.

"You did keep her pretty level last time you got stick time," Duncan said. "Go ahead. Get in and don't touch *anything* unless I say so."

Cade passed Daymon the scrap of paper containing the scrawled GPS coordinates then climbed aboard and slid the door shut behind him. He looked around and chose a seat between Jamie and Lev where he could see both Daymon and Duncan. Swapped helmets and plugged the cord into the overhead jack and, taking into consideration the bird's suspect maintenance record, strapped himself in extra tight.

Clutching his M4 vertically between his knees with its business end resting on the cabin floor, Cade said a quick prayer and crossed himself. Sensing Jamie's gaze on him, he looked up and right a degree and met it.

"Thank you," she said, barely audible over the whirring of a starter located somewhere aft in the airframe.

The Black Hawk shuddered and then there was a low growl that quickly built to a banshee-like whine. Saving his breath, Cade nodded at Jamie then looked out the port window, above the tree tops, at the brightening western sky.

Chapter 28

No rest for the wicked, thought Nash as she peeled the foil from the bottle and rattled a 200-milligram caffeine pill into her palm and, against the dire warnings on the bottle, washed it down with a big gulp of tepid coffee.

She'd already spent most of the early evening hours in the 50th Space Wing's TOC rooting for the dead as the Chinese tried time and again to retrieve their helicopter from the horde that had surrounded and damaged its tail rotor moments after it landed on shore in Norfolk. As Nash watched in real-time the crew lasted all of four or five minutes inside before bolting from the inert craft and being torn apart limb from limb by the dead. The folly continued as the warships shelled a series of buildings a quarter mile distant, likely just a diversion, then sent, one at a time, half a dozen landing parties ashore only to suffer the same fate as their airborne comrades. After several hours of this, without retrieving their fallen or the damaged helicopter, the warships turned tail and steamed out of Norfolk Harbor.

The early morning hours were fraught with heartache as the same satellite transmitted footage back to the TOC of an hours-long life and death struggle between a platoon of Marines and the living dead that had them easily outnumbered 100 to 1.

Though their objective was achieved and they'd fought their way from their LZ in the rolling hills of Bluemont, Virginia, through throngs of dead and into the top-secret fortified stronghold constructed beneath FEMA's Mount Weather complex, the man they had come to rescue, Vice Chairman of the Joint Chiefs of Staff, United States Marine General Tommy (Two-Guns) McTiernan, was in poor health. The Marine commander on the ground relayed to the TOC that the sixty-five-year-old veteran of nearly every military action from Vietnam on up to the previous wars in the desert had suffered a mild stroke two days prior and was receiving medical attention.

Watching the Marines hustle the litter containing their top man to a nearby grassy knoll and seeing them surround the living legend with an outward facing phalanx brought Nash a modicum of hope that Two-Guns would live to fight another day. There wasn't a dry eye in the TOC as the muzzle flashes continued lancing outward and the Zs kept falling in waves. It hadn't been lost on Nash at the time that thousands upon thousands of Americans, Confederate and Union, had fallen during the battles for nearby Shenandoah Valley. And like Stonewall Jackson who had held the area against numerically superior Union forces nearly one hundred and fifty years before, President Clay was hoping the ailing man they were bringing back to Schriever was well enough to devise a strategy to turn the tide on the dead with a disparity in numbers far outweighing those that Stonewall had faced.

The caffeine hit Nash like a mule kick as she reminisced over the cheer that went up when the trio of Ospreys flared and landed and the harried extraction commenced in real time.

"Chalk one up for the good guys," she had said aloud at the time. In fact, Two-Gun was the third high ranking official to be rescued as a direct result of her brilliant idea in which she searched for the signals her satellites never received in the days and weeks following Z-Day when the country went mostly dark—figuratively and literally. Theory was most of the persons essential to the continuity of government had been lulled into complacency due to the sitting President's initial waffling and indecision. That the living dead had gotten such a quick foothold in the District of Columbia—causing the city to fall that first weekend—made getting to nearby Joint Base Andrews in Maryland—let alone relocating to the numerous pre-fortified bunkers scattered about the massively populated eastern sea board—nearly impossible.

So with the help of her best and brightest, and armed with the President's password, they accessed the NSA's supercomputers located somewhere in the ten-thousand-square-foot labyrinth underneath Fort Meade, fifteen miles south of Baltimore, Maryland. Stored digitally behind multiple firewalls Nash found the conduit to terabytes of metadata collected from every cell provider in the United States and abroad from the late nineties to present day. Every benign call. Every drunk dial. Even accidental butt calls had been archived and stamped with unique metadata pointing to when and where the call was placed. The latter being the info Nash coveted. And the way it worked was that every individual cell call went through the nearest tower, the phone first pinging the apparatus affixed to the tower before bumping the signal to the overhead telecommunications satellites that in milliseconds bounced the signal back down, no matter the distance, to the cell tower nearest the call's recipient.

While searching the metadata for cell pings from essential high-ranking personnel, Nash got to thinking and those thoughts led directly to the off-the-books mission about to launch a quarter mile away.

Zero-dark-thirty. The time when most humans naturally lower their guard. Complacency builds and alertness wanes.

She pictured the SOAR pilots readying their birds. Checking the nuts and bolts and software pertinent to remaining airborne. Running diagnostics checks and, hopefully, receiving the green light meaning *all systems go.*

An hour earlier the distant low rumble of the refueling package consisting of a pair of KC-130 tankers taking to air rattled the windows. She had noticed the pitch of the spinning props change as they bit into the cold Colorado air as the planes banked and lumbered away south by west.

The second package, due to launch any minute, would not make a sound. At least not the kind that would travel from Whipper's tarmacs to her ears. So the only way she would ultimately know the mission was not scrubbed would be by the continued silence of the two land-line telephones on her desk, one red and one black.

Chapter 29

Glenda awoke but remained supine with her eyes still shut tight. Her mind's eye, however, snapped wide open. And she was certain, standing within arm's reach, only a flimsy pane of automotive glass and an unlocked door between her and certain death, were a dozen hungry zombies. As her imagination took the ball and ran, the listless horde advanced, moaning and hissing, one awkward step at a time. Soon the wicked screech of cracked nails against sheet metal sounded and she screamed and opened her eyes and craned around. There were no pale leering faces pressed to the windows. So, chest still heaving, she hinged up slowly, wincing from aches and pains resulting from a lifetime of never giving up.

She peered over the dash, eyes narrowed against the light spilling in around the edges of the battered and bowed rollup. The tagline from a watchmaker came to mind: *Took a licking and kept on ticking.* Then she noticed the nearest edge where the door had been forced from its tracks and saw long vertical runners of dried blood.

She looked left and saw corrugated metal and signs on the wall pointing to the brands of oil and air cleaners and long-life batteries the garage's former owner favored. Fram, STP, and Eveready—all familiar names that brought back fond memories of her wannabe-gearhead husband. Grateful nothing was waiting for her in the shadows there, she flicked her eyes to the rearview and saw only a low workbench and on the wall a calendar still pinned to July displaying a scantily clad girl and a shiny red roadster. *Far from the truth*, thought Glenda. Based on her experiences she'd forever remember July for its surprise gift of traffic snarls full of ordinary passenger cars and the living corpses entombed inside of them.

She scooted over the transmission hump on her butt and shouldered the door open. Stepped onto the concrete and shut the door behind her, the resonant creak spurring more of the same hair-raising rasp of bone on metal she'd slept through most of the night. With the renewed heaving of her chest exasperating the stitch in her side, she looked dead ahead and it suddenly dawned on her that the walking briquette was still inside the store and had just been aroused by the noisy door hinge.

Out came the knitting needles and Glenda crept to the door. She mounted the step and rose on her tiptoes. Put her face to the glass pane but saw nothing on the other side. As she took a step back to think through her options, whatever had slammed into the door a moment ago did so again and then inexplicably the knob started rattling.

From her new vantage point a step down she saw only the top of the creature's head through the soot-streaked window. It was wavering back and forth while the knob continued rotating slowly left and right in small increments. With the prospect of the thing actually opening the door and catching her flat-footed, Glenda decided to seize the initiative and turn the tables on the persistent son of a gun. So, throwing caution to the wind, she counted down from three, gripped the knob, and pulled the door towards her.

At once Kingsford stepped over the threshold, juddered stiffly on the pair of steps, and collapsed in a vertical heap on the garage floor.

Glenda forgot all about the needles in her hands. Focusing solely on the blue sky showing between the roof joists, she held her breath and waded through the cloud of gray dust roiling off the struggling creature. Fully expecting a pair of hands to lock on to her lower extremities, she stepped over its twitching legs and into the store and pulled the door closed, trapping it in the garage.

She stood in the store, hands on knees, back pressed to the door and, while catching her breath, looked the three points of the compass. North, to her right, the rear parking lot was choked with burned hulks of cars and trucks, but no walking dead. To the west, dead ahead past the aisles and out the empty pane behind the check stand she could see a small group of dead tottering away, a long hill climb ahead of them. And, much to her relief, the parking lot in front of the store was empty as was the roadway beyond it. In the distant field, however, she saw a pair of deer cautiously picking their way through the grass, left to right.

Then the scratching resumed. She imagined the bony nubs punching through the door and raking her back. Throwing a shiver, she turned around and saw through the soot the white paint of the door from where the thing had been relentlessly pawing at it. In addition to the vertical stripes there were three rough circles. Two where her shoulders had rested against it. And another oblong shape lower down where her backside had rubbed the black coating off the metal surface.

Letting her conscience get the better of her, Glenda wet her finger and scribed the words *Do Not Enter* on the door in three-inch-high letters.

She listened hard for a moment and, hearing nothing moving out of her line of sight, went back into character. Head cocked to one side, she shuffled to the blown-out door, ducked clumsily under the push bar, and stepped into the morning chill. Moving like a zombie, she turned her head left ever so slowly and regarded her handiwork. Mombie, the three younger zombies and the Deer Hunters lay in a heap, limbs askew, near the garage's southeast corner.

As Glenda scanned her surroundings for any signs of Van Man, she heard two things simultaneously. From the grassy median there came a hollow rasp and the crawler she'd first crossed paths with at the roadblock miles back inched slowly hand over hand onto the blacktop. And, causing the deer in the field to start and bolt for the forest edge, she heard the unmistakable noise of rotor blades beating the air somewhere to the east.

Chapter 30

As the Black Hawk got light on its wheels and wavered slightly, Cade kept his eyes locked on the spot in the forest where the compound's hidden entrance would be. Then, as the chopper gained altitude and it became apparent the noisy launch hadn't drawn everyone topside, he shifted his gaze to the familiar strip of SR-39 below his port side window. A tick later, drawing his attention to the cockpit, Duncan's voice sounded in his helmet. "Where to, D-Boy?"

"Former—" said Cade over the comms.

There was a brief silence and Daymon looked over his right shoulder, cocked his head as if saying: *I'm waiting.*

Weighing some kind of decision, Cade waited another beat then said decisively, "Daymon, I want you to hold off on inputting those coordinates until we top the tanks off."

Duncan said, "Morgan County Muni, here we come."

Cade felt the chopper start the bank to port and, deciding a five-minute detour was in order, said, "Keep to the westerly heading."

More statement than question, Duncan said, "You want me to overfly Huntsville."

Cade said, "For future reference only."

"Nothing to see there, Cade," added Jamie. "I've been. And Eden, too. The fires drew the monsters from the compromised roadblock. Both towns are pretty much rubble and ashes and overrun with crispy walking corpses."

As the Black Hawk slipped back around to the previous heading, Cade locked eyes with the fiery brunette and asked, "Did you make it all the way to the Conex barricade at the pass?"

Jamie answered no by shaking her helmeted head. Then said, "I was on foot. A little too far and too dangerous to go all by myself."

Lev said, "Still. It wouldn't hurt to give it a flyby. Like you said ... for future reference."

"I concur," said Cade. "What's the situation like on the ground on your side, Lev?"

"Shit show, sir," he said, accidentally slipping back into a previous role from a previous war. A war against an enemy he'd found easy to hate. And even easier to kill. The things pressing against Daymon's felled trees passing by down below, not so much. In fact, the walking dead, no matter how far down the road of decay they'd travelled, were constant daily reminders of family members who'd balked at leaving their homes in an already overrun Salt Lake City. His mom, dad, older sister, brother-in-law, two nieces and a nephew—all gone. Then inexplicably he heard Adam Duritz's familiar raspy voice singing a favorite and suddenly prescient lyric from a Counting Crows track. And the unexpected gut punch came in the form of five words in the first verse reminding him that all of his memories were now just films about ghosts.

"Are you all right?" asked Jamie, placing a gloved hand on his thigh.

Lev jumped from the touch and strained forward against his belt.

Nodding toward the starboard window, Jamie mouthed, "What do you see?"

Lev recovered and, without missing a beat, said, "Death and more death. But Daymon's roadblock was holding. I counted a couple of dozen rotters hanging around. Easy enough to cull. And now we're coming up on Huntsville ... and more death—" His voice trailed off and his gaze shifted back outside where he saw a lush forested hillside gliding past.

Cade peered out his window. Watched fallow fields and scattered farmhouses and rusty vehicles and swaybacked outbuildings blip by.

Duncan made a fist. Offered it to Daymon and said, "Good call on the roadblock, Urch."

After reciprocating the bump with Duncan, Daymon leaned forward, squinting to make something out in the glare below.

A minute later, with the shimmering reservoir filling up the starboard side window, Cade said, "Huntsville is gone. Fire spared a few commercial buildings down by the water. The docks as well, and looks like maybe a block or two of houses on the high ground east of there."

Steiners pressed to his face, Daymon added, "Looks like the fire flushed out a few survivors. There's half a dozen boats anchored off shore. And we've got movement."

The Black Hawk slowed and descended slightly. Then Duncan nosed the bird left a few degrees and brought her back around perpendicular to the reservoir.

"Yep ... one craft with five adults topside," reported Daymon. He watched the group rush to one side of the sailboat he guessed to be a forty-footer, half of them waving white scraps of fabric. A couple of them threw themselves to the deck as if rescue was imminent. He panned over the other watercraft and added, "All of the other vessels appear abandoned."

"Appear," muttered Duncan into the comms. He fixed his gaze on the water between the boats and the shore where hundreds of Zs, excited by the now hovering chopper, had shifted their attention from the survivors in the sailboat and were now looking expectantly skyward. The charred creatures created a sharp contrast intermingling among scores of pale waterlogged bodies at the water's edge—some moving—most not. Having seen enough and knowing without asking that there was no way to help the survivors without jeopardizing the mission and the safety of everyone aboard, Duncan looked towards the pass and said, "Delta ... you want to get a close-up of the barricade?"

Cade didn't immediately answer. He fished his binoculars from the ruck near his feet and trained them on the four-lane winding up into the canyon to the west. He adjusted the focus ring and walked the field glasses up while panning left and right in tight little increments. Spent a handful of seconds scrutinizing something there, then, dropping the Steiners in his lap, said abruptly, "No. I've seen enough to know that the breach has widened."

"Rotters?"

"Hundreds ... if not a thousand or more have tumbled and ended up at the bottom of the canyon. No threat from *them* ... *yet*."

Duncan nudged the stick left and forward. Responding to the input, the Black Hawk turned hard on a dime and lost fifty feet of altitude before leveling out and hammering south low to the water. Then, not really wanting to hear the answer, he asked, "How many are there on the road?"

A heavy silence descended over the cabin.

Lev and Jamie traded worried looks.

The rotor blades continued chopping the crisp air overhead as the reservoir's silver surface gave way to land.

And, staring out the window at the verdant triple canopy rushing by, Cade quietly said, "You don't want to know."

Glenda went still as a statue as the helicopter passed overhead and continued onward, presumably, towards Huntsville without missing a beat. With the imagery of the half-dozen black helicopters descending on the mayor's mansion, and the ensuing carnage still fresh on her mind, she said a little prayer asking God to will whoever was in the noisy aircraft to ignore her and keep on going. And, as if she had traded one threat for another, once the helicopter was out of earshot, the crawler's incessant peals were back.

Cursing herself for not putting it out of its misery when she'd had the chance, she crossed the blacktop and stopped a foot shy of the persistent creature. Out came one of the needles and she bent down and pushed the sharpened aluminum into its temple, instantly stilling it. Wiping the shaft on the robe's sleeve she blinked away a tear, then put the needle away, and putting one foot in front of the other, continued east on SR-39.

Chapter 31

In order to better get a feel for what might be waiting for them at the Morgan County Airport, Cade had Duncan keep the Black Hawk low and slow and follow Old Trapper Road south, starting at its terminus with State Route 39 near the banks of the Pineview Reservoir.

Almost immediately Cade could see that conditions on the ten-mile-long stretch of mostly two-lane blacktop cutting through the Utah back country had deteriorated exponentially since he'd last traversed it.

Three weeks ago, save for the freeway near the Morgan airport, the road had been virtually free of Zs. But that was then and this was now and not a mile blipped by where the road itself, and the open range it bordered, was not dotted with roving bands of decaying corpses.

Five miles in and for the second time in as many minutes, Cade said, "I've seen enough."

Taking the cue, Duncan nudged the Black Hawk left a few degrees and simultaneously increased the power and dipped her nose slightly. "What do you think we're going to find at the airport?" he asked.

And for the second time in six minutes, Cade uttered the same five words, "You don't want to know." Only this time, like a wakeup call, he delivered them slowly—all business.

Believing everyone's fate on this rock was preordained from birth, Duncan shrugged off the warning and said calmly into the shipwide comms, *"Two mikes out."*

There was a metallic snick from Jamie's M4 as she pulled the charging handle, chambering a round. Fully aware Cade and Lev were watching, she slipped the Beretta from its drop leg holster, confirmed it too had a round chambered, then *snicked* off the safety and snugged it home. Still feeling eyes on her, she donned a helmet and comms and tucked some free strands of her dark bangs in before cinching the chin strap. Finally, unable to control herself, she looked coyly at Cade and Lev, winked, patted the tomahawk riding on the other, then gave it a couple of sensual-looking strokes.

Swapping out the bulky flight helmet for his tactical bump helmet, Cade leaned close and asked her, "Are you good to go?"

Forcing a half smile, Jamie leaned forward and, loud enough to be heard over the thumping of the slowing rotors, replied, "Yep. I'm going to *get some.*"

Smiling inwardly at the exchange, Lev followed Cade's lead, swapping his flight helmet for a comms set and a tan Kevlar item Cade had taken off the dead National Guardsmen weeks ago. He tightened the chin strap then ejected the magazine from his M4 and, performing an Eleven-Bravo ritual once practiced the world over, tapped it against his palm to seat the rounds and then slapped it back into the magwell where it seated with a satisfying click. Following the other's lead he charged his weapon, set the safety, and closed his eyes in preparation for insertion into a very different type of hot landing zone. The kind he hated most. Because here, though no one would be shooting at him, every threat on the ground would be in his face and equally as deadly. *Tooth and nail deadly.* He shuddered at the forming visual, then, like a good soldier, flicked a mental switch, banishing it from his mind.

"One mike," called Duncan.

After adjusting the volume on his comms set, Cade looked up and, mimicking a popular commercial from the old world, said, "Can you hear me now?"

Getting the joke, Jamie smiled and nodded.

138

Nearly simultaneously, Lev, Daymon, and Duncan flashed a thumbs up, the universal semaphore for *good to go* understood by men going into battle the world over.

Daymon looked into the cabin and exchanged a knowing look with Cade. Held it for a tick then swiveled forward and his voice came over the comms describing the scene on the ground at the airport in great detail, not one of them good.

Looking out his port side window, Cade saw one of the points of entry the dead had utilized. A full five-foot run of the chain-link surrounding the parking lot on the airport's northwest corner had been laid flat, and blades of brittle, browned grass poked through the diamond-shaped openings. On either side of the breach, where the fencing was still attached to the vertical posts, colorful scraps of fabric and what looked to Cade like tufts of human hair were being windblown in the same direction as the day-glo windsock dancing high up on a pole at the end of the nearby runway.

Swiveling his head left, Duncan retracted the smoked visor and, through his orange-framed glasses, eyed his passengers. "Are we a go?" he asked.

Matching Duncan's gaze while trying mightily to ignore the colorful specs , Cade bit his lip and nodded subtly.

In the left-hand seat, as he unplugged his helmet, Daymon saw the rotters freeze in place. In the next instant, as Duncan brought the Black Hawk in hot over the forty-foot-tall trees west of the single asphalt landing strip, the multitude of marble-white faces looked skyward and panned a steady arc, their dead eyes locked onto the noisily approaching metal contraption.

"*Kindness*, don't fail me now," said Daymon as he drew his machete from its scabbard and placed it on his lap. His gloved hands went to the harness release as volumes of dust were suddenly sent airborne by the wildly spinning rotors.

Incredulous, Duncan simultaneously flared the helicopter and said, "You named it?"

"Just now," answered Daymon, grinning wickedly.

"But ... Kindness?"

"Yeah. You know ... as in killing them with—"

Over the comms, Jamie said, "Double entendre. I *like* it."

139

Lev added, "Very original, I'll give you that."

Duncan shook his head, then intoned, "You know your job, Urch?"

With a metallic click, Daymon was free of the belt and reciting the mantra in a sing-song voice. "Keep the rotters from martyring themselves with your tail rotor."

"Correct," said Duncan. "Take my shotgun ... I insist."

After circling far and wide of the static fuel bowser and finding a patch of grass free of dead and large enough to set the chopper down, Duncan said, "Wheels down."

Before the wheels were in the tall grass, Cade had yanked the starboard door back in its tracks and had jumped out and was kneeling on the tarmac, M4 sweeping to the south. A tick later he began engaging targets, careful not to walk his fire too close to the tank truck holding their precious aviation fuel.

The DHS chopper settled softly on the grass northeast of the fuel bowser and, breaking every rule in the book, Duncan kept the turbines lit and the rotors spooled up. In his side vision he saw Cade, Jamie and Daymon burst out of the chopper near simultaneously and felt the hot blast of carrion- and jet-fuel-tainted air infiltrate the cabin. He saw Jamie peel left to assist Cade in clearing a path between the chopper and bowser while Daymon disappeared from view on his way to secure the area around the Black Hawk's fragile tail rotor.

Once Daymon reached his position on the starboard side of the tail boom, he put the whirring and near invisible rotor disc at his back and went to one knee. He crunched a round into the stubby combat shotgun and heard Cade saying, *We will be in and out in five,* in his head.

But this wasn't nearly the situation they'd encountered refueling here weeks ago. This was much worse. A hasty headcount from the air told him that there had to be hundreds of rotters spread out across the acres of asphalt and unruly grass. And looking under the tail boom towards the failed fencing he could see that dozens more, drawn by the Siren's song of the noisy Black Hawk, were streaming towards them on their left flank.

First things first, though. He leveled the pump gun at a trio of presumably moaning creatures at his three o'clock position. With the bowser in his left side vision and the deadly blades nearby on the right he let loose, the storm of buckshot dissolving the first monster's face.

Mouth formed in a silent O, the next Z, a young girl with puckered bite wounds up and down her arms, came at him faster than the first.

Stepping forward to meet the threat, Daymon jacked another round into the chamber and, with the utmost care, lined the sights up with the bridge of the stumbling four-footer's nose. A tactical move based on an assumption that, if he knew Old Man as well as he thought he did, the next round in the chamber was a slug.

Daymon held his fire until the Z was within a dozen feet. He drew a breath and thought to himself, *The kid is already dead*. When he finally pulled the trigger his gut feeling was validated when the single hunk of lead found its mark where he'd been aiming and sheared off the top third of the waifish corpse's skull. The resulting kinetic energy snapped the body up and back and through the drifting cloud of cerebral fluid and aerated brain matter.

Before the girl's corpse had time to bounce Daymon had crunched another shell into the shotgun. Holding true to the *every-other-pattern*, the next shell was buckshot which didn't have the time nor distance to spread as it left the shotgun's smooth bore barrel with tremendous velocity. Barely the size of a basketball and only sixteen inches removed from the muzzle, the swarm of tiny pellets struck the right two-thirds of the next rotter's face leaving behind only scraps of shredded flesh hanging from a crescent-shaped sliver of skull. Barely attached at the neck, the hair-covered rind bobbed momentarily on the stalk of exposed vertebrae until the final orders from its already compromised brain reached its feet and the near headless corpse did the splits, collapsing in place.

In the next heartbeat Daymon kept two more ambling corpses away from the tail rotor, felling them one right after the other—slug to the forehead and buckshot to the temple.

As the last one through the open door, and with Duncan barking a reminder over the shipwide comms, Lev closed it at his back and went into a combat crouch near the bird's landing gear. He quickly got his bearings and slow-walked toward his objective, head on a swivel and constantly firing and reloading as he covered the distance to the gun-shaped nozzle lying flat on the nearby tarmac. Halfway to the stretched-out length of hose, time seemed to slow for him and three things happened simultaneously. To his left he saw Jamie swiping at the encroaching dead, the tomahawk cutting a blurring arc, and a look of utter disgust parked on her face. One by one, in the blink of an eye, she caved a trio of faces in, the crunch of bone and thud of bodies impacting the tarmac all but drowned out by the Black Hawk's turbine whine. Then suddenly Cade was crouched low and walking forward and firing by her side. A beat later he had her rifle in his hands and appeared to be working on it.

Lev paused and looked over his left shoulder. Unexpectedly he caught Cade's eye then read his lips: *Failure to feed* then heard his voice saying, "Go, go, go," over the comms. With Cade's admonition spurring him to get the lead out, Lev did just that, emptying a half-dozen rounds into the Zs in his path. He changed mags and picked his way through the fallen bodies. slipping and sliding on clumps of brain and hair-covered skull along the way. He charged the rifle then let it hang from its sling and snatched up the fuel nozzle two-handed. With the hose draped over his shoulder and inadvertently dragging his rifle's muzzle through the pooling blood, he leaned forward and began running towards the chopper where he saw Daymon standing amid a growing pile of Z bodies and swinging a machete wildly one-handed.

In the couple of seconds it had taken Cade to clear Jamie's rifle of the misfed round, pull the charging handle and hand the M4 back to her, a Z had risen to its knees from the tall grass, gotten ahold of his hydration pack, and was climbing his body. In the next beat Cade was twisting around and collapsing sideways with the thing's cold hands groping for his neck.

On the way to the ground two things happened. First, without looking or thinking, Cade reached for the dagger on his hip. Next he heard two pops and the crackle of live rounds passing closely as the rotter's shoulder disintegrated into a horizontal fan of sinew and congealed blood which momentarily blotted out the spinning blue sky.

Upon hitting the ground, Cade felt the water-filled bladder strapped to his back mercifully cushion his fall and then, as the snarling creature's dead weight landed squarely atop him, the plate carrier and spare magazines and M4 carbine still strapped to his chest provided a five-inch buffer between his face and its snapping teeth.

Having missed the Z's head by a less than a hand's width, Jamie relinquished her rifle to gravity and charged hard towards the falling tangle of flailing limbs.

Supine and nearly enveloped in long grass, Cade got the dagger clear of the scabbard and rolled right to free up his left arm. A beat later the Gerber was arcing up from his side, a deadly blur of matte black clutched in his gloved hand. A fraction of a second later, pushing air in front of it from the opposite side, a second glint of metal entered Cade's peripheral. Finally, all inside of the latter half of that same second, Cade's blade plunged upward through the triangle of soft flesh under the Z's chin and the spiked end of Jamie's tomahawk embedded in its left temple with a wet *thunk*.

In one fluid movement Jamie released her tomahawk and kicked the leaking corpse off of Cade, who had let go of his Gerber and was already going for his Glock. "It's dead," she stated, helping him up with her free hand. "Are you bit?"

Cade shook his head and got to his knees. Starting at the Black Hawk, he walked his gaze around his immediate vicinity, nearly a full three-sixty sweep.

Through the Black Hawk's canopy he saw Duncan looking at him expectantly, mouth opened wide as if he was about to shout a warning or maybe a tidbit of what—usually already three sheets to the wind—he liked to call *sage advice*.

Expecting the former, Cade continued his visual sweep and noted the handful of walking dead vectoring toward the cockpit from the east.

He grabbed his M4's grip and got to his feet and saw that Lev was nearly to the bird, the fuel hose spooled out dozens of feet behind him. Then, finishing the revolution, Cade spotted another dozen Zs emerging from the right side of the bowser. So he tapped

Jamie on the shoulder, pointed towards the first turns looping around the chopper's nose, and said, "Do them first ... but be careful not to hit our ride." And as he sprinted away from her, he registered a vague nod, a half-turn, then the rifle swinging up and snugging tight to her shoulder.

Cade reached the bowser and, starting at the top, tapped its rounded flank with the buttstock of his M4. The initial hollow report sounded to the halfway point and remained unchanged another twelve inches past that when finally his steady taps returned a heavy noise with a slight ringing to it. Grimacing, he said, "I've got a third of a tank here, Duncan."

"We better let her drink until she's full."

"Copy that," replied Lev as he inserted the nozzle. "Commencing hot refuel."

Cade looked towards the tail rotor and saw the shotgun still slung over Daymon's shoulder. Saw the man tense and lash out with the machete and drop a rail-thin female Z dangerously close to the whirring vertical rotor disc. Then, as the upper half of the thing's head spun a lazy arc away from the blades, Cade looked away and over the fuel bowser's hood and watched Jamie walking rifle fire into the moaning throng.

He glanced at his Suunto and saw that two long minutes had slipped into the past since the Black Hawk's wheels hit the tarmac. The first minute was burned surviving the sneak attack by the lurker in the grass. Another one slipped by as he simultaneously checked the fuel level and watched Lev plug the hose into the chopper.

The next three minutes would prove to be a hairball wrapped inside of a shitstorm. While the fuel surged into the Black Hawk, he was on one knee firing and reloading, burning through three magazines in the process. Two minutes had passed and ninety rounds were down range by the time he looked away from the fallen corpses of fifty or sixty formerly fellow Americans and heard Duncan say over the comms, "Launching in one mike."

He didn't have to be told twice. Cade rose and trudged through the tall grass. He tapped Jamie's shoulder and said, "We're done here, now." Unmoved, Jamie said nothing and continued firing. So, dodging hot spent brass, Cade walked behind her from right-to-left and tapped her other shoulder. Still no response. She kept on firing head high and the rotters kept crumpling in vertical heaps. One. Two. Then three in rapid succession. Covering his mic, Cade gripped her shoulder firmly and, bellowing near her ear, said, "Cease your firing ... *now!*"

Her body went rigid at his touch. Then a second later she raised the smoking carbine and flicked the selector to safe. Turning, she flashed him the look a kid gives a parent when he or she doesn't want to leave someplace special like Disneyland or the Ringling Brothers Circus. Even before the exchange, Cade could tell by her body language and the imagined English she was putting on each shot that she was having a hell of a lot of fun killing them. To Jamie this was her E-Ticket and invitation to share the center ring with the lions all rolled up into one, and to Cade it was apparent that she was visualizing Ian Bishop's face on every one of the rotters.

After dragging Jamie's mind from the fray, Cade watched their six as he hustled alongside her on the way back to the Black Hawk where they met Daymon at the open door just as Lev had finished the hot refuel and was placing the nozzle on the tarmac.

Cade helped Jamie board ahead of Lev then backed up against the vibrating chopper's warm fuselage. He let Daymon pass in front of him then sighted down the M4 and emptied the last eight rounds from the magazine into the nearest walking corpses before clambering aboard, slightly winded and stinking of gunpowder and death.

Daymon looped around in front of the cockpit and hauled open the port side door, passed the shotgun back to a waiting hand and leapt in. Wasting no time, he shrugged on his belt and plugged in his helmet. Finally, out of breath, he looked at Duncan and said, "The tail is clear. But you've only got about a ten-second buffer until the next wave."

"Copy that," said Duncan as the turbine whine reached a crescendo and the grass on the helo's starboard side flattened into a large semi-circle under the intense downdraft created by the four composite Nomex- and Kevlar-wrapped rotor blades.

Feeling the bird get light on the gear, Duncan pulled pitch and applied a little pedal, spinning them a few degrees left as the ground dropped away. Hovering there for a second, nose pointed due east, he surveyed the carnage that hadn't been fully evident from his vantage point on the ground.

Crushing strange forms into the grass, dozens of bodies with limbs askew were arrayed like spokes on a wheel between the edge of the tarmac where the helo had initially set down and the fuel bowser roughly twenty yards to the south.

In smaller groups of twos and threes to packs numbering a dozen or more, the zombies kept coming in from the east where Duncan presumed there was another breach in the fence.

"Yep," he said nudging the stick forward. "Good thing the bowser was already half empty. 'Cause I don't think anybody with a pulse will be setting down here again anytime soon."

Cade removed his helmet and wiped the sweat from his brow. Took off his clear ballistic glasses and gloves and then rubbed both eyes with the back of his hands.

"Here," Jamie said. "Let me help you." She reached across the cabin and raked her fingers through both sideburns.

Bits and pieces of flesh and bone rained to the cabin floor, the latter skittering away toward the starboard door as Duncan banked the helo in that direction.

Seeing the morning sun swing past the port windows, Cade sat back and thanked Jamie for saving his ass at the airport. He donned a flight helmet, secured the chin strap, then more to prove a point than chastise, asked her when she'd last disassembled and cleaned her carbine.

She shrugged, a blank look on her face.

He said, "The correct answer is: Immediately after I finished shooting it the last time."

Across the cabin Lev nodded his approval.

Daymon piped in. He said, "That's why I kind of like the bow and the blade. Little maintenance necessary."

Lev smiled at that.

Both responses—verbal and visual—earned each of the meddlers a middle finger from Jamie.

Lost in thoughts of Raven and Brook, Cade pulled his rucksack near and rooted around and came out with a handful of shiny new 5.56 rounds. He asked Jamie for her empty mags and quickly reloaded her three and then the four he had emptied into the Zs. Finished, he snugged his four into their slots on his chest, Velcroed them in place and, with Jamie watching his every move, stuffed her mags into his cargo pockets.

"What the?" she mouthed.

Sitting back, he closed his eyes and said, "You'll see."

***

Forty-five minutes had gone by when Daymon said over the shipwide comms, "We're almost to the waypoint coordinates."

Looking out his starboard side glass, Lev saw nothing but reddish-orange earth, tumble weeds, and low scrub.

Jamie opened her eyes, lolled her head left and peered out the opposite side. There she saw much of the same rushing by her window until the helo neared the canyon rim and slowed considerably. Down below a river snaked north to south through a nameless burg. And in the slow-flowing water she saw scores of zombies sloshing around in the shallows, heads down and stalking fish, she presumed. Still more creatures were trapped in the brush at the river's edge, their ashen limbs beating the water to a white froth. Abutting the river on both sides was a triangle of green hemmed in by cliffs on three sides: west, north, and east. On the periphery of town there were mostly single family homes on treed lots. The businesses she could make out were clustered on both sides of a two-block stretch in the center of town. For some reason most of the homes near the main thoroughfare through town looked like they had been imploded, with roofs mostly intact, but the walls reduced to splintered two by fours, dislodged siding and powdery scraps of fractured drywall.

As if frozen mid-scatter from something or somebody, a couple of dozen inert vehicles littered the narrow side streets. Some were opened up like sardine tins and others were burned to metal and sitting on warped rims. All of the cars and trucks and SUVs sported gaping holes in their upward-facing sheet metal and had been stopped dead in their tracks heading north, away from the distant Interstate.

West of the town center a giant U.S. flag flew over a steel frame building full of windows and ringed on three sides by empty parking spaces. On the street in front of the building with the flag that Jamie had pegged for the town's post office, a handful of decaying bodies lay in death poses here and there, Rorschach-like lakes of blood dried to black ringing each and every one of them.

She imagined death coming from above and realized the destruction she was looking at was identical to what the rangers had wrought on Bishop's men and his lakeside redoubt.

At the lake there had been smoking wreckage of fleeing SUVs with immolated bodies hanging from shattered windows and crispy getaway drivers with their hands still clutching what remained of the steering wheels. And like the destroyed houses here, dozens of camouflage-clad corpses had been sprawled outside of the two lakeside houses that had burned down around whoever had been stupid enough to mount a last stand from within them. All together what she saw then and what she was looking at now left no doubt in her mind that highly trained soldiers did this too. In the next instant an icy chill traced her spine and she wondered how long she would last if she ever came up against a similar fighting force.

Just as the creatures below heard the helicopter and lifted their gaze skyward, Jamie shoved the *what-ifs* from her mind and directed her attention farther east where impressive rock formations running perpendicular to the Black Hawk's flight path rose up hundreds of feet from the desert floor.

"Hate to have to raft that white water," quipped Daymon.

Cade didn't need to sneak a peek to know what the man was referring to. Everything had been imprinted indelibly during the *thunder run* down the Interstate weeks earlier. Combat had a way of doing that to him. And knowing firsthand from Beeson's own generalized accounting of the operation that cleansed Green River of the two-legged vermin who had poked the hornets' nest one time too many, he resumed his meditation. Unless his old mentor had softened with age or the SF soldiers under his command had for some reason pulled their punches—which based on previous experience, Cade deemed highly unlikely—everything he'd already imagined in his mind's eye would correlate perfectly with what the others were seeing.

Certainly there had been no warning. No offer to surrender would have been extended. It just wasn't Beeson's style. He'd earned the reputation of being a straight shooter for two reasons. First, there was no marksman with a better record than him during that first war in the desert. And secondly, he didn't pussyfoot around. Wrong him and he was shooting straight for the legs to make you beg for mercy or straight for the head to put you down for good. No winning of hearts and minds happened in Green River. Based on what Cade had seen, and Beeson had warned prior, the city was a cesspool before the failed attack on he and the Kids exposed the bandits' real agenda. Therefore Beeson's boys would have snuck in under cover of night and, through direct violence of action, and using night vision and silenced weapons to their advantage, sniped the sentries and patrols first before using standoff weapons to destroy any buildings deemed too dangerous to breach and/or clear on foot. No quarter would have been given and no stone left unturned. Lastly, before leaving in a flurry of beating rotor blades and roiling dust—exactly opposite a manner in which they'd arrived—for reasons both tactical and to send a message to anyone else who thought brutality and rape and stealing would be tolerated, the bodies would be allowed to lay where they fell for the buzzards and every single one of the bandit's vehicles would be left sitting on rims with their tires slashed or burned to the ground. Definitely the tactic Cade would have employed if he were in charge. More dramatic than cleaning things up. Like a warning, but with a double exclamation mark.

But he hadn't been in control of anything for quite some time. Hadn't led men into harm's way for nearly a month. Nor would he be in control of much more going forward.

Duncan's low, drawn-out whistling jogged Cade's mind to the present. Then the aviator commented about the *shit show* that had taken place on the ground below. Reiterating that *he wouldn't wish an ass whipping like that on his worst enemy.*

Cade smiled but said nothing.

A tick later Duncan was business as usual and, in a skeptic's voice, wondering aloud if the GPS coordinates Urch inputted were accurate. Then he said calmly, "Wheels down ... two minutes."

Still preparing himself mentally for the next part of the mission, Cade said nothing.

Sounding equal measures confused and exasperated, Daymon said, "Two minutes?"

Hearing this, Cade opened his eyes and saw Lev unbuckling his harness and readying his tactical helmet. A half-beat later, on the other side of Lev, Jamie was out of her seatbelt and readying her ruck. On the latter half of the same heartbeat she was gripping her M4 two-handed and looking a question at Cade that said: *What about my magazines?*

Smiling at her and putting a hand up, like he expected order in the court, Cade said, "I hate to drop this on you, but—"

Interjecting, Daymon said, "There's always a *but* with you, Sarge."

Ignoring the barb, Cade continued, "I'm going *solo* from here on out. I hope I won't be needing them ... but just in case ... they're going with me."

Obviously blindsided by the news, Jamie's eyes went wide and her jaw dropped. In the next beat, as the helicopter slowed, as if she'd embarrassed herself again, her mouth snapped shut and her jaw muscles bulged. After a second of looking like she was about to attack Cade, she crossed her arms and sat back hard in her seat without uttering another word.

Taking the revelation in stride, Lev placed his tactical helmet on the cabin floor and, looking at Cade, said, "I'll help hold down the fort while you're gone." He handed over three of his own magazines. All full. Ninety rounds in total. "Just in case."

Cade pocketed the mags. Then, with a modicum of regret for not coming clean earlier, he nodded toward the cockpit and mimed hoisting a flask to his lips. And to make himself crystal clear—while enduring a withering barrage of stink eye from Jamie—he covered Lev's boom mic with one hand, pulled the earpiece away with the other, and whispered, "Watch the Old Man's drinking. And keep an eye on the satellite phone for me, will you?"

Lev nodded. And though it was already an unspoken protocol among all of the Eden compound survivors to watch each other's backs, he said, "I'll look out for Brook and Raven."

"Thanks," said Cade. He thought: *Brook can take of herself. And Raven's getting there.*

After a moment of silent introspection, he added, "Much appreciated."

Unexpectedly Jamie clicked out of her harness and leaned forward, her face growing several shades of red. "I saved *your* ass," she said, her voice rising an octave.

Cade said nothing. Gave his M4 a once over and patted the magazines on his chest, making sure the hook and loop was holding.

Speaking directly at Jamie, Daymon said, "I saved his ass too, *once*. And I'm as pissed off about being left out as you are. Truth is, though, I should be grateful for him putting the heat on Christian and Bishop. If he hadn't I would have never seen Heidi again ... *alive.*"

"I saved his ass too," said Duncan. "Welcome to the club, Jamie. It'll pay off in spades. Dollars to doughnuts before all is said and done that humble fella sitting back there with you ... and, I'd like to note for the record, saying nothing to his own defense ... will one day save our asses ten times over. I'm already over the snub. Now quit yer grumbling so I can land this tub o' tin."

A shroud of silence descended on the cabin.

Bleeding off airspeed, Duncan flared the Black Hawk and leveled off ten feet above the desert.

Cade removed the flight helmet and passed it to Lev. Then he pulled out a pen and quickly scribbled something akin to a small novel on the other half of the scrap of paper that the first set of GPS numbers were written on. Handed it forward to Daymon just as the Black Hawk touched terra firma and its heavy duty suspension swallowed up the uneven ground. Still saying nothing, Cade shouldered his ruck and donned his tactical helmet. M4 in one hand, he hauled open the starboard door, squinted against the gritty rotor driven blast, and leaped out.

Once his boots hit the ground, Cade turned and helped Lev close the door. Felt the latch catch and through the scuffed Plexiglas saw the younger man flashing him a textbook salute. Which he promptly reciprocated. Suddenly movement over Lev's left shoulder caught Cade's eye. Craning his neck, he noticed Daymon staring at him through the channel between the cockpit and crew cabin. His visor was up and, incredulous, he was shaking his head and mouthing the words: *Thanks a lot.*

"Sorry," mouthed Cade, palms up and shrugging, the universal semaphore for *it's beyond my control.* Without warning, the rotor revolutions increased rapidly until the disc was a blur and sand was once again abrading every square inch of his exposed skin. Imagining how bad Daymon must be feeling for once again being excluded from the mission, and hearing in his head the verbal tantrum likely taking place inside the Black Hawk, Cade made a mental note to thank everyone later for working so well together as a team at the airport. And as he ducked away from the forty grit facial peel and subconsciously put a hand atop his helmet, it came to him that the right thing to do when next they spoke would be to make amends to not only Daymon, but all parties involved for him not being forthright from the start.

And then, to add insult to injury, he recalled telling Raven that withholding information is just the same as lying.

What's good for the goose ... hypocrite.

In the Black Hawk, which was now a dozen feet off the desert floor, Jamie buckled in and promptly apologized for her outburst. Then, singling out Daymon, she said, "Want me to try and talk to Heidi when we get back?"

Daymon snapped the visor down, craned right and peered back into the cabin but said nothing.

"I've been where she was," added Jamie. "I don't know exactly what went on at the mansion, but I can guess. I'll go slow."

Behind the smoked visor Daymon's eyes misted over. Nodding, he said, "At this point I'm open to anything."

Perplexed, but not surprised that Cade had thrown them all a late-breaking curve ball, Duncan leveled the helo thirty feet above the rocky ground, looked at Daymon, and shrugged as if saying: *Let's make the best of this.* As he spun the helicopter on a flat plane the better part of ninety degrees to the left, he caught a brief glimpse of Cade sitting near the canyon edge, left hand still raised against the blowing sand. Once the turn was complete and the juddering helo was pointing into the sun, Duncan pulled his visor down over his eyes and stole a last glance through the toe bubble at the lone operator who was now flashing a thumbs up.

Sure you're good to go, thought Duncan. With the uncertainty of leaving Cade alone in the desert with little water and the hottest hours of the day ahead, he was hit with an intense and nearly overwhelming desire to extract the flask. Like energy coursing through a breaking wave, the urge grew and then ebbed but never fully dissipated. With his intellect losing the pitched battle in his head, he looked at Daymon and said, "Punch in the new waypoint."

Daymon said nothing as he carefully unfolded the scrap of paper Cade had given him and began punching in the new string of GPS numbers. A tick later, sensing the lack of forward movement, he looked up from his task and said, "Old Man. You're sandblasting the poor guy."

Releasing his grip on the cool smooth metal of the flask, Duncan removed his left hand—which seemed to be acting of its own volition—from his cargo pocket and rested it on the controls. With the craving momentarily vanquished, he flicked a quick salute at the operator and nudged the stick forward.

A few seconds after leaving Cade alone in the Utah desert, Daymon read the message scrawled below the GPS coordinates. "Looks like we're heading to a base called Bastion. Cade wrote here that you need to talk to a Commander Beeson. Says he agreed to have his men do a remote-field once-over on the helicopter before we go back to the compound."

Chuckling, Lev said, "PMS."

Arms still crossed over her chest and crushing the empty fabric sleeves where she should be feeling the reassuring hard edges of *her* three fully loaded magazines, Jamie shot Lev a death look and mouthed, "Don't go there."

Chapter 32

Cade watched the Black Hawk drop below the canyon rim and thunder off to the east, hugging the undulating contours of the land until it was a tiny speck. Then, as if a switch had been thrown, the crisp morning air suddenly lost its edge. In the next half beat Cade's exposed skin and gear started to soak up the heat from the rising sun. In the latter half of the beat he felt a fat bead of sweat roll from under his helmet and down his spine.

With the rotor noise still banging off the ancient arroyos and sandstone mesas, he continued squinting into the sun until the helicopter and its trailing shadow was lost altogether in the ground clutter. A few more seconds slipped into the past and a heavy silence fell over his elevated perch. He swiveled his head, taking inventory of his surroundings at all points of the compass. Behind him nothing stood taller than the exposed rocks and ground-hugging sage and tumbleweeds he'd already surveyed from the helo. To his right a tiny lizard of some sort scurried from the flat stone where it had been basking in the sun to another that offered a little more in the way of concealment. Farther off to the right, beyond his newfound friend's hiding place, the mesa he was on continued west for a quarter mile before dropping off into what he presumed was the canyon with State Route 6 cut through it south to north before meandering on a northeast tack. And down there on the road somewhere were the trashed cars and festering bodies of the Green River bandits that he and Brook and the Kids had dealt with handily. Dead ahead was the Green River basin, where ridges and veins cut by ancient runoff had left the sandstone features looking like giant overlapping ochre-colored waves. And less than a mile as the crow flies, off to his left, was the newly created ghost town of Green River.

Thankful the sun wasn't as brutal now as it had been the first time through these parts, he removed his helmet and glasses. Tapped the excess dust from both and fished a microfiber cloth from a pocket and first gave his glasses a thorough wipe. Then he cleaned the optics on his M4 beginning with the flip away 3x magnifier and finishing with the EOTech holographic sight perched atop the carbine's upper rail.

Finished, he tucked away the cloth and shrugged off his hydration pack then the ruck. Rifled through a side pocket and extracted his armored Bushnells and the satellite phone which he'd left locked and powered on. He keyed in the code and watched the screen come to life. After noting the time and seeing there were no messages or missed calls, he found Beeson's number and sent a lengthy text message. After sending the message he thumbed the screen dark and slipped the phone into a cargo pocket where it'd be easier to access. *No turning back now*, he thought as he snugged the binoculars tight and began glassing the city and valley below.

Off in the distance, south by east, he recognized the tablelike rock formation and I-70 which ran through it west to east towards the FOB Bastion and Mack, Colorado, ninety miles distant. And in the shadow where the blacktop cut through the red rock formation he spotted someone staring back at him through an impossibly large pair of field glasses. A staring match ensued until the camo-clad soldier dropped the glasses from her face and he recognized the sergeant named Andreason whom he'd met previously at Bastion. She was leaning over the hood of a desert tan Humvee sporting a pair of whip antennas reaching a dozen feet into the sky. She was accompanied by five heavily armed soldiers and nearby was another Humvee with a turret mounted .50 caliber heavy machine gun, one of the five soldiers manning it.

Message received, thought Cade. *Don't fuck with Beeson. The town of Green River now belongs to the Big Green Machine.*

With nothing else to do but sweat it out and wait, both literally and figuratively, he leaned back on his ruck and fixed his gaze dead ahead.

Chapter 33

Still a fair distance out, Duncan saw that what was once just a single strip facility perched atop a desert mesa was now a bustling base servicing fixed and rotor wing craft. A handful of static aircraft sat in a neat line near a row of windowless hangers, all identical and rust-streaked and abutting the north fence line. A safe distance from the flight line were four fuel bowsers, and going by the logos painted on the side of the rounded tanks, two of them hailed from Grand Junction Regional Airport a few miles to the east.

All around the base, running parallel with the hurricane fencing, a deep moat-like trench roughly the width of a Humvee had been carved into the red soil. As Duncan reduced altitude and airspeed, more details emerged. First impressions went out the door as it became evident the trenches were not empty. He saw dead eyes staring up and pale hands clawing at the smooth walls. In places he saw rotters that had managed to crawl out and were either still clutching the fence or in the process of being culled by roaming pairs of armed soldiers.

East of the airstrip Duncan saw a pair of armored personnel carriers reentering the base over a mobile bridge system, its retractable apparatus currently deployed across the trench.

Bringing the Black Hawk low and slow over the west fence line, Duncan saw the welcoming party at the same instant Lev said into the comms, "We've got company. And it looks like they're meeting us at the flight line locked and loaded."

"Couple of Humvees is all," added Daymon from the left seat.

"Lev's right," conceded Duncan, "Those things sticking out of the turrets are fifty cals with shells big enough to knock us out of the sky."

Jamie said, "They're just like the Humvee at the compound."

"Only they're here and they're manned and that makes them twenty times as deadly," stated Lev.

"We'll be OK," Duncan said. "Cade wouldn't send us into an ambush."

A hush fell over the cabin as the Black Hawk entered the airspace over the base.

Just past the fence line, sitting idle near the row of squat hangars, was a matte black twin rotor Osprey and, as Duncan applied left pedal and leveled upon seeing a vacant landing pad, he also spotted a Ghost Hawk helicopter crouched low on the bigger aircraft's lee side, its black skin and angular lines adding to its already menacing appearance.

The static aircraft slid by on the left and Duncan shifted his gaze forward and saw a person on the ground waving him in. Following the directions doled out silently via the day-glo batons clutched in the helmeted figure's gloved hands, he set the helicopter down parallel to the Ghost Hawk atop a square of blacktop marked out as a landing pad. A beat later the pair of Humvees jammed to a quick stop nearby. But the passengers remained inside with the doors closed.

By the time Duncan had powered the DHS bird down and the rotor chop diminished he saw why nobody was coming to greet them. Nearby, the Ghost Hawk's rotors were making lazy revolutions. Seconds later, with no discernable sound entering the Black Hawk's cabin or cockpit, the stealth helo's overhead disc was nearly a black blur.

Duncan thought it a strange sight. Dust kicking up but no rotor sound nor the usual heat mirage produced by hard-working turbine engines. There was, however, a strange harmonic vibration he could feel deep in his chest. Before long the silent black craft was hovering a dozen feet over the tarmac. In the next couple of seconds the wheels disappeared inside the airframe and, concealing them, a triangular black panel motored into place.

Duncan imagined himself at the controls as he watched the helicopter ascend and glide slowly over the hangers and pick up speed, its prism-shaped nose aimed at Grand Junction and the rambling Rocky Mountain range a hundred miles distant.

Steeling himself for the upcoming meeting with base commander Major Greg Beeson, Duncan unbuckled and removed his flight helmet, setting it on the console between the seats. Then, with the need to see clearly more important than keeping his ego intact, he removed the yellow and orange oddities, gave both lenses a meticulous cleaning, and squared them away on his face.

Stating the obvious, Daymon said, "We're keeping the guys with the gun trucks waiting."

Flask in hand, Duncan unscrewed the lid with a flick of his thumb. He growled, "Let 'em wait," and took a prolonged drink just as the behemoth tiltrotor's engines roared to life and, slowly at first, the trio of composite blades making up each prop began chopping the air overhead. In the span of a few seconds the revolutions increased and a hurricane-like roar was picking up outside the Black Hawk.

"That's what our welcoming party was waiting for," said Lev, pressing his face against the cabin glass while pointing out more of the obvious.

Barely two minutes after starting its engines and while churning up twin clouds of blowing gravel and ochre dust, the matte black Osprey rose into the air with a thunderous fury.

"Like night and day," stated Jamie.

More of the obvious, thought Duncan, taking another swallow from the flask.

Once at hover, a hundred feet above the flight line, the twin teardrop nacelles swiveled slowly forward, increasing the engine roar ten-fold.

In one moment, as Duncan watched through the overhead cockpit glass, the aircraft above and now to the fore of the Black Hawk seemed to go weightless. In the next, the rotors became forward facing propellers and the VTOL (Vertical Takeoff and

Landing) bird was nose down and charging south by southeast, the rising sun glinting sharply off the port side windows.

As the dust slowly settled, Duncan continued watching the Osprey as it rapidly closed with the Ghost Hawk. In a few seconds the two silhouettes had grown so small he had to squint to see them. He was just about to look away when he detected a flare of light. In the next second he saw the two aircraft make what he thought was a drastic change in course.

"Binocs," said Duncan, holding a hand out, eyes locked on the two black dots.

By the time Lev had handed his Steiners forward, a gray-haired man in faded MultiCam patterned fatigues had leapt out of the lead Humvee and was striding purposefully towards the Black Hawk.

"What do you see?" asked Daymon, squinting at the retreating aircraft.

"I see some sleight of hand. And now I know why Cade had us drop him off alone where we did."

"At least where he is there's almost no chance of him encountering Zs *or* humans," proffered Jamie.

"He'll have what ... an hour or so with nothing but tumbleweeds and geckos for company," added Daymon, removing his flight helmet. "And I hope he gets sunburned after the crap he just pulled on us all."

Out of the corner of his eye Duncan saw the approaching soldier wave and loop around to his side. Acting as if he hadn't seen the greeting, he said, "We served our purpose. Sometimes, that's just how it's got to be. Me ... I'm getting too old to be tear-assing all over the country anyway. I just want to kick back and count off the days and leave the fighting—" he looked away from the two in the cabin and fixed his gaze on Daymon sitting next to him "—and the *flying* to you younger folk."

"I'm down. And I've been poring over the manual," Daymon said. "Just give me the stick time."

There was a knock on the Plexiglas and when Duncan looked over his shoulder and saw the man's name on the tape on his breast and the black oak leaf front and center on his fatigue blouse, everything fell into place. He opened the door and said, "Major

Beeson, pleased to finally meet you. Cade's had nothing but good to say about you."

"*Bullshit*," Beeson growled. "Cade is a man of few words. And if he were spending some of 'em, he sure as hell wouldn't be puffing up my old carcass."

Daymon leaned forward and ran a hand through his stubby dreads. Then he said matter-of-factly, "Don't mind Duncan. He's been drinking."

Staring daggers at the dreadlocked tattletale, Duncan drawled, "Now that's *bullshit*. I better get my hip waders on ... it's getting deep in here."

Interrupting the spat, Beeson said jokingly, "Pleased to meet you, Duncan. Why don't you give the keys to Sergeant Clare there and come along with me. We'll get some coffee and while my men give your bird a checkup I'll give you the nickel tour. How's that sound?"

Duncan nodded. Shrugged off his flight harness and felt his hand brush the hard outline of the flask. *Empty*, he thought. *And hours to kill*. But he said, "Show us around? Sure. I want to thank you for having this old girl in for her physical. Lord knows she needs it. And yes, I could use some fresh brewed pick-me-up."

Daymon found himself staring at the razor wire atop the perimeter fencing. Subconsciously he slipped a hand under his shirt and rubbed the vertical scars on his chest and had a sudden and brief flashback to the pit of death outside of Schriever. How he'd wallowed amongst the corpses, not all of them fully dead. He imagined hearing the ghostly moans again. How they'd filtered up between the cold and intertwined rigor-affected limbs. A shiver ran up his spine. Finally he looked at the base commander and nodded. *Nothing else to do out here in the middle of nowhere*, he reasoned as he opened the door and a stiff cross breeze polluted the cabin with a super-concentrated blast of carrion-infused hot air.

Voicing her displeasure at the stench and clamping a hand over her nose, Jamie yanked open the side door and piled out, coughing and dry heaving.

Lev grabbed their rifles and Duncan's shotgun and met the others on the tarmac.

Once everyone was out of the helicopter and assembled, Beeson said, "Follow me," turned on his heel and stalked away with the comportment only a lifetime in the military could instill in a person.

Chapter 34

Brook awoke with a start. The nightmare in which she and Cade had been starring had been so vivid and hyper-realistic that for an instant the pitch black environs of her quarters had her fooled into thinking her weapon had failed and they were seconds away from becoming zombie food. In her confused state she called out for Cade and Raven, which in turn caused the diminutive twelve-year-old who had recently snuck back in to the Grayson quarters to sit up so fast the thin sheet covering her went flying. In the next instant Raven was lashing out in the inky black, fighting anything and everything, real and imagined. Her left fist found something soft with a sharp ridge running down its center. Her other hand, also curled into a fist, struck one of the vertical bars attaching the upper bunk to the lower, causing her to call out for Mom and Dad.

Suddenly Brook remembered where she was and the realization that she was being pummeled dawned on her. Smarting from a perfectly placed blow to her spine, she rolled to the right and wrapped a sobbing Raven up in a bear hug.

Face to face with her only offspring and most important person in the world, Brook shushed her and whispered, "It was only a bad dream, sweetie."

Raven said nothing. She was in the midst of a full blown asthma attack. The labored breathing and wheezing continued for a minute or two before Brook's soothing words and motherly caresses paid off and Raven found her breath.

"I'm alright, Mom," she said, her coiled muscles relaxing. "And I'm sorry I hit you. I thought they were getting me."

"Me too," Brook said. "When did you sneak back in?"

Raven mumbled something incoherent.

Brook shrugged and rose from the bunk. Found the string and clicked the single bulb to life. She pulled Raven close and kissed her forehead. Then the details of her own nightmare came flooding back. In it she and Cade had somehow lost Raven and were frantically searching a vast warehouse with dozens of gloomy never-ending halls and hundreds of closed doors with ravenous Zs lurking behind every one. She recalled red and green laser beams lancing from their weapons and monsters falling everywhere as they continued on, and on, and on, to no avail.

Propped up on one elbow, Raven chewed her lip and asked, "What does it mean?"

Brook thought: *A premonition I don't want to interpret.* She said, "Probably nothing." Then her brow furrowed and her gaze went to a widening bloom of crimson on the pillow. "You're cut."

Raven's wheezing returned immediately. And though she had grown accustomed to the sight of bloodied bodies—walking or not—a drop of her own blood was still a catastrophic occurrence. And anything more than a little scratch had her requesting the biggest bandage available and a Life Flight evacuation to the nearest ER.

Eyes wide, Raven asked, "Where did it all come from? Am I going to need an *infusion?*"

Wrapping her up in a tight embrace, Brook said, "You'll be fine. You cut your elbow flailing at the monsters in your nightmare." Then she smiled. "And no ... you won't be needing a *transfusion.*"

Brook made a trip down to the room used to store the group's food and gear recently taken from the quarry. She returned with a couple of bandages and saw Raven with the pillow held in front of her face and spitting on the crimson stain. Afraid to ask what she was up to, Brook took the pillow and said, "Don't worry about the blood. I'll take care of it later."

Raven examined the soiled pillow. Shook her head while saying, "I'm the only one who can do it."

Brook quickly bandaged Raven's elbow. Then, unable to let it go, asked, "What do you mean by only *you* can clean the pillow?"

"Tran said that saliva takes the blood stain out. But only *our* saliva works on *our* blood. Cause of *endives* or something."

"*Enzymes*," corrected Brook. "*Endive* is a leafy vegetable. Like lettuce ... sort of. When did Tran tell you that, anyway?"

"The other day. He cut himself dressing a boar."

"It's nice he's pulling his own weight *finally*. But it's not true, sweetie."

"He said Daymon told him about it. He said it took the blood out of his clothes before."

Wetting the bottom of Raven's tee shirt with her own spit, Brook rubbed the stain, lessening it considerably. Then she fetched a bottled water. Wet another part of the shirt and repeated the process. The stain now barely noticeable, she said, "The lesson you just learned is *never* take everything you see at face value. The moisture defeated the stain ... that's all. The *enzyme* in our spit thing is an old wives' tale."

"Wives' what?" asked Raven, her vivid imagination conjuring an image of a geriatric woman with a graying prehensile tail.

"Never mind," answered Brook. "The second lesson you take away from this is that adults don't always know everything about everything. Daymon knows pretty much everything about the forest and fighting fires—"

Raven interrupted saying, "But health stuff, not so much ..."

"Leave that to me."

"'Cause you're a nurse. And the radios and stuff technology is Foley's specialty."

"Correct, Bird."

"And security to Dad and Lev and Chief ... right?"

"And Mom and Jamie and Taryn sort of ..."

"She's the driver. And Sasha said Wilson is pretty much worthless ... right?"

Brook looked at the ceiling. Said nothing for a handful of seconds. Then she stared at Raven and saw her features softened by the single bulb's glow. Saw the innocence there and said, "Third lesson for the day. I want you to apply lesson one and two and come to your own conclusion about Wilson."

"Right now?"

"Yes."

Once again Raven's face contorted and she looked at the ceiling, head cocked right a degree.

"Well?"

"He's done a lot more than Sasha. That means I shouldn't believe jealous teenagers. Right?"

Laughing, Brook thought: *A+ for today's lesson*. But not wanting to set the bar too high, she said, "Pretty much. Let's get some breakfast and bang out our daily chores. Get dressed and grab your rifle."

"My rifle?"

"Gotta have it for lesson four."

Brook dressed and strapped on her pistol. She picked up the Glock 19 Cade left behind. Stowed the compact semiautomatic in her cargo pocket, then retrieved her M4 from near the door and went through the motions, making sure it was locked and loaded, the selector on *Safe*. Seeing that Raven was ready and had mimicked her entirely, rifle check and all, Brook looked down at her watch and wondered what her man was doing at this exact moment.

Two hundred and twenty miles away, Cade had the rubber stalk between his teeth and was taking a sip from his hydration pack when movement to his right caught his eye. Just ninety minutes after he'd first made its acquaintance, the little lizard poked its head from behind its new rock, paused briefly and then scurried from the shadow, stopping smartly on the nearest patch of sun-splashed soil where it fixed one beady eye in Cade's direction. Remaining stock-still as if not even a hungry raptor circling overhead could see it out in the open, the lizard rotated the eye facing Cade ever so slowly towards the flat sunning rock, presumably its favorite, before surreptitiously letting it wander back and settle on the silent camo-clad intruder.

As if moving his lips might scare the critter away, through clenched teeth Cade said, "Carpe diem, little guy."

166

The words elicited nothing. No shifting gaze on the lizard's part. No little feint towards the cover of the nearest rock. Nothing was happening. It was a silly sort of Mexican standoff in Utah's high desert. And worst of all, Cade had no witness to corroborate that it was even happening.

The staring contest ensued for another couple of minutes until the gecko shifted its slender body a few degrees to the right and locked both meandering eyes at something far away, beyond the canyon rim, in a general easterly direction.

Cade clamped down on the bite valve and took a long pull, then secured the drink tube to his shoulder strap. He raised the field glasses again and instantly saw what the gecko was already wise to. And it was an awesome sight. Filling up the slot across the way and tearing down I-70 ridiculously fast and low only a handful of feet above Andreason's roadblock was a cinder-black, sunlight-absorbing, sight for sore eyes.

Chapter 35
Eden Compound

"Really? Lemon poppy seed pound cake for breakfast," said Brook with a tilt of her head.

"No different than a doughnut," replied Raven, stuffing another piece of the yellow morsel into her nearly full mouth. She divided the last piece into two squares and fed one to Max, who gobbled it down hungrily.

Brook feigned grabbing the last square from the foil packet on Raven's lap, causing Max to leap to all fours and the girl to laugh and inadvertently inhale some of the moist cake. Coughing, Raven scooted away on her butt until the outer edge of Duncan's faux crop circle was at her back. She caught her breath and smiled and waved the cake tantalizingly at her mom.

Brook feigned like she was standing up.

Max stood equidistant from the drama playing out, his eyes connecting the dots from Brook to Raven to the pound cake in the girl's hand.

Without missing a beat, Raven popped the cake into her mouth, crumpled the foil packaging and made slow exaggerated chewing motions.

"Huckleberries would have been a better choice, young lady," said Brook as she popped a handful she'd just spent twenty minutes collecting into her mouth. Offering some to Raven, she added, "You have a nurse for a mom. How often have I let you eat a doughnut over something healthy?"

Answering the question with a question as her dad often did, Raven said, "Who says I like huckleberries? And—" she paused for a second and swallowed "—I don't even remember what fresh melon or strawberries or bananas taste like. And we can't exactly walk on down to the local farmer's market, last I checked. So what's the harm?"

"I earned these," said Brook, again offering the tin of berries. "Take some ... I insist."

Grudgingly, Raven accepted the offering. Ate the red berries and washed them down with a swallow of water. Not wanting to let the argument go, she said, "Dad *let* me have doughnuts for breakfast now and again."

"When?"

"After he retired and was home for good. We'd go to Krispy Kreme just about every late opening during the school year. Dad said it was for the coffee ... but he always had two of their glazed doughnuts. Three if they were fresh made and still warm."

That's a helluva lot of doughnuts, thought Brook. Then she factored in *No-school-vember* when it seemed like every other day was a late arrival or a teacher's in-service day. She said, "Better stop digging, Raven. 'Cause as it stands, your dad is going to get it when he returns."

Classic diversion, thought Raven. Then she heard voices and saw just the people who were going to get her off the hook.

Max growled as Sasha stepped onto the expanse of beaten-down grass. "What time did you go home?" she asked.

Raven shrugged and wagged her head side-to-side.

Brook greeted the Kids and smiled when she saw Sasha's getup. With the small caliber 10/22 in hand and clad in a set of tiger-striped camos taken from the quarry, the redheaded teen looked like an extra from Apocalypse Now. Following close behind, wearing woodland-camouflage-patterned BDUs circa the late '80s, Wilson and Taryn jogged an altogether different memory.

With guns slung over their shoulders and walking arm-in-arm, they looked more like they'd just stepped from wardrobe dressed for the movie Red Dawn than a young couple trying to survive a zombie apocalypse. The brown, black, and green scheme worked well at concealing a person in the forest. However, Wilson's red hair, even tucked under the ever-present boonie hat, totally defeated their purpose.

At their feet Max spun a full circle, stub tail going a mile-a-minute. His exuberance lasted a dozen revolutions before he lay back down in the grass and locked his bicolored eyes on Raven.

"What's up?" said Brook, offering up the tin of huckleberries.

"No thanks," said Sasha. "I've got pound cake."

Perking up, Raven asked, "Lemon poppy seed?"

"Vanilla," answered Sasha as she plopped down and offered Raven a piece.

"We're going on patrol," said Wilson, crunching his hat down subconsciously. He took a small handful of berries and gave them to Taryn. Then he helped himself to some, said "Thanks," and wolfed them down.

Taryn rolled up her sleeves, exposing the black skulls and dragons. Pushed them above her elbows and said, "We figured we'd go ahead and check the inner fence for rotters and then maybe go pump some water from the creek. Mind if we leave Sasha here with you?"

Sasha shot Taryn a look that said: *You're not my mom.* Then, acting as if it was her decision, she said, "I don't want to *pump* anything. Besides, Wilson fixed the bike he found at the quarry." She looked at Raven. "We could ride."

The sun emerged from behind a slow scudding bank of clouds and Brook removed her ball cap. As she fanned her face with it she fixed her gaze on Wilson and Taryn and said, "I owe you guys one for letting Raven hang out in your quarters yesterday and *half* the night." Then she grinned and added rather cryptically, "Go ahead ... take *allll* the time you need."

Kicking at a stray blade of grass, Taryn said, "We've each got a radio set to channel ten-one. Call if anything comes up."

If anything comes up it won't be here at the compound, thought Brook, the grin now a full on smile. *Oh to be young again.* Then, nodding at the slung carbines, she said, "You have *protection* I see."

Wilson's face flushed a crimson nearly a match for his hair.

170

Taryn fidgeted and patted the Beretta strapped to her hip. "We'll be careful," she answered, returning Brook's knowing look.

"Don't do anything *I* wouldn't do," called Sasha at the retreating pair's backs.

Grateful the doughnut talk had been averted, Raven patted Max on the backside and hopped to her feet.

"Let's ride," said Sasha theatrically, like the bike was a trail-wise steed and she was heading up a posse.

"But it's a *boy's* bike," Raven answered with a subtle eye roll. "I'll share my *flying purple people eater* with you."

"I still hate that you call it that ... so *no*."

Raven said, "Suit yourself," and bounded off to get her bike with Max keeping pace.

After watching the girls and Max head to the compound entrance where the bikes were parked, and seeing Taryn and Wilson melt into the tree line behind the patch of level ground where the Black Hawk usually sat, Brook was blindsided by a wave of emotion and suddenly yearned for Cade's embrace. So with nothing to do but kill time and wait for his eventual return, she lay back on the grass and perched her black ball cap on her face to block out the sun and closed her eyes. Instantly she started to relive the last three weeks. The only thing violent about them had come when she was asleep. Cade had been around almost non-stop. It had been like the thirteen months of bliss she'd enjoyed in Portland before some dumbass let a bug out and started a chain reaction that changed billions of lives in a very short time. Then her mind drifted off to her childhood and, as she slipped into sleep's embrace, her parents and her brother seemed to be there with her. Only the images weren't entirely formed. They were like apparitions, soft and shimmering around the edges.

Chapter 36

The gecko held out, standing impossibly still until the near silent craft halved the distance from where it had first appeared between the natural cut in the rock formation across the vast expanse of desert. Then, as if the largest flying predator it had ever set eyes on was homing in for the kill, mister gecko was off. Forsaking the safety of cover underneath the nearest rock, the scaly rocket zig-zagged across the hot sand towards the canyon rim and disappeared over the edge. Instead of embracing the notion that it had fallen to its doom, Cade envisioned the little survivor clinging to the vertical face and flashing the approaching Ghost Hawk a defiant one-fingered salute.

Shielding his face with one hand, Cade scooped up his carbine, shrugged on his rucksack, and walked towards the spot where he last saw the reptile. He reached the edge just as the stealth helicopter flared and commenced a rock-solid hover with its flat underbelly level with the mesa top, but still a hundred feet or so off the canyon floor.

The first thing Cade noticed was the obvious wear and tear on the bird. Like war paint on an Appaloosa, her black outer skin was dirt streaked as if she'd been flown through a rain shower and then hovered in a cloud of dust before drying completely. Around the irregular edges of the many maintenance panels, the radar-absorbing paint was chipped and peeling. Pencil-thin fingers of dried ochre-colored dirt streaked the three starboard-side windows. And up front he saw the cockpit glass was sullied by the greasy remnants of hundreds of bug strikes.

As the helo sideslipped closer Cade felt the familiar pressure in his chest from the noise-cancelling rotors cutting the air closely overhead. Then he got a face full of the foul jet-fuel-smelling exhaust rising up the canyon wall.

Abruptly the starboard-side door slid back in its tracks and the crew-chief, wearing a matte black helmet complete with smoked visor and face mask painted with a wicked set of red teeth, reached a gloved hand out and called, "Welcome aboard, sir."

Still holding his breath against the noxious fumes, Cade hustled the last couple of feet to the edge of the earth, grasped the man's outstretched hand, and leapt across the sliver of daylight without a downward glance.

Once aboard, Cade was directed by the crew chief to the eighteen-inch-wide swath of canvas not so affectionately known as the bitch seat. Which he didn't mind. With his back pressed against the bulkhead, amidships and facing straight ahead, he could see out both sides of the helo as well as a good portion of the cockpit glass between the two pilots. He registered the door shutting then moved his gaze around the cabin, pausing for a tick on each face, familiar or not.

The pilot in the left seat, an athletic-looking African American man whom Cade hadn't seen before, cracked a toothy smile under his visor and flashed a thumbs up. Cade reciprocated while craning to see who was in the right-hand seat and, judging by the spot-on flying he'd already witnessed, was prepared to bet his left nut that Ari Silver was strapped in up there, armed heavily with a number of one-liners and at least a half-dozen razor-sharp quips.

But he couldn't quite see without stepping on some toes, so he panned left and saw Javier "Lowrider" Lopez, his stocky Hispanic friend who'd been the first to volunteer for the mission. Moving on from the freshly minted Delta captain he saw a bushy out-of-control beard mostly concealing a face he thought looked familiar. The man's eyes narrowed and wrinkled at the corners—like he knew something Cade didn't and was waiting for some kind of recognition. Then Cade read the name tape on the Special Forces sergeant's MultiCam blouse, *Lasseigne*, and it all came back to him. Aboard the Ghost Hawk at the tail end of Cade's previous mission weeks ago, Lopez had addressed the man as *'Lasagna,'* a nickname no doubt. Instantly Lasseigne noted the change in Cade's face and extended his fist for a bump. "You're *shit hot*, Cade Grayson. All high speed, low drag is what they say. I'm Kelly, group ten. Everyone calls me Lasagna. Met you a few weeks ago in Idaho." He paused a beat and said real slowly, "And you lost the beard ..."

Cade nodded and bumped fists. "I remember," he said. "You and your guys took it to Bishop's crew."

Lasseigne flashed a look that said: *All in a day's work*, then pulled a lightweight rucksack from under his seat.

Cade turned and nudged the man sitting on his right. Tanned as always, dressed in all black fatigues and wearing a pair of black shades darker than obsidian, Special Agent Adam Cross flashed a smile of recognition.

"Cade Grayson," he said. "How the hell's civilian life been treating you? Minus the dead walking around and all, of course."

"Just keeping busy crossing T's and dotting I's, is all. You?"

"Clay has reassigned me permanently with your old team. Griffin here too. We've been going non-stop since you killed Bishop."

And he looked it. Like he'd been running on Rip It and adrenaline since Cade saw him last. His face was no longer clean shaven and the blonde hair curling from under his tactical helmet showed the three weeks' worth of new growth. And though the man was slumped a little, showing fatigue, perhaps, sitting shoulder to shoulder with him made the half a head advantage the chiseled Adonis normally had over Cade much more pronounced.

That he was here and no longer at the Cheyenne Mountain Complex guarding Clay came as no surprise. For Nash had a way of endearing herself to all of the men in Special Operations, no matter the branch or rank of the individual she came into contact with. And seeing as how the leaders at Special Operations Command— SOCOM—had scattered into the wind in the days and weeks after MacDill Air Force Base in Florida had fallen to the dead, Cade guessed the petite officer—who, along with General Cornelius Shrill, had been overseeing current operations—was the one who had convinced the President to release the highly capable jack of all trades.

But that was none of Cade's concern so he strapped in and cast a glance at the man to his left. The MultiCam he wore had no rank or insignia. Just an American flag and name tape that read *Griffin*. Like the mythological Greek creature with an eagle's head and the body of a lion. It suited the man to a T. His chiseled nose, high cheekbones and dark brown eyes jived with the former part of the creature. His wiry compact frame was all juvenile lion, coiled and ready to pounce. But the man was in his early forties—at least—and Cade swore that he'd seen him before. Perhaps in passing in Iraq or Afghanistan—in the same garb for sure—but without introduction and minus the name tape. DEVGRU or Navy Development Group. In layman's terms, *SEAL Team 6*, Cade decided a beat before Cross introduced the man as 'Griff' and rattled off who they all knew in common. Information that once Cade cross-referenced in his mind all but confirmed his earlier suspicion.

Feeling his stomach drop as the helicopter rose rapidly and banked hard left, putting Green River out the port windows and in clear view, Cade offered his left fist and bumped knuckles with the fellow Tier-1 operator. As the craft leveled off, Lasseigne handed Cade a comms set identical to the ones fielded by the rest of the team. "Freqs are already set," he said, pulling a five by seven photo from a pocket which he passed silently across the cabin to Cade.

Cade stared at the photo for a full minute, committing it to memory, then folded it in half and slipped it in his breast pocket.

Lasseigne said, "We're going to be needing our NODs. No power where we're going."

Cade removed his helmet, swapped headsets, and adjusted the boom mic. He checked his night vision equipment and when he was finished, powered them off and looked quizzically at Lasseigne. After a prolonged pause, he said incredulously, "Someplace *has* power?"

Lasseigne smiled. He said, "Springs has juice now."

"Wow," was Cade's reply. "And it's been totally cleared of Zs?"

Shaking his head, Lopez chimed in, "President Clay promised power before the first day of autumn. She never said all the Zs would be gone. However, the Second ID and a couple of hundred MARSOC guys who made it overland from Lejeune are taking it to them hard ... making one hell of a dent in their numbers."

Cade asked, "And the nuke plants?"

"We shut down the ones near enough to Springs to cause any problems. Cooper and Fort Calhoun in Nebraska and Wolf Creek in Burlington, Kansas."

"How about the Eastern seaboard?"

Shaking his head again, Lopez said, "We're going to have a slew of China Syndromes on our hands before long. Lost two teams and a bunch of Rangers and a couple of nuclear engineers trying to shut down the ones nearest DC. On the ground, in the heavily urbanized cities from Maine to Florida, the conditions are worse than anyone theorized."

Cade grimaced and shook his head. Then, resting his helmet upside down on his lap, plugged his comms wire into the overhead jack and said, "Comms check." After receiving a flurry of *'copy that's'* and seeing heads nod around the cabin, he said, "Ari ... is that you up there?"

"That you, Wyatt?" replied Ari, feigning surprise. "I thought Elvira went a little heavy on the stick back there. Did you give up your pre-dawn PT or something?"

"Or something. I've been eating real good," quipped Cade. "*Elvira* ... that's what you're calling this dirty bird now?"

"She works her magic at night and still looks good in the morning," said Ari.

Cade saw the other pilot chuckling and shaking his head. The reaction to the banter got him wondering if the big man had been exposed to Ari's entire stand-up routine yet. Then he decided to add fuel to the fire just in case he hadn't. "Elvira needs a bath and a couple of hours in the makeup chair," Cade said. "If you ask me ... looks like Whipper's been slacking. You need me to go back to Schriever and reaffirm to him *how it works?*"

"You going soft on us, Grayson?" quipped Cross. "Last I heard Whipper was on his final warning. What's this crap about giving him a final, final warning?"

Cade made no response. Didn't want to stoke the fires too much before the long flight.

Suddenly serious, Ari said, "We've been running non-stop missions for the last three weeks. Lots of trips back east and south. Can't go into it right here and now, but rest assured Whipper and the 2As are taking great care with all of the SOAR birds. Besides, I want them to stay in the air, not win best in show at the Concours d'Elegance."

"Ari's sugar-coating it. It's been pretty hairy lately," added Cross. "Good to have you back, bro."

"Given the circumstances, I'm glad to be back working with you again. Think you can give me a redacted Cliff's Notes version of the last three weeks?"

Cross leaned forward and said, "I'd rather let Griff bring you up to speed. He was there at the start."

Save for the crew chief who was keeping an eye on the ground flashing by on the starboard side, all eyes swung from Cross and parked on the seemingly reserved Navy SEAL.

Griff twisted the boom mic out of the way, leaned in and spoke loud enough to be heard over the turbine whine and muffled rotor thump. He prefaced his firsthand account by starting at the beginning and pointing out how quickly comms had been lost in the Middle East. Blamed it on an unknown number of EMP devices being popped off over Israel and Saudi Arabia by still unknown actors. Then he said, "We were pulling a special reconnaissance mission on a couple of high level AQ types in Karachi, Pakistan when the shit hit the fan."

Lasseigne asked, "Biters?"

"Not at first. Just after we received confirmation of the use of EMPs, our local who was highly trusted by the agency started getting agitated. Totally unlike him. Then his face went white and he ripped off his headset and said all he was hearing on the police scanner was *adam khor*. He said it over and over to himself *adam khor, adam khor* while shaking his head and cycling through all the known frequencies searching for something. Finally, he pulled it together a bit and said there were reports of widespread cannibalism in Peshawar, Abbottabad, and Lahore."

Cade said, "Adam khor?"

"It's Urdu. Translated it literally means *man eater*. Then the local said very ominously *'It's here,'* mentioned something about his wife and kids and was out the door." Griffin shook his head. "No way of stopping him. He had those crazy eyes. We *had* to let him go."

The helicopter made a slight course correction and Cross said, "Griff ... tell em how you got out."

"Quick as we could," said Griffin. "Put on our man dresses and scooted."

There was a long pause. Five seconds. Ten. Then twenty slipped by and Cade watched the man absentmindedly kneading the pair of tactical gloves he'd been clutching. Working them like a set of worry beads as he stared out the port side window at the slick red rocks of Moab passing by and radiating an ethereal measure of warmth six hundred feet below the stealth helo.

Finally Griffin met Cross's gaze and his jaw took a hard set. "We were split into two teams of four. Opposite sides of a thoroughfare where we could cover ingress and egress of the HVT's safe house," he said. "We watched our targets squirt. They sped out of there in a half dozen white Land Cruisers like their seventy-two virgins were in trouble somewhere and needed help." A ripple of laughter went around the cabin. "Five minutes later we got a call confirming this cannibal thing and were given the details not one of us could comprehend ... nor believe. *At first.*"

"Been there," said Lopez, performing the sign of the cross over his chest.

Griffin sighed. Said, "You know. It's too bad the virus *really* took hold during daylight hours. If it had been after dark we could have just used our night vision and boogied on out of Dodge without having to tangle with so many of them."

Knowing how the debrief after the debrief helped him get his keel straightened out after a mission, Cade asked, "How far did you get before encountering Zs?"

"Jolly and Diesel got bit before we made it three blocks. The *adam khor,* as we'd heard the Zs called, were everywhere. Skinny little walkers biting anything that moved. We were still following Rules Of Engagement. No one was shooting and we didn't know the full scope of Omega yet. We only killed the few Zs that attacked us ... which at the time we still thought of as just sick locals. So we forced our way into a closed shop and I bandaged my teammates." He paused for a few seconds then went on, "Jolly was bit on the neck. Had a nicked carotid. He bled out and died in the shop so I put him on my shoulders and carried him the rest of the way. By the time we rendezvoused at our vehicles ... less than twenty minutes had passed and ... craziest shit I ever saw happened. Diesel, who was still ambulatory, fell down and stopped breathing. He died just like that from a couple of bite wounds on his arm." Griffin paused again.

"Take your time," said Cross, handing over a bottled water.

Griffin cracked the seal and slugged half of the water down in one pull. He capped the remainder and went on, "No way we're leaving our bros behind. So we put their bodies in the trunk. Halfway to the docks they both came alive back there. They're kicking and moaning real loud ... both of them are crammed in Cog's trunk when we hit a checkpoint at the dock entrance. What was usually manned by one keystone cop lackey is now being manned by half a dozen hajjis trying hard to encourage us with their AKs to go elsewhere. Because he has a fair grasp of conversational Urdu, Cog's in the lead car and he isn't taking no for an answer. He gave one guard all the local currency he had to let us through. I watched the hajji pocket the wad, expecting him to play it off and go about business as usual, but he went ahead and waved us through. Both cars ... didn't check Cog's trunk or ours or ask any of us for papers. Didn't seem to care. We found out why a few seconds later. Around the corner are more soldiers in hazmat suits and they have six or seven cars pulled over. People are zip-tied and lying on the ground, foaming at the mouth and fighting the cuffs like crazed animals ... which wasn't far off. Shit, we thought we were home free. The six of us that were left were about to get out of the biggest shit storm we'd ever seen. Made Fallujah look like a kid's birthday party. Adults eating kids in the street ... just tearing in and ripping out their guts. There were people getting run over, seemingly on purpose—"

Interrupting, Lasseigne said, "So you had an American-flagged ship waiting off shore?"

"No ... some CIA guy on a fast mover was going to scoop us up at the docks. Thirty-eight foot Scarab off shore racer, supposedly. Didn't matter, though. The Pakis in the level four bio-suits wanted us to strip before going any further. All of us had passed for locals dressed like we were, but they wanted us to first prove that none of us had been bitten."

In a knowing tone, Cade said, "Tattoos..."

"We all had em. Some specific ... most not. No way we're taking off our *Paki pajamas*, so Nilla, who's driving our Suzuki, takes out the three nearest with his Sig and the shit goes from zero to a hundred in one breath. I'm in back of the Suzuki when the shit starts hitting the fan and Stewie and Cooper fire up the Hajjis from the Hyundai ahead of us and we're all on our way. But by now ... so is the rest of the line ahead of us."

Cade said, "They all panicked?"

"Yeah. Two or three drivers popped the clutch so to speak and tried to drive away. That's when the cops ... or ISI ... that are left start sprayin' them and us down and then Snip buys the farm ... and he drives the car right over the cops. Grinds a few of them into the road. That's when they got Coop and Stew. Had to be a hundred rounds peppered their little Hyundai. Then the trunk pops open and I see Diesel roll out. He's six-two and all muscle and pale as a ghost. Unfazed, he walks through a hail of bullets. Pieces are falling off of him and he's jerking forward and ... and then he just lifts this little brown fucker into the air and eats his face off. Then Jolly ... he's not green and he's no giant. He's this wiry white guy who tans good and can grow a full black beard in a week ... looks just like a native when he's in country. Anyway, he's out of the trunk now and walking all stiff and he's white as Elvira's ass—" He cracked a sad half-smile at the visual. "Jolly, he distracted them and didn't even know he was getting our backs. But there wasn't time to put them down," said Griffin, again shaking his head. "We had to leave 'em there tearing shit up."

"I know the feeling," said Cade. "I had to make the same decision ... had to leave a good man behind at Grand Junction Regional."

Griffin said nothing.

Cade sees that the SEAL is sweating. No doubt reliving the moment as if he was still there. More statement than question, he asked, "So you and your other two teammates made it to the Scarab."

Shaking his head, Griffin said, "Negative. Just me and Nilla. One round found Snip. Right in the head. Golden effin BB. He died instantly. I know this 'cause I was wearing his brains."

The helicopter made another course correction and Cade said to Griffin, "Just you and Nilla made it to the Scarab?"

"Yep. We get aboard and below deck and the spook, who has already bribed the dock workers to look the other way, he takes us just to the other side of international waters and kills the engine and we wait. Had a lot of time to think about how everyone died and how we couldn't bring their bodies out. And all that time while we're lolling and seeing Paki patrol boats we're trying to wrap our minds around everything and we can't make the shit we saw jive with reality. Still hard to believe five weeks after the fact." Griffin went silent again.

The helo had been in the air for thirty minutes and everyone had been listening to the story with rapt attention—especially Cade, who had been privy to little, save for the missions he was on, up until three weeks ago—and had been totally in the dark since. "So who picked you up?" he asked.

"The *USS Texas*, a Virginia Class attack sub, she surfaces right beside us in broad daylight in the Arabian Sea with no apparent concern about being spotted. So we ditch our ride without scuttling it and board the sub. That was Z-Day plus two ... and it got worse after that. The *Texas* sets course for, we were told at the time, Hawaii. I figure it should be pretty safe there but the commander tells us as soon as we're underway that it's a shit show there too. Pearl is holding their own ... but the virus jumped from the mainland already. Came on commercial airliners and was spreading like wildfire."

"Same in Portland, Oregon," said Cade.

"D.C. fell like a fat lady on roller skates," said Cross. "Fast and hard, and though I feel nothing for the lobbyists and most of the government types inside the Beltway ... it hurt to watch it happen."

Lopez said, "Frisco and L.A. and San Diego didn't last long. I lost a lot of family—"

Lasseigne said through clenched teeth, "New Orleans, I heard, looked like it did after Katrina ... minus the missing roofs and boats thrown up on shore. Again people were looting and killing and FEMA and DHS were nowhere to be found. Then my girl leaves a message saying the *biters* were everywhere. Talked to her only once after that ... just prior to the phones going down. She was scared to death and I'm hundreds of miles away protecting the lowlifes in D.C." He shook his head and pounded a fist on his thigh. "Nothing I coulda done to help her. And I have no idea where she is now—"

Griffin said, "The quick spread that swallowed everyone up I think can be attributed to *normalcy bias*. The notion that the first responders were going to swoop in and right the ship is what did most of the population in." He shook his head and looked around the cabin. "Just like our man in Karachi, nobody had an inkling of the true nature of the virus. Thus the danger wasn't real to them. Hell, half of the crew on the sub were talking like everything was going to be fine and their families would be waiting at Pearl when the boat docked. Wasn't the case, though—"

Lopez asked, "Where's the *Texas* now?"

"No idea. I got off and caught a Galaxy to Springs. I presume she was resupplied and is out hunting our *new* enemies."

"Back to *your* story, Griff. *Nilla* ... what happened to him. And who are our *new* enemies?" asked Ari, who had obviously been listening in over the comms and whose pay grade wasn't high enough to afford him more intel than what he'd already seen from the air during the dozens of missions he'd been on since Z-Day.

"Nilla got a little bite when we were fighting our way out of the store. More like a scratch from a canine tooth we figured later. But it was enough to kill him slowly. He got sick and was put into four-point restraints in the infirmary. Later I heard someone call the way he turned a '*slow burn.*' Lucky him ... he wasn't around when the shit hit the fan again."

Cade said, "Again?"

Ari said, "New enemies ... let the man talk."

"We rendezvoused with the Fifth Fleet near New Guinea and then inexplicably we're about facing and word is we're heading back towards the Torres Strait to go silent and escort a boomer ... never heard which one, though. Not long after that the Fifth Fleet is in an all-out surface engagement with both remnants of the Chinese North Sea fleet and a few destroyers and frigates of Russia's Black Sea Fleet."

Cade found himself sitting on the edge of his seat, straining against his shoulder straps. So much for the Cliff's Notes version. He wanted to know as many details as possible. "What happened then?"

"Kicked the shit out of them," Griff said, all serious and unsmiling. "Tomahawks flying everywhere. Thirty or forty Marine FA-18 Hornets in the air and taking it to them." Griffin went silent again.

"Sorry I asked," said Cade, looking out the window and seeing the terrain had changed from smooth horizontal wave-like rock flows to knobby spires and arches eroded from the earth, monuments all eons in the making.

Meanwhile, two hundred miles away at FOB Bastion, Jamie and Lev were in the same single-wide Cade and the Kids had spent the night in weeks ago. The wall-mounted A\C unit was rumbling and their weapons were in pieces on a blanket spread out on the floor. There was little small talk; for a long while both seemed content to solemn introspection until Jamie brought up the sailboat full of survivors anchored in the Pineview Reservoir.

"It looked like those folks on the sailboat were in big trouble," Jamie said. "You know ... the way they were jumping up and down ... waving at us."

Lev said, "They were just reacting that way because of the helicopter's markings."

"What do you mean?"

"They thought we were an arm of the government finally coming to their rescue."

"DHS," she said, nodding. "Department of Homeland Security. Some security they provided."

"You see Cade's point, though? There really was no way we could have picked up all of them."

"It just sucks," Jamie said. She brushed some dirt off her carbine's bolt carrier group then paused and looked up, adding, "And it sucks how Cade scolded me in front of you and Daymon."

"He was right. You've got to keep your weapon clean."

The two-way radio sitting on the blanket amidst the rifle parts and spare magazines came to life. It buzzed on as both Lev and Jamie stared at it.

"You get it."

Shaking his head, Lev said, "No. You."

And she did. She snatched it up, said, "Jamie."

She nodded as Daymon told them they were needed at the hangars. "What for?" she asked.

He said, "Bring Lev. It'll be fun."

Grumbling, she set the radio down and went back to reassembling the carbine.

A short walk away from the single-wide, inside a much smaller hangar than the ones at Schriever, Daymon was sitting on a plastic chair, bending its legs back and forth as he craned around doing his best to watch the techs and learn a little about the DHS Black Hawk without getting in the way.

Thinking about the trap he'd just baited, he smiled and put the radio away in his pocket.

Four hundred yards east of the row of hangars, inside a building once used as a waiting area for outbound travelers but now converted to a sort of base PX, Duncan was all alone and sniffing around for something with a little more of a kick than watery coffee or a Rip It energy drink.

He walked the *aisles,* which consisted of a couple of rows of opened cardboard boxes that no one had seen fit to cut the tops off. There were energy bars and applesauce in single-serve squeeze containers and Slim Jims jerky sticks and processed cheese and crackers, but no booze. Seeing as how the zombie apocalypse had rendered paper money good for only two things—burning and wiping—Duncan figured anyone *shopping* here was operating on the honor system. So he took a couple of each. Left with a wide enough variety to share with Jamie and Lev with a few leftovers earmarked for Sasha and Raven. He mined some Snickers bars and M&Ms from another row of boxes, stuffed his pockets and exited the building.

He stood outside, trying to get his bearings while lamenting the fact that his buzz was wearing off and the shakes were close behind.

A staccato burst of gunfire, presumably coming from the distant front gate, gave him something to orient from. He took a left tack and after a few minute walk was in front of the nondescript cement block building Beeson called headquarters.

He loitered outside the door, his hands beginning to tremor, until the tractor-beam-like pull of the bottle of Scotch he'd spotted behind the major's desk overrode the last scintilla of willpower in his body.

Four hundred feet above Staircase National Monument, inside the speeding Ghost Hawk, Cade burned the minutes of uneasy silence looking out the starboard side window. Suddenly some movement on the desert floor caught his eye and he shifted forward and craned his neck. He saw a shadow far ahead and right of their position and it was keeping steady pace with the Ghost Hawk's shadow, which was riding along the broken ground a little ahead and right of the outer edge of the helicopter's whirring rotor disc.

He was about to mention to Lopez that the black Osprey was forming up on their port side when Griffin picked up where he'd left off.

The Navy SEAL said, "In an act of desperation, with their carriers already on the way to the bottom and their frigates and destroyers burning ... someone in the Russian or Chinese fleet got skittish and made a calculated decision. At least that's what our sub's XO assumed. Hell, communications had already been spotty since the EMP airbursts, and he said he couldn't get permission to pop a nuke even if he wanted to. By that time I guess President Odero, his cabinet and the Joint Chiefs had all gone dark. There was no government. So the bastards launched from a nearby sub. The sonar operator pegged it for what it was and the entire boat went silent. Like we were all attending a funeral ... only the poor bastards weren't dead yet. We heard the airburst nuke that took out the entire Fifth fleet ... fifteen, twenty thousand sailors, airmen, Marines. Heard the blast two hundred feet deep. Didn't even need an acoustic listening device to hear the hulls popping when they hit crush depth. Thank God we didn't hear any screaming when they were on their way to the bottom."

Cade asked, "Did you guys get the other sub?"

"Yeah. Took about an hour of running silent before they made a mistake."

Lasseigne asked, "The *Texas* torpedoed them?"

"The cocky bastards went to periscope depth. Just as they were nearing the surface, we let go a couple of Mk-48 torpedoes that were on the money. Broke the *Akula's* back. The commie bastards got the longest ride possible ... all the way from spitting distance with the horizon to the ocean floor. That one, though," Griffin said, nodding. "Wish I would have been listening in when it hit crush depth and imploded." He went silent and looked towards the cabin floor.

"Don't mess with Texas," Ari said over the comms.

Cade peered past him and out the window. Everything was a red blur. He heard the SEAL draw a breath and then the man said in a funeral voice, "It would've been satisfying hearing them suffer. Softened the loss of my platoon. Jolly, Cog, Diesel, Snip, Stewie, and Cooper ... I wouldn't have traded three subs full of Russian sailors for a hair on any one of their heads."

Cross gave his old friend a squeeze on the shoulder. "If they come anywhere near the CONUS we'll deal out some payback for them."

Sitting back, Cade thought how heavy a burden the news of the loss of an entire carrier battle group and all of the supporting ships must have been for the new President Valerie Clay, Nash, and Shrill while they already had their hands full dealing with traitorous snakes on American soil. Wouldn't have wished that kind of pressure on anyone. And that they'd kept their cards close to their vest even when China's hunter killer satellites were attacking the International Space Station caused Cade's analytical brain to wonder what else they knew and weren't letting on.

Chapter 37

Eight miles east of the garage, her feet and ankles throbbing like she'd just been hobbled by Annie Wilkes, the specks of flesh and blood and dermis clinging to Glenda's body started attracting unwanted guests. Treating her like a native in a National Geographic documentary, the greedy insects lit on her face, nosed around her unblinking eyes, and crawled into her nostrils and mouth without remorse. Before long Glenda was host to an undulating green and black carpet of hungrily feeding common houseflies. And though she looked and smelled like one of the dead, and her winged passengers were undoubtedly exposing her to all of their diseases, the myriad of six decades' worth of accumulated aches and pains was telling her different. With each new step the pain radiating from the soles of her feet had her convinced that this was what it must feel like to have a belt sander loaded with forty grit paper taken to them. Not one pass, but several, until the once pink pads there were gone and, like the exposed innards of a Grand piano, she imagined she would be able to see the tendons and metatarsals stretching and retracting with each pain-filled step.

Keep going, Glenda, she told herself, praying the endorphins— Mother Nature's answer to pain—would continue building and eventually bring on the euphoria she remembered from her days as a world class cross-country runner.

But something better fell in her lap before she'd reached that necessary plateau of pain. She saw the glint of sun off of chrome to her left. Saw whitewall tires and the red outline of a bike frame propped against a stately pine. She slowed her gait ever so slightly to allow the collection of charred and bloated creatures to overtake her.

Keeping her eyes locked on the ham-sized hunk of pink uncooked flesh jiggling on the nearest creature's backside, she continued shaving off steps until the lurching cadaver was a few paces beyond the gravel drive in the pine's long shadow.

Keep going, you bastards. Don't look back. Nothing to see here, she thought to herself as if those words would have any effect on the pack of dead or the ultimate outcome of her next move. She figured one of two things would happen. Either bare buttocks walker would see her deviate from the State Route and turn and follow suit, the primeval part of its brain fooled into thinking prey must be nearby. Or the train wreck would be none the wiser and continue slogging ahead with the others until its oozing butt literally calved off and met the roadway with a wet resonant slap.

Time would tell. *Six more steps.* She could almost hear the power tool's whine and smell the caustic stench of abraded flesh. *Four. Three. Two. And one.* Inadvertently her left turn became more of an about face than the dumb shuffle she was aiming for, which resulted in a sharp *squelch* as a handful of gravel shifted under her hiker. She knew a millisecond later that she was in trouble and, like dominos falling, this sudden revelation started the familiar cold blast in her gut that radiated to her limbs, mercifully delivering some of the comfort she'd been praying for.

Alerted by the out of place sound, bare buttocks walker and his two crisped friends performed wooden, near-simultaneous pirouettes and stalked her way, their low mournful moans preceding them.

Get a move on, Glenda. They're gaining.

Heeding her inner voice and with the hair on her neck standing at attention, Glenda straightened up and set her arms and legs to pumping, leaving a cloud of pissed-off insects swirling and diving in her wake. Though she was certain her socks were one fine bloodied mess by now, she started into a slow jog that, as the moans and grunts of her pursuers intensified, became a frantic uphill slog.

From the turnoff to the house the drive was fairly steep and rutted by parallel tire tracks. For every hard-earned ten yards Glenda covered the dead managed only two or three steps, and by the time she could clearly see the object of her attention she figured she had maybe a minute or two before the zombies caught up with her.

Though it didn't dawn on Glenda at first, the house, which was set back in the trees and partially hidden by shrubs growing out of control, was well known to her. She'd had a friend named Violet who had lived with her husband in the dilapidated two-story affair until his passing some years before and the pull of family drew her back east.

Many a raucous game of Bunko had taken place behind the darkened picture window staring down on her. And many a bottle of wine had been uncorked there as well. At first the camaraderie and gossip had been just what Glenda needed. Later on it was just the wine. Then, after one too many game nights when she didn't stop when the dice did, she found she'd worn her welcome out.

After her self-inflicted ouster from Bunko, *game night* continued at home and she drank alone and unencumbered by social mores while Louie worked graveyard at his plant job in Ogden.

Violet's husband died the next summer and by autumn she was also gone, the home up for sale and a U-Haul hitched to the old Caprice. Not much had changed at Violet's place, though. The siding showing through the bushes was still a shade of blue, chalky and fading from the accumulative effect of past winters and new owners who cared more about slinging paint on stretched canvas than on their new place. *Priorities*, thought Glenda. The screen on the front door was closed and the Huntsville Times had piled up on the stoop, unread, a week's worth at least. Newly installed stained glass windows flanked the door, and in the other windows Violet's God-awful olive green velveteen curtains had been replaced by those horizontal aluminum things that screamed modern and were hard to keep dusted.

Nosed in at an angle on the oil-stained cement pad was the kind of boxy foreign station wagon favored by the artistic set in Ogden. On the back tailgate, below the oversized window, were dozens of stickers attesting to some of the places the young couple who'd bought Violet's house had ventured. Mixed in among the colorful tributes to *Glacier National Park*, *Yellowstone*, and *Bryce Canyon* was a who's who of stickers giving voice to activist groups whose social values fell farther to the left of Glenda's—*much farther*.

Watching the dead over her shoulder, she misjudged the distance and bounced off the Volvo's passenger-side quarter panel at as near to a full sprint as her shredded feet—and partial suit of magazine armor—would allow. Knitting needles in hand, her heart in her throat and a sheen of sweat wetting her face, she paused to catch her breath.

Leaning on the car, hands on knees and with her chest heaving uncontrollably, she glanced left and saw the doors to the small swaybacked garage at the rear of the property hanging wide open. Save for the cobwebs strung between the rafters, a recycling bin full of newspaper, and an old-fashioned push mower leaning against the back wall, the structure was empty. However, Glenda quickly ruled it out as a place to hide due to the suspect-looking hinges and handful of vertical planks missing from the outward opening doors.

The house was looking better and better with each passing second. The blinds in the rear-facing windows were all closed. On the side of the house the small bay window above the kitchen sink where Violet had sprung her failed intervention so many years ago held a trio of houseplants, their leaves browned and drooping in defeat. She craned left and saw no movement behind the dining room's large plate window.

Her breath returning, Glenda limped to the side gate and looked the length of the house and spotted the trio of corpses twenty yards distant and struggling mightily to navigate the uneven pitted tracks and raised hump of grass running down the center of them. In an almost comical manner, the zombie with half its ass falling off would straddle the center ridge then step into a rut and stagger forward a short distance and repeat the move in the opposite direction in a kind of perpetual motion, zigging and zagging in front of the other two rotters.

Blinking the stinging drops of sweat from her eyes, Glenda tore off the bathrobe and tossed it on the ground. *Served your purpose.* Then, with her flight instinct winning out over the idea of spending another night alone with the nightmares inside her head and the hungering dead lingering outside, she looped around the car's squared-off front end and snatched up the bike by its red vinyl grips. Grunting, she lifted the heavy art-deco-inspired behemoth and pointed the front wheel towards the State Route fifty yards downhill and felt her stomach sink when she saw that the rest of the staggering pus bags were coming to the dinner party.

Without checking the tires for pressure or even looking to see if the thing had a chain, she straddled the red rust bucket and, while hoping the pendulum of good fortune was still on her side, planted one aching foot on a pedal and pushed off downhill.

As the nearly flat front tire bounced over rocks the size of baseballs and was tugged left and right, Glenda focused on keeping her butt centered on the spring-cushioned seat, the bike tracking straight with only one hand on the bars and her eyes fixed on the closest zombie.

With the front wheel juddering in the right side rut Glenda saw the wobbling cadaver step over the center ridge and simultaneously applied the rear brake, leveled the knitting needle like a jousting stick, and plunged it inches deep into the moving target's left eye socket.

Instantly there was a sharp pain in her wrist and before she could release the needle it was ripped violently from her hand. Then, dangerously close to putting the bike on its side, she regained control with both hands, rode up on the center ridge and pedaled hard for three full revolutions. At the last moment, with the other two walkers taking slow telegraphed swipes for her head, she bent low over the bars and, with the grass threatening to hang up in the spokes and chain, passed right between the moaning ghouls with no room to spare.

She sat up and, with the wind buffeting her face and the drying sweat giving her a chill, nosed the rattle trap off the ridge and back into the right side rut.

Total time elapsed from mounting the bike and reaching the bottom of the hill, Glenda guessed, was no more than ten seconds, but probably closer to five. Ducking low to the bike when the drive connected with the State Route, she leaned left and zippered through the ragged knot of walking corpses while letting loose with a guttural war whoop.

With her victory peal hanging in the air, she angled the bike left on the smooth blacktop and never looked back.

Eden Compound

Raven walked her mountain bike through the tangled grass near the compound's hidden entrance and waited in the shade at the forest's edge while Sasha fetched hers.

"You're going to have a big advantage over me," said Sasha. Then, referring to the antiquated, battered and rusty piece of work she was pushing, added, "This thing is a *tank*."

"Well you're bigger and stronger than me," countered Raven, crossing her arms. "*I* should get a head start."

"Not going to happen," said Sasha with a flip of her hair. "Bragging rights are at stake. And I like to brag."

Raven thought: *Yes you do. And then some.* Parroting something she'd heard uttered by her mom, or dad, or perhaps both, she said, "It would probably level the playing field if you filled your designer handbags with rocks and put one on each arm."

Shaking her head, Sasha threw a leg over her bike, pushed off and, in a move some would call cheating, hollered, "Go," when she was already a couple of yards ahead of Raven.

***

Raven lost the first race which consisted of ten full laps around the clearing, keeping only to the beaten-down grass oval. Slightly winded and with a subtle rattle evident with each exhale, Raven dismounted her bike and began pestering Sasha for a rematch.

Shaking her head, Sasha said, "Not yet. I need some water."

Raven smiled and nodded toward the crop circle where Brook was. "Follow me," she said with a noticeable gleam in her eye.

The girls laid their bikes down and crept to the edge of the crop circle where they covertly took a knee and peered between the stalks of grass.

Still breathing hard, while suppressing the urge to giggle, Raven mouthed: *The bear's still sleeping.*

"You get it."

"No. You," Sasha whispered.

So Raven stepped onto the tamped down grass. Snuck up to her snoring mom and plucked a sun-warmed bottled water off the spread out sheet. Snickering, she turned slowly and, with four exaggerated high-steps, made her way back to the side of her partner in crime.

Sasha wiped the sweat from her brow and regarded the sun which was climbing steadily towards its high noon position. She took the bottle from Raven, cracked the cap and took a long pull. Then, passing the bottle back, she whispered, "Rematch time."

Eden compound motor pool

Foley drove. Not because he wanted to. On the contrary. Initially, when he'd learned they would be going in Daymon's pick-up on account that all the gear was stored in its box, he had parked himself riding shotgun. But all that had accomplished was to warm the seat for Chief, who had insisted he was *not* driving.

So when Tran balked as well, by default the former IT worker slid behind the wheel and, since his legs were nowhere near the length of Daymon's, made the necessary adjustments to the seat and all three mirrors.

Foley waited for the girls to zip by on their bikes, then nosed the truck up the gravel drive. At the inner fence Chief delegated the job of seeing them through to Tran. They followed the same routine at the outer gate and, while Tran was locking the gate behind them and arranging the wall of camouflage foliage, Chief hailed Seth back at the compound and Phillip who was up the hill at the over watch and informed them that he and Foley and Tran would be at the roadblock for two, maybe three hours at the most.

Glad that the formalities were taken care of by someone other than him and coming to accept the fact that he was the new guy and thusly should do what he was told, Foley—though he'd been nearly bald since the early '90s—decided to let his hair down a little. Smiling, he wheeled the powerful Chevy west, aimed the steel brushguard at a pair of rotters loping down the road, and tromped the gas, saying, "Let's see what this baby will do."

"I wouldn't," warned Chief. "Gonna piss Daymon off if you break anything."

Tran said nothing. Just held onto the grab handle near his head and braced for impact.

As the engine propelled the truck rapidly from a near standstill to thirty-five miles per hour, Chief was doing the same. He had his left hand splayed out on the dash and his other wrapped white-knuckle tight around the front A-pillar-mounted grab-handle.

The speedometer hit forty and Foley pinned the accelerator to the floor. There was a whine from the engine and the truck reached fifty just as it entered a stretch of the road where spring runoff had settled the rock and gravel bed which in turn caused the asphalt to take a subtle dive. At the bottom of the depression the springs went taut, pressing everyone's butts into the seats. On the upslope the suspension unloaded and by that time the two male zombies had turned a one-eighty and brought their arms up, ready to embrace the speeding Chevy.

Seeing visions of an infected body lodged in the windshield, legs kicking like a diver out of water, Foley blinked first. He braked hard and jinked the truck right; there was a sharp crack and the hollow thunk of cranium meeting tempered steel. Chief shook his head and grimaced as he saw the damage the glancing blow inflicted on the undead pair. One stick-thin arm trailing tendon and veins spun away towards the far ditch. The rest of the creature that had just lost the battle with the tubular grill guard hinged backwards directly into the path of the passenger-side tires. A millisecond later the front quarter panel nailed rotter number two sending it over the truck, head, heels, head, heels amidst a shower of glass from the destroyed headlight.

Slowing the truck to thirty, Foley said accusingly, "You made me drive." He flicked his eyes to the rear-view mirror making sure the gear was intact and there were no unwanted passengers in the bed.

Chief reached over and started the wipers spreading the clumps of brain on the windshield like a thin greasy cataract. "Juvenile move, Foley," he said. "Hit the washer fluid."

As an electric pump whined somewhere under the hood and a liberal shower of blue fluid splashed the glass, Foley replied, "At least we know she's got some giddy up."

The radio crackled and Phillip, who had apparently witnessed the whole thing, said, "Oooh. Daymon's going to be pissed when he gets back."

Chief ignored the radio.

Foley said nothing in his defense and after driving in silence for a few short minutes Daymon's late summer project, a myriad of fallen trees and sharpened boughs designed to keep a large contingent of walking corpses at bay, was blocking the road dead ahead.

"Park it pointing east," said Chief, racking a round into his pump twelve gauge. "I'll get the saws and spare chain. Bring all of the fuel and oil ... we've got a lot of work ahead of us."

Foley wheeled the truck around with a three-point turn and killed the engine.

Lugging a backpack filled with food and bottled waters, Tran exited the truck through the door behind Foley's and closed it behind him. Without a word he crossed the road, navigated the ditch, took a seat on the guardrail and waited.

Foley donned his pack and Chief threw the chainsaw over his shoulder. They hiked across the blacktop, formed up with Tran and the three of them entered the forest heading south, perpendicular from the road. A dozen feet in, Chief hooked a right and they walked for a while, passing a long row of fresh stumps leaking sap, each one's circumference bigger around than a wagon wheel. On their right were the expertly felled trees making up the base of the blockade.

They walked until they heard the rasps of the dead milling about the blockade's westernmost end where the next layer, a phalanx of mainly smaller lodge pole pines, was to be started. *Lay them down like pick up sticks, interwoven. The more tangled, the better,* Daymon had said at dinner the night before.

Chief planned to work both flanks of the road, felling many of the smaller trees and leaving an interlocked layer atop the entire east-west run. The theory being that the prolific thicket of branches would inhibit the still few and far between self-aware first-turns from clawing up on each other and making their way along the top.

At first sight of the barrier, Tran adjusted his pack and craned around Foley and asked, "What's keeping the demons from going around ... through the forest?"

Chief lowered the chainsaw to the ground and shrugged off his pack. Placed his shotgun within easy reach. Finally, he motioned beyond the dead crowded around the pair of SUVs abutting the barrier a dozen feet away. "This bridge spans a sixty-foot deep gorge. There are dozens of snags and impenetrable undergrowth flanking the dry riverbed down there. Any rotters that fall off end up getting trapped."

Tran stepped up on a fallen log to see the crossing from a better vantage point. Constructed of poured white cement and taking a gentle curve away from the break in the treed canopy, the two-lane affair looked like some kind of public works project from the '60s. After a few seconds of scrutiny, he proffered, "What's to stop a person from picking their way through the trees?"

"There are no *living* people in Huntsville," replied Foley.

Chief added ominously, "But there are thousands of walking dead."

"And the vehicles?"

Chief said, "Keys are on the driver's side rear tire. They're gassed up and ready. Just in case we need to go to Huntsville or Eden."

Tran said nothing. He dumped the pack and, with the shallow exhaust burble from Chief trying to start the chainsaw exciting the dead, set off into the woods in search of dinner's accompaniments.

Chapter 38

Leaving behind the southeastern corner of Zion National Park with its red rock spires and canyons harboring patches of green and rivers that from the air looked like mere trickles of water, the Ghost Hawk cut across the northwest corner of Arizona, all of sixty short miles, and then entered Nevada's airspace with Lake Mead glittering like polished silver dead ahead.

To Ari's naked eye it looked as if the lake's water level had risen. Still, there were mud flats showing near shore where hundreds of Zs had become hopelessly mired, no doubt lured there by the staggering number of personal watercraft anchored in the lake and languishing under the hot sun. On shore, walking corpses were everywhere. The boat launch beside the deserted marina was thoroughly snarled with abandoned vehicles, most hitched to empty boat trailers. And catching Cade's eye north of there, reminiscent of the scene at the Flaming Gorge Recreational Area in Utah, was a sizeable campground bursting at the seams with tents of every size, shape, and color of the rainbow.

Cade walked his gaze towards the lake's southwest end and recognized the gently curved top of Hoover Dam jutting from the lake and silently holding back millions of gallons of blue-green water. That there was just a trickle spilling out the back side told him the turbines weren't operating. Therefore the dam was not supplying electricity to Los Angeles 266 miles away.

Lasseigne tapped the window nearest him. He said, "Check out the mound of bodies in the spillway south of the span."

Cross said, "I hope my eyes are deceiving me. Looks like a whole lot of dead kids down there."

Cade shifted his attention to the scene passing below. Running parallel left of the dam and high over the spillway was a four-lane bridge dotted with inert vehicles, most of which were crowding the railing. Nothing moved there, living or dead. He noted the mass of tangled bodies and suddenly it dawned on him what he was seeing. He thought: *No better place to stop and end it all than one of the Seven Wonders of the World.*

Simultaneously coming to the same conclusion, the operators and SOAR crew went silent. For a few long seconds there was only the steady resonant whirr of the rotors and various sounds as the mechanicals did their thing behind the scenes.

Then, for the first time since Cade came aboard, and presumably to distract everyone from dwelling on what they had just witnessed, the heavily muscled African American pilot in the left-seat uttered something not pertinent to the mission. "Who remembers this?" he said. He cleared his throat and, with his baritone voice rising a couple of octaves, went on, "Welcome everyone, I am your *dam* guide, *Arnie.*"

"I know what movie it's from," said Ari, chuckling. "Hit us with another quote won't you please, Chief Warrant Officer Haynes."

Acquiescing, Haynes said, "Please, take all the *dam* pictures that you want. Now, are there any *dam* questions?"

Playing along, Griffin took his eyes off of the marvel of modern engineering slipping away to their six and said, "Where can I get some *dam* bait?"

"That's great, Doc. But who remembers this one?" said Ari. He cleared his throat. "Where the hell is the damn *dam* tour?"

That one rang a bell, finally, and Cade realized they were riffing on Vegas Vacation. Not his personal favorite of the series. Sure, Cousin Eddie was funny in that one. And the Griswold family did get some nice exotic rides off the casino in the end. But nothing compared to Christmas Vacation. His train of thought totally removed from the grim scene below the bridge, Cade smiled, remembering the hilarity that ensued when the Griswold family went Christmas tree hunting. "Too easy," answered Haynes, his voice dragging Cade's attention back to the previous conversation. "That was Clark Griswold's line after he gets separated from the group at the Hoover dam."

"Bingo," said Ari. "Next stop, one-armed bandits, no armed Zs, and the world famous, undead choked, Fremont Street."

Hearing this, and without fanfare, Lopez unbuckled and reached into the canvas bag near his feet and came out with a handful of metallic cylinders. He sat up straight, his body language changing. His jaw took a hard set and he looked around the cabin, meeting each man's gaze. He finished the circuit and stared at Cade and said, "You all have been drilled on how to use these so I'm not going to repeat the gory details."

Though he had a good idea what Lopez was up to, Cade still craned forward to get a better look at what was in Low-Rider's hand. Each item was about five inches long, had a screw-on-type lid, and, judging by the dull sheen and tinny sound they made rubbing together in the Delta commander's gloved hand, Cade guessed they were made out of aluminum or titanium or some other exotic metal.

Lopez handed one to Cade then doled the rest out around the cabin counterclockwise. Then he rooted in the bag and brought out four more cylinders and a handful of black heavy duty zip-ties already fashioned loosely into figure-eight-shaped handcuffs. Silently, he passed the cuffs around then put one of the cylinders away in his blouse pocket. He looked at Cade for a few seconds. Finally he handed the remaining three over and said, "All of these are for you as per whatever agreement you have with Nash. Damn, *Wyatt*. You must be as good at negotiating as you are with that *pistola* of yours. 'Cause I heard these things are far from being produced in any kind of large quantities."

"They're far from being perfected, is what I heard," countered Cade. "I just pray we'll never have to use them."

After concurring with a nod, Lopez looked around the cabin again, settling his gaze on each man for a tick. Finally, in a no nonsense tone, he said, "If you get bit you *must* administer the antiserum as soon as possible. And there's no need to sterilize the injection site first ... you get to this point, that's the least of your worries. Please remember, if you do not immediately experience the euphoric rush that our egghead friends at Schriever briefed us about then presume that you are in the lower percentile and there will be little to zero probability of avoiding Omega's ultimate outcome. In the event you have crapped out, so to speak, it is your duty to fight your way to somewhere safe and practice proper containment procedures. If you *cannot* cuff yourself ... if you're injured and bleeding out, call for Griff and he'll do it for you."

Worrying the zip-ties in one gloved hand, Lasseigne looked at Lopez and said, "Copy that."

Griffin nodded and gazed out the window as the terror-stricken faces of the soldiers he'd patched up in the field cycled through his head like a jittery movie. Their eyes darted about, looking for salvation. To a man their mouths emitted choked pleas for a mercy bullet. But not before calling out for those already lost. Echoing in his head at all hours were the specific names of spouses and children and moms and dads. Most were carried in tortured screams. Some came out in a whisper and a last breath.

Next to Cade, Cross patted the P229 Sig Sauer pistol strapped to his right thigh and said, "I got my own *containment* protocol right here. If I get bit and the dose doesn't take hold, no way I'm saddling Griff with that responsibility ... not with those kind of long odds. I'll take as many of them out first as I can, and save the last round for myself."

"Hope for the best, bro. At least with the antiserum you've got better odds of surviving a bite than bringing money home from Vegas," said Ari over the comms. "And speaking of the Devil ... on our starboard side you will see, in all of its former glory, the city that never sleeps."

Noting the ant-sized forms staggering here and there on the residential side streets northwest of the strip, Cross said, "The city that never dies is more like it."

"Beat me to it," said Ari, faking a rim shot by tapping his index finger on his mike. Then, in his best Andrew Dice Clay, added, "What *dies* in Vegas ... *stays* in Vegas. *Ohhhh.*"

Cade was looking out the window and marveling at the contrast between the red tiled roofs—which seemed to be the norm for Vegas's suburbs—and the glimmering aquamarine waters of hundreds of swimming pools. He grimaced at the bad joke but said nothing because he knew how far a little levity went towards keeping one's sanity intact in the face of so much wanton death and destruction.

"You've got the stick, Haynes. I want to work the FLIR pod," Ari said.

"Copy. Taking the stick," Haynes stated coolly.

Ari's hands flew over the touch screen monitor, pressing the appropriate pixelated buttons to engage the gimbal-mounted optics pod. He thumbed the hat switch to the right. Consequently the pod panned right and the distant mountains gave way and the Vegas skyline graced the color monitor to his fore. He zoomed in a few stops and informed the *customers* in back to watch their flat panel because they would soon be seeing *Lost Wages* up close and personal, closing with his customary, *'Courtesy of Night Stalker Air.'*

As Haynes nosed the Ghost Hawk smoothly south by west, Cade removed the satellite phone, glanced at the screen and saw there was nothing new. No text. No voice mail. So he slipped it back into his cargo pocket, glanced up at the large rear-facing monitor above the crew chief's seat and saw in full color and with outstanding clarity the Vegas strip in all its gaudy splendor. From a trip there in 1998, a month before he and Brook were married, Cade vaguely remembered a hotel with crazy fountains out front and a circus-themed casino complete with three rings laid out inside a vast high-ceilinged building. In his mind he could still see the towering Luxor pyramid and the eye candy that was Treasure Island with its staged battles between damn near life-sized pirate ships simulating cannon fire on a lake of water fronting another mega monument built with gambling revenue.

But the one thing that would forever stick with him on that first visit to Sin City was how stupid wasting hours and hard earned money inside a windowless air-conditioned dungeon seemed to him.

Brook, on the other hand, let her hair down and lost a whopping twenty dollars before her better judgment kicked in and she began bemoaning the fact they'd gone to the *'armpit in the desert'* in the first place. *'Disneyland would have been a wiser choice,'* she had said at the time.

A sentiment to which Cade had instantly and wholeheartedly concurred.

Now the entire place seemed radically altered. He was nearly blinded when Ari trained the camera on a number of buildings skinned with more mirrored glass than he thought existed. There was a copper-hued slab of a skyscraper, its entire southeast side lit up marvelously by the high-hanging sun, and emblazoned prominently on the top floor, but almost lost in the glare, was a sign with huge gilded letters spelling out the name TRUMP.

"You're fired," said Ari, chuckling.

Griffin covered his mic and leaned towards Cross. "Is that guy ever serious?" he asked, shooting a glare towards the cockpit.

Smiling, Cross looked the question at Cade.

"He's all business ... most of the time," replied Cade, the crash in South Dakota still fresh in his mind.

"I'd ride into hell with him," said Lopez. He crossed himself and motioned for Cade to take the open seat next to him.

Without hesitating, Cade unbuckled and took a seat. Said, "What's up?"

Lopez unplugged Cade's comms, then did the same with his. Cupping a hand next to Cade's ear, he said, "What's your take on the intel?"

***

Two minutes later Vegas was behind them. However, the images of the car-choked strip, bloated bodies floating in the fountains and waterparks, partially burned skyscrapers with curtains flapping from their broken-out windows, and the tens of thousands of Zs still caught in the city's gravitational pull would be forever imprinted in the Delta team and SOAR aircrew's collective memories.

Chapter 39

Enveloped in a brown cloud of dust and with the raucous sound of a mini avalanche nipping at her heels, Glenda reached the bottom of the decline without twisting an ankle or even a scratch for that matter.

She hobbled the last twenty feet across uneven ground strewn about with rocks and tree limbs, fell to her hands and knees and plunged her face in the water and drank greedily.

When she'd had her fill, she rolled over onto her back and sat up and scrunched around until the water was running by in front of her left to right. She washed her face and neck vigorously, using sand to abrade away the stubborn dried bits of internals still clinging to her skin. She did the same to her hands and wrists and watched the oil-slickened water carry away the scraps of decayed skin and flesh.

She unlaced her hikers, wrenched them off, and tossed them to the side. Didn't bother removing the blood-soaked socks with any kind of restraint. Just peeled them away, sloughed off skin and all, and unceremoniously tossed them atop one another in the sand.

Perspiring profusely, she decided the soiled sweatpants had to go. Careful not to disturb the taped-on magazines, she pulled the long-sleeved shirt over her head. As she placed it on the ground near her socks, she couldn't help noticing the horizontal black streaks on both arms and the sooty palm prints incurred when the throng of zombies at the foot of Violet's drive had nearly knocked her from the bike.

She threw a hard shiver as it hit her full on how close she had been to death. Not once, but three times in one day. Four, if she counted Louie. But that was in proximity only. She had been in no jeopardy in the presence of her bound undead husband.

Counting her lucky stars, and wondering how much longer they'd be aligned in her favor, she eyed the crystalline water that had been so close, yet so far, and subliminally calling her name for miles. Little more than a creek at this location, the burbling water and smooth stones were just what she had envisioned. She let out a little yelp and cast a nervous glance uphill when her bare feet finally hit the ice cold water. Thrust her toes into the sand and rubbed her heels and arches gently back and forth on the pea-sized pebbles. Twice, over the creek's gentle murmur, she thought she heard the rasps of the dead coming from the State Route above. And both times she held her breath unnecessarily, looked up expecting to see flesh eaters, but, thankfully, only saw the red bike leaning against the guardrail precisely where she'd left it.

She read page 1 through 164 in her blue book and by the time she closed the dog-eared and highlighter-marked tome she figured she'd been soaking her feet for close to an hour. She stuffed the book between her jeans and the small of her back and the sound of her grumbling stomach convinced her it was time to tie on the crimson-splashed Hi-Tecs and tackle the shale incline rising steeply behind her.

Sliding down the hill had been fun—sort of. Equal parts gravity and bravado combined with the near orgasm-inducing sight of the running water made tackling the dangerous decline seem like nothing to Glenda.

Climbing out, however, was a monumentally harder task than the former cross-country runner could have fathomed. Halfway to the road she stopped, feet planted and hands splayed out in the sharp stones, and spewed every ounce of water she'd consumed—and then some.

One step forward and three steps back was how the latter half of what had become Glenda's own personal Everest played out.

She scaled the last ten feet commando-crawling on her stomach until the squared-off wood post and attached guardrail was within arm's reach.

Then she rested her eyes.

Chapter 40

Raven won the second race by a nose, her front tire crossing the poorly marked finish line just ahead of Sasha's.

Chest heaving, Raven jammed to a stop and between ragged gulps of air said, "Best of three?"

"Let's rest for a few minutes."

Let's not, thought Raven. Then she heard Sasha's whiny voice in her head: *Bragging rights are at stake*. "Now," called Raven over her shoulder.

"After a water break?"

Shaking her head side-to-side, Raven said forcefully, "*Now*."

"Let's up the ante," said Sasha. "How about the loser cleans the winner's gun next time."

Still shaking her head, Raven answered, "Dad would be pissed if I didn't clean mine myself."

Screwing her face up, Sasha thought hard for a few seconds. She said, "Loser makes the other person's bed for a week."

"Deal." Mimicking something she'd seen the fifth grade boys do, Raven spit on her palm and offered Sasha her hand.

"Uggghhh. I'll trust you on this one."

Face a mask of concentration, Raven stood hard on the upright pedal and counted down from *three*.

At *one* they were off and pedaling hard.

By lap two Raven had pulled away but multi-colored tracers were flashing in front of her eyes.

By lap three she was still in the lead but breathing was becoming difficult.

Lap four was when Sasha made her move, passing Raven on the far corner near the parked vehicles.

Casting her gaze over her shoulder and following the redhead left to right as she passed by was distraction enough to cause Raven to miss the turn. She swiveled her head forward and registered the tree trunks rushing at her and, without thinking about the lesser of two evils, jinked the bike right, putting it on a collision course with several hundred pounds of gore-encrusted steel bumper.

She remembered the blue Ford oval rushing at her face. Then the coiled cable wound vertically on the winch drum flashed by in her side vision as the bike slid from under her and the whirr of the tall grass whipped against her back side. Lastly, she let out a yelp and the angular bumper disappeared under her upthrust arms and met her ribs with breath-stealing force.

The air blasted from her lungs wasn't replaced. Instead she tasted copper as a fine sheen of blood rimed her lips. And as she struggled to inhale, her forehead met the bumper. In the next beat her body rolled over the bike and a burst of white hot pain flooded her brain, causing it to turn off and sending her mercifully into darkness's warm embrace.

Feeling like he was being watched was an understatement. The forest seemingly had eyes, and lying there naked on the soft bed of needles under the low branches of a Douglas fir, Wilson could feel his skin begin to crawl.

Taryn ran her hand through Wilson's hair and then moved to his cheek, and with the pad of her index finger traced over the scar where Cade's bullet had grazed him three weeks ago. It had healed to a colorless line of corded tissue four inches in length and stood out in stark contrast on his perpetually sunburned face. She continued the journey down and dragged a fingernail over the uneven line demarking her man's reddened forearm from the rest of his alabaster torso. Sensing him tensing up, she asked, "What's wrong, Mister Farmer Tan?"

"I thought I heard something out of place."

"From where?"

"Back towards the camp."

"What did it sound like?"

"I don't know," Wilson said, the inquisition obviously getting to him. "Something like a hammer banging metal, I guess."

"Well we all know the rotters aren't using tools," she said, propping herself up on one elbow.

"Yet," countered Wilson as he cast an anxious glance towards the nearby inner fence. "I saw that thing get over the top yesterday. That was no accident. I have a theory."

"And?" said Taryn. She shrugged on her bra. Made a mental note to keep her eye out for a couple of new pairs, sports bras preferably, next time she left the perimeter. She grabbed her shirt and, seeing Wilson averting his eyes—a gentlemanly trait she had come to admire—pulled it over her head and then gave him a quick peck on the scar on his cheek.

Wilson waited for Taryn to finish dressing then said, "I think some of these things ... at least the ones that turned early on ... are getting smarter."

"It'd look awfully strange if someone stumbled upon us and only you were naked," said Taryn. "Get dressed while you elaborate."

He laid flat, arched his back, and pulled his fatigue pants on. Covered his supernova bright upper body with a neon green short-sleeved shirt emblazoned with a giant Mountain Dew logo. Then, thinking about how best to articulate his hypothesis to Taryn, took his time lacing his boots.

Tired of waiting for the slow poke, Taryn helped him out on both accounts. While tying his left boot, she said, "I think the rotters are acting *mostly* on instinct and their desire to feed. However ..." She paused and watched Wilson tie a double knot on the other boot. Saw the corded muscles under his shirt rippling on his sides. He looked up and she continued, "... if they see something they've done a ton of times it's like Deja vu or something. A certain sight or familiar location dislodges a little bit of something from their memory and they just act on it."

"So they're *not* learning?"

"I don't think so," Taryn said. "Remember Captain Kirk at the four-wheel-drive shop? That wrench was in his hand because he was just going through the motions ... like muscle memory. We ever go back there again I'd be willing to bet you a month's worth of laundry duty he's still got that same tool in his hand and all of those bolts holding the shelving together down there will not have been touched."

Wilson smiled. He arched a brow and said, "Throw in two shifts of body disposal duty ... digging and burying *both*, and you're on."

Taryn rose and shouldered her carbine. She reached out her hand to shake on the bet just as a shrill scream rang out.

Looking in the direction of the sound, Wilson sprang from the ground with his fatigue top in hand, grabbed his carbine and sprinted that way, bellowing, "Sasha," at the top of his voice.

Chapter 41

Beginning to end, Glenda's climb from the creek bed back to the road burned thirty minutes of daylight. Ninety minutes total squandered since she'd left the old Schwinn on the road.

She wasted another five catching her breath. Then listened hard for almost as long. But between the white noise of the distant creek and the steady breeze jostling the pines and firs rising up on the far side of the road there was no telling whether she was alone or not. So she commando-crawled forward a few more inches and peered through the opening between the frost-heaved roadbed and the underside of the guardrail. What she saw twenty feet away, and stretching at least a hundred feet in the direction from which she'd come, stole her breath away. Between the bicycle's warped spokes, distorted by the heatwaves rising off the blacktop, she saw an army of dead shuffling left to right—towards Woodruff. Close to a hundred souls were following hot on the heels of the monsters she'd recently given the slip. Cursing under her breath, she put her cheek to the warm ground, did her best to appear twice dead, and watched them pass.

It was a mixed lot, that much was clear. The zombies in the lead, for the most part, appeared to be from Huntsville. However, as badly burnt as they were, trying to tell one apart from another would be an exercise in futility. More than twenty, dispersed throughout the undead parade, were newer specimens, all showing no more than two or three weeks' worth of rot. And looking like wet linen, the alabaster skin clinging to their bloated bodies contrasted sharply with their brethren's crunchy, coal black dermis.

Moving with purpose, the stealthy procession passed mere feet from Glenda's prostrate form. She gave them a five-minute lead and, having learned from past experience, made certain there were no stragglers around to give her away before peeling herself off the hillside and surmounting the guardrail.

Being careful to keep the chain from rattling—which up to now had proven nearly impossible—Glenda wheeled the bike off the gravel shoulder and onto the blacktop. She hopped aboard but refrained from sitting on the seat lest the springs give her away. Slowly she pushed off and stood on both pedals. Let the momentum carry her a short while until she hit the left-hand sweeper and the tail end of the Woodruff death march.

Then, drawing on all of her reserves, she began pedaling like her life depended on it—which it most definitely did. Picking her route in advance, she steered left and right, zippering with ease through the first twenty or so cadavers. However, the rasps and moans began the moment she entered their midst, and in seconds, like a train lurching to a slow-speed halt, the front two-thirds of the herd began stopping. The monsters turned their heads to see what the ruckus was about, and when they fixed their milky eyes on the meat on the bike the clumsy chain reaction only got worse.

Going wide right and risking being shoved over the guardrail and ending up back down the ravine with broken bones or paralysis, Glenda repeated her earlier move, tucked her elbows and knees in tight and became one with the bike.

The move only further confused the zombies on her immediate left, but the throng's lead element—not so much.

With only thirty feet and about as many flesh eaters between her and the open road, she raised her paper-wrapped left arm, ready to fend off the closest of her attackers.

Twenty feet to go. She leaned left, hoping her weight and momentum would be sufficient to parry the first creature's lunge. The female, judging by two sagging breasts that looked like a first timer's failed attempt at roasting marshmallows, missed grabbing her head by a few inches, but still received a forearm shiver and an up close look at the July copy of National Enquirer.

Ten feet to go and a trio of carbon copies of Kingsford were near enough to make a grab. With one eye on the ever deepening ravine, Glenda braced for contact. A tick later, left arm up in a defensive posture, she saw the tips of their burnt fingers—perhaps the same ones that had soiled her shirt earlier—make contact with her forearm, bend back and snap off, one at a time, hollow little pops that left all three creatures with far fewer digits on each hand than they brought to the fight.

Desperate times call for drastic measures, thought Glenda. With only ten feet to go and freedom looking her in the face, she took her left foot off the pedal, straightened her leg, and stared the last cadaver in the eyes. Saw a spark of knowing there. Not cunning, but just a feeling that the thing knew what was in store for it. And it wasn't pretty. Newton's Law was in effect. The action part came into play as her hiker hit a glancing blow on the naked zombie's package. She felt a great deal of give, like the bloated thing there was a rotten melon. Instantly, started by the impact and furthered by the zombie's reaction to it, the pasty abomination brought its arms up and began spinning away slowly to her left. The opposite reaction piece of Sir Isaac's law played out when a torrent of brackish fluid squirted onto the blacktop and the two pus-engorged testes, now freed but still attached by the testicular artery and smaller veins, dropped and swung around like mini wrecking balls. As Glenda wheeled past, inexplicably, caught in her side vision, she witnessed the zombie make a slow motion play at protecting its ruined family jewels.

Some things never change. And some things you just can't unsee, thought Glenda, as she pumped her legs and pulled away. Once she'd put a little distance between her and the persistent parade of death, and the bike was coasting smoothly on the blacktop, she looked down at the paper armor, saw a number of teeth embedded there, and realized how close she'd come to becoming one of them.

Chapter 42

The Ghost Hawk encountered a bit of turbulence and shimmied and lost a dozen feet of altitude, the latter sending Cade's stomach into his throat and jolting him from his power nap. He vaguely remembered nodding off shortly after Vegas and was awakened twice since.

The first time when there had been changes in airspeed and he heard mechanical whirrs and clunks and a rushing sound under his feet, all sounds that from experience told him an aerial refueling was taking place.

The second time he was rudely awakened was when, presumably, based on song choice alone, the flight of two crossed over the Nevada border and someone next to him—Cross, he guessed, though he didn't bother to check—started singing the Eagle's hit song Hotel California, rather poorly. Then, with everyone aboard save him belting out the last line of the song: *You can check out any time you want, but you can never leave,* his eyes again got heavy, and with the aid of the droning aircraft he drifted back off to sleep. But that proved to be short-lived because according to the Suunto on his wrist he'd been sawing logs for less than thirty minutes when Ari's voice interrupted, informing everyone aboard that they were five minutes out.

Holding the five by seven in his gloved hand, Cross asked Lopez, "What's the building the target is standing in front of?"

"Nash called it the Widney Alumni house."

"But her daughter wasn't an alum yet."

"Nope. That was orientation day ... three years ago."

Cade sat up straight and corralled his carbine, trapping it between his knees. He yawned and stretched and looked out both side windows. Then cracked his neck and placed his clasped hands on the M4's collapsed buttstock. Parking his chin on his glove's rigid knuckle protection, he gazed straight ahead through the cockpit glass, back among the living. Why the bitch seat was abhorred by Lopez and then by the late CIA nuke specialist Scott Tice after he'd been forced into it was beyond Cade. There was great situational awareness to be had from here. Plus, with the bulkhead at his back and the sensation of forward momentum not contradicted by terrain moving in opposition, overall, he felt more in control.

As Cade looked out over the quiet city he couldn't believe how far south and north he could see. The lack of traffic, both air and ground, and the emissions produced by the hundreds of thousands of vehicles in and around the sprawling metropolis had left the skies shining brilliant blue. Gone was the chaotic hustle and bustle and with it the gray, city-obscuring haze.

Out the port side glass Cade saw the unmistakable oval of poured concrete housing tens of thousands of red and white seats. *Los Angeles Memorial Coliseum.* Home to an Olympics games in the thirties and again more recently in 1984 when at the height of the Cold War the then USSR balked at attending and eventually boycotted them. The rectangular natural grass playing field was now a honey-colored shade of brown, the yellow USC logos and crimson end zones standing out like brilliantly colored bookends.

Through the starboard windows, way off in the distance, Cade saw the expansive Pacific Ocean, deep blue and appearing deceptively calm from this altitude. Ari began a gradual descent and a couple of minutes later banked left. He leveled the Jedi Ride out until the ocean was completely filling the windows on Cade's right. So he craned past Griffin, looked down and saw palm trees and a cement bike path bisecting the white sand. And jutting out into the ocean bordered by nearly empty parking lots was a wooden pier, home to a handful of one- and two-story structures shoehorned in between the beach and a four-lane highway. Beyond the buildings was a Ferris wheel and a dozen other amusement rides, all colorful and seemingly out of place when compared to the nearby traffic jam of death clogging what he guessed was the Santa Monica Freeway.

"Santa Monica Pier," said Haynes to no one in particular.

Just south of Santa Monica, Venice Beach complete with its zombie-crowded skate park and sun-baked sports courts slid by. The helicopter's shadow clipped along the ribbon of sand and the men sat inside in a brooding silence, the ocean's serene Yin on their right not near enough to balance out the chaotic Yang exemplified by the picket of fire-scorched skyscrapers scrolling by on their left.

Dead ahead through the cockpit glass Cade could see the shoreline gradually curling right and noticed a vast marina and another long pier built on wooden pilings jutting out into the ocean. And as the pier grew in size it became apparent that like Santa Monica and Venice Beach it also belonged to the dead. The marina, however, was nearly deserted and it looked as if all of the vessels once moored there were now anchored and lolling in the waterway separated from the ocean by a curving, mile-long, man-made rock jetty. Putting the numerous yachts and their blood-streaked decks from his mind, Cade continued his counter-clockwise one-eighty recon and locked eyes with Lopez. Saw the knowing look in them. And then knew that though the Delta captain hadn't acknowledged it publicly, he was in agreement with Cade's interpretation of the intel and, somewhere between Vegas and the California border, had reversed the order of importance of their two objectives which resulted in Ari altering their flight plan.

Chapter 43

Figuring she was past the halfway point to Woodruff and knowing there was a down grade after the looming challenge, Glenda tackled the steep hill with a renewed vigor. "Go, girl," she said aloud over and over until her breathing became labored and forced the verbal mantra into her head.

To her left was dense forest consisting of firs and pines with an occasional aspen or oak breaking up the monopoly. The opposite side of the road was more of the same, a ravine gradually getting steeper and deeper, but instead of the creek and its cold waters beckoning below there was more forest, the tree tops nearly level with the roadway in places.

Taking a much needed break at the crest of the hill, she straddled the bike and followed the road ahead with her eye. After the long downhill stretch she was going to savor like a Godiva chocolate, there was a gradual right hand turn and beyond it a bridge crossing yet another chasm with what she guessed would be a creek running perpendicular to the road. But shambling away from her, currently passing through the trees' angular shadows, was a group of about a dozen dead, their attention seemingly directed at something around the bend.

"Now or never," she said, putting her throbbing left foot on the pedal. Oh what she would have done for an Ibuprofen—or six— at that moment. In fact, if the herd of flesh-eaters weren't still following somewhere back there she would have been inclined to strip off the hikers, found a shady spot and cooled them in the afternoon breeze. But the hungry beasts were at her back and Woodruff, and hopefully one or two survivors—or if there really was a God, a whole town full of them—was beyond the ones she *could* see.

Then the realization that she had not seen a living soul for weeks hit her. The loneliness came roaring back as did memories of Louie. As she stood there cooling off, a dull throb started behind her eyes and moved to her shoulders. Then the cramping in her calves started and a tenseness radiated up her back until it felt like all of the skin covering her skull was slowly being drawn tight. She imagined her eyes as slits and the corners of her mouth tugged into a straight, thin line. Not wanting to be caught by her pursuers curled up in a fetal ball and looking like a cosmetic surgery addict—at least in her mind concerning the latter—she forced herself to straddle the bike and let gravity have her.

Compared to the Pike's-Peak-like hill climb, the lee side run out was better than any Godiva's chocolate. The pain in her feet lessened as the wind rushing by invaded her Hi-Tecs. The minor relief of the wind cooling her feet relaxed her back and, by the end of the run out, she was feeling like she could ride to New York if need be.

The Glenda Glide had served her again. She whooped it up in her head as she sped silently by the group of dead. Not wanting to lose the momentum gained from the long downhill, she tucked and pedaled hard, cutting the right-hand turn by degrees, the bike leaning over substantially.

With the trees on her left coming to an abrupt end and a wide slice of daylight taking their place, she wheeled onto the two-lane bridge. As the bike's rubber tires met the smooth white surface, the steady humming ceased and somewhere around the bend in the road she heard an out-of-place murmuring and, overriding it, the whiny peal of a two-stroke engine.

In the second or two it took Glenda to process the new sounds and conclude the latter was coming from a chainsaw engine running somewhere in the nearby woods, the bike had carried her another thirty feet and she spotted the source of the former. Which was a waist-high drift of pale corpses and the writhing black bodies of hundreds of feeding ravens and crows slowly winnowing it down. And then her stomach clenched and a cold finger of dread traced her spine as she saw a pair of SUVs, then, standing in an uneven line crowding in on a head-high snarl of fallen trees, another two dozen flesh-eaters and no obvious way of getting around them.

With the dead she'd just zipped by now lost from sight, and the ones to her fore still oblivious to her presence, Glenda let her momentum bleed off and, once she'd cleared the short span, veered left and quietly laid the bike down on the shoulder. She cast a furtive glance toward the static SUVs and the shelter they might afford, but quickly ruled them out based on their proximity to the dead. She shifted her gaze west and heard hollow moans riding the wind. *Between a rock and a hard place.*

So, with no other logical course of action and risking sliding into the ravine, she scurried into the underbrush and said a silent prayer.

SR-39 Roadblock

Chief placed the chainsaw gently in the truck bed along with the empty gas cans and tools and spare parts, and then sat on the tailgate wiping sawdust and woodchips from his shirt and face.

Foley climbed over the guardrail and traipsed slowly across the road towards the truck, drinking from a bottled water. "These are going to run out pretty soon," he said. "What are we going to do then?"

"What we always did," said Chief. He retrieved a military surplus canteen from the jumble in the bed, screwed off the cap and drank heartily. The water was tepid and tasted of plastic but hit the spot and he let Foley know as much.

"I'm no yuppie," said Foley defensively. "Just used to the convenience. That's all."

"Just razzing you," Chief said.

The sound of twigs cracking preceded Tran as he emerged from the forest. Slung over his shoulder and bulging with something he'd foraged was one of those reusable shopping bags, and screened on its side in colorful island-themed graphics Jimmy Buffet would be proud of was the name Trader Joe's.

"What did you find this time?" asked Foley.

"Mushrooms," answered Tran, flashing a toothy grin.

"For sustenance or hallucinogenic purposes?"

Tran didn't answer Foley. He threw the bag in back of the truck and came out with a water of his own. Cracked the top and drank greedily.

"What do you say we make sure our rifles are zeroed in, city boy?"

"I may look like I'm just a plump computer guy," Foley said. "Truth is ... you don't really know me, Chief."

The fifty-five-year-old Native American smiled at that but said nothing. He turned his ball cap around, rose to standing and, with his Les Baer carbine in hand, shuffled along the bed and braced his butt against the cab's sliding rear window.

Tran moved backward a few paces and covered his ears.

Showing a little shooter's savvy, Foley rose and formed up next to the pickup's bed on Chief's left where he wouldn't be catching hot brass in the face.

Chief shouldered the rifle, put his eye to the scope, flicked the selector to *Fire* and exhaled slowly while squeezing the trigger. His first round missed its intended target, going right judging by the puff of dust that leapt off the roadside beyond the bridge. He waited for a second or two while the sky went black as the birds winged off, cawing in displeasure. Aiming for the tops of the bobbing heads, Chief snapped off four more shots, dropping one rotter to the roadway beyond the fallen trees for each 5.56 round expended.

"Gotta be a nice pile of those things over there by now."

"Bird food," replied Chief, snugging his rifle in tight, his finger drawing back the trigger.

Bringing the binoculars up and focusing on something beyond the 4Runner's hood, Foley said, "Do you remember seeing a bicycle on the shoulder?"

Keeping his eye glued to the scope, Chief tracked the barrel up a couple of degrees and said, "That red piece of work?" He looked over his shoulder at Foley with one brow raised and a hint of concern on his face and shook his head slowly side-to-side.

Chapter 44

The screams jerked Brook from a deep spell of REM sleep. Her eyes snapped open to a gray gloom punched through with needle-thin shafts of light. As consciousness gripped her firmly her first reflex was to jerk upright, a move that sent the ball cap flying from her face as if shot from a catapult. The thought that the shrieks were somehow a manifestation of a forgotten nightmare or just figments of her imagination were quickly dispelled when she heard Sasha's unmistakable voice calling her name.

The shouts of "Brook, help" continued as she sprung up from the crushed grass circle, carbine in hand.

Following the sounds, Brook ran towards the motor pool, her legs making a swishing sound against the grass. Suddenly Max was nearby, a blur of brown and white leaping gazelle-like on a divergent course.

Max made the scene first.

Brook was there a few seconds later. The screams continued and she saw Sasha, hysterical, kneeling down and tugging at the purple and white mountain bike.

"Back off, Sash," Brook said calmly. She gripped the teen's shoulder and sat her on her butt and out of the way. She looked back and saw Raven face down, limbs all akimbo and tangled in the bike's handlebars.

Heavy footfalls came from the forest behind the vehicles. They were followed by a flurry of movement as Taryn and Wilson looped around front of the F-650 and skidded to a halt.

222

Motioning Taryn over, Brook said, "Help me with the bike." She looked at Wilson and nodded towards Sasha, mouthing: *She needs you.*

Feet seemingly rooted in place, Wilson's head swiveled slowly towards Sasha but returned at once, his eyes falling on Raven's motionless form.

"She's dead. And it's all my fault," cried Sasha. "I saw her crash in the grass. But I kept going around. This is how I found her." She bit her lip, turning it white, then added, "I think she hit the bumper head on."

Brook turned her head towards Wilson and through clenched teeth said, "Take your sister and sit her in the grass and come right back."

While Taryn held the weight of the bicycle off of Raven, Brook supported her daughter's head with one hand and straightened her legs and arms out on the grass with the other.

Straining against the weight, Taryn said, "Now?"

Brook shook her head side-to-side and helped brace the bike with her free hand. A few seconds later when Wilson returned, she said, "Real easy now ... lift it off of her."

Taryn picked the bike up, moved it aside, and let it fall into the grass. When she turned back and saw Raven's bloodied face, she let out a gasp, believing that Sasha was right in her assessment. But a tick later Brook said, "She's alive. Wilson, I need your shirt."

Without hesitation he stripped it off and handed it over.

Brook said, "I'm afraid she may have punctured a lung. I need my stethoscope and the biggest syringe and needle you can find."

Nodding, Wilson sprang into action.

Brook called out, "Bring a sleeping bag." Then she hunched over and checked Raven's pupils, seeing instant dilation. She peered down Raven's airway, finding it clear. Next Brook walked her fingers, spider-like, around Raven's slender neck. Then, without the luxury of a backboard, Brook enlisted Taryn's help and, working together, they turned Raven over gently on her side and Brook quickly traced her fingers from the base of Raven's skull on down to her tailbone.

After helping place Raven back flat on her back, Taryn asked, "Is anything broken?"

"Her neck and spine ... I don't think so," replied Brook, grimacing. "But I can tell by the way she's breathing that something isn't right internally."

Raven's eyes fluttered open just as Wilson returned from the compound with Heidi and Seth in tow.

Brook cleared a lock of hair from Raven's face and said, "You're going to be alright, sweetie."

Wilson handed over the stethoscope and the only syringe he could find. It was a small item without a needle, useful only for flushing eyes and irrigating wounds.

Brook took the stethoscope and syringe from him. Turned the syringe over in her hand and looked up, confused. "That's it?" she said.

"Yep," answered Wilson. He unfurled an olive-drab sleeping bag. "Where do you want this?"

Ignoring him, Brook looked at Seth and then to Heidi and said, "Who's in the security container?"

They looked at each other and said simultaneously: "*Nobody.*" Then Seth went on. He held up the two-way radio and said, "Phillip is at the hide. He's going to call me if he sees anything out of the ordinary."

Relaxing somewhat, Brook put her hand under Raven's shirt. Spent a moment moving the stethoscope over her chest, stopping occasionally and looking up and grimacing. Finally, with no kind of good expression on her face, she addressed Wilson. "Lay the bag next to her." She scooted over and took a knee near the crown of Raven's head. "Everyone get a hand under her body. On three we'll *gently* transfer her to the bag."

With Taryn, Wilson, Seth, and Heidi positioned equidistant around Raven, and Brook supporting her head and neck, the former nurse started the count.

Once the transfer was complete Brook took Heidi's spot, grabbed hold of the bag, and with the others' help began moving her to the compound.

The radio in Seth's pocket warbled and he looked a question at Brook.

"Sasha," Brook said. "Get the radio from Seth's pocket."

As the group moved across the clearing in a herky jerky manner with Raven wrapped up in the bag hammock-like and swaying side-to-side, Sasha tried to match their speed and gait. Nonplussed by the prospect of sticking her hand into a man's front pocket, she finally got over herself, rooted around in there and came out with the radio just as it went silent. Sasha held her arms out and looked a question at Taryn that said: *What do I do now?*

Brow furrowed, Taryn looked Sasha in the eye and said, "Call them back."

Not quite sure how to work the thing, Sasha fiddled with the buttons.

Meanwhile, at the roadblock, Chief was peering through the scope and trying to make heads or tails of the bike and the rustling in the bushes next to it when the radio chimed in his pocket. He looked at Foley and shrugged. Propped the carbine against the bed and fished out the Motorola.

Chief thumbed the *talk* button. He whispered, "I can't talk now. We have company at the block."

Sasha asked, "What do you mean by ... *company*?"

As Chief came back on, Phillip's voice also emanated from the speaker saying, "All clear at the entrance. How come Seth's not answering?"

To which Sasha said, "He's here. This is his radio. Bye, Phillip."

After Phillip signed off Chief waited for a two-count and described the bicycle's mysterious appearance and after a brief pause mentioned the movement in the underbrush.

Excitedly, Sasha said, "Do you see the person who was riding it?"

Still moving across the clearing, Brook, who had been listening in, tightened her grip on one corner of the sleeping bag and said incredulously, "Chief and Foley can play hide and seek with whoever it is later. I need them here five minutes ago." She looked down at Raven and saw that her lips were pursed into a thin blue line. Shifted her gaze toward Sasha and said, "Hit that damn talk button and tell them to get back here ASAP. I *have* to load up the truck and leave. And when you're done with that I need you to *run* ahead to the compound and get me the satellite phone."

Trying her best to duplicate the urgency in Brook's voice, Sasha depressed the Talk button and relayed the message. A tick later the gears were in motion and she was hightailing it to the compound.

At the roadblock

Chief turned the volume down and slipped the radio into his pocket. He whispered, "I think there is someone trying to hide in the bushes near the bike."

"Or *something*," said Foley, glassing the undergrowth near the bicycle.

In a rare display of humor, Chief replied, "Rotters don't ride ... as far as I know. So I'll give whoever or whatever is wearing those hikers a warning shot."

"Brook said she needs us back at the compound ASAP."

"If there's a person over there we can't just abandon them," answered Chief as he snugged the carbine to his shoulder and sighted down the scope. "Besides, if we step on it we can be back there in three or four minutes with no one the wiser."

Foley pressed a button on his watch that started the numbers on the stopwatch scrolling. He trained the binoculars on the road ahead and said, "What do you make of it?"

"Let's find out."

Foley nodded then trained the field-glasses on the scuffed leather hikers.

There was one single loud report from Chief's carbine and a geyser of gravel erupted near the stationary pair of boots.

The sensation of tiny bits of asphalt shrapnel peppering the magazines taped to Glenda's shins did little to warn her of what was coming next. However, the report rolling over her head left no doubt in her mind that somehow she had become the shooter's target.

Two courses of action sprang to mind. One, she could burrow further into the underbrush and still risk taking a bullet, or worse, make too much noise and die at the hands and teeth of the moaning corpses crossing the bridge behind her. Or, number two, she could spring up and rely on the Glenda Glide to see her quickly and silently to the fallen trees on the far side of the road and then scramble over the jam to take her chances with the living, whomever they might be.

She winced as more debris pelted her and had made up her mind even before the second sharp report was echoing off the tree branches overhead.

One moment Chief was tracking the rifle to the right, preparing to make the next shot, and the next a gaunt and gray-haired thing was rising out of the foliage and before he could process what he was seeing it had risen to its feet and was standing erect, waving its arms mutely.

Foley asked, "Are those *magazines* taped around its arms and legs?"

"Question is," Chef said incredulously, "*what* is it?"

Before Foley could answer to that the rotters were turning and starting off towards the gesticulating figure.

"It's alive. And I think—

"It's a woman," said Chief, finishing Foley's thought for him.

Remembering his ordeal walking among the dead from the road below Robert Christian's mansion all the way to the Teton Pass, Tran blurted, "We have to save her."

Chief nodded and said to Foley, "Grab your rifle. Let's see what you've got."

***

After a thirty-second volley, a changing of magazines, and then another spate of closely spaced single shots, a blue-gray gun smoke haze hung in the air, and the knot of walking dead were felled and in an unmoving tangle stretching across the bridge's east end.

"Good shooting," said Chief. "I stand corrected on my first impression of you."

227

With a pair of binoculars pressed to his face, Tran announced, "It's a woman."

Foley looked through the scope atop his rifle and watched the woman mount the bike and pedal the distance to the blockage. She was lost from view for a tick; then he saw her haul her slight frame up on a horizontal tree and begin picking her way gingerly through the tangled mess of branches.

He looked at his stopwatch and said, "Three minutes gone."

"She'll be here in half that, the way she's moving. Must be scared as heck."

Foley said, "Let's see. She probably just pedaled through that group of rotters that came up behind her. Then she comes upon our roadblock and you start shooting at her. Wouldn't you be?"

"Good point," said Chief.

Foley took his eye from the scope and spotted Tran moving across the fallen trees. He moved with an economy, picking and choosing handholds and places for his feet with care, but not wasting any time as he did so.

Chief tossed his rifle in the truck. He said, "I'll go meet them in the woods and check her for bites. You fire up the truck."

"Back in ten?"

"Call it five," said Chief.

At the compound

Brook traded her corner of the sleeping bag to Sasha for the satellite phone and said to Taryn, "Take her to your quarters so you don't have to deal with getting her past the clutter in the security container. I'll be there in a few seconds."

Nodding, Taryn disappeared into the gloom with Seth squeezing through the doorway right behind her. Bringing up the rear, both clutching a handful of sleeping bag, Wilson and Sasha negotiated the doorway and, once they'd cleared the threshold, Wilson reached back with one hand and pulled the door shut behind them.

Biting her knuckles, Brook cycled through the menus searching for the one labeled *Contacts*. "Come on. Come on. Come on," she chanted until she spotted it. She chose the sub-menu labeled *Compose Text Message* and with the speed of a tween planning a sleepover her thumbs flew over the keys as she banged out a message for Cade. Without reviewing the inputted text she hit the *Send* button, pocketed the phone, and rushed into the compound with a full head of steam.

Chapter 45

Four minutes out from what was initially going to be objective number two, Ari said, "Nash couldn't wrangle updated satellite imagery so here's the bird's eye view of Long Beach Naval Shipyards, also known as Terminal Island." A moment later an image flashed up on the cabin monitor. And as they got closer to the manmade island he swung Jedi One-One wide right out to sea, leaving the black Osprey behind. A few seconds later Ari had the near silent stealth helo in a steady hover eight hundred feet over open water.

"Looks like the FEMA folks had the National Guard drop the bridges," proffered Haynes.

Manning the FLIR controls, Ari zoomed in on the nearest fallen span and quipped, "Pardon the pun, but looks like somebody was forced to take extreme measures to keep the undead citizens of Los Angeles at *bay*."

A collective groan sounded in the passenger cabin.

Ignoring the quip and unable to see the full scope of the damage through the port window, Cade shifted his gaze to the monitor and watched as the camera zoomed out from the fractured concrete pilings and panned slowly left to right. The place looked deserted and, sure enough, as Ari had already alluded to, all three bridges—one coming in from the north, another from the east, and a third from south—had been reduced to rubble, the tons of concrete and rebar now sitting on the bay floor.

The camera zoomed in to the northwest corner of the operation where what looked like a couple of acres of once bare concrete, surrounded by a smattering of shipping containers and rust-streaked cranes on rails, had been covered completely by thousands of body bags, many of them containing reanimated corpses. South of the undulating sea of body bags were more dead bodies than Cade had seen in one place. Heaped two stories high and host to thousands of white seagulls, the monument to Omega's ruthless efficiency was exponentially bigger than the mound of dead Americans he had come across near the coal plant at the junction to State Route 6 east of Salt Lake City. And hard as it was for him to wrap his mind around, there were even more corpses in the water here than there had been lodged against the spillway of the Flaming Gorge Dam in southern Utah. Of all the monuments to humanity's suffering he had seen since Z-Day, this one, by far, troubled him most.

"No wonder they abandoned the place," said Lasseigne, breaking a long silence. "Hell of a biohazard down there."

"Not as bad as this one here," said Ari over the comms. "'Cause these ones are still ambulatory." The camera moved in its gimbal and zoomed in and focused on the far end of what remained of the east bridge once connecting the naval yard to the mainland. The crowd of flesh-eaters amassed there probably could have filled the mall in Washington D.C. ten times over. They were moving south and filling up both sides of the freeway, their bodies pressed close enough together to create the illusion that the whole lot of them were rippling like a human wave at a ball game, only on a much grander scale.

"Wouldn't want to be anywhere near that thing," said Cross. "That would swallow up the Pueblo horde."

"Copy that," said Cade. "Its mass is almost incomprehensible ... probably double the size of the Denver horde Lopez and the boys nuked at Castle Rock. I'd guess there's one ... one point five million Zs down there, at least."

Griffin added, "And that's just a fraction of the population that used to call Los Angeles home."

The men suddenly went silent and their stomachs and testicles relocated inside their bodies as the helicopter nosed down and their altitude and distance to the artificial island was quickly halved. A handful of seconds later, sending everyone's anatomy in the opposite direction, Ari flared Jedi One-One hard and commenced a hover over the southwest portion of the yards bordered on two sides by water being beaten to a froth by hundreds of pasty white and horribly bloated reanimated corpses.

Back in the cabin Cade swallowed hard and took a calming breath. He glanced at the monitor and saw that what had initially looked like tiny multicolored Legos from their standoff distance were actually hundreds of intermodal shipping containers like the type the Eden compound was constructed of. And like the cranes and wheeled contraptions that moved the containers from the back of long-haul trucks to waiting ships, they were rust-streaked and showed lots of wear and tear. Stacked three high and several deep, they completely ringed the FEMA facility. And in the center of the castle-like walls, erected on what had to be several acres of flat ground crisscrossed by train tracks and marked up with numbers and letters that amounted to little more than longshoreman hieroglyphics to the layperson, were white semi-rigid tents too numerous to count. The first three rows of twelve abutting the seawall to the south were lined up precisely and looked to have been erected with care, most likely before the full scale of the outbreak was known. The next dozen or so rows had been thrown up hastily and stood in ragged formation, roofs sagging and door flaps waving lazily in the offshore breeze.

A pair of large recreational vehicles, the kind which snowbirds often traded their homes for in retirement—FEMA command centers, Cade guessed—were parked nose to tail near the southwestern corner of the seawall, extensions bulging from their sides. Nearby were a dozen smaller panel vans tagged with bold blue FEMA logos. Roughly fifty yards north of the tent city and inert command vehicles, surrounded by temporary chain-link fencing held in place by removable cement anchors, was a trio of FEMA COWs—Cell tower On Wheels. The COW trailers were hitched to identical white Peterbilt tractors and each had a telephone-pole-sized tower rising up through its roof. Sporting all kinds of shiny angular panels and cylinders all connected by wires and insulators, the tower looked like a giant-sized royal scepter minus the ubiquitous gilding and encrusted jewels.

Parked in a semi-circle nose-to-nose near the COW trailers were three white Econoline style vans also with FEMA emblazoned in blue on their roofs and sides. Hitched to each van was a white windowless single-axle trailer, and connected to each trailer, umbilical-like by a thick black cable, was a white satellite dish the size of a backyard trampoline.

The ground from the command vehicles to the fencing surrounding the COW was littered with shell casings all glittering in the sun. And here and there among the tents and vehicles were dozens of Zs clothed mostly in civilian attire or still wearing their blue and white FEMA garb. And scattered amongst the herd were a number of soldiers who had died clad for all eternity in their MultiCam fatigues.

Most of the walking dead were covered in blood, theirs or others. The blood had dried to a glossy black and threw the sun as they moved about aimlessly. Even viewed from afar and relayed to a monitor in a hovering aircraft the defensive wounds to hands and arms, likely received during the frantic egress when ammo was low and tensions were running high, was clearly evident.

"This is the last known location of our target," said Lopez, breaking the shroud of silence. "Z-Day plus five, I believe. These temporary cell sites known as COWs were still operable then. Same deal though ... the cell tower here did its part but the commercial communications sats didn't relay the signal."

"Or somebody jammed them," said Griffin. "With all due respect, Sir. Z-Day plus five was a *long* time ago. The target could be anywhere. Palm Desert. Balboa Island. In one of those ... body bags."

"We're going on what we *do* know. We're starting here because we know the facility was secure a week out. After that ... it's highly likely that some survivors were relocated to other camps inland by helo. Also reports indicate that a larger number of civilians and essential government personnel were evacuated by sea."

Incredulous, Griff said, "You're telling me Nash was able to sweet talk President Clay into allowing this mission but couldn't pull any strings between days one and five to get a lone chopper and team of shooters in here to secure the target?"

Lopez shook his head. He said, "She had her hands full moving satellites around D.C. searching for President Odero, who had gone dark. So proof of life for Nash amounts to only a handful of voice messages all stamped by the location services in the target's phone as having originated from the USC area."

Cross said, "Doesn't explain why we're starting here and not the target's last known location."

Cade said, "Lopez is working up to it."

Griffin pressed, "So if there was an open line of communication, why wasn't the target instructed to egress to a safe exfil point?"

"Sure the messages came in when the sats were still up," answered Lopez. "But you're going to have to ask Nash why she didn't call back. You and I both know that from the get go cell lines were overloaded. Land lines were overloaded. The Iridium satellite array was overloaded."

"I can sympathize," said Cade. "I was in Nash's shoes by day two. My phone was working sporadically. The messages I did get out ... I had no idea if they'd been received or not. And I didn't find out until days later."

Ari broke in over the comms, "How'd Nash get a trace on the pings this far out from Z-day in the first place?"

"Being the computer whiz that she is, somehow she got ahold of a log of all of the cell tower pings in Southern California ... whether the calls serviced by the towers were received by the cellular sats and bounced to another cell tower somewhere in CONUS or not. I don't know how she thought of this ... pretty brilliant if you ask me. She went through the pings that weren't passed on ... or transmitted, if you will, by the carrier satellites until she located the target's number which she found to have sent out numerous pings after the cellular communication sats went down."

Lasseigne said, "So the target was here?" He pointed to the white mast below. "And the phone in question pinged off of *that* mobile tower?"

"Yes," replied Lopez. "The pings start up north near USC and then the target's phone pinged off of different towers in multiple locations, and if you connected the dots you'd find a straight line north to south from USC to here." He paused for a tick. Then finished by saying, "And here is where they ceased."

Cade looked at Lopez, then Lasseigne and finally Griffin and said, "First off, the *target's* name is Nadia. Nash's daughter was a senior at USC. Secondly, during the shit show that those first few days was there was continuity of government to worry about ... she oversaw President Odero's rescue while D.C. was still going through its final death throes. And when that rescue went sideways she was the main person responsible for locating Speaker Valerie Clay. *She* sent Desantos and Lopez to the Greenbrier in West Virginia to secure our new president and bring her back to Springs. So, with all due respect, *Griff*, I think second guessing Nash at this point after we've all already volunteered to find *Nadia* is foolish."

Griffin put his hands up in mock surrender. He said, "No disrespect intended."

Nodding, Lopez went on, "So we do a quick search of the tents with the intent of finding Nadia alive. While you're at it keep your eyes open for *anything* resembling Nadia."

Cade thought: *Anything?* But he said, "Call them what they are, Lopez. They're zombies, not humans. They weren't brought back by the Devil to stalk the living. God's not smiting us either. This was a colossal fuck up started by a man or woman in a bug-making facility thousands of miles away. No doubt Omega was being weaponized and they succeeded ... but it got out. So as my theory goes, the Chinese generals, having already been working up plans for an invasion of Taiwan and possibly Japan anyway, decided to send the Alpha and an unknown number of human missiles here ... carrying the already escaped virus as their payload."

Cross said, "I agree. Just like their and the Russian's nuke doctrine. They still subscribe to—or at least they did forty-three days ago—mutually assured destruction. Use 'em or lose 'em. And that's no different than a martyr strapping on an explosive vest embedded with nails and ball bearings and hoping to take as many innocents at a wedding or bazaar or government checkpoint with him as possible."

Lasseigne chimed in, "Omega was ... *is* ... terror on an epic scale."

"They may have succeeded. And I'm sure we haven't seen the last of them," replied Cade as the satellite phone in his cargo pocket vibrated against his thigh. He extracted it, thumbed a button and, when the screen lit up, read the brief text message. Finished, he cycled through the half-dozen contacts, finding *Greg Beeson* just ahead of the entry labeled *Nash*. He punched out a two-paragraph message, the first three words reading: *For Duncan Winters*. He finished the message with two words: *Stay frosty*. He hit the green pad marked *Send* and once he saw the message had been transmitted, he thumbed the *End* button and watched the screen go dark. Still clutching the phone two-handed, he looked out over the Pacific Ocean and revisited Brook's message in his mind. The words *concussion, collapsed lung and possible asthma* didn't put the fear of God in him; however, the part when Brook indicated that all three together is *like a perfect storm taxing her remaining good lung* set off the first tingles of worry in his gut. And compounding that apprehension was Brook's sentence indicating that she had no choice but to make a run outside the wire to Woodruff—a town far from the Eden compound and seemingly light years from Los Angeles.

Ari came over the comms and said, "Seen enough, Lopez?"

Lopez said, "Affirmative. And much more than I wanted to."

Ari asked, "Where do you want to infil your team?"

Lopez leaned against the port side glass. Spent a couple of beats taking in the sight below.

Quietly, Cade said, "Want to use the Osprey as a diversion?"

Nodding, Lopez said, "Ari ... have Ripley move her Osprey to the northeast corner and hover close to the deck and call out *Nadia*. If there's no response, have her pipe some *Wagner* or *Disturbed* outside to draw the dead to her position.

A wicked grin spreading on his face, Griffin said, "Or *Five Finger Death Punch* ... Jeremy Spencer's drum work will flush 'em out if the hurricane from the Osprey doesn't." He racked a round into his M4, looked around the cabin, and added, "Stay frosty. And I don't want to hear anyone calling for a *corpsman*. You hear?"

Cade smiled at that and said to Lopez, "After all we've seen, I don't think Nadia is here, living or dead. I think she made it to the east bridge and saw that it was blown. She's no dummy. That's Nash's kid we're talking about. So it might be smart to forgo searching the tents and drop in near the command trucks and see if they left any intel behind. What do *you* think?"

Lopez covered his mic and said, "You've got a point about Nadia using her smarts. But why would FEMA workers leave anything sensitive like that behind?"

"Just doing Nash's bidding. She has her reasons ... two birds, one stone. That's all. I assume like the guard dropping the Golden Gate and the Bay Bridge that she figured FEMA blowing these was the same ... a last resort action," answered Cade. "No one's getting their paychecks deposited on Monday, that's for sure. You think a civil servant is going to go above and beyond with everyone around them turning? Would you lag behind and take the time to deal with the minutiae?"

Lopez mouthed: *Good point.* He removed his hand from his mic and looked at the monitor. He said, "Insert us near the command trucks."

"Roger that," said Ari. "I've got the stick."

Haynes said, "Copy that. Handing this black beauty back over to you."

"That's *Elvira* to you, Haynes."

Ignoring the banter, Lopez said, "Cade and I will clear the trailers, south to north. Cross, you and Griff cover our flanks. Lasagna, you've got our six while we're inside the trailers. And watch those tents to the east real close."

Helmeted heads nodded and thumbs up were flashed.

Simultaneously Cade felt his stomach heading to his throat and saw the ground rushing up. He chambered a round and, leaving his rifle *hot*, said a silent prayer for Raven.

Chapter 46

Forgoing Brook's orders, Chief quickly checked the woman's exposed skin for any signs that she'd been bitten. Aside from a number of fresh scratches and abrasions incurred during her scramble through the felled fir trees the woman seemed healthy.

Chief and Tran walked her to the truck in silence. Tran opened the rear passenger door for her and offered her a helping hand up.

The woman hesitated. Looked at Tran then Foley and finally fixed her gaze on Chief and said, "You *are* good people ... aren't you?"

"I do my best, lady," answered Chief.

Glenda smiled and accepted Tran's hand. She climbed up and fell into the seat, obviously exhausted.

After loping around front and hauling his weary frame in and slamming his door, Chief reached to the floorboards and grabbed the last of the bottled waters. He passed it over his shoulder to Tran, looked sidelong at Foley and said, "Home, James."

As the big engine throbbed to life, Chief extracted his radio and called ahead to Phillip with instructions to have the gate open in two minutes *by any means necessary.*

Foley jammed the shifter into *Drive* and pinned the pedal. Hands on the wheel at the proper ten and two, he pronated his wrist and glanced at the watch and saw that since Brook's harried call a little less than eight minutes had slipped away. *A well spent eight minutes,* he thought. Because though he didn't know a thing about their passenger, she was one of the living and to boot she did have a good aura about her.

***

Five minutes after leaving the roadblock, and thirteen total after receiving word of Raven's injury, the black Chevy blazed past Phillip near the hidden entrance on SR-39, juddered over a handful of Zs prostrate in the road and, tires screeching, made the hard turn into the open gate.

Holding on for dear life, Glenda began second guessing this lesser of two evils thing. "Who was that man with the gun and where are you taking me?" she asked loudly enough to be heard over the thrumming tires and gravel pinging off the undercarriage. "And why the hurry?" she added as an afterthought.

Chief swiveled around and said, "We just got word that one of our group was injured ... one of the kids."

A kid, thought Glenda. Suddenly she slumped back into her seat. Stopped worrying about who these men were or what might happen. She stopped worrying about anything and everything. It suited her best that way.

For a long minute the forest whipped by and scratched both sides of the truck. Suddenly, as if they'd been shot out of a cannon, her field of view opened up wide and she saw an ocean of tall grass capped by a vast bluebird sky. Then she saw some younger people carrying guns and the truck she was in slewed sideways and ground to a halt. She looked to her right and noticed a number of SUVs and pick-ups, one of them much larger than the rest, parked under cover of the trees near the clearing's edge.

"Fourteen minutes and thirteen seconds," said Foley. "A little longer than the normal commute."

"Good driving," said Chief. "Now let's see how we can help Brook." He opened his door and was hit by the instantly recognizable stink of hot motor oil. Which momentarily overpowered the stench radiating from their passenger then was gone with the restless afternoon breeze.

Remembering how on occasion Louie used to speed along the State Route throwing the Austin Healy around some of those very same curves, Glenda said, "Took more than fourteen minutes and thirteen seconds off this old girl's life. But I enjoyed every moment. Well ... maybe not the sounds of breaking bones and stuff. Was running over those biters on the road really necessary?"

Foley said, "Couldn't be helped, ma'am. Time was of the essence." He reached out his hand, which was covered in pitch and had abraded knuckles the size of acorns. "James Foley. You can call me Jimmy. Or James. Or Foley. Whatever floats your boat."

She took his hand. Felt the hard-earned calluses scrape against her palms, which were recently rubbed raw from the bicycle's unforgiving fifty-year-old plastic handgrips. "Glenda Gladson," she said. "Pleased to meet you. And thanks for saving my bacon back there."

Shrugging away the accolades, Foley just smiled.

Chief introduced himself next.

"Just Chief ... really?" said Glenda, intrigued. "Of what tribe?"

Remaining stoic, Chief said, "This is my tribe now. And there are no chiefs here."

"Workers among workers," she said in a matronly tone. "I like that. Now run along. You better see what your friend Brook needs."

Chief looked at Foley, who apparently was reading his mind.

Foley said, "I'll stay with Mrs. Gladson." He patted his thigh. "I've got a radio. Call me if you need anything."

Chief nodded and started off towards the compound, carbine in hand.

Glenda turned to Tran, who had just clicked out of his seat belt. "Where did you boys get the *assault* weapons?"

Tran, being the lone pacifist of the group, shrugged and looked the question at Foley. He opened the door and took his bag of mushrooms and greens and left the two alone.

After Tran closed the door behind him and was on his way to the compound, Foley hitched an elbow over the seatback and said, "They just *look* menacing. Most of them have less kick than a hunting rifle." He pulled a folding knife from his pocket. Thumbed the stud on the blade and it flicked open and locked with an audible *snik* which was amplified to a menacing level inside the truck.

Glenda frowned, trying to place the sound. Her eyes went wide when she spotted the blade in Foley's hand. In the next instant she was pressing her back into her seat and stammering, "Wh ... wh ... what's that for?"

Foley's brow furrowed. He looked her square in the face. Noticed how it was lean and angular and traced with lines of age. Her thin lips were chapped and pursed and quivering. There were dark bags under her green eyes and up close he could tell the reason for her death-like pallor was a base of oily makeup that was streaked in places yet still threw off an unusual sheen. He smiled, hoping to put her at ease, and, pointing the knife tip at the magazines on her forearms, said, "To cut those things off of you. What'd you think ... I was getting ready to gut you?"

"After seeing what some of Huntsville's more unsavory citizens were capable of ... I'd be lying if I said that wasn't my first thought."

"Put your arms up here ... please."

Glenda draped both arms over the black leather seatbacks and let her hands dangle limply.

Eyes focused on Glenda's right arm, Foley said, "I have two questions for you before I get started."

"Go ahead," she said, visibly relaxing. "I've got nothing to hide." A curious smile replaced her frown and she nodded her head, waiting.

Using the knife as a pointer, Foley tapped one of the half-dozen yellow, jagged items protruding from the magazine. Speaking slowly, he asked, "What - are - these?"

"Teeth."

"I'm afraid to ask ... but I'm going to. How'd the *teeth* end up there?"

"Simple," she said. "Fast Glenda. Slow biter."

Nodding to show he understood, Foley said, "I've heard of the *Irrational Enquirer* here. But what in the heck is a ..." he traced the smaller magazine's title with the knife tip "... Grapevine?"

"AA-approved literature."

He visibly recoiled. Said, "*You* were an alcoholic and had to go to AA?"

241

"Still am ... always will be. But I put the *plug in the jug* years ago. And yes, James, at first I *had* to go to AA."

Foley set the knife aside and rubbed his hands together. They made a scraping sound and tiny flecks of dead dermis filled the air. He leaned in and said, "I have someone I want you to meet. And I even think you'll like him. Or at the least he'll grow on you over time. That's my experience."

"But?" said Glenda in the same matronly tone she'd used before.

Foley wrestled with the question of how much he should divulge to this stranger. His inner voice said: *Jimmy, she has a good aura.* And that broke the dam and he multitasked, cutting off the other magazines while spilling the beans on Duncan's worsening addiction to Old No. 7.

When he was finished, Glenda pulled up her sleeves and rubbed her raw palms up and down her clammy damp forearms. Then she rubbed her palms together and said, "We usually wait for the person to come to us. It's AA's policy of attraction rather than promotion. Also we usually only work with persons of the same sex." She closed her eyes and kept them that way for a few seconds. When she finally reopened them Foley saw a twinkle there and her face had softened somewhat. She said, "*But* ... seeing as how there are probably damn fewer of us now thanks to the Omega thing, I don't see how I can't in good conscience make an exception on both counts."

Foley smiled and nudged the driver's door open.

Glenda opened her own door and turned back and said, "Plus ... Lord knows Glenda Gladson loves a challenge."

Before Foley could answer to that, the two-way radio in his pocket vibrated.

Chapter 47
Terminal Island

The numbers on Cade's Suunto told him the Osprey had been hovering over the northeast corner of the yard for five minutes. He imagined a little Metallica blaring over the bird's loudspeaker and in his mind's eye saw the chalk of Rangers sitting inside facing each other and itching to '*get some.*' But he hoped the search of the command vehicles wouldn't devolve to that. And seeing the dead responding to the diversion, trudging lockstep towards the cacophony like so many army ants, gave him a feeling in his gut that maybe Mister Murphy was busy whipping up a shitstorm on some other poor individuals somewhere else in the Z-plagued nation.

The Ghost Hawk started a slow slide to the right and the nose soon dipped and the rest of the craft followed.

Cross, Lasseigne, and Griff, busy securing their weapons, dialing in their comms gear, and powering up their NVGs, paused for a tick and nodded simultaneously.

Lopez grabbed a nylon gear bag and stuffed it in a cargo pocket. Disregarding Cade's theory of God's involvement in this whole mess, he signed a cross on his chest and squared up with the door, ready to be first on the ground.

Cade watched the hovering Osprey slip from view and saw the tents then FEMA trucks filling up the port side windows. Without warning, Ari banked the craft hard left and brought them in fast from the south, flaring at the last second as the mechanical clunk of landing gear locking into place vibrated through the floor. In the next instant the crew chief had opened his port, deployed the starboard minigun, and was scanning the ground for threats.

Haynes said, "Be advised. The LZ is cold."

Ari said, "I concur."

Haynes answered, "Touching down in three, two—"

'One' didn't register in Cade's ears. He was focused intently on the thirty yards of shell-casing-littered asphalt between the helo and the twin RVs at his twelve o'clock.

By the time Haynes's count hit 'One' Lopez had wrenched the cabin door back in its track and was in mid-air. A millisecond later he was boots on the ground and moving forward in a combat crouch, weapon at the low ready and totally oblivious of the brass rolling away from him in a near perfect arc.

Semi-propelled by the rotor wash at his back, Cade leaped out and hit the wall of carrion-infused air. It was thick and sweet in a gut-churning way. Bent over at the waist, he moved ahead a few paces, took a knee, and covered three points of the compass until he felt Cross tap his left shoulder and, near simultaneously, Griffin do the same.

From his side vision Cade saw Lasseigne crab-walking towards his position, weapon trained on the nearby tents and his head on a swivel. Then the electric minigun's barrel began spinning and its noisy whine registered over the baffled rotors chopping the air overhead. He heard Lasseigne and the two SEALS on his flanks indicate that they were "in place." Which was his cue to continue on to the command vehicle, following in Lopez's footsteps.

Head swinging an arc left to right, like a Secret Service man scanning a crowd, Cade saw the Osprey a half mile distant, its dual spinning rotors producing a muted ripsaw buzz and holding the craft aloft twenty or thirty feet from the deck. He then took into account the number of dead streaming toward it from the tents erected on the premises and figured there had to be more Zs lurking around somewhere.

Lopez arrived at the command vehicles and pressed his back to the southernmost RV's door. Tried the handle at once and found it unlocked.

Cade formed up a second later and saw Lopez nodding and looking at the handle. He mouthed, "Unlocked," and once Cade was ready, started another countdown.

When Lopez's count reached 'one' he flung the door wide.

Crouched six feet away with the silenced M4 tucked in tight, Cade trained the Eotech optic's holographic red pip on a spot in the darkened doorway he imagined would be head-high on a person of average height.

They waited a full second but nothing dead or living exited the trailer.

So Lopez said, "Going in." He mounted the metal fold-down steps one at a time, slowly, and leaned in, cutting the corner by degrees, M4 leading the way.

Cade watched Lopez hesitate momentarily. Then a bright cone of light lanced from the tactical light affixed to the entry man's carbine. The light spill walked right as Lopez's head and upper torso torqued in that direction. Then the stocky Delta operator moved left and out of sight and the doorway went dark again. A beat later Lopez reemerged and motioned for Cade to join him.

The windowless RV was much more plush on the inside than Cade would have guessed. In fact it was quite opulent, by cousin Eddie Griswold's standards. There were multiple flat panel monitors along the driver's side wall and six expensive-looking leather and fabric office chairs fronting them. The floor covering was several notches in quality above the usual AstroTurf-like carpet in most Winnebagos. The walls were a gray Formica, or its modern equivalent, and placed at intervals underneath a real wood counter running along the same wall as the monitors were three networked computer towers.

Without a word, Lopez let his carbine dangle from its sling, yanked the three black CPUs off of the shelf, opened them up and quickly harvested their hard drives.

While Lopez was filling his nylon sack with computer hardware and thumb drives, Cade poked his head out the door and looked right and saw that a number of the dead had doubled back and were steadily cutting the distance to the awaiting helicopter. A tick later, in his headset, Cade heard Cross say "Engaging" and saw the first burst of gunfire lance from the SEAL's compact HK-MP7.

Ducking back inside, Cade heard a dry rasp and the rustling of fabric against fabric emanating from behind a blackout curtain to his right. Sliding the heavy hanging partition aside with the stubby suppressor revealed a lone zombie belted in behind the steering wheel and disturbed the shiny black carpet of flies feasting on it.

Cade let the curtain down and said, "Looks like someone left their FEMA co-worker here to turn all by his lonesome." He turned to Lopez and went on, "Question is ... why didn't you put it down?"

Lopez threw the half-full bag of computer parts over his shoulder and replied, "It's no threat to us."

Cade said, "It's a threat to the next person who stumbles upon it." He drew his Gerber and parted the curtain a foot or so, releasing a buzzing squadron of tiny carrion feeders. He leaned between the heavily upholstered captain's style chairs, stared into the dead thing's clouded eyes and saw just hunger and want. Nothing to summon even an ounce of remorse for what he was about to do. Sure the bloated corpse had once been human. Sure it had suffered horribly on its first death judging by the hunk of meat missing from its neck and the dozens of raised purple bite marks disfiguring both arms. But the hissing thing was a threat nonetheless. So Cade put it to sleep, burying the dagger into its temple all the way to the hilt.

"Clear," called Cade with a trace of sarcasm in his voice, a veil of flies dipping and diving around his head. "Please don't let that happen again."

Forgoing the folding steps, and batting the insects away, Lopez leaped to the ground and said over his shoulder, "You clear the next one then."

And that's what Cade did. With brief volleys of suppressed gunfire sounding behind them, the pair approached the task of entering the second RV in reverse order from the first. Cade got the door while Lopez covered the doorway. Cade counted down and flung the door open and instantly a pair of zombies in FEMA hazmat suits stumbled out and into a lethal hail of 5.56 NATO hardball.

Cade brushed a quarter-sized scrap of hair-covered skull from his shoulder, put his back to the cool aluminum skin and listened hard.

Nothing.

So wiping droplets of blood from his ballistic glasses with a sleeve, Cade thumbed the switch activating his tactical light and mounted the stairs. Once inside, he found the layout the same as the first. Same monitors and chairs and flooring. Same trio of computers, and he had their hard drives extricated in no time. As he rose from kneeling and turned towards the door, two things happened. He heard Lopez say, "We gotta go." Then a stream of hot spent brass arced through the doorway and pinged noisily off the wall and ceiling and struck him about the head and chest.

"Coming out," he said into his boom mike. Then, with his M4's business end leading the way, he was out the door, down the steps, and immediately saw Lopez in the midst of swapping magazines.

Cade looked over his left shoulder and, near the Ghost Hawk, saw the other three members of his team tightened into a rough semi-circle. They were nearly back-to-back and throwing volumes of lead downrange into an advancing horde numbering in the hundreds and inexplicably consisting of mostly kids. Simultaneously Cade heard Lopez say "Mount up," and the Osprey's shadow was darkening the ground around them all as it passed overhead trailing hurricane force winds and dumping a waterfall's worth of spent brass in its wake.

Emptying a magazine, all thirty rounds, in controlled single shots while *making them count* as he'd been taught in basic, Cade followed Lopez, who was curling around behind the other shooters and tapping each on the shoulder as he passed.

Doing the same, Cade hauled himself into the cabin and met the door gunner's gaze. His visor was up and there was a glimmer of primal fear in his eyes. Then Cade noticed the big man's gloved hands kneading the minigun's scuffed metal grips.

Finally Cross and Griffin were on the move with Lasseigne on their six.

The three operators covered the distance in a loose knot, firing as they moved. Brass was flying in glittering arcs and the soft pops of skulls bursting could be heard over the soft rotor thrum.

As the smaller and therefore much faster members of the undead noose closed around the operators, Lasseigne covered Cross and Griffin while they broke for the open door and log rolled across the cabin floor to safety.

After seeing the men leap inside and with only five feet to go to the chopper, Lasseigne's magazine ran dry and the bolt locked open. With no time to access his chest rig and rip free a fresh magazine he instead flipped the carbine around and backpedaled, all the while bashing zombie skulls with the rifle's buttstock. Teeth gnashed and gnarled fingers were tearing at the lone operator's uniform as he made it to the door. Prying a snarling Z's bony fingers from his forearm, he felt gloved hands grab him from behind and suddenly he was light on his feet and in the next instant impacting the chopper's deck with a heavy wind-robbing *thud*.

Cade let go of Lasseigne's left arm, leaned over top of the shaken operator and, shutting out the rising crescendo of wails and moans, slammed the cabin door closed.

"Bastards were waiting for us," stammered the crew chief. "They were in the tents. Didn't come streaming out until you and Lopez were inside the second RV."

As the turbine roar increased, as if validating the crew chief's statement, a mad flurry of white palms hit the starboard fuselage. Tinny-sounding pings were followed by the hair-raising peal of nails raking the outer skin. Then a number of gaunt faces mashed against the Plexi, their rheumy eyes regarding the soldiers inside hungrily.

Haynes was looking out the starboard side door glass. Calmly he stated, "The Zs are going to get our tail rotor."

Without thought behind his actions, Ari rotated Jedi One-One to the right so her tail boom was sticking out over the seawall, nothing but water below it.

Before Cade was back in his seat against the bulkhead two things happened. Ari pulled pitch and the helo leapt from the blacktop, and a loud tearing sound filled the cabin as the crew chief let loose with a split-second burst from the minigun. Normally rated at six thousand rounds a minute, the electric-assisted Gatling-style gun spit a hundred and sixty lethal missiles in the fraction thereof. The rounds scythed into the Zs chest-high and screamed out the other side and, still packing quite a kinetic punch, a number of the bullets entered the RV's gas tanks, touching off a huge fireball.

"That was close," said Lopez as his stomach reeled from the rapid launch and a flash of orange from outside lit up his face. "You could have warned us sooner."

"Close only counts in horseshoes and hand grenades, friend," answered Ari, finessing the controls while applying enough power to get them clear of the rising roiling cloud of black. "In all seriousness, you got the same lead time ... neither me nor Haynes saw them initially. You have the Osprey driver to thank. Ripley saw them streaming out of the tents and warned us immediately. Then broke her own hover and her gunner started lighting them up."

Watching some of the dead advancing dumbly for the dancing flames while others had stopped in their tracks and were looking skyward got Cade to wondering why their behaviors had become so varied and unpredictable since Z-Day.

He processed that for a second and proffered, "It's not the first time she's acted as savior. Remember Operation Slapshot ... all the dead at the NBC?"

Nosing Jedi One-One north by east, Ari said, "Worst day of my life. Thanks a lot, Wyatt. I had purged that from my memory. *Had* being the operative word."

Cade said nothing. Watched the unintentional self-immolations taking place on the ground until the forms might as well been ants burning under a magnifying glass.

Cross said, "That was no easy day. I'm going to buy her two drinks when we get back to Schriever."

"Not if I get to her first," said Griffin, buckling in as the G-forces pressed him into his seat.

Cade clicked his belt and said, "What happened back there, Lasagna?"

The bearded operator was rubbing his forearm. He stopped and looked at Cade but was unable to come up with the words.

"Failure to fire?"

"My mag went dry and they were on me before I could reload or switch from primary to secondary."

"Well you improvised, that's for sure," said Cross.

Nodding agreeably, Griffin said, "And you didn't even have to holler *corpsman*. I'm very impressed." He unzipped one of the pouches on the medical kit hanging from his MOLLE gear. Dug in there for a second. Looked up and added, "The way you were swinging that rifle of yours at those things ... it's probably a biohazard now. Better take a minute to clean it." He tossed an alcohol swab across the cabin, which Lasagna snatched from mid-air with one hand. The SF soldier peeled the packet open and set to removing hair and bone and generally disinfecting his carbine's polymer SOPMOD buttstock.

Cade fished the sat-phone from his pocket and thumbed it alive. Once the screen refreshed and he saw there were no new messages he was hit with mixed emotions. On one hand he was grateful. On the other he felt a measure of worry building. The former because no update from Brook presumably meant Raven was holding her own. The latter because Beeson didn't cut corners and should have passed the message to Duncan by now. And given his troubled friend's growing propensity for the drink, even if the message had made it to him, the lack of response could mean that he was in no kind of shape to fly the Black Hawk back to the compound anyway.

Pushing the baggage he couldn't control from his mind, Cade inched forward on his jump seat and, straining against his belt, watched the concrete jungle glide silently beneath Jedi One-One.

Chapter 48

"The lead mechanic tells me that bird of yours has been ridden hard and put away wet. She's going to need some extra TLC before she's good to go." Beeson removed his black beret and plopped it on the desk blotter. Leaned back in the old-school wooden office chair and, with the seventy-year-old fasteners creaking and groaning, put his boots up on the corner of his equally rustic desk. "I gather she'll be airworthy in a few hours."

Duncan chewed on the prospect of spending another minute here, let alone a few more hours. Then he realized the creep of alcohol withdrawal he was feeling now would soon manifest itself in the form of tremors and shakes that would not go unnoticed. He shifted in his chair, thinking through his options. The PX was dry. As were the three uniformed guards at the gate, because no matter how he cajoled or what he offered up in trade not one of them would take it upon themselves to get him a bottle or point him in the direction of one. So an hour spent walking around the base and now he was here with nothing to show for it. And to add insult to injury there was a bottle of Scotch or the American or Canadian equivalent just a few feet away from him. Feeling a little self-conscious of his new glasses, more so due to their garish color than the abnormal size of the prescription lenses, he took them off and pinched the bridge of his nose.

"Are they uncomfortable?"

"Beggars can't be choosers," drawled Duncan.

"I like 'em," said Beeson.

Duncan thought: *Bullshit. You're busting balls now. Feeling me out for an intervention.*

"Things look better on you than those *aviator* glasses all the SOAR boys wear. And you and I both know they wear them just to let us ground pounders know who they are."

"So being cocky is a bad thing?"

"Not at all. That's how they perform flawlessly while riding the razor's edge and keep coming back for more," explained Beeson. "They say Night Stalkers never quit."

Cut to the chase, thought Duncan as his gaze wandered to the unopened bottle of booze sitting on a shelf behind the reclined base commander. He sat up straight and said, "Tell it to me straight. Will our bird be ready for launch before dark?"

"Can you stay the night if it isn't?"

"I've got a feeling Cade isn't going to make it back to the compound from his mission tonight. That would leave us a little thin in the Delta operator department."

"Mission?"

Duncan's eyes locked with Beeson's; then, as if someone was working him like a hand puppet, his gaze inexplicably, almost of its own volition, again shifted to the booze on the shelf.

"You got a lazy eye *and* a hearing problem, son?"

Duncan couldn't believe his ears. He thought: *Son? Maybe the graying and semi-paunchy commander has five years on me. But son? That's pushing the edge of the envelope.*

"Eyes, ears, and now problems of the mind, huh, Duncan. Do I need to get you drunk to get you to elaborate on this mission?"

Duncan eyed the booze for another second before declining the drink, and when he did it took immeasurable concentration to make his mouth open just so he could croak out a none too convincing, "No."

"Then lay it on me. I'm sure my security clearance will cover whatever cloak and dagger stuff is going on."

Duncan turned his chair so the bottle wouldn't be in his direct line of sight. Then, looking at the wall full of framed certificates and business licenses bearing the airport's former civilian moniker, he recounted the mysterious call to Cade's sat-phone. He spilled about Cade setting up the man-portable satellite dish and relay unit and then consequently receiving some sort of transmission. He paused for ten long seconds and added, "But I think you know all about it and you're just playing dumb with this *good ol' boy*."

"What makes you say that?" asked Beeson.

Hell of a poker face this guy has, thought Duncan. But he said, "Cade had me drop him off on a mesa in the middle of the desert eighty plus miles from here ... by himself. That was the first thing to set off my bullshit alarm."

Beeson didn't answer to that. He just ran his fingers through his close-cropped hair, all the while staring at Duncan.

"Those two aircraft that launched after we came in. I watched them heading eastbound through my binoculars. Only they should have flown a little farther towards Schriever before doubling back." He snatched up his glasses. Put them on, insecurities be damned, and added, "I know what I saw." Then he fixed a steely gaze on Beeson until the commander took his feet off the desk, leaned forward in the creaky chair, and threw his hands up in resignation.

Beeson said, "Nash isn't going behind the President's back on this one. But it's supposed to look that way. Let's call it what it is. An under-the-table deal."

"I'm not following."

"President Valerie Clay never served, so she really doesn't understand the *leave no man behind* concept. Same with President Odero ... he couldn't comprehend or he didn't want to believe what the Joint Chiefs were telling him had to be done to stop Omega. So Nash made an overture to the President from that angle. Then I heard she added a little wrinkle. Something to sweeten the pot."

"And the President bit?"

"Nash has her by the short hairs. Nobody is better at what she does than Nash. If you had need-to-know clearance we could crack that bottle behind me and I could tell you stories I wouldn't expect you to believe."

"So ... we're talking plausible deniability. In case the thing goes sideways."

"Roger that," Beeson conceded. "Once a politician, always a politician. And I had the two birds make that feint to keep the tongues from wagging here on base."

Duncan wasn't surprised about all of the attached strings. He'd served in Vietnam. The politicians lost that war. He paused for a beat in thought, then said, "So where are those birds taking Cade?"

Obviously anticipating the question, Beeson immediately said, "Do you have an hour?"

But before Duncan could answer, a look crossed Beeson's face. Raised eyebrows. Pursed lips. And a dead giveaway wag of the head followed by a couple of choice curse words muttered under his breath. He pulled open the top desk drawer and came out with a slim black item. He extended a stubby antenna and powered the thing on. He worked a button, cycling through the messages and then saw the first three words to the one sent by Cade and, hoping his transgression hadn't put anyone's lives in jeopardy, handed the phone to the man across from him.

Chapter 49

Brook closed the door to her quarters and froze there, listening hard. Once she detected the distinctive metal-on-metal rasp of the inside lock falling into place, she turned on a heel and stalked down the corridor and into the security container. She squeezed behind Seth, reached over his head and plucked the pair of ultra-long-range CB radios off the shelf. She verified they both held a full charge and set them to the same frequency. She handed one to Seth and stressed to him, seeing as how Cade and the others were still incommunicado, how important it was to monitor the radio and sat-phone closely while keeping his eagle-eyes glued to the entrance.

"Just a tiny bit of pressure," she said in a joking manner. Then she got serious and broke it to him that Chief was going with her to Woodruff, softening the blow with the caveat that they wouldn't be gone long.

Seemingly unaffected by the news, Seth asked, "Taking the kids?"

"Yeah ... I figure it's best to have the two vehicles and a couple of extra guns ... just in case. I tried to tell Sasha she was needed here, but she wasn't having it. Said it's still a *free country.*" Brook said the last part with air quotes and added, "You and I both know how stubborn she can be."

Seth nodded. He looked up at Brook and said, "That only leaves Heidi or Tran to watch Raven."

"I buried the hatchet with Heidi. It was hard but I went to her, tail between my legs."

"And?"

"She was equally sorry. At least she said as much. She and Tran both volunteered to sit with Raven round-the-clock. I wrote down detailed instructions letting them know what warning signs to be on the lookout for." Brook dragged her forearm across her eyes. Slung her carbine over her shoulder and, gesturing with the brick-shaped radio, said, "Listen ..." She paused, her eyes twinkling with newly formed tears, "I only want to hear this thing go off if her condition worsens."

"Copy that," said Seth. He removed his Utah Jazz ball cap and ran a hand through the shock of greasy black hair. "When are the others coming back?"

"Cade, I don't know. I just got a text on the sat-phone from Duncan saying he, Lev, and Jamie will be back before dark. I guess they diverted to Bastion where the helicopter is getting some much needed maintenance."

"And Cade just left them there?"

Without going into detail, she said, "That was the plan from the start. He didn't have the heart to break it to them until the last minute."

"I bet that twisted Dunc and Daymon into pissed-off pretzels."

"I bet it did," conceded Brook. "Lev and Jamie too, I'd bet."

"Think Dunc will be good to fly when they get done working on the chopper?"

"Beeson won't let him fly if he isn't. However, if they do get back here before us, I need you to make sure he gets a proper introduction to the new girl Tran told me about. Her name's Glenda Gladson." She slapped the younger man on the shoulder, and before he could object to his new role as matchmaker, she ambled off towards the entrance, a half-smile curling her lip.

Chapter 50

Terminal Island rotated below the Ghost Hawk as Ari spun it ninety degrees on axis and nudged the stick, putting them on an easterly course. As the northernmost bridge grew larger he turned the helicopter ninety degrees back to the north and slowed the aircraft to a veritable crawl over the channel separating Terminal Island from the mainland.

Close in, clearly, the demolitions, used to drop the bridge had not only done their job but had also caused catastrophic damage to the nearby railroad crossing. Huge I-beams once laser straight and capable of bearing the weight of a shipping-container-laden locomotive were now twisted like gnarled arthritic fingers after having been sheared off by the blast and intense overpressure.

Cade looked away momentarily and saw the last man in the ship worrying his forearm through his fatigue sleeve. Shifting his gaze back to the bridge, he noticed a twenty-foot-run of the vehicular bridge sticking vertically from the strait's murky water. And like a ragged assemblage of stepping stones across a creek, dozens of colorful automobile rooftops were visible just under the water's surface, with no doubt scores more settled on the sea floor beneath them.

North of the bridge, on a tract of land stretching off into the distance, was what looked to Cade like a traveling carnival or some kind of an impromptu renaissance fair. And just like the campground near Lake Meade, every spare square inch of ground was occupied by brightly hued tents. Unsecured nylon doors flapped freely in the offshore breeze and, like urban tumbleweeds, trash was piling up against them.

Near the makeshift shanty town on a triangle of ground bordered on two sides by water and empty marinas and hemmed in on the other by the 710 Freeway sat a sea of abandoned vehicles.

As Ari overflew the refugee camp and began a gradual turn to the west, Cade saw thousands of Zs milling about and became acutely aware that there was no way anyone could still be alive down there.

Pulling Cade's attention from the disheartening scene below, Ari came over the comms and announced they'd be coming back around and then following the 710 Freeway north to the USC campus where they would rendezvous with the Osprey carrying their QRF (Quick Reaction Force).

Across from Cade, the two Navy SEALs, Cross and Griffin, were busy reloading their magazines and checking their other equipment. The crew chief to his right was scanning the ground; periodically he would look up and swivel his head around, checking the sky off of the starboard side. And directly across from him Lasseigne had taken off his right glove and was rolling up his sleeve. Seeing this conjured up a bad memory that sent a cold chill down Cade's spine. Then he met eyes with the SF soldier and detected a measure of concern in them.

Shaking his head, Lasseigne rotated his forearm towards Cade and said, "They got me."

"Zip-ties," said Cade to Cross even before he was out of his seatbelt. Then he leaned forward and spoke directly into the cockpit. "Keep her steady, Ari. We've got a situation." Twisting towards Lasseigne, he grabbed the man's arm, looked closely, and saw what looked like two pin pricks, about an inch and a half apart, oozing blood. He took the zip-ties and looped one around the operator's thickly muscled bicep and cinched it tight, like a tourniquet.

"I'm already getting cold," Lasseigne said.

"Do it now," Cade ordered. "Or I will."

With a sheen of sweat blooming on his forehead, and a barely perceptible palsy affecting his hands, Lasseigne pulled the cylinder from a pocket and twisted off the cap. Looked a question at Lopez as he dumped the auto injector into his left palm.

"Here," said Lopez, stabbing a finger at his own right thigh, roughly eight inches north of his patella.

With no further questions or any hesitation Lasseigne jabbed the business end of the slender device into his muscled thigh, then, whispering some kind of prayer, leaned back and secured the infected injector in its container.

"Hands," Cross said. "We have to do it, brother."

Complying, the Special Forces operator clasped his hands in his lap and closed his eyes.

As Cross secured Lasseigne's hands at the wrists there was an audible *zip* as the plastic teeth ripped through the locking mechanism. He said, "Mask," and reached one arm across the cabin.

The crew chief ripped the wicked-looking face shield from his flight helmet and handed it over.

Cross accepted the spare flight helmet handed to him by Lopez and affixed the mask. He then removed Lasseigne's tactical bump helmet and snugged the flight helmet over the stricken shooter's sweat-drenched hair and buckled the chin strap.

Feeling totally helpless, Lasseigne let out the breath he'd been holding and said, "I'm sorry, fellas. There were just too many of them."

"Forget about it," Cade said. "How are you feeling? Any of the euphoria the tutorial spoke of?"

"Not yet."

Cade said, "Hang in there ... and keep us posted."

Near simultaneously Cade and Lopez started the stopwatch functions on their watches.

Ari said over the comms, "Four minutes."

Cade caught sight of the crew chief sans the mask and noted his clean-shaven face and easy smile, conceding inwardly that both were miles apart from his first impression.

Over the comms, Haynes said, "Oh my Lord."

Cade could only see the back of the aviator's helmet, so he leaned forward and peered out the port windows and couldn't believe what he was seeing.

Down below he saw dozens of bomb craters big enough to swallow up a small compact car. The bombs, five hundred pounders he guessed, seemed to have been walked the length of the freeway from the south, where a number of ramps met to a point a half of a mile north where an overpass had been dropped to the roadway and covered all eight lanes, remaining mostly intact. Thrown about on the southbound side of the freeway were hundreds of barely recognizable vehicles. Roofs were bowed up like the tops of so many soup cans way past their expiration dates. Hatches and doors here and there had been ripped away, some flung as far away as the northbound median. And to add insult to injury not an intact pane of glass remained in any of the blackened and twisted shells.

Hundreds of civilians had died in the obvious attempt to seal off Terminal Island. As the scene blipped by, Cade could make out vague forms still hunched over steering wheels. There were dozens of lifeless corpses sprawled out on the oil-stippled-pavement near their cars, and surrounding most were pools of dried blood from mortal injuries received from indiscriminant hunks of shrapnel or the initial explosions themselves.

Zombies were few and far between on this particular stretch of the Interstate. The seagulls, crows, and ravens, however, were not lacking for food. Nor would they be for weeks to come.

"Does Basra ring a bell?" asked Haynes, referring to the highway of death leading away from Kuwait towards Basra where miles and miles of fleeing Iraqi Republican Guards had been trapped and decimated by Coalition air power.

"Those were mostly old Soviet tanks and BMPs and Hilux trucks," Ari replied. "Besides, we were all still in high school. Except for maybe Griff there. The old man was probably already in BUDs training."

Ignoring the quip, Griffin placed two fingers on Lasseigne's carotid. Held them there for a second then sat back in his seat, a grimace on his face.

Chapter 51

The sun was high and the clouds were moving in quickly from the southeast. A long white band of them growing pewter around the edges and threatening rain looked to be on a collision course with Woodruff. *A bad day about to get worse,* thought Brook. She opened the F-650's door and tossed her M4 on the seat. As she climbed into the cab, the other door hinged open and Chief was joining her, his silhouette fully blocking out the light spill.

"We're leaving a light crew behind, so I suggest we not rush into Woodruff without giving it a once-over from a distance."

"What Cade would have said for five hundred, Alex," Brook said. She turned the engine over and listened to the low burble for a second.

Chief propped his carbine on the seat barrel down next to Brook's M4 and snugged on his belt.

Finally Brook looked his way and said in a low voice, "This isn't my first rodeo."

"What Cade would have said for six hundred," Chief said. "I wasn't trying to sound patronizing. Just thinking aloud."

"Copy that," said Brook, then smiled. "Also what Cade would have said."

"The Kids are in," said Chief, mercifully stopping the running gag in its tracks. He picked up the radio and keyed the Talk button. "You guys ready?" He heard a whistle and craned around and saw Max hop into the bed of the idling Raptor.

"We are now," Wilson said over the radio. "I'll get both of the gates."

"What's your gut saying to you about Glenda?"

"I think she's on the level," Chief said. "And that part about her husband ... who would make something like that up?"

"Yeah," conceded Brook. "Plus she knew about the dirtbags who let the Zs into our fence a while back. And then she was able to describe Bishop's men and their helicopters to a T." She went silent and watched in the rearview while Taryn backed the mud- and blood-spattered Raptor around and then smiled when the best driver in their small band gunned the off-road rig towards the feeder road, sending up a rooster tail of dirt and rocks and uprooted grass.

"Give them a second head start," Chief said.

"Why?"

"What do you think we should do about Heidi?"

"I've already given that some thought. While I look for the stuff I need for Raven, I want you to keep your eyes open for Celexa or Zoloft or Citalopram ... all antidepressants. It'll be a starting place, at least. Her PTSD is going to take time to overcome."

"Gives me something to do," Chief said with a smile. "Now we better catch the Kids."

***

A freshly killed rotter was propped up against the inner fence and Wilson was waiting to seal it up behind them all when Brook squeezed the oversized Ford between the two posts. She slowed and opened her window and said, "It was waiting for us here?"

Wilson nodded. "It was stuck in the fence. I walked the perimeter fence in both directions last night and didn't see any other breaches. I'm pretty confident it's just a straggler from the group we culled yesterday."

Brook made a face. She looked long and hard down the fence line in both directions. Then she said, "We'll call it in. Just in case," and wheeled the Ford ahead a few feet.

While Wilson closed the fence, Chief called Seth and told him about the encounter. Seth came back on the radio and said that he'd seen very little rotter activity on the State Route since morning.

Sure enough, when both trucks arrived at SR-39 the road was free of rotters. Wilson had the gate yawning open for them in no time and both trucks wheeled through and formed up on the road facing east. After playfully flipping the nearby camera the middle finger, Wilson closed the gate and in seconds he was back riding shotgun and the two Fords were rolling in the direction of Woodruff, the F-650 in the lead.

***

Fifteen minutes had slipped into the past by the time the red bluff, rising several hundred feet above the road and casting a shadow on the nearby Ogden River, came into view. Brook looked up at the depressing knuckle of earth as they blazed past and her heart hurt when she thought about the pain, both physical and emotional, Jordan, Logan, and Gus had endured while they were dying up there.

For the first time since turning on to the two-lane blacktop she noticed how the weeks-long accumulation of pine needles covering it had been recently disturbed. There were two wide tire marks, some distance apart, tracking straight and true and equidistant from both shoulders. As she slowed to negotiate the corner her eye was drawn to the horizon where, judging by the smattering of oranges and russets and muted yellows showing on the trees blanketing the rolling hills, autumn was right around the corner. In fact, Brook thought, if she remembered correctly, the first day of fall was September 22nd. *Around the corner, indeed.*

Brook and Chief sat tight lipped as the miles ticked off. Along the way the two-vehicle convoy passed a handful of walking dead, and either blew by them at speed or slowed and bulled them aside where there was no room to pass.

Knowing that 39 met up with State Route 16 at the end of a short straightaway around the next bend, Brook halved her speed and flicked her eyes to the rearview where she saw the Raptor's black grill filling the mirror, the word Ford spelled out in the cooling vents there.

The scene ahead was revealed in degrees as the F-650's massive snout cut the corner. Seeing a clutch of rotters near the overturned bus dead ahead, Brook pulled to the right-side shoulder and jammed to a stop. A tick later she saw a flash of white in her side vision as the Raptor pulled in tight next to her door. The Raptor's passenger side window whirred down and Wilson looked a question at Brook.

She said nothing; pressed a pair of binoculars to her face and glassed the intersection.

Peering through a pair of his own, Chief asked, "You see that?"

Brook exhaled then put the binoculars on the center console. Finally, she met Chief's steady gaze and nodded, a pained look on her face.

Head hanging half out of his window, Wilson waved his arms at Brook and said, "Well?"

Sasha's voice filtered up from the back seat. She was going on about stopping, whining and fretting about the Zs patrolling the road ahead of them.

Brook craned and shot Sasha a look that momentarily silenced the teen. Then she passed her Bushnells through the window to Wilson and said, "Better look for yourself. And those are yours to keep."

With the faraway murmurs of the dead competing gamely with the sound of the two idling motors, Wilson glassed the scene for a full minute. When he lowered the binoculars his mouth was hanging open and, as if what he had just seen was but a heat mirage or a figment of his imagination and in no way reality, he looked up and flashed Brook an incredulous look.

Suddenly Taryn picked the black and white vehicle out of the clutter. Quietly, she said, "That's Chief Jenkins's cruiser ... isn't it?"

Wilson sighed and slumped in his seat. "It's the Tahoe all right."

Sasha asked, "Is he there?"

Wilson said, "Thankfully, I didn't see him."

"Maybe he's just trapped inside," said Sasha, wild-eyed, her upper body hanging over the seatback. She looked left at Taryn. Let her gaze linger. Then she panned her head to the right, locked eyes with Wilson, and added breathlessly, "We have to help him."

Taryn said, "We owe him as much. Ask Brook if we can check it out."

In a low voice, Wilson said, "There's a lot of rotters there."

Taryn squared up in her seat and shot back, "He'd do it for us."

Wilson nodded and leaned as close as he could to Brook's window and ran the idea by her.

A ten-second huddle ensued between Brook and Chief. Finished, she ran the window down and nodded in Wilson's direction. Said, "Better open the slider and let Max in with Sasha." Then her window pulsed up and the F-650 pulled ahead of the Raptor at little more than walking speed.

Sasha opened the sliding window and called Max inside.

Following Brook's lead, Taryn slipped the transmission into *Drive,* caught up to the larger Ford, and tucked her ride in close to its bumper.

Inside the F-650 Chief recommended having the Kids stay at the intersection while he and Brook motored down the State Highway to get a closer look.

In response, Brook said, "I don't think I want to know the final outcome."

He said, "All the more reason for the Kids to hang back."

She responded at once, "Put a positive spin on it, though. Say we need them to watch our backs."

Which wasn't altogether a lie.

While Brook swerved in order to bypass the first of the rotters, Chief grabbed the radio and broke the news which, as expected, went over inside the Raptor like a lead balloon.

Keying off the radio, Chief said to Brook, "That's not going to fly with them very much longer. One of these days ... real soon ... you're going to have to let them go. Let them sink or swim."

"Not right now," Brook said as she tapped the brakes and squeezed the F-650 past the overturned school bus that had been there since before the *incident.* With barely an inch to spare between the right side mirror and bell housing protruding from the bus's massive rear axle, the Ford slipped past and Woodruff's small town center, just a short distance ahead, came into view. But she fought the urge to just motor on through and start the search. Instead she turned right onto State Highway 16, the Ford tracking straight for the grim task awaiting her. Thirty feet south of the school bus's crumpled front end, facing away from them and high centered on a mass of writhing bodies, was Jenkins's Tahoe. Standing near the driver's side window was a large male Z. And clutched in its clawlike hands was a smooth river rock the size of a cantaloupe.

Brook pulled up twenty feet short and watched as the big rotter bashed the rock repeatedly against the SUV's B-pillar, to no great effect.

"It's using a tool," Chief whispered, as if saying it any louder would prompt the handful of Zs approaching the idling Ford to find a like-sized rock and adopt the practice themselves.

Meanwhile, in the Raptor, which was parked diagonally on the junction where 39 and 16 met, Wilson was watching the action through binoculars and providing a play-by-play of what he was seeing.

Shaking her head, Taryn said in a skeptical tone, "A rock?"

"Yes ... a rock," confirmed Wilson without looking away from the surreal scene. "A pretty large one, too."

"Why is it still attacking the truck if the window's already shattered?" Sasha asked.

Wilson said, "I have no idea. But it looks like Brook and Chief are going to intervene." He kept the binoculars glued on the F-650. He saw Chief's boots hit the roadway a second ahead of Brook's and, when their doors closed behind them near simultaneously, fifteen gaunt faces swung away from whatever had their attention in the Tahoe. Quickly rising to a crescendo, their plaintive murmurs became a strained chorus of throaty moans.

Arm hairs standing at attention, Brook picked her targets as she stalked through the minefield of pulped body parts leading up to the inert Tahoe. The oversized rotter wielding the rock went to his second death first. A quick double tap from Brook's M4 sent the rear half of its skull spinning away in front of a rapidly expanding cloud of pink mist. Zs number two and three each caught a pair of lethal 5.56

266

mm hardballs traveling at 3,100 feet per second. The kinetic energy absorbed by the second and much smaller female Z was sufficient to send it flying into the SUV's rear hatch, its newly misshapen head absorbing the full brunt of the impact. And as the sheet of glass imploded with a bang that nearly drowned out Chief's steady controlled fire, Brook's second volley smacked the next rotter in the mouth and right eye and exited out back of its skull with another aerated spritz of gray matter and tooth and finely flecked bone.

To clear his side of the Tahoe, Chief moved in a crouch, firing continually, and by the time he reached the dented passenger door more than his share of the rotters were sprawled on the roadway, rivers of their bodily fluids trickling slowly toward the dusty shoulder.

Simultaneously, leaving a trail of bodies sprawled on the center-line, Brook fought her way to the driver's side door where from underneath the listing vehicle pale hands reached out and groped her shins and ankles. Ignoring the grabby Zs wedged under the rig, she went to her tiptoes, looked through the bashed-in window and saw Jenkins. She lowered her weapon and was hit by a wave of grief when she realized he was dead. That feeling lingered for but a second and then strangely enough she felt gratitude for the simple fact that he wasn't coming back as one of them. He had spared himself from that hell on earth. That was for sure. The flesh that was once his lips and cheeks was specked black from the blowback of superheated gunpowder. The back of his skull was sitting nearly intact, ring of graying hair and all, next to a gym bag full of his clothes in the back seat. His blood and brains painted the headliner crimson, and here and there dangling tendrils of semi-dried detritus provided the flies a place to land and feed.

Looking in the passenger side, Chief saw that the semi-automatic belonging to the dead former Jackson Hole Chief of Police was still clutched in his lifeless right hand. And in the other was a cherished picture of his wife and daughter, at Christmas time, wrapped up in his loving embrace. Seeing it clearly for what it was, he called to Brook, "Charlie told me he knew he was never going to find them."

Brook bit her lip. Said, "He gave it a shot."

"Gotta hand it to him," Chief answered back. "At least he went out on his own terms."

"They'll meet again ... somewhere," Brook said, swiping at a runaway tear.

Chief said nothing. He snugged his carbine to his shoulder and methodically culled a trio of dead lurching toward them from the south. Changed the magazine and racked a fresh round into the chamber and then began the long walk back to the F-650.

Dreading the sad task of breaking the news of their grim find to the Kids face-to-face, Brook was about to call ahead to Chief and ask if he would do it when the radio vibrated in her pocket. Taking it as a sign, she answered and, as she followed Chief back to the truck, provided the Kids with all the gory details.

As Brook neared the F-650 she saw a south facing sign marked *Randolph 11.*

"If Woodruff doesn't bear fruit we'll have no choice but to go there," she called ahead.

Chief slowed his gait. "Refresh my memory. What kind of place are we looking for?"

"Any kind of medical facility or veterinarian's office," said Brook.

"Me and Logan and the others did most of our foraging west and north of the compound. If I remember right from a couple of trips I made through here before the outbreak there's really not much to see. It's like an unincorporated town. Post office, a couple of fix-it shops, and a gas station."

"Won't hurt to look," Brook said. "I've only seen it on a map. The Kids have never been this way either."

When they got back to the Ford they stowed their weapons and climbed in, Brook still driving. She turned the engine over and stole one last look at the black and white. The place where Charlie Jenkins made his last stand. Feeling a second round of tears threatening to spill, she nudged the shifter into *Drive* and made a K-turn in the center of road. Then, wheeling north past the Raptor, she braked alongside, powered her window down, and said to Taryn,

"Let's keep a little more spacing between the trucks when we're in Woodruff."

Taryn nodded. She said, "Are you sure both trucks will fit in Woodruff? Looked like only three blocks of Main Street before we're back on the State Highway."

"We'll make do," said Brook as she released the brake and powered her window up.

They passed a couple of turn-of-the-century farmhouses with spacious tracts of grass surrounding them like moats guarding against the desert's approach. A little farther down the road, 16 became Main Street and all concerned discovered that Woodruff truly was a blink-and-you-miss-it kind of town. It was nothing like the towns south of Huntsville where smaller one- and two-story brick structures with awnings protruding over the sidewalks were the norm. Instead the places of commerce here were spread apart, sometimes by a block or more.

The post office on Main Street was a single-level affair painted an awful cream color with an off-putting red shingle roof. It was separated from the two-lane State Road by a wide pothole-dotted shoulder and, beyond it, a single strip of sun-baked grass. A flagless pole was planted in the ground on the corner of an empty L-shaped parking lot and, continuing the red theme, a sea of crushed lava rock surrounded it all.

Across the street on the left was an automobile repair shop. A trio of goose neck lights affixed to the flat roof hung out over its gravel parking lot. Vinyl banners touting cheap and quick repairs and listing their prices were strung on one side of the building and rippled lazily after a little gust of wind.

There were early model rust buckets covering two-thirds of the lot and, like the gas station preceding it, the neon signage in the window was darkened and the mini-blinds behind were snapped shut, leaving the contents of its interior up to Brook's imagination. She slowed the truck and at the next corner turned right off of Main Street. Head on a swivel, she wheeled the black Ford slowly around a pair of horribly burned walking dead.

Chief pointed diagonally across Brook's field of vision. He said, "My eyes aren't the best. Does that say physical therapy?"

Brook slowed the truck to walking speed hunched over the wheel and gazed at the two-story home turned business. In front was a pair of gnarled bushes flanking a wide cement walk. The walk ran ten feet from the sidewalk to a half-dozen stairs leading up to a small porch. A wide wheelchair ramp branched off right from the walk, switched back once, and ran uphill at a gradual grade to the right side of the porch. The front door was some kind of dark wood and in its center at eye-level the business name was spelled out in three descending rows with what looked like raised bronze letters. Sheer white curtains covered the vertical windows on either side of the door. The curtains for the two picture windows flanking the entry were also drawn. Hanging from eyehooks above the front stairs was a hand-painted sign. Red letters over a white background. Brook read it aloud: *Back in the Saddle Physical Therapy.*

"Do you think they'll have what you need?"

"Doubtful," said Brook. "But it's the closest thing to a medical practice we're likely to come across in Woodruff."

"Where do you think folks used to take themselves to be seen by a doctor?"

Brook said, "Ogden for specialized medicine, surgeries, and diagnostic type stuff ... X-rays, CT scans, MRIs and the like."

Chief looked at her and half-jokingly said, "How about shots then."

"Most likely a doctor in Huntsville or Randolph would hold a clinic for flu shots and immunizations once or twice a year. And that's assuming the high cost of malpractice insurance didn't put all of the private practitioners here in the boonies out of business."

Chief said nothing.

Brook asked, "What do you think the odds are that there's anything dead inside?"

Still eyeing the building, Chief said, "Slim to none. But if there is ... clearing the place shouldn't be difficult. I'm guessing there's four ... maybe five rooms downstairs. With probably the same floor plan above."

Simultaneously two radios vibrated. The one deep in Brook's pocket and the backup Chief had brought and placed in the center console.

Chief retrieved the one from the console, pressed the *Talk* button and said, "We're going to check out this physical therapy business."

"That's not what I'm calling you for," Wilson said testily. "While you two were sitting in the middle of the road burning fuel and daydreaming, a couple of rotters got wind of us."

Brook craned around and saw their unwanted visitors approaching. The same two horribly burned corpses she'd just passed by. Sex indeterminable. No hair or clothing or shoes. Just crisped skin and gaunt faces with pickets of off-white teeth and yellowed orbs for eyes staring straight away. And they were moving forward undaunted. Like a pair of hungry fire-and-forget missiles.

She took her foot off the brake and made a low speed U-turn. Pulled past the Zs, causing a clumsy shuffling about-face in the center of Main Street U.S.A. She parked the truck near the curb in front of the fix-it-shop and, leaving the motor running, set the brake.

Knowing the crispy Zs would follow them to the ends of the earth and that a bullet to the brain would be the only thing stopping them, Chief said, "You doing this or me?"

Letting her actions do the talking, Brook drew the Glock and deftly screwed the suppressor onto the muzzle. One and a half twists of the wrist later she punched the button bringing the window down and patiently eyed the approaching undead duo in the side mirror.

Behind the staggering ghouls she saw the Raptor roll to a silent halt.

Once the snarling creatures reached the rear tire on the driver's side, Brook stuck her arm out the window and, like she'd seen Cade do, waited until the first rotter reached for the pistol.

The awful crackling sound the crisped dermis made when the abomination raised its arms made her cringe. With her own skin crawling and tingling, she waited until it wrapped its skeletal hands around the cylindrical suppressor then helped guide it along into its mouth and, with a forceful thrust, deeper yet into its throat.

She pulled the trigger. Said, "Sleep well," as the creature's eyes bugged in its skull and inexplicably two puffs of fine black powder exited the recesses where its ears used to be. And whereas the suppressor usually rendered the Glock's normal report to little more than a light hand clap, the creature's abdomen silenced the shot entirely as the bullet severed its spinal cord and the remaining gasses dissipated to places inside.

As the Z fell to the roadway in a heap amid a swirling cloud of carbonized dermis, Brook raised the pistol by a degree and shot the other shambling mess between its darting eyes.

Cocking his head and checking the mirrors for more interlopers, Chief asked, "Only one shot each?"

Brook leaned out the window and the gun chugged twice more. "I was taking my time," she said, flashing Chief a fake smile. The gun went under her thigh and she picked up the radio, keyed the *Talk* button, and thanked Wilson for the heads up.

Brook released the brake and pulled another U-turn, running over one of the fallen corpses in the process. With the sickening crunch reverberating through the truck's undercarriage she heard Cade in her head reminding her to *Always double tap.*

The drive to the rehab place was short, and pulling into the cracked asphalt lot behind the white-and-gray-trimmed building they came across a car with its door ajar. Still trapped behind the wheel was a corpse, glistening streamers of muscle and flesh and veins hanging from its neck. As the Z struggled against its seatbelt, a torrent of white maggots spilled from its working maw and all of the flesh on the left side of its face bounced and jiggled like an ill-fitting Halloween mask, threatening to slide off its skull completely.

Chief grabbed his carbine and said, "I wonder why the things don't finish their kills once they've turned."

Brook had no answer to that. She pulled the truck in left of the compact, set the brake, and killed the motor.

The Raptor slid into the spot right of the little car, and Wilson hopped out and strode to the thrashing cadaver, brandishing his beloved Todd Helton Louisville Slugger.

Before Brook could say anything the redhead was teeing off on the Z's head. The beating went on until a white sheen of pulped maggots painted the inside of the windshield and there was nothing recognizable above the corpse's collar bone.

Wilson wiped the barrel of his bat in some tall grass growing up through the cracked asphalt next to the building.

"What was that all about?" called Brook, her tone confrontational.

"Payback for Charlie. I had just started to click with the old guy."

Though he knew the answer, Chief asked, "Why the bat?"

Sasha was out of the truck by now and she answered for her brother. "He saves it for special occasions like this."

Brook smiled coyly. Said, "Better than taking it home to Taryn." Then her tone changed. All business as she hopped down from the F-650, she added, "Let's go Chief."

Bat in hand and with cheeks still redder than the blood-splashed seats in the small compact, Wilson fell in behind.

Brook stopped mid-stride, turned, and shot him a look that said: *Where do you think you are going?*

"What?" said Wilson, arms spread, the bat still dripping some of the gore he'd missed.

Brook put one hand on her hip. A move that conveyed she meant business. One that always worked on Raven. She said, "Stay behind with the ladies ... *please.*"

Wilson threw the petite brunette a smart ass salute and turned on his heel feeling like some kind of private in her personal army. Then, without a word to the contrary, he placed the bat in the Raptor's bed and climbed in next to Taryn.

Chapter 52

Just a handful of minutes removed from surveying the damage several five-hundred-pound bombs could inflict on a jam of cars on a United States freeway, Cade was trying to wrap his mind around the numbers of dead he was seeing patrolling the sunbaked Southern California sidewalks. They owned Rodeo Drive and Sunset Boulevard. There had to have been a hundred or more languishing in the tar pits of La Brea.

The only part of L.A. that seemed unchanged to Cade when they overflew it was West Hollywood, a seedy area east of Santa Monica known for its eccentric nightlife and tattoo parlors and the place—from watching TMZ, which was a hidden guilty pleasure of his—he associated with fighting in the streets and drugs and prostitutes and bad boy actors in handcuffs.

Down below, like partiers leaving the clubs at closing, Zs were staggering down the sidewalks and streets and caroming off of palm trunks and inert vehicles.

Putting words to Cade's thoughts, Lopez said, "Place hasn't changed much. I wonder how Ronnie's old stomping grounds look."

"All the guns in Compton and Inglewood," said Cross. "No way the Zs stood a chance against 'em. I bet there's BBQ shops still cooking brisket in drum smokers."

Yet another good man gone too soon, thought Cade, trying to tune out the banter. Like Mike Desantos, Ronnie *'Ghost'* Gaines had pretty much died in Cade's arms too. Bled out real quick after the helo crash in South Dakota.

"One of you needs to do it before we set down," said Ari over the comms.

"Enough small talk," said Cade. "Should be Lopez ... but we're all volunteers here. So who's going to step up? Who knew him best?"

Nothing.

There was a long stretch of silence. Fifteen seconds during which Cade felt the helicopter start to bank right and then watched Lasseigne fighting gravity as the bird carved out a big chunk of sky leaning hard to starboard. When the craft finally righted, the SF operator's helmeted head lolled right and banged against the bulkhead and instantly his bound hands were up and pale fingers groped the air in a futile effort to get ahold of Cross and Griff. Through the cockpit glass Cade saw the downtown skyline and Dodger Stadium materializing, slowly, like an oncoming car emerging from a distant heat shimmer. Then where the automobile-choked 110 Freeway took a slight right-hand bend, Los Angeles Stadium came back into view. And even from this distance, thanks to the lack of airborne particulates, he could see clear as day the numbers on the field and, sitting smack dab on the fifty-yard line, the Osprey with its slow spinning rotors.

Knowing they had little time to spare before they reached their final objective, Cade decided to heap the unenviable task upon himself. He'd met the guy once before and the Special Forces sergeant deserved no less than a quick release from his dead body. So Cade unbuckled from his seat and unsheathed his Gerber. He retracted the smoked visor and peered into Lasseigne's rapidly clouding eyes. And as the undead man strained and his teeth snapped out an unnerving cadence behind the painted facemask, Cade raised the dagger and poised its tip an inch from one of the undead operator's wildly roving eyes. "I'm sorry, friend," he said. Shifting his weight forward, he plunged the blade in and, with a copious amount of blood sluicing around the hilt, twisted his wrist once or twice for good measure.

Cade extracted the blade and placed the visor in the down position. He left the zip-ties on. No feelings left in the empty shell to hurt. He arranged the dead man's limp legs so they were out of the way, then returned to his own seat, heavy of heart.

After buckling back in, he said, "A moment of silence for our fallen brother," and bowed his head.

Ten long seconds ticked by then the team raised their heads one at a time. The SEALs peered out their respective windows.

Lopez performed the sign of the cross, his lips moving as he uttered a final prayer for the dead warrior.

Cade stared at the lifeless body for a second then filed all of his feelings away. He reached in a pocket, ripped open the square of foil with his teeth, and went at his dagger with the alcohol swab.

While Ari and Haynes made plans for their next-to-last aerial refueling, the crew chief unbuckled and moved across the cabin. Cade watched the sergeant reach into a recessed cubby, come out with an American flag, and then was caught off-guard when it was offered to him without a word out of the crew chief.

Also saying nothing, Cade took it with both hands. It was folded tight into a triangle. Three long equal sides with a handful of stars floating on a field of blue showing. He found a grommet, pulled a corner, and unfurled Old Glory.

Lopez removed the fallen soldier's dog tags and pocketed them. Then he watched in silence while Cade wrapped the upright body in the flag, being careful to tuck the ends in just so.

The crew chief turned away first. Returned to his vigil near the starboard hip window, silent, eyes on the lookout for ground fire that would probably never come.

***

It was quiet inside the cabin for a long minute and then Ari said, "Watch the monitor."

The screen on the bulkhead went blue for a millisecond. Then an image splashed on the screen. "Four Palms Apartments. Nadia's off-campus abode," Ari said. "That's the Santa Monica Freeway north of it. And to the east is the 110 Harbor Freeway; that's what we're following now."

A tick later, someone, probably Haynes, manipulated the FLIR pod and the building's roof snapped into view. There were no bulky AC units or vents to speak of. Just a single ridge running its entire length with red clay tiles falling away at a steep pitch on both sides.

Griffin said, "There's no stairway access to the roof. No skylights. And it looks like there's too much of an overhang to rappel off and go in through a window."

"You'd be a dangling treat in front of them anyway," said Griffin. "Hell, there's not even so much as a satellite dish to anchor to."

"At only six stories," Lopez said. "I was half-expecting this."

Ari cut the helicopter's airspeed and started a slow orbit of the building.

"Courtyard looks to be out of the running," said Cade. "With those tall palms and their wide fronds I doubt if even Ari can get us close enough to rope in."

"One block south by east," said Cross, who, thanks to time spent on Secret Service advance teams, had a great eye for detail and was an expert in identifying areas of opportunity. Some chink or another in the layers of protective armor around the principal. A vulnerability. Most notably, anywhere a threat to the person he was tasked with protecting might ingress and egress. "Zoom in east of the building. On the crossing over the 110 ... if that's what I think it is, then we're golden."

Griffin was checking his weapon. He paused and looked up and said matter-of-factly, "As long as we don't get trapped up there."

Lopez said, "Can you put us in there, Ari?"

"I can put you in the bed of a moving pick-up if you want me to."

"Settled," Lopez said. "There's our ingress point then. Show us the back of the Four Palms first."

"Copy that," said Ari.

The image on the screen grew larger and began a slow and lazy counter-clockwise rotation.

A quick look told Cade that the off-campus apartment was a for-profit venture meant to appeal to those intent on independence by any means necessary. Just looking at the hemmed-in property he could almost hear the whoosh of passing cars in his imagination.

Noisy place. Hard to rent to just anyone, he thought. *Perfect for young people prone to making noise of their own.*

The building was shaped like a geometric boomerang. No soft curvature. Just hard angles and lots of windows and a liberal coating of pastel orange paint. There was a fenced-in courtyard with a rectangular swimming pool, its murky green water a far cry from the crystal blue one would expect to see. And hampering their insertion by fast rope, four majestic palms rose from tired landscaping to bracket each corner of the swimming pool.

There were glass doors off the courtyard and a pair of solid doors with no outside handles on the west side opposite the pool.

As the helicopter kept up the distant orbit the rear of the building came into view. Under the building's vertical spine was an entrance to what looked to be an underground garage; however, from the angle and low light Cade couldn't see whether it was gated or not. Above ground was a parking lot with enough spaces to accommodate maybe twenty vehicles. Miserly by L.A. standards. But impressive considering that most of the nearby dwellings didn't have any off-street parking.

The helo slowed and sideslipped and instantly the insertion point Cross had identified was just below them.

With Ari expertly holding the Ghost Hawk in a steady hover, the crew chief hauled open the door and a blast of hot-carrion-and-kerosene-tinged air slapped Cade full on in the face. Through his side vision he saw Lopez kick the thick nylon fast-rope out his side door. Then as the crew chief deployed the second rope, Cade checked his gear again out of habit. Satisfied, he watched the coils at his feet unspooling over the metal sill and then quickly walked his gaze over the maze of unmoving vehicles on the sunken eight-lane freeway sixty feet below. He thought: *Focus on the landing, not the dead.* He mouthed to the crew chief, *"I'm good to go."*

Once the pair of ropes unfurled completely Cade felt the crew chief tap his shoulder. He nodded and gripped the rope with gloved hands and stepped into thin air. In the next instant his palms and fingers were heating up from friction as gravity yanked his hundred and eighty pound frame—encumbered with an extra forty pounds of gun, gear, and ammo—the thirty feet from the helo's open door to the narrow elevated walkway below.

The moment his boots hit cement he released the rope and, in one smooth motion, side-stepped a handful of feet, took a knee, and swung his rifle into a ready position.

Looking the length of his carbine, Cade trained the red holographic pip on a point near the east end of the elevated pedestrian bridge where the walkway curled out of sight. Seeing nothing there, he called out, "East ramp is clear."

A tick later Cade heard the hollow thud of Cross landing on the same spot he had just vacated. And then Lopez was on the comms and calmly calling out, "We've got Zs inbound. Nine o'clock underneath the west entry ramp."

Then, also over the comms, there was a grunt followed by the unmistakable sound of someone gasping for breath.

Cade glanced over his shoulder and saw the Navy SEAL, Griffin, lying on his left side and just in the process of righting himself. And as the fast-rope jerked and bobbed in the rotor wash over the fallen man's head Cade quickly deduced that on the way down Griff had brushed the spikes atop the bridge's protective fencing. Confirming the hunch, he noticed that the operator's MultiCam blouse was torn and showing through the yawning hole in the fabric was a horrible six-inch gash running down from his right shoulder to just above his tactical elbow pad. Dark crimson blood spilled from the wound, instantly misting as the fabric and jagged tear in the skin flapped wildly in the down blast.

Lopez moved quickly to assess the wound. A beat later he looked skyward and flashed a thumbs up to the crew chief looking on.

In the next instant the crew chief had pulled the pin on the starboard fast rope and it plummeted by the skywalk and landed audibly on the vehicles below. A half-beat later the port-side rope also fell, but instead of joining the other on the 110 it got hung up in the same run of security fence that had just taken a bite out of Griffin.

With the Ghost Hawk peeling away, Cade hustled west and formed up next to Cross, who was on one knee and training his carbine on the nearby ramp where anything approaching would initially emerge.

"How bad is it?" Cross asked.

"Just gotta rub some dirt on it," Griff said, grimacing.

Cade kept his eyes and weapon trained westward while Lopez tended to the injured SEAL. Every couple of seconds he would check their six to the east. And every thirty seconds or so he would say, "All clear."

Two minutes after roping from the helicopter, with a cacophony of moans and groans rising from the freeway below, Lopez had the unlucky SEAL's bicep wrapped in three layers of gauze and secured with white tape and was zippering up the corpsman's med-kit.

Cade turned his attention to Griffin. Looked him in the eye. "Good to go?"

Griffin said nothing. Instead, his eyes widened and he calmly scooped up his suppressed carbine and nodded west.

Woodruff

A quick rap on the back door followed by a long hard listen had Chief and Brook convinced that there was nothing dead banging around inside the ground floor.

So Chief felled the wood core door with one kick from his lug-soled boot. Then, carbines leading the way, they quickly cleared the lower level starting with a nearby bathroom and small storage closet adjacent to it.

A quick check of the closet revealed only toilet paper for the bathroom and a myriad of cleaning supplies and a good amount of disinfectant wipes, no doubt used to clean equipment or mats of sweat and tears after strenuous rehab exercises.

Moving on, they entered a wide open twenty by forty foot room awash with natural light spilling in through a pair of windows bookending a floor-to-ceiling wall-length mirror on the left wall. Parallel to the mirror was a freestanding piece of equipment with a pair of adjustable wooden ballet-style grab bars. The floor was tiled with light green squares and in front of the mirror was a row of thick blue mats secured together by strips of hook and loop tape. In one corner near the front door was a pair of yoga balls, large and neon green. Nearby was a dark brown medicine ball, smaller and partially squashed and no doubt much heavier than it looked.

Like the items sold in the Scandinavian furniture stores, floor-to-ceiling cabinetry finished with a faux oak laminate dominated the wall on their right. And inside their doors, some of which had been hanging open, Brook found dozens of individual drawers and plastic storage boxes—none of them labeled with any kind of consistency. Without counting, she guessed there had to be twenty or thirty of them in each of the ten cabinets.

"I'll start left," Brook said. "You work your way over from the right."

Chief said, "And we'll meet in the middle."

"Remember ... we need a syringe and needle."

***

Ten minutes later, after rifling through every drawer and cupboard and cubby and bin, the floor was littered with glossy handouts detailing every therapeutic exercise imaginable. Colorful tangles of rubber resistance bands were heaped where they'd been thrown. Dozens of hand-held therapy balls made of highly pliable Nerf-like foam, near bullet-proof hard rubber and everything in between lay on the floor wherever they'd come to rest.

Brook slammed a door, sending a trio of rubber balls bouncing away. She looked at Chief and said, "Nothing. Not even a pump and needle for the effin yoga balls."

"That would work?" asked Chief, his brow scrunched up.

"No ... I'm just frustrated. That's all."

Chief picked his carbine off the padded floor and straightened up. He moved close to Brook and placed a finger vertically to his lips. Cocked his head and looked at the ceiling. A tick later he gazed at the short flight of stairs at the corner opposite the room from the front door. The narrow treads rose up several feet into the gloom to what was likely a landing at the back wall where the only way to go from there was to the right and up.

Nodding, Brook went quiet and jabbed a finger at the ceiling and then pinched her earlobe. "*I heard it too*," she mouthed. Then she pulled out the two-way radio and made sure the volume was turned low.

Chief motioned for her to follow and picked his way quietly through the mess of their own making. He ascended the stairs, keeping his feet wide and placing them where he imagined they were nailed to the solid wood stringer underneath.

With a minimal amount of noise the pair made the first landing and paused there while Chief thumbed on the tactical light affixed to his carbine. Gripping the stubby foregrip and snugging the rifle in tight, he took the remaining dozen stairs in the same fashion as the others, but for expediency, two at a time.

At the top of the stairs the cone of light lancing from Chief's rifle illuminated a wooden door with five inset horizontal panels and a rubbed oil knob set on the right. The striker plate looked original to the building and it appeared he would be needing either a skeleton key or most likely—seeing as how kicking in a door is virtually impossible with no handrails to hold on to and only an eight-inch tread on which to stand—a couple of rounds from his carbine.

But first things first. Chief put his ear to the door and heard nothing. Then he tried the handle, and lo and behold it turned. So he pushed in a bit and felt the heavy wooden door catch on the sill and make a grating sound before finally swinging inward freely on its hinges. He held it in a partially closed position and looked down the stairs at Brook and held up his free hand, three fingers splayed out like a pitchfork, and began ticking off a countdown.

On one he shouldered the door open, pivoted right, and brought his rifle to bear. Half-expecting to come face-to-face with a rotter, he instead found himself alone in a long hallway and squinting against the sun pouring in from a distant gabled window. Equidistant from the stairs and window on the left hand wall was a closed door. On the right wall were two doors, evenly spaced, and also closed. The walls were bare and the ceiling came to a point far above their heads. *Definitely some kind of a renovation happened here*, thought Chief.

When Brook closed the door behind her two things happened. Again she heard the same wood-on-metal squeal and then the radio in her pocket vibrated against her thigh. It went on as she watched Chief pad to the front of the building and duck his head through the curtains over the window then crane left and right, surveying the street through the wavy glass.

At the end of the hall Chief hinged up at the waist, turned around, and said, "We have to hurry. Same thing as before. You get the left. I'll get the right." Training his rifle on the nearest door, he tested the knob and found it unlocked. Pushed it inward and stepped forward while walking the cone of light about the shadowy interior. The curtain was drawn on the window facing him and allowed only a thin bar of diffuse light. Below the sill were cardboard boxes brimming with paperwork. *Strike one*, he thought as the spill illuminated a personal computer, monitor, and printer all perched on a desk pushed against a wall to his left.

As Chief disappeared into the first room Brook answered the radio and learned that a small herd was heading their way from the north. *About a hundred of them. Figure you've got five minutes, max*, Wilson said.

Calm before the storm, Brook thought. She padded across the creaking floorboards and stopped in front of the lone door on her side of the hall. She smelled the faint scent of carrion seeping around the door frame. Held her breath and placed her ear against the door and listened hard. There was a barely audible rustle and the same squeaking she'd heard from downstairs, only the responsible party was no mouse.

She tested the knob and it turned freely. Seeing Chief emerge from the far door, she waited to catch his eye then pointed at the door and mouthed, "Rotter inside."

Chief stood nearby, rifle trained on the door, as Brook pushed it inward and stepped aside.

He said, "Clear," then lowered his rifle and covered his nose with his free hand.

Brook walked through the wall of stench and felt bile rising in her throat when she saw what was making the noise.

An arm's length to her left, standing half a head over the top of its crib, was a withered and cadaverous undead toddler. A girl. Maybe two or three at the most. An electrical cord was knotted tightly around the thing's wrist-thin neck. One dainty bicep was wrapped with a crude gauze and tape bandage. Blood had soaked through and dried to black in a perfect oval. *A bite*, thought Brook.

Chief said, "Looks like she was bitten first."

Reacting to Chief's voice, the thing bared its teeth and hissed and, reaching for the source, slammed its tiny frame against the headboard.

"I'm sure Mommy did her best," said Brook as the squeaking she had heard from downstairs started up again and quickly rose in tempo and volume. She walked to the center of what looked like a break room for the owner or staff—probably one and the same. There was a kitchen table near the window and on top of it was a microwave and a salt and pepper shaker. Tea packets were stuffed into a large paper cup. There were wooden stir sticks and creamer and sugar. One of the four chairs was missing from the table.

The little Z, now with both pale hands wrapped around the bars, was shaking the drop-down crib gate, which produced a shrill nonstop metal on metal peal.

Then, coming from the front of the long room behind the large piece of fabric dividing it into two equal parts, the other noise intensified.

Standing in the middle of some kind of macabre orchestra of the dead, with the incessant rattling on her left and the nerve-jangling squeaking to her right, and a good idea of what was beyond the divider, Brook took a handful of burgundy fabric in one hand and said, "I'll pull. You cover."

Nodding, Chief raised his carbine and took a few steps to his left to better the angle.

With its little feet slipping on the slickened bedding, the undead toddler hissed and strained and somehow got both arms hooked over the rail.

Brook yanked the curtain back and her initial expectation was shattered. Time seemed to slow and again the radio in her pocket vibrated. In the next second her salivary glands went into overdrive, flooding her mouth with a bitter acidic taste and she fell to her knees, willing the rising tide of bile down. Breathing hard through her mouth, she looked at Chief and said, "This could have been me ... and Raven."

Suddenly she was reliving Myrtle Beach. Her mother and father were zombies. Mom was stalking her down the hall. Then a horn blaring in the parking lot behind the building snapped her back.

Chief said, "We need to get moving. There's nothing for us here."

Brook keyed the radio and said, "Grow a pair and handle them, Wilson. I've got a couple of things to take care of." She released the *Talk* button and pocketed the radio.

Outside, the Raptor's horn blipped once.

"You sure you want to?"

Rising up from the floor, Brook shot Chief a look that said: *Don't go there.* Then she cast her gaze on the young brunette woman who had obviously not been privy to the rules of the new world. The missing dining chair was lying on its side a yard distant. On the floor next to it was the white panel that had been removed from the drop-down ceiling overhead. The writhing corpse was hanging from a nylon rope knotted around its alabaster neck and, judging by the non-stop squeaking, secured to a loose ceiling joist somewhere up there in the gloom.

Partially stuck in the bodily fluids that had pooled and dried under the dangling flesh eater was a single sheet of white paper, folded in half.

Brook crouched and took the paper between two fingers and unfolded it carefully.

Chief saw her eyes moving back and forth, reading something. Then she looked up at him and, tears welling in her eyes, said, "Her name is Carol. The little girl is Mia."

"*Was*," said Chief. "Let me have your pistol." He held his hand out to receive the suppressed Glock.

The horn blared again. Urgent sounding. Three sharp reports.

Chief pointed toward the stairs. Framed by dark hair which was perpetually pulled back into a tight ponytail, his ruddy tanned face showed no emotion. No fear. No apprehension. Nothing. He said, "Go. *Now.*"

Brook shook her head. Drew the Glock and checked the chamber. Seeing the glint of fat brass, she let the slide snap back and raised her gun arm. With her free hand she spun the twitching corpse around a few degrees and, with the Glock's suppressor hovering inches from the base of its skull, squeezed off two quick shots. Instantly a spritz of congealed blood and other viscous fluid spattered the ceiling tiles in two wide overlapping arcs. A millisecond later a cloud of aerated gray matter burst from the ruptured skull and joined the roiling dust motes riding the once still air. On the back side of the initial second the weapon's dual coughs had toured the room and receded to nothingness and the oak wood flooring was receiving a fine misting of both. Chest heaving under the bulky MOLLE gear, Brook strode the length of the room and, sensing a little more of her humanity slipping away, grabbed a tuft of Mia's wispy straw-colored hair, forced her face down onto the soiled mattress, and in one quick motion drew her hand back and put two rounds behind the undead girl's tiny button of an ear.

With tears flowing fully down her cheeks and awash in a feeling of foreboding from not finding the supplies necessary to save her own daughter, Brook followed Chief out of the building, wary of what awaited them.

Chapter 53

In his mind's eye, Cade pictured Nadia tooling her little white Miata down the L.A. side streets, confused and terrified and trying to get to one of the promised FEMA safe havens mentioned in the looping radio broadcasts that had initially instructed everyone to shelter in place.

He imagined her skirting the freeway south with nothing but her cell phone and a desire to be reunited with her mom.

He supposed seeing the bridges out and coming to the realization that all overland access to Terminal Island was gone must have been a hell of a gut punch. And how the feeling of dread upon seeing the freeway under attack, or, more than likely, stumbling across the aftermath, must have been monumental for someone her age to fathom.

Enduring all of this knowing the power and position her mom held. The unfettered access to spy satellites and secure phones and high-level government officials—yet nobody had contacted her or come to her rescue.

What a knockout blow that must have been.

Then he put himself in her shoes and instantly came to the conclusion that if this apple fell anywhere within a mile's radius of the tree that was Freda Nash, the young woman was sheltering in place somewhere familiar. The one place she could eventually be found if her mom mounted a search. And that place loomed just three blocks to the west.

He looked beyond the curving ramp, over the bobbing heads of the walking dead at the V-shaped apartment building, and felt in his gut that she was still alive.

The first salvo of gunfire lanced from Lopez's carbine. Pumping suppressed rounds into the dead two at a time, he advanced down the narrow ramp, stepping over the leaking bodies until he had expended thirty rounds and the carbine's bolt locked open. "Next," he said into the comms. Standing aside, the stubby suppressor still smoking, he raised the barrel and changed mags.

Cross squeezed past Lopez and took up where he left off. The dead were falling and rolling down the widening ramp. A pair dropped side-by-side, semi-upright and limbs akimbo, blocking the team's passage. Improvising on the fly, Cross halted and kicked them onto their backs and then padded across their prostrate forms.

Bringing up the rear, Cade kept one eye on Griffin and the other on their six. He noticed the SEAL's dressing was completely blood-soaked and asked, "How's the arm?"

Grimacing from the pain of raising his arm, Griffin flashed a thumbs up and hung his upper torso over the cement rail and started raining lead down on the dead from above.

Inside the hovering Ghost Hawk two hundred feet above a cluster of small two-story homes north of the insertion point, Ari looked on with a healthy dose of apprehension. Though this was a sticky situation since the dead had gotten wind of the team, there was nothing he could do. The bird's minigun wasn't suited for the kind of help the team could use. For one, the noise would only draw more dead to the AO (Area of Operations). Secondly, the term *danger close* in this situation was a hell of an understatement. The dead were nearly draping themselves on the advancing team. But such was the nature of CQB (Close Quarters Battle). And the chalk of rangers swooping in aboard the noisy Osprey would only add to the confusion. They were along at Nash's behest solely as insurance should the cobbled-together team find themselves trapped in a building like the *Four Palms* where a rooftop extraction was not an option. So he held the steady hover and drew his own little crowd of Zs.

***

The fight from the pedestrian walk to the east/west street leading to the Four Palms lasted five minutes during which Haynes was watching from the helicopter and calling out targets and threats for the team. Twice it looked as if the dead had them surrounded. Once when the team reached the base of the ramp, when Haynes did his best smooth talking to dissuade the door gunner from entering the fight as the team had to resort to a *mad minute* of gunfire to break contact. And then again half a block from the apartment building where finally he could take it no longer and bellowed, "Guns free," to his crew chief.

"That's danger close," Ari replied. "Disregard. We've got a different set of rules now, Haynes. Those things aren't firing back. So *close* has a different definition to the guys on the ground."

Then Cade's voice filled the comms, urging the team to turn and follow him.

"Hold fire until they break," Ari said. "One quick burst is all. That should give them the buffer they need."

The crew chief on the minigun acknowledged with a quick, "Copy that."

Keeping the front of the Four Palms in sight, Cade broke for the corner at a dead sprint. He didn't look back. Didn't need to. The sound of boots and breathing and the subtle rustle of gear and fabric told him the others were with him.

Then another sound filled the air. A friendly sound comforting to any foot soldier in harm's way. The chainsaw-like ripping noise lasted less than a second. Then hot shell casings were pinging and bouncing off the cul-de-sac's circle of blacktop a block off of his left shoulder. He thought: *There's the dinner bell.*

Once the Dillon fell silent, Ari sideslipped the helo two blocks east, dumped altitude until the helo was just above the pedestrian bridge, and then descended another twenty feet. Keeping Jedi One-One just below the lip of the man-made concrete canyon, he flew over top of the jammed up vehicles for a block or two. A handful of seconds after pouring a hundred and fifty 7.62 mm NATO rounds into the throng of Zs, the stealth helicopter had skimmed the inert vehicles and risen from cover and was holding a steady hover.

To Ari, from the helo's right seat roughly a block southeast and a hundred feet above the rear roofline of the Four Palms, the place looked entirely deserted.

The sun and sky and tops of nearby palms were reflected in the windows on the southeast wing. On the other wing, displayed in the mostly westward-facing glass, was a snapshot of the neighborhood and, rising above it, the azure Pacific Ocean. And as if the city was under some kind of a mandatory blackout order every window on every floor of the Four Palms was drawn tight.

"Nobody's home," cracked Ari.

"Except for the dead," echoed Haynes.

"I think we're going to make a good team, Haynes."

"As if I have a choice," answered the big African American.

Ari smiled. He said, "Good restraint back there, Doctor Silence."

Haynes said, "Boom. I think we have a nickname for the quiet sergeant."

"Let's go with Doctor. Or Doc for short," Ari said. "What do you think ... you like the sound of that, Doc?"

Sergeant James Skipper's eyes narrowed behind the smoked visor. Then, still gripping the minigun and with Lasseigne's corpse his only company, he nodded subtly, but said nothing.

High-stepping through the tangle of Zs littering the sidewalk took Cade right back to basic training. Only this wasn't a phalanx of old sun-hardened automobile tires where a misstep meant at best a little hurt pride or at worst a twisted ankle or knee. No, these were dangerous bio hazards with blown-apart skulls and broken bones protruding from previous damage. One scrape from a green stick fracture and it was anti-serum time for the unfortunate victim. And so far Cade didn't like the odds of survival Fuentes's concoction offered. The cooling corpse in the helicopter above was deadly proof enough.

He led the team along the front of the Palms the way they'd come for half a block and, with the pedestrian bridge two blocks dead ahead, took the next right. They moved south for another block, passing by a picket of palms on the left and a wall of manicured shrubs growing up next to the apartment building's east-facing wall which rose more than a hundred feet skyward on their right.

"Wait one," said Lopez. "I need to check something."

Cade raised a closed fist and came to a halt and went down to one knee. He looked up and noticed the Four Palm's metal fire escape twisting back and forth on itself all the way to the top floor.

Filing that bit of info away for later, he looked left past Cross and Griffin, who had their backs to the shaped shrubs and the barrels of their suppressed carbines pointing out at opposite angles.

A few feet beyond the SEALs, Lopez was leaning between the bushes with only his legs and backside visible.

Curious, Cade did the same and found himself peering through decorative holes designed into the cement block supports and into the Four Palms's underground garage. There in the gloom he saw a game-changing sight that buoyed his hopes and, short of proof of life, all but backed up his gut feeling.

"There's a white Miata in the garage here," said Lopez. "Has to be Nadia's."

"Can't be too many white Miatas in Southern California ... can there?" answered Cade, tongue-in-cheek.

Ignoring the quip, Lopez said, "There's a few more vehicles." He paused for a second. Drew a breath and went on, "And a mess of *demonios*."

Either the building has been compromised entirely and the things got down there through an open stairway, thought Cade. *Or if the garage entrance is gated, which, presumably, it would be, then hopefully someone left it open.* Cade hoped for the latter, because if it was gated and that gate was down and locked, figuring a way to breach it and then secure it behind them once they were inside might prove to be a deal breaker.

Still running the contingencies through his head, Cade started off at a trot past the shrubs. When the foliage abruptly ended and the building angled away to the right and a low cement wall bordering the outside parking lot became his only cover, he went into a low-combat crouch and hurried a dozen yards farther to the corner, where, again, he went to one knee and raised a closed fist. A moment later three pairs of boots scuffed to a stop on the sidewalk behind him and the team came to a stop. Given the shit storm they'd gone through covering the first three blocks of the incursion, that they hadn't encountered a walking corpse for an entire city block was refreshing as hell—but not long-lived.

Feeling the sweat pouring down his back and pockets of liquid pooling against his chest underneath his body armor, Cade peeked around the corner, looked the length of the low wall bordering the lot's south side, and saw a dozen dead things looking skyward. Following their gaze, he saw the Ghost Hawk, silent, black, and menacing. It was partially blocking out the sun and hovering parallel to the building with the starboard minigun deployed and covering the team's approach.

"I count thirteen Zs southwest of your position," announced Haynes. "I repeat, one-three Zulus to your southwest. The Zulus you just broke contact with are now turning the corner at your six o'clock."

"Copy that," said Cade. "I have the point now."

"Do we have an Anvil Actual sighting?" said Ari over the comms.

Cade said nothing to that. He snugged his carbine to his shoulder and, looking over the barrel, rounded the corner low of profile and searching for targets.

Leading the team quick and quiet westbound, Cade slowed to a walk once he was within ten yards of the dead. He put his finger on the trigger and, with the others at his back, started dealing out lethal double-taps. And the dead didn't know what had hit them. They fell vertically. The first five in a jumbled heap, their near naked bodies intertwined in second death. The next half-dozen went down in succession, like dominos, as they turned to face the advancing footfalls. With audible pops their heads exploded one after the other and Cade stepped over their prone forms and did the final two— execution style—two rounds each from behind as he rushed by them. In fifteen short seconds all thirteen rotters littered the sidewalk and parking lot entrance, their heads caved in from thirteen unlucky pairs of rapidly decelerating and tumbling 62 grain hardball.

Lopez, Cross, and Griffin rushed through the open gate in a tight knot and, as planned, Cade stopped underneath it and jumped and grabbed ahold of its sharp metal lower lip. As the other three continued running down the ramp there was a strobe light effect on the walls and low ceiling from their weapons discharging.

Cade felt his rifle banging him in the crotch as he curled his legs and held on, dangling two-handed from the gate.

But nothing happened immediately.

So, feeling useless as teats on a boar, simultaneously he watched a new throng of Zs vectoring in from the street and worked out a couple of hard-earned pull-ups.

Meanwhile, behind him, the distinct soft chugs of suppressed weapons throwing lead downrange competed with the echoing moans of the dead, the tinny tinkle of brass on concrete, and the wet slaps of bullets striking flesh and bone.

As he eyed the staggering corpses homing in from the street, Cade felt something give in the mechanism somewhere overhead as the combined weight of his body and gear started the gate moving, achingly slow, on its downward journey.

Chapter 54

The scene behind *Back in the Saddle Rehab* wasn't quite as bad as Brook had envisioned prior to stepping out the back door. Immediately she learned Wilson couldn't count—at least not from the shotgun seat of the Raptor.

There were dozens of rotters advancing from three points of the compass: north, east and south—not hundreds. And she learned another thing—Wilson had grown a pair as she'd recommended and was standing alongside Taryn in the Raptor's bed bludgeoning the creatures crowding the truck with his Louisville Slugger.

Black Beretta pistol in hand, Taryn was crouched low and firing point blank into the dead.

Then more gunfire rang out and Sasha was shooting at the Zs with her .22 caliber rifle from her usual perch right behind the driver's seat.

Before Brook could react, Chief was down the stairs to the left, rifle leveled at the Zs and running and firing.

So she turned right, ran down the shallow ramp and at the sidewalk came face-to-face with a putrefying first turn. Without breaking stride she swept it out of her way with the M4's buttstock, skidded to a stop, tracked the stubby rifle around, and put two bullets into its brain before it could rise up off the ground. She stepped over the mess of blood and brains and cleared the corner of the building unchallenged. She looked right toward the State Highway and saw a handful of dead a dozen yards away. Sweeping her gaze to her left, she spotted three more Zs blocking her path. Beyond the trio of first turns, near the rear of the F-650, another ten to fifteen walking corpses were angling straight for her in little clusters of twos and threes.

Feeling his ponytail thump against his back with each stride, Chief peeled left around the Raptor at a slow trot. Rounding the bumper, he saw the clutch of zombies reaching up towards Wilson and Taryn and began pumping round after round into their heads at near point-blank range.

Suddenly the sporadic gunfire coming from the Raptor's cab ceased and in his peripheral Chief saw Taryn holster her pistol and dive head first into the open slider. He saw her feet kicking the air and watched her dark form disappear inside. A tick later the big V8 throbbed to life and Chief's eye was drawn to Wilson, who had stopped swinging the bat and seemed to be focusing on something out of sight. Recognizing this for what it was, Chief made his way by the idling Raptor's rear bumper, stepped through the fallen corpses, and rounded the F-650's towering tailgate.

Simultaneously two things happened. Chief heard a clunk and roar as the Raptor's transmission engaged behind him and the motor revved. In the next instant, with exhaust fumes mingling with the stench of the dead, he rounded the F-650's bumper and saw Brook in danger of being surrounded near the truck's left front fender.

Ignoring a still-writhing corpse nearby, he took a knee and peered through his rifle's holographic sight. He put the red pip on the back of the head of the flesh-eater closest to Brook and caressed the trigger. Bone and brain went airborne, and without verifying the kill he repeated the process, walking his fire to the left away from her.

When Brook saw the rotters start crumpling to the ground right in front of her, she immediately went into a crouch and crabbed left towards the tiny Z blocking her path to the truck. Judging by the way the skin had tightened around its eyes and mouth, and taking into consideration the condition of the clothes hanging off its emaciated frame, she guessed the undead pre-adolescent had turned near the very beginning of it all.

Fearful of a stray round finding one of the truck's gas tanks, she lashed out with the M4's buttstock and connected solidly, sending shards of yellowed teeth into the air and the little monster on a one-way trip to the blacktop. Coming around on the follow-through she saw a lone rotter trip over the yellow wheel chock under the Ford's front tire and come stumbling at her, head down, arms flailing, and on the verge of a major face plant. Never one to look a gift horse in the mouth, she stepped back, shouldered the M4 and, with an arm's length to spare, stilled the floundering creature with a quick double-tap to the top of its head.

However, her gift horse turned Trojan the second she spun back towards the truck and saw that the juvenile Z was already up and facing her with a sneering mouthful of jagged teeth.

Brook felt a cold shiver rack her body and time seemed to come to a screeching halt as two things happened simultaneously. First off the undead kid found another gear and closed the distance and had the front of her cotton shirt wrapped up in a two-handed death grip. Then Max came flying out of nowhere, clamped his teeth around the thing's thin neck and took it down to the pavement all in one fluid movement.

Still not one to look a gift horse in the mouth—even after the last surprise—Brook leaped over the prostrate Z and lunged for the F-650's door handle.

Still crouched in the Raptor's bed and unable to see Brook, Wilson witnessed Max squirm from the cab through the slider, leap from the truck bed to the compact car's roof and, in one final bound, clear the F-650's bed and disappear from sight. And before his brain could process what he was seeing, the Raptor lurched backwards at tremendous speed and he was flat on his back and rocketing towards the cab. A fraction of a second later when the truck finally jammed to an abrupt stop, he sat upright, stomach reeling from the unexpected spin cycle, and saw Chief prying a twice-dead rotter off of his leg. Then, to his relief, Wilson saw the stocky Native American reach the other truck's passenger door, open it unaccosted, and climb up on the running board. But before he made it inside, Max had slinked out from under the truck and wormed his way past the man's legs and inside the cab. Then again, without any kind of warning, tires were screeching, the Raptor was moving forward, and Wilson was sliding uncontrollably towards the tailgate. Like a kid in a bouncy house, he found himself being thrown up and down along with his bloody Louisville Slugger and a couple dozen loose shell casings.

The F-650's cab smelled of gunpowder and dog and sweat laced with fear when Brook finally slid her petite frame into the driver's seat and slammed the door. She glanced at Max as she started the motor and said, "You saved me, boy. I owe you a venison steak ... or three."

"I think we spent a little too much time upstairs," said Chief, his hands visibly shaking.

"No comment," replied Brook, breathlessly, as she slapped the transmission into reverse. "But I bet that was you who saved my ass, wasn't it? None of the Kids can shoot like that."

Chief said nothing. He had kicked off his boots, loosened his wide leather belt, and was busy stripping off his denim jeans.

Sensing Brook's eyes on him, Chief said, "Avert your eyes, please. And get us away from here."

And she did. Following Taryn's lead, Brook reversed hard and left the compact car and dead rotters alone in the shadow of the two-story. The F-650's big knobby tires pulped the corpses and spewed meat out the back as she pinned the accelerator and, ignoring the driveway entrance, drove over the sidewalk and grass parking strip. Threatening to get away from her, the Ford lurched and bounced and skittered sideways before she reined it in.

At the junction with 16, Brook let off the gas, braked hard and, with the tinny pinging sounds of dead hands striking the sheet metal, jerked the wheel hard right, putting the rig into an unintentional power slide. Once she got the truck tracking straight again and was closing the distance to the Raptor's white tailgate, Wilson rose up from the bed. Instantly the slipstream grabbed his boonie hat, ripping it off his head. But he didn't lose it entirely. The camouflage number was arrested by its thin leather chinstrap, which was now wound around his neck and chafing his Adam's apple. As he worked his way toward the cab, the hat spun wildly to and fro, battering his back and head like a parachute deployed behind a dragster.

Taking her eyes from the road for a beat, Brook said, "Are you OK?"

"I don't know yet," replied Chief. "You have a mirror?" Then, sitting there in his boxers, he stripped off his socks.

As Brook watched Wilson squeeze his lanky frame through the back window, she said, "I'll pull over in a minute and check you for bites. Once I declare you *good to go*, we'll pull Randolph up on the navigation system and see how far they made it into the twenty first century before Omega slapped them back into the dark ages."

Chief said nothing. He was contorting his body trying to see the back of his calves. There were deep red welts running vertically up and down his right leg from mid-calf to just below his groin. "At the least these wounds are going to need some antibiotic."

Brook didn't even want to think about the worst case because Cade was hours—at least—from returning with the antiserum. And that was assuming Nash had come through and given Cade some in the first place.

So with the grain of salt accompanying Nash's word growing boulder-sized the more Brook thought about the antiserum's very existence, she snared the radio from the console and, though she had a good idea who was responsible for the transgression, keyed *Talk* and said, "I don't know *who* laid on the horn back there ... but it *cannot* happen again. Shoot the bastards for Christ's sake. *Do not* invite them to dinner." She chucked the radio back where she got it and listened as the apologies poured in over the open channel.

Chapter 55

Cade hung from the lip for thirty long seconds while the gate traveled the advertised ninety-six inches from ceiling to floor. By the time the metallic clang signaling his task's completion was echoing through the subterranean garage, the rest of the team's weapons had gone silent and the Zs were slamming their decayed torsos against the gate and thrusting their pale arms through its horizontally aligned metal links.

With fingers grasping at air inches from Cade's chest, the dozen hissing first turns strained mightily against the gate, bowing it inward.

Ignoring the gathering crowd, Cade turned and faced Lopez, Cross, and Griffin. He proceeded to swap out magazines and then asked Lopez what he knew about the stairs.

Letting his carbine dangle from its tactical nylon sling, Lopez spread his arms like he was preparing to fly. He answered, "One in each corner. I heard movement behind the door to the west wing. It was closed but unlocked like someone might be coming back. I left it the way I found it."

Cade nodded. "And the east?"

Shaking his head, Lopez said, "Locked."

Cross held up a small leather pouch. He said, "That's why I brought these."

Cade reached into a cargo pocket. Tossed Cross the lock-picking gun. "Use that. It'll save us all a lot of time."

"And headache," conceded Cross, holding up his gloved left hand. "I've got these big ol' mitts. Not very conducive to doing the old *pick* and *tensioner* two-step."

Now that he was out of the sun and not running for his life, Cade noticed that the temperature twelve feet underground was a good ten degrees cooler than topside. For that he was grateful, but as the adrenaline surge of a few minutes ago ebbed he felt his body cooling off a touch and the damp shirt under his armor making his skin go clammy.

While Lopez and the SEALs swapped magazines and readied their weapons for the next push, Cade formed a three-dimensional image of the building above them in his head. He saw the inverted V-shaped structure from the front. Two glass-enclosed elevators ran up the outside of the building, and on the first flyby he'd noticed that both were parked on the bottom floor. He saw the wide sidewalk leading to a metal mesh security gate and the barricaded front entry beyond. To the right of the gate, behind a high wall paralleling the entry walk, was a pool ringed by palms and a sea of stark white cement on which all kinds of outdoor furniture was arranged. And though it was far from Olympic size, when viewed from the air, the rectangular-shaped pool area dominated the front two-thirds of the property. And like most of the oddities he'd seen so far in Southern California, the need for an amenity like that at off-campus student housing totally escaped all reason.

Thanks to the rudimentary floor plan Nash had beamed via satellite to his laptop, Cade had a decent grasp of the building's layout. For instance, he knew that the first five floors had twenty-four units each, mostly efficiencies that were divided among the front and back of the V and separated by a central hall with the elevators located where the east and west wings met. And according to the architectural plans the sixth floor where Nadia's apartment was located housed eighteen two-bedroom units, nine to a side. He figured whoever designed the place numbered the rooms like every high-rise building he'd been in. Conditioning from the way we read or dictated by some universal building code, he hadn't a clue. However, the numbers invariably started lowest on the left and counted higher to the right. So Cade figured, if past experience held true within the Four Palms, the rooms on the ground floor would be numbered 101-124 with the apartments of the identical floor above numbered 201-224. On the *penthouse* level, Nadia's floor, the two-bedrooms would also be numbered, presumably, left to right, 601-618. And if that assumption was correct, Nadia's room, 610, should be near the elevators. Cade thought: *Only the best view for a fourth year student and daughter of a major in the United States Air Force. A bigwig in the 50th Space Satellite Warfare, to be more specific.*

Once he'd finished with his preps, Lopez called Ari with a brief situation report, letting him know they were about to ascend the stairs and that their comms might be compromised by the inches-thick steel-reinforced concrete walls once they entered the well.

Nearby, Cross and Griffin stood facing the rectangle of daylight. Scrutinizing the mass of Zs and going over options of egress aloud and wondering how, if they had to leave the way they had entered, they were going to get past the crowd with Nadia Nash in tow.

Suddenly remembering Raven's situation, Cade faced Lopez, raised his hands, and stated the obvious, "Time to make a call ... *east* or *west?* We need to get a move on."

Lopez didn't immediately speak. Instead, he looked to the SEALs for input.

Holding his suppressed carbine at a low ready, and shifting his weight from foot to foot unconsciously, Griffin said, "I'm thinking east wing first."

"I concur," said Cross. "We pick the lock and back away. See what comes out."

Nodding his approval, Cade glanced at the hollow-eyed corpses gathered at the gate. He said, "And if there are a hundred of those things in the stairway?"

Smiling and patting the half-dozen magazines Velcroed snugly in their sleeves on his chest, Lopez said, "I've got a hundred rounds of five ... five ... six for the demonios, right here."

With the metal gate rattling discordantly at their backs, the team powered on their night-vision devices. Leaving them flipped up, for now, they zippered single-file through the fallen corpses at a fast trot while taking care to avoid slipping on the pooled blood and detritus covering the already oil-stained cement.

Running point, Lopez ignored the elevator, hooked a right, and led the team through the gloom to the scratched and dented fireproof metal door.

"Opens outward," said Cross.

The door was labeled: *Stairs East to Floors 1-6*. Below that, most likely to alert emergency personnel, a warning—*NO ROOF ACCESS*—was emblazoned in large raised white lettering. And just outside the door, rising vertically from the cement floor, was a waist-high concrete pole sheathed with thin steel. About as wide around as Cade's arm, he figured it was placed there to protect a tenant who might happen to be emerging from the stairwell into the path of a moving vehicle. Or to spare the door from careless backing.

While Cross worked on the lock, Cade checked the sat-phone for any new messages. Finding nothing recent on the screen, he stowed it away in a thigh pocket.

Seconds later Cross had the lock defeated, passed the pick gun back to Cade, and was striking the door lightly with his open palm.

"Dinner bell for the dead," he said, looking back at the assembled team. But there was no immediate reaction from within. However, ten seconds later, when Cross reached out for the knob, a slight shuffling noise sounded from the other side of the windowless door. As the men brandishing guns and wrapped in body armor looked questions at one another, a repetitious scratching sound started up. Faint but determined. Like a woodworker finishing a prized piece with the finest grit paper.

"There's *something* in there," said Lopez, swallowing hard. "Wish Tice was here with his high-tech periscope thingy." Then, seeing a brief flash of the stairwell of death at the National Microbiology Laboratory in Winnipeg in his mind's eye, he shivered and performed the sign of the cross on himself and prayed to God that he wasn't about to relive that foray through Hell all over again.

"I just wish the Spook was still with us, *period*," stated Cade. "*Let's do this.*"

With the other three operators standing a few feet back, in a semicircle a shoulder's width apart, and training their weapons on the door, Cross hauled it open and crouched down and crabbed sideways out of the line of fire.

But the rifle fire never came.

However, the something that was on the other side of the door, a dirty orange tabby cat—easily fifteen pounds of purring, fur-covered fat—strutted past Lopez and into the garage. Green luminescent eyes sized up the team. Then the feline eyeballed the flesh-eaters rattling the gate. After a few seconds spent licking futilely at its fur and paws, the cat turned a circle and trotted nonchalantly back into the darkened stairwell.

Lopez shook his head and released the breath trapped in his chest. He initiated a quick comms check and, as the replies came in, he saw the rest of the team lowering their night vision devices in front of their eyes. Seeing the faint eerie green ovals reflecting off the others' eyes, he pulled his own down and said, "Weapons hot."

A series of soft clicks followed as safeties were thrown and lasers were powered on.

Assuming tacit approval, Cade stepped past Lopez. Without looking back he crossed the threshold and, with the wavering green laser beam probing the well ahead of him, started up the stairs.

The cat was nowhere to be found, and inside the roomy stairwell the stench of death was heavy on the cool air. Rendered in light green, the stairs were much wider than most he'd seen. In fact, three grown men could stand comfortably on the same tread. *For ease of moving larger pieces of furniture in-and-out*, Cade guessed. There were traction strips on the edges of all seventeen stairs between landings. Sturdy handrails were bolted into the walls on the left. On the right, the inner rail was bolted to the floor and followed the run up and bent around the blind corner at the mid-floor landing.

Taking the stairs slowly, one at a time, Cade made the landing and cut the corner by degrees. Held a hand up, craned his head around the inner rail, and simultaneously walked his gaze and laser beam up the run to the next rise.

"Clear," he whispered into the comms.

***

Ten minutes after entering the garage, the team was gathered together on the landing between floors two and three and, thankfully, since decimating the walkers in the garage, hadn't had to discharge their weapons since.

However, peering down on a sight that made him want to puke, Cade's finger was itching to pull the trigger. What he saw in front of his face rendered in a dozen shades of green made his heart skip a beat. He wasn't ready for it to end this way. But it was closure. Of that he was certain. Until he extracted his tactical flashlight, flipped up his NVGs, and looked at the scene from a different perspective and in a more revealing light.

Illuminated there on the landing was the fat tabby. And splayed out in a pool of dried blood, surrounded by dozens of crimson paw prints and an abundance of wilted flowers—their aromatic properties long dormant—was a young woman's corpse. Like Nadia, the blonde looked to have been in her early twenties. She had died on her back and, judging from the look of surprise frozen on her pallid face, she had been alive and free of the Omega virus when she passed.

Looking closer, Cade noticed that her neck was bent unnaturally, nearly ninety-degrees from vertical, and her face was turned in a direction contrary to the rest of her body. Nearly lost in the bright cone of light, and scattered about the landing in a wide arc radiating out from her gaping mouth, were numerous shiny white jagged shards of what Cade presumed were teeth that used to reside in her mouth.

Like a Slinky race halted mid-descent, clumps of clothing still on hangars littered the run of stairs from where the body had come to rest to the landing below. And clutched in the cadaver's right arm was more of the same, mainly blouses and tanks, also still on their plastic hangers.

Still suppressing the urge to blast all nine lives out of the opportunist feline, Cade barked, "*Git*," and nudged the fat tabby away from the decaying corpse with the business end of his carbine.

As the tabby scooted past his boots and up the stairs, Cross, who was standing over the corpse, said matter-of-factly, "Looks like this one died moving out."

"At least she didn't forget to *feed* the cat," said Griffin.

Lopez bowed his head.

Even Cross shot his SEAL brother a look that said: *Really?*

"That's uncalled for," Cade said as he went to a knee on the top stair. He removed the photo of Nadia from a pocket and compared it with the corpse. *Same build. Same hair.* Grateful he'd initially been mistaken, he took a fistful of blonde locks and craned the head around. *Close, but no cigar.* He let the head down to the cement easy then looked the body over from head-to-toe. The corpse's once bare midriff was now just a mass of flayed flesh, and snaking from a tear near the navel was a short length of intestine, glistening white and still wet with dark splotches of congealed blood.

The dead co-ed's eyes, earlobes, and lips were gone. *Hence the fat ass cat*, Cade thought morbidly.

But the nose was intact. So, to be certain, Cade compared it with the photo. Concluded that it was hooked a little. Not a cute button like Nadia's and Nash's.

"Not her," Cade said, total confidence in his voice. He rose up and pocketed the photo. Thumbed the light off and put it with the photo.

"Cat's a survivor, though," said Cross.

"In here it is," said Cade, drawing his NVGs back down over his eyes.

"Out there—" added Lopez, his voice soft and distant "—with the *demonios* ... it'd be nothing but gnawed-on bones before day's end."

"My money is on the cat," stated Griffin, adjusting his NVGs.

Already on the move, Cade said over the comms, "Couple of hundred stairs to go and a length of hall and we'll probably know one way or the other how Nadia fared."

Silently the others fell in behind and, after tackling the next several flights as cautiously as the first, they were on the top landing in front of a door identical to all of the others from the parking garage on up. It was wide and windowless and the dents and scratches marring the skin dispelled any notion that they were inside a hotel as the building's clean facade and swimming pool might suggest.

Cade put his ear to the door. Listened hard and detected what he thought were soft footfalls. Many of them in fact. And they were coming and going and seemingly stopping and starting at random.

Zs.

Lots of them.

Cade relayed his suspicions to the team in a hushed voice and called them into a huddle, and together they formed a semblance of a plan.

When the brief strategy session concluded, Cade turned away and retrieved the pick gun from his pocket. Without another word he took a knee by the door next to the bold tabby cat and attacked the lock.

Chapter 56

Three miles north of Woodruff, Brook hailed the Kids on the radio. Thirty seconds later the two trucks were pulled over tight on the shoulder, bumper to bumper, on a straight uphill stretch of 16, the Raptor still in the lead. Grasslands dominated on the right and there were no Zs or cars or dwellings for as far as the eye could see. A good distance away to the east some unnamed mountains rose up from the already high elevation of central Rich County. To the left, close in, hardscrabble foothills of another small range rose gently up and away from the road. Hardy ground-hugging plants dotted the ochre soil from the road to where the muted tan of the hills began.

Brook threw the transmission into *Park* and said, "Let's get this over with." She opened her door and jumped down to the road. Stalked the length of the truck, approached the idling Raptor and held a brief conversation with Taryn, informing her why they had stopped. When Brook walked away and looped around back of the Raptor, all three of its passengers were picking their jaws off the floorboards and a heated argument was underway—the topic: whether any of the businesses in Randolph would bear fruit. With Sasha the major proponent of them continuing on.

"No matter what," she said, both arms hanging over the seats, her red hair unruly and moving proportionately with her arms and hands, which were going in all directions as she pled her case. "It was my fault Raven got hurt in the first place. I should have known better ... I'm two and a half years older than her. And now Chief is hurt too."

"Don't beat yourself up," said Taryn. "Chief is an adult. He knew what he was getting himself into. And Raven ... she rides that bike like the devil whether she's in competition or not. Hell, she's Cade's daughter."

Wilson flicked his eyes to the rearview mirror. Said, "Brook's no slouch herself. I've seen her mad."

"What we're saying, Sash ..." Taryn glanced over her shoulder and saw the F-650's slab of a passenger door hinge open, Chief emerge, sans pants, and assume a stance against the front fender that looked more like something from an episode of *Cops* than a cursory inspection for zombie bites.

Wilson said, "I think what Taryn was trying to say is that the apple didn't fall far from the tree. Raven is going to be just fine when all is said and done."

Sasha shot him a glance that seemed to say: *What the hell does this have to do with fruit and gravity?*

Eyes still on Brook and Chief, Taryn added, "Wilson has a point, Sash. She'll probably kick your butt in the same race tomorrow with one hand tied behind her back. Let's all just pray that Brook is right about Chief and he's only got a few scratches and all he needs is a little antibiotic ointment."

Sasha said nothing. With the fate of two people resting on her shoulders, she melted back into her seat.

***

A full minute passed and not a word was spoken in the Raptor.

Wilson sat back tight against the seat and felt a rising tide of embarrassment for what Brook was having to do. Then he saw Chief's features. The tightly drawn lips and clenched jaw. Then Chief shifted, stretched out and put his palms up on the side of the hood. Empathizing wholly with the man for the indignation he was likely feeling from having to *drop trou* in front of God and nature while Cade's wife stooped near his dangling junk, Wilson tried his best to look away. But just like happening upon the broken glass and torn metal and yellow tarps of a fatal car wreck, he just couldn't tear his eyes from the life and death measures taking place.

When all was said and done and Chief was cinching his belt tight, Wilson didn't know any more about his status than when Brook had dropped the bombshell in their collective laps and turned and walked away without fielding questions.

All three Kids craned and watched Brook and Chief get back into the big truck. Then three heads swiveled forward and down and stared at the two-way radio in the console. Which remained silent even as the black Ford F-650 pulled onto the road and passed them by on the left.

Chapter 57

The band of light painting the first quarter-inch of chipped concrete in front of the sixth floor doors was proof enough the team would not be needing their night vision goggles from here on out. So each man took a second to flip them out of the way and then stacked up in a tight bunch next to the inward-swinging door. Each operator had his weapon at a low ready position and his free hand resting on the shooter's shoulder to his fore. A tactic employed for situational awareness, mainly. But also to keep the target four soldiers in bulky gear represented as small as possible. A vertical rectangle, two feet wide by four tall, ideally.

But a small target was the least of their problems. The dead wouldn't be shooting at them when they flowed through the doorway in a move rehearsed by each man hundreds of times over their varied careers. The flesh-eaters would, however, be onto them at once, '*Like stink on shit*,' as Desantos would have so eloquently put it if he were here.

Cade looked at the strip of light on the floor and waited for the shadow to transit past, then ticked off thirty seconds in his head to give whatever it was plenty of time to move off to the west, away from the stairwell door.

Having volunteered for point—or first man through the door—Cade counted down quietly from *five* and upon arriving at *one* hauled the door toward him, letting it skim close to his nose and chest before releasing the handle and creeping over the threshold, full of barely harnessed adrenaline and a healthy dose of fear.

He saw a sliver of threadbare mustard yellow carpet first. Saw that swirls and dots in a light turquoise were staggered here and there. *Paisley*, he had heard it called. Then he saw the blood trail. Or to be precise, blood trails. Plural. And that they were almost black and stood out starkly, like the paisley pattern, against the awful base color, told him that whatever had caused them was over and done.

Halfway through the door and moving, Cade tightened his grip on his carbine and swung the stubby suppressor right. He took a quick snap shot in his mind of everything there and saw only a door with a plastic sign featuring white stairs and next to them someone's stylized representation of licking flames—universal semaphore for fire escape. With no immediate threat in the short hall right, and seeing that the door opposite the stairwell labeled 601 was closed, Cade ducked low and craned his head left.

In the split second he spent assessing the danger in the hall, the gloved hand on his shoulder belonging to Cross never moved. In his peripheral Cade saw the four-inch suppressor attached to the pig snout of a barrel on the SEAL's MP7 holding steady. *Cool as ice*, thought Cade as he took a step left and swept his weapon with his line of sight, his situational awareness ratcheting up ten notches and everything in his cone of vision sharpening and seemingly slowing to a crawl. A fifth of a second later additional training kicked in and he said, "Right clear. Contact, left. Numerous Zulus ... three yards. Engaging," into the comms and a steady stream of brass began spewing from his carbine's ejection port.

The once beige walls and white ceiling instantly received a makeover as Cade took a knee near door 601 and walked accurate fire into the phalanx of Zs angling his way. He dropped three in quick succession. All co-eds. The brains and blood once contained inside the skulls of a pair of twenty-something males struck door 602 with a wet smack and instantly began a slow slide towards the carpeted floor. The third monster, a once darkly tanned bleached blonde with a large pair of paid-for boobs crammed into a blood-smeared tank, stumbled over the recently fallen and fell face first into a rectangle of light spilling from a nearby open door. Cade aimed for the crown of her head where a stripe of black roots presented a perfect vertical target amidst the peroxide affected tangle of hair. As he drew up the last couple of pounds of trigger pull the tabby cat bounced off his leg, took two long, stretched-out strides, and used the flailing undead student as a springboard. Tail big as a feather duster, the cat bounded down the hall, passed through a half-dozen similar bars of light streaming in through still more doors that had been left ajar, and disappeared through an inches-wide fissure at the base of a makeshift wall of furniture.

A half beat after the tabby made its escape, the rest of the team was in the hallway and a quick three-round burst from Cross's weapon stilled the Barbie-doll-looking Z.

Lopez and Griffin checked fire and watched as Cade and Cross dumped the rest of their ammo into the advancing dead.

Sticking to the plan, the first two through the door fell back to change mags and Lopez and Griffin filed ahead and engaged the remaining rotting corpses, leaving another half-dozen human shells leaking brains and body fluids on the soiled carpet.

While the Delta boys covered the hall, the SEALs cleared the four rooms on the left, starting at the nearest door which was labeled 602 and hanging wide open.

The pair was inside for a hard two-count before one of them bellowed *clear* and they were both exiting, weapons at a low ready, Cross in the lead, with Griff leaving the door hanging open to take advantage of the added light.

The door to 604 was locked so Cross picked it with Cade's tool. Inside he found the lone occupant in the bathtub. Cause of death: one jagged vertical wound starting at the left wrist and ending mid-inner forearm. Imperfect in its execution. But deadly just the same, resulting in a tub full of crimson water that contrasted sharply with the young male's alabaster pallor.

Rivulets of colorful melted wax from a handful of burned-out candles ringing the tub streaked its sides to the water line. The blade used to seal the deal was nowhere to be found. Cross guessed it had to be in with the wrinkled, decomposing corpse.

"Clear," Cross said into the comms. Then, taking a page from Lopez's book, performed the sign of the cross and said a prayer for the kid, both uncharacteristic moves for the laid-back operator.

The doors to rooms 606 and 608 were open. Once again Cross and Griff did the honors. Both rooms showed signs of being lived in after the outbreak. And, like the two apartments they'd already cleared, the toilet tanks here were bone dry and empty water bottles and junk food wrappers littered the floor.

Both rooms also showed signs of some kind of struggle. There were bloody handprints on the carpet and crimson black smears on the walls. Dirty clothing was strewn about and most of the inexpensive fiberboard furniture was overturned and in splinters.

In the hall Cross said to no one in particular, "Someone rode it out for quite a while in zero six and zero eight."

Lopez said, "And?"

"They bought it ... of course. Signs of a struggle. Blood. Same old same old."

"The domino effect," said Griff. "Seen it a hundred times. One turns and nobody has the stomach to do it in ..."

Cade said, "Eventually that one gets another, and another, and so on."

"Rinse and repeat," said Lopez, shaking his head. "Four down, five to go. Know what that means?"

Across the hall with his ear pressed to 603, Cade answered, "610 is on the other side of the elevator banks."

"Correct," said Lopez. He let his carbine hang from its tactical sling and sipped from his hydration pack. Clipped the tube to his shoulder, craned his head at the bend sixty feet in front of them. And finally, in a low voice tinged with impending doom, added. "To get to the west wing we're going to have to go through *that*."

Chapter 58

Looking directly at Chief while keeping the F-650's monstrous tires tracking true, Brook flat-out lied, "Yes ... *really*. I don't think any of them look like bites or even puncture wounds for that matter. Those are gouges made by fingernails. Hell, if I had a phone I'd take a picture and show you. Short of me tearing one of the mirrors off this beast ... as if I even had the strength to accomplish a feat like that ... you're going to have to take my word for it."

There was a ten-second stretch of silence filled only with the sound of tires thrumming on asphalt. Then the radio came alive. It was on low volume and the needy voice sounded distant.

Ignoring the radio, Brook went on, "But to be safe ... you know the drill. You do your part. And I promise. If it comes to it. I'll do my part." She could feel Chief's eyes boring into her.

He said, "*Promise?*"

Although she wanted so badly to tell Chief about the most important reason for Cade going on his latest mission, she held back and said only, "Cross my heart."

Adding to that, Chief said, "And hope to die ... a natural death."

Brook snatched up the Motorola two-way. "What?" she said, sounding annoyed.

Wilson said, "Sasha has to pee."

Having a hard time holding her tongue, Brook said, "OK. There's a real clear stretch coming up. Max could use a pit stop, I'm sure." She pulled over gradually. By the time the gravel crunched under the tires Max was on the seat beside Brook and sniffing Chief up and down, paying particular attention to his lower extremities.

Chief scratched Max between the ears. Said, "Turning crotch hound on us?" Oblivious to his condition, he opened his door and let the dog out. "Let's see what resides in the next town." He powered on the truck's navigation device and found some kind of an error code splashed on the screen. Short of calling the 1-888 number connected to it he was at a loss getting it to work.

**

Chief hit Brook with the bad news when she returned to the truck. "Just going to have to keep our eyes open, then," she said, still avoiding eye contact.

A beat later they were on the road. Same thrumming of the tires. Same uneasy silence. And the same driving order. The F-650 in the lead, with Taryn keeping the Raptor tucked in tight to the black truck's blood-streaked bumper.

All the while the three purple punctures Brook had located under Chief's right butt cheek wouldn't leave her mind. Not a good liar, she was surprised he hadn't called her on it.

So she locked her eyes forward and prayed for two things. One, that she was wrong about the wound. And two, if she wasn't, that Cade was on his way home with the proper remedy.

**

Three minutes later, a bullet-riddled road sign, the words on it reading *Randolph, Pop. 476*, zipped by on the right. The State Highway became another Main Street. It seemed to Brook some old rule book must have mandated every town and city include a Main Street in order to be recognized by the state or perhaps even the Union itself. But she knew that that was probably incorrect. The abundance of Main Streets was probably due to equal parts lack of imagination and mankind's natural inclination to cling to the familiar.

Some farmhouses with rusting farm implements and more broken-down cars than one residence needed sat near the town's outskirts. Barbed wire fences, some constraining small numbers of Zs inside their perimeter, bordered the road. Telephone poles, wires drooping under the weight of dozens of ravens and crows, paralleled the fencing overhead.

They crossed over a winding creek on a flat two-lane bridge with narrow sidewalks bordered by waist-high railings. Main Street stretched ahead of them and was lined with more telephone poles with thin wires crossing perpendicular to the road every few hundred feet.

Craning his head and peering east down a side street, Chief said, "Not much to this town either."

"It's all I've got," replied Brook.

"There's no other way to help Raven?"

"There are a couple of last resort things I think might work. But due to the fact she's pre-asthmatic I don't want to go that route unless I have to. Risk of infection runs pretty high." She slowed the F-650 to walking speed and let the truck's bumper nudge a small group of rotters out of their path. The hollow bangs of palms slapping along the truck's side rang out but thankfully the spine-tingling crunch and squelch of bone and internals pasted under the Ford F-650's tonnage never came.

Seeing Taryn successfully negotiate the cluster, Brook sped up to match the posted thirty-mile-an-hour limit. The end of town came and a Zions Bank and auto parts place slid by left and right, respectively. Brook continued on 16 looking for a place to turn around. Ahead, the low hills on their left curled around and caressed the horizon. A patchwork of some kind of crop, inexplicably still green, swung by outside the windows as Brook cranked the wheel and pulled a modified U-turn.

With the Ford's grill pointing south now, Brook stopped in the right lane, let the motor idle, and powered her window down.

The white rig pulled tight next to the black rig and Taryn pulsed her own window down. She said, "What now?"

"Hate to do it," Brook answered. "Since time is of the essence we have to split up."

The window aft of Taryn's rolled down and Sasha's tightened features framed by her wild red mane filled the opening. She asked softly, "How *is* Raven?" She thought: *And Chief?* But deathly afraid of the answer she might receive, couldn't bring herself to ask.

"No word yet," Brook answered. "But for now ... I'm taking that as good news."

Sasha nodded. Swallowed hard but still couldn't find the courage or words.

Taryn asked, "Where do you want us to search?"

"I'm going to canvas the town east to west starting with the first cross street. You go one more street south and start off to the right and then skip every other street."

"A modified grid pattern," added Chief.

Wilson's brow furrowed. He looked past Taryn, locked eyes with Chief, and asked, "Are you OK?"

Unsmiling, Chief merely nodded and again powered on the navigation unit to no positive result.

Seeing this, Brook released the brake and made room then waited while Taryn put the Raptor into a K-turn in the middle of North Main Street. When she saw the white truck's grill with its big black lettering spelling out FORD in her side mirror, she tromped the gas and was off to the races.

The first pass on East Field Street took Brook and Chief by a number of them on the left, fallow and brown, and then a few two-story houses ringed mostly with white picket fencing on the right. Another pass took them by a high school with darkened windows and brown grass and ringed by a six-foot-tall run of chain link. In there somewhere was a Mormon tabernacle. The tallest structure by far, and obviously the reason the town had continued growing for, presumably, an entire century after the building's foundation had been laid.

There were few Zs and even fewer places resembling a medical office. The only one of note was a squat brick building with a shingle hanging outside with one name on it—Jerry Layne—and the letters MD preceding it. *Private practice*, thought Brook as she pulled into the lot.

Chief hailed the Kids and filled them in. A beat later he and Brook were armed and picking their way over broken glass and ducking through the still locked but windowless front door.

Mainly to rouse any dead lurking in the gloom, Chief called out, "Hello," and trained his carbine at the darkened doorway to their fore.

Ten long seconds ticked by during which they heard nothing coming from the rooms in back. No moans. No rasps. No footfalls.

Then the unmistakable low rumble of the Raptor's motor filtered in from the street.

The radio crackled, and in case Brook and Chief had suddenly been struck deaf, Wilson said, "We're here. Want us to wait ... same as before?"

Chief keyed the radio and, adopting a firm tone, said, "No honking. And stay in the cab."

"Copy that," said Wilson.

***

Three minutes later Brook was in the parking lot, her chin touching her chest and both hands on her hips. To say she was utterly dejected would be an understatement. Old magazines and medical records weren't going to do her daughter, or Chief for that matter, any good.

Understandably, the place had been cleaned out of anything of use. There wasn't so much as one tiny gauge needle used for administering a diabetic a dose of insulin. And there wasn't even a tube of Neosporin that had gone overlooked.

However, in one drawer Brook had found, and quickly pocketed, a few blister packs of Celexa meant to be distributed as samples only. Twenty-four pills in total that she hoped to pass discretely to Daymon or Heidi as soon as possible.

"Nothing?"

"Nope, Taryn," Brook said, lying again. "Just a couple of six-year-old Sunset magazines and handouts pushing Viagra."

"I'm sorry," said Sasha, tears running down her cheeks.

"For the last time, Sasha. It was not your fault."

"How can I help?"

"Keep your eyes open for anything you think might have what we're looking for ... a store, vet's office, anything," answered Brook. She clambered aboard the Ford and slammed the door. She looked into the Raptor and locked eyes with Sasha, who was biting her quivering lower lip and nodding in acceptance to the task given her.

***

They'd been back trolling side streets for a couple of minutes and passed by the courthouse, a squat structure with far fewer stairs than its cousins in larger cities. There were no cars with county plates in the lot and so far the two-vehicle convoy had come across not one emergency vehicle in the entire town.

Trash, however, had accumulated underneath the front and rear bumpers of the handful of static cars left in places against the low—almost non-existent—curbs bordering both sides of Main. On one corner up ahead Brook saw what looked like a mom and pop general store. *Promising*, she thought to herself. But the positive feeling she'd felt in her gut disappeared a beat later when she spotted the twinkle of broken glass and realized the place had already been looted—and set fire to afterward. The door hung from one hinge and the flames had blackened the overhead sign leaving inky vertical streaks of soot obscuring the business's name.

Brook snatched up the radio. "Find anything?" she growled.

"Negative," said Wilson. "Just more rotters."

Brook hissed into the radio. "We're done here."

"Where to now?" asked Chief.

"Depends upon how you feel."

"I'm a little shaky," he conceded. "Probably because I haven't eaten for hours." And to confirm that his stomach made a low rumble.

Chapter 59
Schriever AFB

The mess dress blues were stored in a garment bag that Nash kept tucked away in a closet. Worn only during very special occasions, much like a civilian's tuxedo or ball gown, the ensemble displayed all of her ribbons and medals and had a frilly satin cummerbund and brass buttons. And as ornate as the thing was, even if it was put away in good shape, it always required special attention.

So Nash laid the uniform out on the small couch in the corner of her office. Then she fetched the lint brush and Brasso out of the garment bag's pouch.

With a dab of the Brasso on a moistened fabric scrap and applying a little elbow grease, Nash shined all of the buttons on her tunic to a high luster.

The lint brush took care of any rough spots, smoothing the navy blue wool out on the top and ankle length skirt with only a couple of passes.

The shoes didn't need much attention. Just a light buffing and they were shiny and reflecting her face all wavy and distorted like a funhouse mirror.

Nash put the shoes on the floor and went to the filing cabinet and retrieved her semiautomatic pistol. On the way back she took the photo of her and Nadia from the wall and placed it and the pistol, side-by-side, on her desk.

She picked up the full shot glass from her desk blotter and, without a toast or even pause, quickly downed the tequila.

After shedding her ACUs, she tossed them in a pile in the corner. She poured another shot and dressed in her mess dress, being careful to remain regulation while doing so.

Lastly, saying screw it to the wrinkles, she sat at her desk, her gaze moving between the photo and the shot glass.

The decision-making process lasted a few seconds and the tequila was downed and Nash was removing the magazine from her weapon. She racked the slide back and found the chamber clear. Next she inserted the magazine and placed the pistol on the blotter next to her open laptop and the satellite phone.

She filled the glass again and started the image running on the laptop's screen and watched D.C. die for what seemed like the twentieth time. And as she did she couldn't help thinking about what was happening 2,300 miles away from the nation's capital when the heartbreaking footage was being recorded.

She picked up the glass and said, "To you, Nadia," and just held it aloft, her eyes misting over.

She downed the shot and thought to herself, "And to you, Cade Grayson. Bring my girl back. And the information on those hard drives. Two birds ... one stone."

Eden Compound

After enduring a thorough full-body inspection from a young blonde woman named Heidi and having been declared bite free as a result, Glenda was given a towel and led to a crudely strung tarpaulin shower stall and given a five-gallon bucket full of sun-warmed water. The thought of sudsing up and rinsing with a commodity she knew was worth its weight in gold for the scattered pockets of humanity trying to ride this mess out made her feel a pang of guilt and she balked at first.

But the thin fellow who relieved Heidi and introduced himself as Tran had insisted. Wouldn't take *no* for an answer. *There's a creek nearby*, he had said. *We'll collect more.* So, reluctantly, again, Glenda stripped away her jeans and top and finished the job she had started in the creek earlier, vigorously scrubbing away the bits and pieces of Louie that still clung to her.

Afterward Tran had given her a full set of sand-colored army fatigues, two sizes too big, and a fresh pair of socks which felt like butter against her bruised and blistered feet. He also provided some kind of a prepackaged meal that was appetizing enough and which she ate hungrily.

Finally, with the promised hot meal of venison and fresh foraged greens and mushrooms keeping her mind occupied, Glenda was handed off to one of her rescuers—a balding man named Jimmy—who gave her a tour of the well-thought-out compound.

From the look of her guide, who was carrying an extra twenty pounds and hiding a double chin and filled-out cheeks behind a close cropped beard, hot meals looked to be a frequent occurrence and something Glenda Gladson could get used to.

After meeting another of the survivors named Seth, a young man with a budding beard and long stringy hair parted in the middle and who looked like he would be more at home at Haight-Ashbury during the Summer of Love than lording it over a high-tech security system, Glenda was shown to a room filled with dry goods and supplies. There, Foley set up a cot for her and started a gentle interrogation. A sort of fact-finding interview sans turning of screws or vicious backhands. If she said anything that sent up a red flag he'd note it and have Duncan or Cade follow up. He learned about the attack by men in helicopters on the brigands who had been terrorizing Huntsville. Immediately he thought of Carson and Bishop's men. Better odds of getting struck by lightning, he thought, than there being another group of killers out there with black helicopters who left death cards scattered about their fallen victims.

The story of her trek from there was remarkable. He was really struck how she'd fashioned her armor from magazines and duct tape and instantly thought of the stacks of Guns and Ammo and Field and Stream magazines sitting in his home back in Idaho.

But the thing that nearly knocked him over was that, like Brook, the matronly soft-spoken woman used to be a nurse. Hopes buoyed, he led her to the Kids' quarters not only to meet Raven, who was awake and had stopped coughing, but to mine her for a second professional opinion. Which after a three-minute exam was relayed to him in private and was precisely what Brook had said before setting out on her foraging mission.

So he left Glenda with Heidi and Raven and went topside to get ahold of Brook and relay the good news. Maybe take a load off the woman's shoulders while she was away from her ailing daughter.

Chapter 60

The navigation system was still glitching and not showing the business, town, or road names, let alone the distances between. But nearing the junction with State Route 39 and with the bust of a town, Woodruff, gliding by, Brook spotted a north-facing sign that indicated Bear River, Wyoming was thirteen miles south and Evanston an additional ten beyond it. *Last resort*, thought Brook.

Then there was a warbling sound she was unaccustomed to hearing. She looked at the two-way radio. Furrowed her brow and took her foot off the accelerator while digging in a pocket for the satellite phone.

Chief wiped his brow and stuffed his handkerchief back into his pocket. He opened the console and the electronic tone intensified, filling the cab. "It's the long range set," he said, fishing out the bulky black half-of-a-brick-sized CB radio.

Brook put the sat-phone aside and took the CB from Chief. She spent a few seconds looking for a way to receive the transmission. Finally she keyed the correct button and listened as Foley caught her up to date on the new arrival.

"What's your gut telling you?" she asked.

"She's legit. I think she'll be a real asset going forward," he answered. "And she's with it too. A real survivor ... for sure."

"Keep an eye on her, though. I crapped out in Woodruff and Randolph."

"Nothing?"

"Nothing," replied Brook. "So we're going south. Maybe Bear Lake or Evanston, which are just over the border in Wyoming, will have what we need."

"Alright," said Foley. "I'll keep this radio close. Supposed to have a forty-mile range. Call if you need anything. And stay frosty."

Suppressing a chuckle, Brook said, "You do the same."

"Why didn't you tell him about me?"

"Because you're not bit," she said, not so sure if the statement was still a lie or not. But she thought: *If you are there's nothing I can do about it until Cade returns with the carrots Nash dangled in front of him.*

Chief said nothing. Instead he peered at the desert outside the window, dabbing at his forehead.

Just before the junction with 39, Brook took her eyes from the road on the gentle right-hand sweeper and set the radio next to the smaller Motorola in the console. She slowed some more and looked at Chief and didn't like what she saw. Applying more brake, she asked him to get on the radio and warn the Kids not to look at Jenkins's corpse. When she returned her eyes to the road ahead, with the F-650 now rolling at a slow crawl, she saw another vehicle pulled up close to Jenkins's high-centered Tahoe and completely blocking the northbound lane, its front end facing directly at her.

After a couple of seconds she decided that the early model SUV, boxy and painted in a woodland camouflage pattern of browns and greens with black splotches simulating shadow, was an old Army surplus Bronco or Blazer.

The Tahoe's driver side door was open and a wiry-looking man, or teenager—Brook couldn't tell from this distance—had his arms wrapped around Jenkins's lifeless body and was manhandling it from behind the steering wheel. At almost the same instant that she saw the person, the person heard the Ford's engine note and looked up, surprise etched on his face. In the next heartbeat the person let go of Jenkins's corpse and Brook saw the blood-soaked upper torso fall the three feet to the road and what was left of the dead man's mangled head strike the blacktop and bounce a couple of times before going still.

With a pair of binoculars already raised to his eyes, Chief said, "There's someone else ... a woman. She's crouched behind the camouflaged rig's passenger-side quarter-panel."

The Ford finally crunched to a halt on the shoulder a third of a football field from the clogged intersection, with its rounded front end partially blocking the right lane at about a sixty-degree angle. A tick later the radio came alive with Wilson chattering excitedly and telling them everything about the situation that they already knew.

Hearing the squelch and pop of gravel as the Raptor pulled in behind the F-650, Chief lowered the binoculars for a tick, snatched up the two-way, and began relaying a play-by-play to the Kids. He said, "I see two bodies. Both of them are armed—" He squinted hard into the field glasses and added, "—rifles and side arms only ... as far as I can tell." There was a pause as he muted the radio and informed Brook that the two would-be scavengers were about Taryn and Wilson's age.

To that Brook shrugged. Age was only a number in the apocalypse.

Still glassing the scene, Chief said, "Now they're taking cover behind their rig. The male is behind the driver's side door. The female is near the rear bumper ... passenger side, crouched down. Be advised ..." He looked at Brook as he spoke the last five words, "... she's wearing a ballistic vest."

"Only the two of them?" whispered Brook.

Chief put the field glasses back to use. He made a ten-second sweep of the vehicle-clogged 39/16 juncture and beyond, paying closer attention to the grassy shoulders and interiors of all three vehicles. The bus was on its side, and running horizontal on its grease-stained underbelly was a thick driveshaft and a mess of exhaust pipes. Splitting them up vertically were the two tree-trunk-sized axles still shod with six oversized commercial grade tires, two up front and four bolted two to a side—dually style—at the rear. Save for the open doors, the Tahoe seemed undisturbed atop the mass of bodies that were now stilled, killed by the scavengers, presumably. Finally, having discerned as much as he could from afar, Chief declared that there was no one else up ahead.

"We're going by them no matter what. Dead or alive ... it's their call," said Brook as she unbelted and kicked open her door.

"What should we do?" asked Wilson over the radio.

Ignoring the radio, Brook turned from where she was crouched near the F-650's left front tire and waved Wilson and Taryn forward.

She conferred with the pair for a second then sent them back to the Raptor, where Taryn slid back behind the wheel and Wilson climbed up into the bed and sat, back against the cab, waiting for his cue.

Come on kids ... throw up a white flag, thought Brook. *You're way outgunned.*

A minute passed and Brook nodded to Chief, who with as much bass as he could muster and doing his best to project his voice down the road, ordered the pair to throw their weapons down and put their hands into the air.

But the only thing being thrown from behind the rattle-can-painted 4x4 were a couple of middle fingers. Then the male declared that they owned Woodruff and everything south. The girl spoke up and in a shrill voice ordered Chief and the others to turn around and leave.

"Can't do it," shouted Chief. "Make way. We're going to pass."

The scavengers' body language changed as they used some colorful words to defame Chief and the proverbial horse he rode in on.

Brook inched her head around the angular metal bumper and was immediately pelted with chips of matte black paint and felt her own blood, hot and sticky, seeping from her hairline and wetting her forehead.

The sound of gunfire his cue, Wilson shouldered his carbine, took a deep breath that did little to calm his nerves, and rose to standing. He planted his elbows on the sun-warmed sheet metal and laid his rifle over the Raptor's moon roof. Pressing his lower body firmly against the back of the cab, he flicked the selector to *Single* and peered through the 3x magnifier, searching for the woman.

A tick after being sprayed in the face with tiny fragments of God knows what, Brook had the shooter's head bracketed in her sights and a volley of answering gunfire erupted from behind and above. Finger tensing on the trigger, Brook heard Cade's voice in her head. *Never use a vehicle's door for cover if there's something else nearby.* Which she'd already done without thinking. However, the kid shooting at her had not. And seeing as how he wasn't a Z, she had no reason to go for a headshot. Much more difficult. Then Cade's voice again, reminding her to shoot for *center mass.*

So she adjusted her aim lower by a couple of degrees, took a calming breath, and drew back the rest of the trigger pressure. And then after the first bullet left the muzzle, repeated the latter part of the process continuously for three seconds until there were six puckered dents grouped closely together chest-high in the 4x4's camouflaged sheet metal.

A surprised look on the kid's face was the first indication that the 5.56 hardball ammo had continued on through the door's internals and penetrated the inner trim and found flesh. And happening near simultaneously, the second indicator, caused by a ripple effect from the projectile's kinetic energy and trailing shockwave, was a violent eruption of pebbled glass and pulped cardboard and flecks of sun-hardened vinyl.

Shots three through six must have struck the body as it melted vertically into the ground, because the initial split-second scream coming from the kid's mouth was silenced mid-collapse.

From his perch in the Raptor's bed Wilson continued taking single potshots at the small form crouched down behind the camo 4x4. He heard Chief's instruction: *Keep her head down so I can flank her.*

Already one step ahead of Wilson, at the onset of gunfire Chief had angled to his right and gone into a low crawl in the nearby ditch. By the time Brook's volley went silent he was a dozen feet beyond the F-650's right front tire, rifle tucked in tight and peering through the roadside grass.

Magnified by the scope atop his carbine Chief could barely make out the woman's knees where they met the asphalt near the camo rig's jacked-up rear end. He hovered the crosshairs on a square foot of air above and behind the diamond plate bumper near where the whip antenna was bolted to the quarter panel. He waited a few seconds and, when Wilson's firing stopped altogether, drew a few pounds of pressure off the trigger. A tick later, as expected, human nature overcame fear and the woman, lips pursed into a thin white line, poked her head out from behind the vehicle.

With his stomach in knots, whether from the deed he was about to commit, or something else entirely, Chief took the shot. The 5.56 left the muzzle traveling 3,100 feet per second and in less than a fifth of that the woman's head snapped back and a halo of pink blossomed where it had been. In the next instant she was flat on her back, one knee pointing skyward, left arm twitching.

The hollow clang of his boots on the truck's metal bed preceded Wilson bellowing, "They're both hit," as he jumped down to the road.

Then in the next beat, with the report of Chief's shot still rolling across the open range, Brook called out for help. Saying she couldn't see.

Chapter 61

The *that* that Cade had alluded to was a barricade made from hardwood desks, rolling ergonomic chairs, computers, printers, monitors, cheap fiberboard drawers and the skeletal dressers they belonged in.

There were comforters and shower curtains and beach towels draped over the jumble making seeing anything on the other side difficult. All in all it looked as if the well-thought-out barrier had been constructed over time. And the fact that (so far) all of the Zs the team had encountered had been on this side of Mount OfficeMax, whoever built the thing deserved to live. Or at the very least—if they hadn't benefitted from the engineering masterpiece—a posthumous medal was in order.

Accentuated by the gun smoke haze, pinpricks of light shone through the barrier here and there. The air smelled of death and gunpowder and the sour pong of fear-laced sweat.

"Let's yank the thing down," Griffin said, bouncing subtly from foot to foot.

"Everything is a nail to you guys," Lopez said. He pulled aside a shower curtain with a floral pattern and black mold growing on the lower six inches. Peered beyond the wheeled base of a high-backed fabric chair. After a second's scrutiny he let the vinyl curtain fall back into place, turned and said, "Let's hammer the dead through this thing first. *Then* you can demo it. What say you, Griff?"

With a wide grin parting his face, Griffin said, "Copy that."

Cade looked behind them only to see the tabby lounging on the paisley carpet and grooming itself. "I have a hunch," he said. "I'm going to check the fire escape. Give me a minute before you start tearing that thing down."

Sipping from his hydration pack, Cross said, "Please share."

Cade held up one finger and said, "One minute." He hustled down the hall past the wildly contorted leaking bodies the way they had come and stopped at the far end near where they'd exited the stairway from the garage. Pressed his ear to the fire escape door and heard only the soft murmur of the dead he knew were out there somewhere. Conditioned to expect the attention- getting wail of an alarm, he threw the deadbolt and slowly cracked the steel door open a few inches. When no alarm blared he pushed ahead, leaned out, and looked down.

The cursory glance told him all he needed to know. Unlike the building's internal stairs, the escape stairs didn't have the benefit of a long run. Therefore the entire run was ridiculously steep and switched back multiple times. About sixty degrees steep, he guessed. Nothing easy to navigate for a group of guys wearing body armor and carrying weapons and gear all over their bodies. And a monumental task to negotiate while lugging a hundred pounds of dead weight in a makeshift litter no matter the garb.

On the street below, through the gently swaying palm fronds, he could see twenty or thirty flesh-eaters. Working the scenario through his head he decided that even if they took Nadia down in a litter their combat boots beating the steel rungs would be enough to get them noticed and draw a bigger crowd before they reached the building's middle floors. And if they somehow successfully fought their way through the crowd at the bottom there was still the matter of getting the girl to the extraction point with hungry Zs in hot pursuit. *It was going to have to be the front entry or the garage*, he thought to himself.

So he closed and locked the door and returned to the barricade. When he arrived he quickly voiced the thought he had just had to the assembled team and let it be known that he was leaning towards going out the way they had come in—but with a little added *wrinkle*.

331

Lopez nodded and the team began tearing down the sheets and towels; in no time walkers had emerged out of, Cade guessed, apartment doors left open beyond the barricade and were hissing and moaning as they approached.

Cade tore down a Hello Kitty bedspread and saw, on the right, the main source of natural light spilling in, the two empty glass elevator bays he'd noticed from the air. And through the staggered panes of glass he noticed the building's west side angling away slightly to the right. Closer in he saw a bank of mirrored windows he pegged as belonging to Apartment 610—Nadia's place. They were all closed, and due to the angle of deflection he couldn't make out any movement behind them.

Sticking his M4 through the newly created opening, Lopez said, "Going hot. Engaging."

There was the sound of brass tinkling off the door and wall to Cade's right and the soft report of the suppressed gunfire echoing off the drop-down ceiling tiles and walls all around the team.

One by one the creatures dropped like marionettes, their strings snipped.

A few long seconds ticked by with Lopez sighting down his weapon and waiting. During those seconds, as eddies of gun smoke danced through the light spill from the elevator windows, the only sound in the hallway was of the men breathing and the rustle of Griffin's uniform as he paced along the barrier.

Changing out the partial magazine, Lopez looked to the SEALs and said, "Hammer time."

On the lookout down the hall for additional flesh-eaters, Cade and Lopez stood as far left as possible, while, with a good deal of huffing and puffing and smashing of furniture, Griffin and Cross created a sizable opening in the barrier near the elevator doors on their right.

Two minutes after Lopez decimated the demonios the team padded through the breach and, while Griff and Cross moved the bloodied corpses from their path, Cade and Lopez conducted a quick sweep of the rest of the east wing hallway, closing any doors that were open.

Once the team reconvened in front of 610, Lopez banged a fist on the door and then pressed his ear to the cool metal skin below the brass numbers and listened hard. A few seconds went by and then he stood up straight, shaking his head and mouthing, "Nothing."

Cade moved forward, took a knee and, using the pick gun, defeated the lock in a matter of seconds.

Just like in the stairwell the team stacked up hand on shoulder: Cade, Lopez, Cross, and Griffin.

The brushed nickel knob made a clicking noise when Cade turned it. He paused and listened again. Still nothing moved inside. So, feeling Lopez's hand resting on his right shoulder, he pushed the door in and stalked over the threshold, taking in everything through the holographic sight mounted atop the M4. Details registered in his mind like scenes cycling through a View Master. A kitchenette full of miniature appliances on the right: Fridge, stove, and dishwasher. A table awash in hardened candle wax and two chairs up against the window. Next to it a water cooler and an upturned plastic bottle attached with not so much as a drop of condensation inside it. On the floor, on its side, was another five-gallon empty, and strewn about were dozens of single serving water bottles, also empty.

Flat light splashed the walls gold as Cade waded through the mess on the floor and curled left. Instantly he saw the living room was barren, its contents no doubt added to the zombie barrier in the hall. He called out, "Clear," and proceeded towards an open door at the far left corner of the room.

Three paces across the carpeted floor and he was at the door, crouching and staring into the gloom. "Nadia," he called.

Nothing.

As his eyes adjusted, he saw there was a twin-size mattress on the floor. On the mattress was a blanket and under the blanket was a small inert form.

"Nadia."

Still nothing.

Cade looked at the men assembled at his six and saw an eagerness to help in Griffin's eyes. Cross was covering the door and staring at the tabby cat staring at him. Lopez was hailing the waiting Ghost Hawk, obviously anxious to offer up a situation report.

A second went by and Lopez said, "Wait one," and looked a question at Cade.

"I've got this," Cade said. He flicked his light on and entered the tiny room. The air was still and smelled of feces and urine. Straight ahead was a second door likely leading to a bathroom and inoperable toilet, which he gathered to be the source of the stench. Since the form didn't react to his presence he spent a half-beat checking the next room. He cut the corner with the business end of his M4 and craned around the door frame looking right. He saw the source of the stench: dark brown water in the toilet bowl. The porcelain tank lid was on the floor and the tank was empty, the flapper in the up position. Beyond it was a tiny wall-mounted sink, also dry.

There were towels strewn about the floor and then he saw the standup shower at the back of the room, minus its curtain and also empty, save for what looked like half a dozen different shampoo bottles. Once again he announced, "Clear," then ducked back into the bedroom and crept to the inert form on the low bed and prodded it gently with the carbine's suppressor. Instantly there was a faint guttural moan. He called, "Nadia?" then bent over the waif-like form and peeled the thin sheet away.

What he saw stirred up a plethora of stuffed emotion. There on the bed was a woman no bigger than Brook, clad in tank top and shorts and staring up at the ceiling. In profile the woman's button nose was unmistakably Nash. And though it was matted and greasy, the mane of blonde hair resembled Nadia's from the photo. However, the eyes staring up at him did not. They were dull and fixed on the ceiling and for a beat he thought she was infected. Until she said, "Mom." It was barely above a whisper but unmistakable.

"It's Nadia. She's still alive," Cade blurted.

Suddenly Lopez was chattering into the comms, filling Ari in and setting up their next course of action.

Then, as if a switch had been flicked, Griffin was in full-on corpsman mode and Cade found himself swept to the wayside. In seconds the SEAL had his rucksack off and was unfurling a rubber tube, tearing packaging with his teeth and spitting the remnants on the floor.

Cade stood up and backed away, giving the man room to work. Watched over Griffin's shoulder as he expertly inserted a tapered needle into Nadia's arm and attached a bag full of a clear solution, likely Ringer's lactate.

Griffin asked, "What's your name?"

Head lolling side to side, Nadia again said, "Mom?"

With Ari standing by and waiting for word to be passed from Griffin to Lopez that Nadia was stabilized and ready to be moved, Cade pulled Cross aside and detailed the *wrinkle* that he had alluded to minutes ago.

Cross nodded an affirmative to Cade. He crabbed past Griffin and said, "We'll be back in a minute with a litter to carry her down the stairs."

Resting one hand on Nadia's wrist and checking her radial pulse, Griffin looked up from what he was doing, nodded, and said, "We can move her whenever you're ready. She looks worse off than she is."

Hearing this, Nadia lifted her head off the pillow and her eyes went to the floor beside the bed. "Someone please bring my phone. All of my pictures of Brian are on there."

Lopez looked at Cade. Tilted his head and mouthed, "Brian?"

Cade shrugged.

Chalking the request up to delirium, Lopez said, "Which stairwell you think is best ... east or west?"

Cade thought about it for a second and said, "The Zs in the hall were probably on another floor and heard the commotion ... bodies falling ... us opening and closing doors. I'd be willing to bet they came up the west stairway. The door was hanging open when I got to it."

"It was open when I cleared the hall," said, Cross. "I didn't hear anything down there when I sealed it up."

Nadia said, "Brian went out that way ten days ago and didn't come back."

"Probably why it was unlocked," Cross said to Cade. "Best to stick with what we know."

"East it is," agreed Cade.

"Copy that," said Lopez. "I'll have Ari move in for the extraction. South of the parking lot?"

"Gonna have to be," answered Cade.

"I'll take care of the west fire escape," said Cross.

Cade shrugged off his pack and retrieved a pair of flashbangs and an olive-green-colored fragmentation grenade. "Let's go," he said, leaving his rifle behind and heading for the door.

"In one mike," said Cross, looking at his watch.

Cade drew his suppressed Glock 17 and, after consulting his Suunto, said, "One mike. On my mark. *Mark.*"

Cade closed the door to 610 behind them, peeled off left, and trotted down the hallway.

Meanwhile Cross padded off in the opposite direction, stepping over fallen Z corpses and heading for the fire escape at the far end of the gloomy corridor.

By the time Cade reached the fire escape door he'd already burned forty seconds negotiating the warren of stacked furniture and zippering through the tangle of twice-dead corpses. He shouldered it open and pulled the pin on a cylindrical flashbang stun-grenade. Held the spoon down and picked out a spot on the ground between the palm trees. Once his watch confirmed a minute had passed he let the flashbang fly. Then, in quick succession, he tossed an egg-shaped fragmentation grenade and a second flashbang over the rail.

The zombies below didn't know what had hit them. First the brilliant light and sharp report given off by the initial flashbang drew them closer to the sidewalk at the foot of the building. Then the frag went off in their midst, sending mostly ineffective shrapnel flying into unfeeling flesh. A millisecond later a concussive blast wave shook the palm fronds and rolled up the building's side. In the next breath Cade saw the second flashbang produce a sun-like flare of light and hopefully the start to a chain reaction drawing Zs to the site from blocks around.

Near simultaneous with the reports of his grenades going off, Cade heard the muffled *pop-whoomph-pop* of Cross's grenades doing their thing on the building's west side.

GHOSTS: SURVIVING THE ZOMBIE APOCALYPSE

Before stepping back inside Cade looked over the fire escape's safety railing and saw the Zs trickling in from three points of the compass. *Mission accomplished*, he thought as he turned and pulled the door behind him, nearly squashing the tabby underfoot. He paused for a second in thought and then cracked the door a few more inches and set the furry survivor free.

"Operation Wrinkle enacted," said Cross, tongue-in-cheek, over the comms. "Heading back to 610."

Cade was already at the Great Wall of furniture with the satellite phone out and finishing up the latter of two text messages. He said, "Roger that. I'll get the sheets for the litter." He finished tapping out the rest of the message and hit the green button, sending it up into space. Then he collected an armful of sheets from a nearby vacated room and hurried back to 610.

***

After picking their way past the dead girl in the east stairwell the team spent ten minutes at the bottom behind the closed door breathing in the cool, carrion-scented air while they waited for the all clear from Jedi One-One so they could make a run for it.

During that time the medicine flowing into Nadia's vein and being absorbed into her system was having the desired effect. A little of her normal color had returned and she had become talkative.

In the time it took Cade to check his weapons and cinch up his pack he learned from Nadia that the Brian whom she had asked about was her twenty-year-old boyfriend. After finding out that there was no way for them to get to the FEMA facility at Terminal Island they had to run a gauntlet of undead and looters just to get back here. Their food ran out three weeks ago and Brian started going outside to look for more. Then, choking back tears, she said he went out ten days ago and came back with only a meager amount of food and water with a fresh bite wound on his forearm. And then the tears really flowed and her sobs echoed in the stairwell as she recounted how, to keep from turning in her presence, he left on his own power and she hadn't seen him since.

***

Still waiting for the *'Go'* call from the chopper, Lopez asked, "What did you do then?"

"Ate the food sparingly but didn't do well rationing out the water," she said, eyes red and watery. "Then four days ago I started drinking my own pee."

"You did what you had to do. Hell, you were at death's door," said Griffin as he discarded the partial and attached a fresh bag of the same solution to the IV line. "And the Pale Rider was just about to usher you in."

Changing the subject, Lopez said, "Your mom will be so happy to see you. She moved heaven and—" he paused mid-sentence and listened as a call came in over the comms. He squeezed Nadia's shoulder, gently. "I'll finish the story for you later. Our freedom bird awaits."

Cade said, "Lock and load," and lowered his M4 and shouldered the door open.

Chapter 62

Handing Brook another of the plastic gas cans, Chief said, "That's the last of them." He took the empty from her and added, "I noticed you took your time bandaging yourself up. And then filling the truck when you know that it has a pair of reserve tanks. I think you're stalling. Even if for a minute or five ... you're consciously or subconsciously delaying the inevitable."

Sticking the flexible spout into the truck's filler neck, Brook said, "What do you mean?"

"We're going to have to move that camo rig and the bodies if we're going any farther south ... and Jenkins will have to be moved off the road."

Wilson tossed an empty gas can into the Raptor's bed and said, "We should take him back and bury him with the others."

"Who's going to do *that?*" said Sasha.

"I will," replied Wilson.

With no hesitation, Taryn said, "I'll help you."

Kicking a pebble off the road with her toe, Sasha looked up and said with a measure of reluctance, "I can help too."

"Sis is growing a pair," Wilson said. He hugged Sasha around the shoulder and started walking her towards the passenger doors. Along the way he added, "Let's get going before she has second thoughts."

With a welling sense of pride, Brook watched the exchange take place. Then she rattled the upside down can, getting every last drop into the Ford's tank. Looked around and called for Max in a low voice. A second later the Shepherd bolted from the tall grass where Chief had been prone and shooting from earlier and launched himself up and into the F-650 through the open passenger door.

Chief climbed into the truck and said to Brook, "I'll put the Bronco ... or whatever that camouflage thing is into neutral and you use this rig to push it out of the way."

Brook tossed the empty can in back and twisted the gas cap closed. Slammed the filler door shut. Climbing behind the wheel, she said, "Works for me. But don't think I'm trying to get out of helping with the bodies." She thought: *Least I can do since I killed the kid.*

As if he were reading her mind at that moment, Chief said, "Don't beat yourself up about the young man. He shot at us first and deserved what he got."

Brook turned the key, cranking the motor to life. Her hand went to the blood-dampened swatch of gauze taped over the gashes on her forehead. She said, "Bleeding out on a lonely stretch of highway is a pretty lopsided tradeoff for a couple of lead fragments to the face."

Chief threw a visible shudder. He coughed and said, "We reap what we sow. Don't we?"

Chapter 63

While Cade and Lopez grabbed onto the roll-up gate, the other two operators lowered Nadia and the thrown-together litter to the ground and readied their weapons.

The half-dozen die hard flesh-eaters that weren't fooled by the twin diversions created by Cade and Cross were gripping the metal links and growling and hissing at the fresh meat just a yard away from them.

Adding to the hair-raising din of the dead, the strange harmonic vibrations given off by the stealth helicopter were felt by all and growing stronger with each passing second.

"On three," said Cade. He set his pistol near his feet, began counting and, on three, working together with Lopez, clean-jerked the gate upward in its tracks.

The resulting clatter seemed to confuse the Zs for a moment. Two of them, still gripping the gate's articulated link panel, took a brief ride upward before the heavy gauge shroud protecting the motor and moving parts sheared their hands off at the wrists. Oblivious to what would prove to be a fatal bleed-out event to a living, breathing person, the Zs crashed to the ground and at once struggled to rise.

No longer held back by the gate, and propelled forward faster than normal because of the slight grade, the four Zs still on their feet staggered into the underground garage. Eyes filled with purpose and radiating an insatiable hunger, like a single-thinking school of piranha, they angled right and converged on the nearest food source that just so happened to be Lopez.

On one knee and sighting down the barrel of his stubby MP7, Cross let loose with two separate three-round-bursts that pulped the pair of rotters nearest the Delta shooter. Casings were pinging and skittering down the ramp, and before the decaying bodies hit the ground Griffin was in the fight, his carbine jumping subtly and silently as he delivered double-taps to the other two ambulatory corpses.

Meanwhile, Cade had snatched up the suppressed Glock and, while the struggling Zs were leaving wet kisses of crimson on the cement with their bloody stumps, he closed the distance and began delivering efficient, near silent, double-taps of his own.

Propelled by gravity and on a collision course with Nadia, one of the four Zs taken out by the SEALs started a slow log roll down the ramp.

Seeing this, Lopez hustled over and planted a boot on the limp corpse, stopping it rolling, and then waited for Griffin and Cross to get ahold of the litter.

Lopez said, "Good to go?"

Cross said, "Thanks."

Lopez hopped over the putrid Z and let gravity finish what it started.

Two blocks south of the Four Palms, Ari was holding the Ghost Hawk in a steady hover and watching the parking lot on the monitor centered on his glass cockpit. Suddenly there was movement in the dark rectangle and he saw a pair of shadowy forms approach the gate. A second later the gate was disappearing upward. Then he saw the monsters on the ramp falling in pairs, six in total, and before he could ask for a sit-rep, the operators were moving out into the light, two of them carrying a body in a litter.

"One mike," said Ari calmly into his boom mic. "You've got Zs vectoring in from the north. They're splitting the building and heading south along both the east and west side. I'm coming in guns hot then setting her down near the white compact car in the parking lot."

Head on a swivel and trying to locate the target vehicle, Cade answered Ari with a clipped, "Copy that." In his left side vision he detected the blur of black swooping in, and like he imagined an anxiety attack might start, he felt the bass note from the baffled rotor threatening to steal his breath. But the thought was fleeting because the tearing sound of the mini-gun started up and set his ears to ringing.

He located the white Honda at about the same time he saw the lick of flame and chain of tracers rip into a throng of Zs rounding the building's west side. The speeding projectiles cleaved rotted body parts off the shambling mass, and as quickly as the cacophony started, the gun went quiet and the chopped-up corpses were sprawled and sullying the sidewalk.

Evidently Doctor Silence wasn't finished. The Dillon came alive again above and behind Cade to the east, and for two long seconds as he ran toward the LZ the sickening sounds of bullets slapping flesh and splintering bone and hundreds of shell casings pinging off the cars and asphalt seemed to be following him. But he didn't look back. He kept pace with Griffin and Cross, felt rotor wash blasting him from directly overhead, and then breathed in a lungful of air lightly scented with kerosene.

Cade saw the SEALs place the litter on the asphalt and each take a knee and place a gloved hand on their helmets. The white Honda was parked sitting on the periphery of what looked to be eight empty spaces.

Then the helo cut the air overhead and made a high-speed turn to the right. As it flared and the engine whine ratcheted up, a pair of foot-locker-sized panels opened below the cabin doors and the landing gear emerged and locked into place.

Cade saw the mini-gun protruding from its port fore of the open starboard side cabin door. The wicked death-dealing snout was still smoking and probing the air in tight little circles, searching for any threats to the chopper or team.

Cade watched the SEALs rise and hustle toward the helo as it touched down and bounced lightly on its bulbous tires. Then he turned to cover Lopez, who had just stopped in his tracks and was looking up at the building, oblivious of the Zs flanking him from the driveway to the south. The Delta operator was shielding his eyes against the mirrored glare and pointing at a person waving a pink towel from a freshly broken-out window four stories up. Then, to be heard over the rotor wash buffeting all of them, Lopez said loudly over the comms, "There's a survivor on the fifth floor."

With the images of withered geriatrics jumping to their deaths from the roof of the old folk's home in Atlanta and then being forced to loiter while mercy kills were delivered still fresh in his mind, Ari broke in over the comms and bellowed, "Get your asses into the helo. I have an idea."

The Delta operators made it to the chopper just as Skipper let loose another quick burst with the Dillon. With the heat from the still-whirring barrel warming the right side of his face, Cade hopped aboard and spun around on one knee. He took one quick glance up at the building and then grabbed ahold of Lopez's gloved hand and pulled him aboard. A beat later Cade was being pressed down by g-forces; his stomach entered his throat and the ground began falling away rapidly outside the open door.

There was a deafening silence when the mini-gun stopped whirring. Cade spun around and planted his backside on his usual seat and felt the helicopter tilt on axis as it rolled back around towards the building. He felt a pang of remorse when he glanced at Lasseigne, whose flag-draped body was still strapped into the seat he died in. The corners of the flag not tucked under his thighs or between his helmet and the bulkhead fluttered in the invasive slipstream.

Then over the comms he heard Ari: *"What do you see, Haynes?"*

The other pilot, apparently controlling the FLIR camera and watching on the glass display, said, "One body. Female. She looks to be alone. Selecting infrared." A second passed and anyone looking at a monitor could see, judging by the reddish yellow glow emanating from the form, that the woman was a breather and alone in the room.

"We're all volunteers here," Ari said over the comms. "May I have five more minutes of your collective time?"

Lopez looked a question at Griffin, who was attaching the IV bottle to a slot in the airframe with a small carabineer.

344

Griffin said, "Nadia's stable, for now."

Remembering the women and kids he was unable to save from the capsized party barge weeks ago, Cade said, "I'm in."

Cross nodded.

***

With Ari piloting the chopper like only a Night Stalker could and Skipper guiding a rope and attached sling towards the window, Cade watched the delicate dance taking place via the cabin monitor.

Twice, the young woman, who was canted forward with a curtain wrapped around one hand and swiping away with the free one, nearly snared the wildly spinning nylon sling. And twice she almost plummeted to her death through the jagged opening. But on the third try the brunette snared the sling with a finger and dragged it inside the room with her.

Also watching the drama on the monitor, Griffin asked, "Won't the glass cut the sling?"

Skipper, who was guiding the rope, shook his head. Said, "Negative."

After holding his breath for a good ninety seconds, Cade exhaled when he saw the lone survivor return to the opening with both hands grasping the rope and wearing the sling correctly.

Ari said, "I'm going to pull her out sideways."

"Copy that," said Skipper, his voice all business.

And Ari did just that. He sideslipped the helo gently to port and the woman had no choice but to step over the dagger-sharp shards of glass and into the void.

In less than a minute the woman, who identified herself as Emily, was in the cabin and drinking greedily from Griffin's hydration pack.

***

Once the newest passenger was strapped into her seat, Ari pulled pitch, curled around to the west, and passed over the front of the apartment building. The four signature palm trees passed under the starboard side and Ari dropped them down over the pedestrian bridge, then nosed the helicopter south and west following just over the Interstate and backtracking the way they'd come.

A few seconds later they were orbiting Los Angeles Coliseum and Cade was watching the Osprey rise up slowly from the faded gridiron. He looked away and asked Griffin about the wound to his arm.

"I'll live," was all the SEAL offered up before going back to tending to the new passengers.

Finally, the Ghost Hawk made a sweeping right turn to the east and after a minute or two the Osprey had cleared the flag standards ringing the coliseum, was formed up off the starboard side and remained there while Ari lined up for the first of two aerial refuels necessary to see them from Los Angeles to Mack and eventually Schriever, and no doubt what was guaranteed to be one hell of a tearful reunion for the small Nash family.

Cade remained awake while both the Ghost Hawk and Osprey drank and then watched the Hercules disappear following a north by east heading. He shifted his gaze from the litter on the floor and got Lopez's attention. He said unashamedly, "Wake me up just before we refuel again."

Lopez nodded and smiled. Cade had no doubt the new captain was pleased after having saved an additional life, especially after having lost Sergeant Kelly *'Lasagna'* Lasseigne to Omega via the smallest of bites.

Chapter 64

With the F-650 nosed in close to the two vehicles blocking the road and the engine idling away, burning copious amounts of precious fuel, Brook stayed in the driver's seat, drumming her fingers on the wheel. Finally, after having come to some kind of decision, she killed the engine. Tapping out a final verse to whatever tune she'd been replicating she faced Chief, turned on her nurse's charm, and convinced the obviously ailing man to stay in the truck and be their lookout.

She grabbed her carbine, popped the door open, and leaped down to the road. Covered the twenty feet to the jam with purposeful strides. Walked around the camouflage K5 Blazer, peering into the windows glazed with road grime and who knows what else. She noticed after finishing her loop that the two-door 4x4 was missing a headlight up front and there was dried blood and hair and scraps of flesh stuck to the grill. Seeing only camping gear and a couple of long guns inside the rig, she trudged back to the driver's side and the body prostrate behind the bullet-riddled door.

She knelt next to the fourth person she'd killed to date, took a deep breath and rolled the corpse over. The body moved easier than she'd anticipated. However, a pile of greasy entrails spilled out onto the road, leaving her face-to-face with a dead man's gaping abdominal cavity and the partially digested remnants of his final meal.

Fighting the urge to vomit, she tore her eyes from the damage the half-dozen bullets fired from her carbine had caused. She shifted her gaze to the upturned face, which had no kind of a calming effect on her gag reflex. To the contrary, it made her think of who he might have been. Made the kill personal. And much like Wilson and Taryn, the kid looked to have been in his late teens or very early twenties. His slim face was framed by a full head of wavy dark hair and similar colored sideburns working their way toward a merger with a week's old growth of beard. Close set brown eyes, an aquiline nose, and thin lips seemed to point to some kind of Slavic descent way back.

The corpse was clad in blue jeans and wearing sturdy leather boots, laced up tight. A simple cotton long-sleeved shirt was blood-soaked and sticking to its pallid skin. For some reason the once white item was hiked up to his sternum. Maybe it caught on the shredded door panel when the kid collapsed vertically to the blacktop. She'd never know. But she would take the sight and smell of the dead man's gutted torso to her grave. That was for sure.

"Wasn't worth it ... was it?" mumbled Brook, closing his staring lifeless eyes with a practiced swipe of two fingers. "Lonely stretch of road and you couldn't share." Grabbing the corpse by the boots, she leaned back and lugged it to the ditch, leaving a slimy trail of guts and organs and streaks of bloody fecal matter.

Walking clear of the gory trail, Brook went around back of the camouflage rig and knelt by the corpse of what looked to have been a young woman in life. The parts pointed to it: small breasts and thin hips that child birth had yet to change. And judging by the long locks of dark hair, Brook guessed this corpse and the other had been related.

But there was no way to be certain. Like its dead friend, this corpse's pockets were also empty. Moreover, Chief's volley had erased its narrow face, leaving a half-moon-like chasm displaying gelatinous clumps of brain and all of the intricacies of the human body's internal cranial structures.

Shivering with disgust, Brook relieved the corpse of the ballistic vest. Knocked it against the road, attempting to dislodge fleshy bits and shards of bone—some with hair and pale dermis still attached. Suddenly overwhelmed by the reality of what had just happened, Brook went to all fours and added the contents of her stomach to the detritus already painting the road.

While Brook moved the bodies, the Kids, staying true to their word, had gone about the grim task of wrapping Jenkins's ruptured head with a patrolman's jacket found in the back of the Tahoe. Then, working together, they managed to man-handle his two-hundred-plus pounds of dead weight to the Raptor and into its bed.

By the time Brook finished emptying everything in her stomach onto the road, the Kids had rounded up all of the useful gear and weapons and loaded it into the back of the F-650.

A few short minutes after the aggressors had initiated the deadly encounter, the Kids were back in the Raptor—waiting patiently. Business as usual.

Wiping her mouth with the back of her hand and with a sadness welling up, Brook rose to standing and made the slow walk to the Blazer's open door. She reached in and rattled the transmission into neutral. Hinged over and found the T-handle and popped the e-brake. Standing on the road, feet a shoulder's width apart, she muscled the wheel, fighting against friction and tonnage and got the big tires moving to the right a few degrees. Still sweating from exertion and the late afternoon heat rising off the road, she hurried back to the F-650 and clambered aboard.

"All in a day's work," said Chief, "And just in time." He pointed past the Blazer across undulating fields and foothills to a point far in the distance where a sliver of road dipped and rose back up. There, silhouetted against the blue-gray horizon, was a giant dust cloud created by what could only be a large contingent of dead which appeared to be bearing north on 16—straight for them.

She placed her carbine next to her, barrel to the floor. She sighed and said, "Can't be that many of them on this lonely stretch of highway. Can there?"

Wisely, Chief made no reply as Brook fired up the motor, engaged the transmission, and popped the e-brake.

Only a gentle nudge from the Ford's heavy-duty bumper was necessary to get the scavengers' Blazer moving. A beat later gravity grabbed the smaller rig and it started a shallow turn towards the ditch, and Brook accelerated briskly through the newly created gap.

"A dirty job. But somebody had to do it," said Brook as she watched the dead kids' truck slow roll backwards into the ditch and lurch to a stop amidst a puff of dust, the whip antennas vibrating madly. She kept the truck rolling slow until she saw the Raptor had successfully negotiated the narrow patch of blacktop flanked on one side by the inert Tahoe and on the other by the listing Blazer.

"Which ... the killing or the cleanup?" asked Chief, feeling the rig accelerate and nose into a right hand sweeper.

Brook returned her gaze to the road. "The killing," she stated softly.

They skirted the west side of Woodruff and after a couple of blocks the overhead lines and power poles kept going straight and Main Street took a hard jog left and then became Highway 16 again. A short drive later the gray strip of two-lane curled right and there was a long straight-away hemmed in by fences bordering fields that pushed up against houses and outbuildings set way back. The scenery was occasionally split up on the left and right by gravel drives and the ubiquitous accoutrements of country living: tired-looking tractors and rusted-out cars. They saw a burn pile stacked high with charred skulls and knobby vertebra and gnarled limbs. Saw lone Zs traipsing the countryside here and there.

But the road was clear for the first couple of miles.

Out of the blue, Chief said, "Thanks for taking care of the girl. That was a girl ... right?"

Brook nodded. Thought about how there was nothing menacing about the pair—save for the fact that they'd fired on her and her friends first. She gripped the wheel tight one-handed and swiped some stray tears away with the other.

"I'm dying," Chief said, his eyes locked on the low hills outside his window.

Brook drove in silence for a while. Finally, when the straightaway was coming up to a slight bend, she said, "I know. But you need to hold on. Don't leave us before the miracle."

Brow furrowed, he said, "What do you mean?"

"Just hang on. I remember you saying you never got sick. How you had the constitution of a bull elephant. Remember that?" She wiped another tear.

"I'm Percy Blackwing and I approved that message." Chief saw Brook do a quick double take.

"That's your real name?"

Nodding, he said, "Yeah. See why I preferred Chief?"

Brook smiled. "You have a valid point."

"Percy was my granddad's name."

"Thanks for sharing that with me. But I was serious when I said *hang on*. Tap that fucking constitution, Chief."

"Does this have something to do with the antiserum everybody was going on about right after you and Raven and Cade arrived?"

Keeping her eyes on the road, Brook nodded and, in a low voice, said, "Just hang on. *Please.*"

Chief pulled his right pants leg up. He showed Brook the pair of zip-ties he'd fashioned into a big loop. It was cinched down below his knee and the ragged scratches below it were blazing red. The rest of his leg, however, from the makeshift tourniquet on down, was turning a troubling shade of blue. With a granite set to his jaw, he said, "I'm one step ahead of you. Took care of it when you were chatting with the Kids. I figured it might help me make it back to the compound ... alive. I've got a special place where I plan to end it."

Brook shook her head. She said, "The bite is below your right buttock."

Inexplicably, he chuckled. "I got bit on the buttocks." He said buttocks all nasally and Forrest-Gump-like.

Brook couldn't smile at that. She just heard: *I've got a special place where I plan to end it* over-and-over and it made her think of the ending to *Where the Red Fern Grows*. Only that was about a boy losing his Redbone Coonhound. This was different. She was on the verge of losing a gentle soul who she'd grown fond of these past few weeks. Not wanting to cry, she kept her eyes ahead and pedal pinned and dodged the trickle of walkers coming at them. A short while later, she slowed and negotiated a pair of wrecked cars and saw another roadblock off in the distance. Only this one wasn't made of metal, glass, and rubber. And there were no warm bodies with trained weapons and shadowy ambitions.

This impediment to further forward travel was the distant movement responsible for the dust cloud Chief had pointed out just minutes ago. It consisted of cold flesh and bone. The weapons: tooth and nail. Shadowy or otherwise, there were no ambitions. Only an unstoppable drive and built-up lock-step momentum fueled by an insatiable hunger for human flesh. And there were thousands of them, shoulder to shoulder, still kicking up dust and grass seed as they came down off the rise nearly a mile distant.

Chief chuckled again and said, "So much for your lonely stretch of highway."

Brook said nothing. She braked hard and whipped the truck into a quick left-hand one-eighty. Gravel was kicked up and pinged the slewing Raptor as the wheels on Chief's side came dangerously close to entering the ditch beyond the shoulder on the southbound lane. But Brook powered through the turn and merely gestured to a startled Taryn and mouthed *follow me* as the two trucks passed side on.

Chapter 65

A little over an hour and roughly two hundred miles from east Los Angeles, Cade was awakened by loud voices. Keeping his eyes closed, he surreptitiously upped the volume on his head set and eavesdropped while Cross and Griff argued over which of the famous Las Vegas Rat Pack was the coolest. After a lengthy period of back and forth banter during which Cross proclaimed adamantly that Dean Martin was *the shit* and Griffin protested by saying that *the warbling drunk couldn't carry Sammy Davis Junior's jock strap*, a God-like voice boomed from the cabin speakers and Ari settled the affair by announcing *Elvis Aaron Presley* as the coolest of them all.

Groans filled the cabin and Haynes's voice rode over them all as he scolded Ari for not knowing the *Rat Pack* from the *Brat Pack*.

Eyes still closed, Cade smiled and tried to tune out the verbal melee as it took a new tangent and the aircrew and team of operators began discussing the cinematic merits of *Weird Science*, *Pretty in Pink*, and finally *The Breakfast Club*. Cade nodded off after hearing Ari declare how much of a crush he had had on Molly Ringwald *back in the day*.

If Cade would have taken a peek before drifting off again he would have seen Nadia sitting on the fold-down seat next to Skipper, the IV bag now hooked to the superstructure overhead, tubes still delivering electrolytes into her arm.

And he would have gotten a morbid chuckle from the permanent look of incredulity projected by Emily, who, ninety minutes into the trip, was still coming to grips with having had the misfortune of being strapped into an uncomfortable seat beside an American-flag-draped dead body inside an aircraft that looked like it had been sent from outer space to rescue her.

But he hadn't. He was asleep and blissfully unaware of the trials and tribulations faced by his better half, roughly four hundred miles away north by east as the crow flies.

Chapter 66

To create some distance from the horde, Brook quickly pushed the F-650 past sixty. With the Raptor keeping pace, she blasted north down 16 for nearly a mile and then braked violently and slewed the rig between a pair of nondescript wooden fence posts, choosing the drive based solely on how far off the road the cluster of buildings representing a modicum of shelter were located.

So as not to create a telltale cloud of dust for the monsters to follow, she kept the speed down as the truck lurched and bucked over the pitted dirt track.

Post and beam fencing, gnarled by time and weather, filed by slowly, left and right. Beyond the fence was a vast beaten-down pasture corralling the gnawed-on remains of dozens of some species of hooved creature. And caught in the patches of barbed thistle slowly retaking the land were softball-sized tufts of fine fur or wool in differing shades of brown and orange.

The radio in the console vibrated. Steering one-handed, Brook snatched it up, keyed to talk, and said, "What?"

"What? That's all you've got? What are you getting us into is what I'd like to know," wailed Wilson.

"It's what I'm trying to get us out of, Wilson. Besides ... I've come this far. I'm not going back without the stuff I came for. After the herd passes, you can get the hell out of here if you like."

"If the herd passes," said Sasha in the background.

There was a second of silence on the open channel before Wilson said, "You saw what happened to Jenkins's Tahoe. You dang well better hope they didn't see us."

"Even if they did, we put enough distance between us and them. We'll lay low and let them pass," Brook said. "After they do ... you can do what you want. Go back to the compound ... whatever suits you."

Ignoring Brook's offer, Wilson said, "I just hope whatever killed those animals in the field aren't still here."

Chief shook his head.

Brook said, "Chief says they're gone. I'm hoping there's no humans here."

Again Chief shook his head.

Brook said nothing.

The truck crested a rise and lurched into a deep pothole and came out the other side with a slight side-to-side shimmy that quickly dissipated. Dead ahead was a dingy white turn-of-the-century farmhouse. The two-story swaybacked affair had a wraparound porch and a white picket railing partially obscuring a pair of wooden rocking chairs. Opposed diagonally, a hundred yards right of the house, was a brick-red barn connected to a towering metal silo. The doors were huge slabs of wood painted red with opposing white timbers marking each with a big X. The doors, which appeared to slide open horizontally from each other—likely on wheels riding inside a hidden overhead track—were secured with a pair of industrial-sized padlocks, their chromed cases gleaming mightily in the sun.

Breaking off from the unimproved approach to the house was a gently curved left-to-right drive, like a hand scythe minus the straight grip. A handful of trees, neither small nor large, lined the south side of the west-facing home. A mess of gravel was strewn about in front for parking on.

Behind the house, providing a natural barrier of sorts east and north, was a narrow winding river, its blue water making a constant lazy churn south to an inevitable merger with the Green River.

Brook keyed the radio and said, "We're here." And after a second glance at the impenetrable-looking barn doors, added, "We'll turn around and park both trucks out of sight beside the barn."

"As if we have a choice," said Wilson. "Wouldn't *inside* the barn be safer?"

Ignoring the comment, Brook put the radio aside and cut the wheel to negotiate the narrow opening between a tilling tool adorned with dozens of rusting discs and a green tractor that looked highly capable of towing it. A tick later she stopped mid-turn when the door to the home opened and out stepped a slightly stooped gray-haired man with a long gun cradled comfortably in his withered hands. The relic, looking to have hailed from the Hatfield vs. McCoy era, had an ornately carved stock and side-by-side blued barrels that were presently moving on a steady upward arc.

Staring down the dual muzzles that looked capable of slinging quarter-sized chunks of lead her way, Brook made a snap decision which was partially dictated by the last encounter, yet mainly a byproduct of what her gut was telling her. She stuck her left hand out the window, palm down, and made a patting motion she hoped the Kids would interpret as *stand down*. With the barrel still aimed at her open window and unwavering, she stilled the engine and smiled at the man.

Eyes moving steadily between the two trucks, the man said, "There's a high-powered rifle trained on the tattooed girl's head. You're trespassing. Turn around and leave now and nobody gets hurt."

Brook grabbed her Glock off the seat and made a show of placing it on the dash. Then she stuck that hand out the door and opened it from outside.

The man took a step closer to the porch's edge, but stayed in its shadow. He said, "You have to five," and started a count.

Brook lowered herself to the ground and moved into the open, hands up. She cast a glance at the Kids and locked her gaze with a wide-eyed Sasha. Slowly, she mouthed, "It's going to be OK," then turned back and took a step towards the old man. "Please let us stay out here, in our trucks, until those things pass. We'll be no trouble ... we won't ask for a thing. And we'll leave the second they pass."

The man was at three when he paused the countdown and said, "If you leave now, you can get ahead of them and go back the way you came from. At least you'll live to see another day."

"We ... I can't. My little girl is dying," she said. "She might not see tomorrow if we don't get to the next town south of here. There has to be a pharmacy or doctor's office still not thoroughly looted."

The count didn't resume. The shotgun barrel drooped a few degrees and the man just stared at Brook.

Brook could almost hear the gears turning. As if the pendulum of fate was once again swinging in her family's direction. Maybe it was her lucky day and the blade had just cleaved Mister Murphy in half for her.

Finally, after a couple glances at the horde, which by now was creating a kind of humming sound from their combined footfalls and low guttural moaning, the old guy rooted in a pocket and tossed a set of keys on the dirt near Brook's feet. "I don't much like tattoos," he said. "The guy in your rig goes with the others. I want you to lock them all inside the barn and then you return *with* the keys... and unarmed."

I'm his insurance policy, thought Brook. She smiled and nodded to the old man and then scooped up the keys and hustled to the barn. She opened both locks and, with Wilson's help, parted the heavy doors.

In seconds she and Taryn had wheeled the trucks inside the barn and, after sharing a few words with Chief and the Kids, Brook was alone outside the red doors and snapping the locks shut.

"Hurry. *Now*," called the man from the porch, gesturing with the shotgun. "They're real close."

Once inside and the man had battened up the door behind them, Brook looked around at the dark wood-paneled walls, letting her gaze settle on the works of art and ceramics scattered here and there. All in all, inside, the place seemed a few decades more modern than the impression she'd gotten upon first seeing the place. Continuing her covert recon, she glanced at a stairway a dozen feet to her right and following the stairs up caught a brief glint of light off of metal. As she squinted, trying to see into the shadowy recesses, the man said, "I'm Ray. I want you to meet my better half, Helena."

There was a creaking from the direction of the stairs and a woman with a cherubic face and rosy cheeks emerged into the bars of light spilling through the rectangular window above the front door. She smiled and lowered the bolt-action hunting rifle Brook presumed had been trained on her the entire time.

"Sit. Sit," said Ray. He motioned to a simple bench pushed against a plate window overlooking the circular drive, barn and highway beyond.

Brook straddled the bench and said, "Thank you. And though she doesn't know it *yet* ... my daughter thanks you, too."

Ray set the shotgun aside and said, "Tell me about your daughter."

***

While Brook was recounting the bicycle accident and the resulting collapsed lung and the type of equipment she needed to fix the problem without making it worse, Helena was banging pots and humming away in the other room which had to be the kitchen, judging from the nice aroma wafting into the parlor.

While the matronly lady set the nearby table with service for three, Brook started at Z day and told Ray how she and her small family had survived that hellish nightmare, all the while praying the multitudes of monsters of their present-day nightmare would stop filing by so she could continue her quest south.

As if he knew what Brook was thinking, Ray cleared his throat and said, "Sometimes it takes the deaders hours to pass. We knew they were coming ... eventually. Helen saw a vehicle pass by shortly before you and your friends showed up. She figured they were being followed. And she was right."

Helen poked her head around the doorway. She said, "I usually am, Raymond."

Brook said, "There *was* a vehicle at the 39 and 16 junction."

"Camouflage paint and Wyoming plates?" asked Helena.

Brook nodded.

Helen entered the parlor and stood in front of Brook, a long kitchen knife in her hand. She hitched a brow and asked, "What happened to them?"

Brook stayed silent for a beat. Then she said, "You want the truth? Or should I tell you what I think you'd want to hear?"

Ray scooped up the shotgun and said, "While I appreciate your concern for our sensibilities ... considering the bandage on your noggin, the truth will do just fine."

Over the course of twenty minutes Brook spilled her guts. Held nothing back. She cried a little and when she was done she felt like she'd just emerged from a confessional. Not rejuvenated. But maybe absolved. At least in her mind.

"You have a trusting look about you," Helen said, gesturing with the knife. "And I think you all did what you had to do in order to survive. And you know, young lady ..." She paused and smiled wide. "I have a feeling Saint Peter will take that one with a grain of salt."

Helen disappeared into the other room.

Ray paced over to the window and said, "You see those carcasses in my pasture?"

Brook followed his gaze and nodded.

"Those *were* Alpacas. Beautiful animals. Me and Helena are ... were ranchers," he said. "Those bones out there *were* our retirement nest egg. Thirty head. Three hundred thousand give or take worth of animals and future stud fees ... all eaten by former humans that just climbed in there overnight. I gather they chased them until the poor things were tired out and then had their fill of them. Most expensive buffet ever were Helen's exact words after we awoke and found the monsters eating them. Hell, *we* were planning on eating a couple of them this winter. They're gone now. No use crying over spilled milk. Besides ... not much to spend a nest egg on going forward. There certainly is no trip to Florida in our future."

Ray liked to talk, that much was clear. As long as he wasn't holding the gun and Helen wasn't hovering nearby with a knife, Brook was happy to continue listening and nodding. Every few minutes, though, she'd look at the Zs filing by and wish she had the satellite phone and handheld CB so she could check in on Raven and maybe throw Cade a text to see if he was alright. But she didn't. So she remained passive and patient and sat looking out the window, willing Ray to keep talking, Helen to keep cooking, and the Zs to move faster.

Chapter 67
FOB Bastion

"We've been jawing for quite some time," Beeson said. He took his boots off the corner of the desk and reached behind him. He came back with the bottle of Scotch.

Perking up like a cat hearing a can opener, Duncan adjusted his butt in the chair and said, "What do we have there?"

"We've talked about every war from Nam on up to the two wars in the desert and the few bubbling in AFRICOM before Omega went and changed everything. The whole time—whether you realize it or not—your eyes kept coming back to this bottle. You have to have memorized the label by now?"

Feigning ignorance while keeping his shaking hands out of sight, Duncan said, "It's got a nice one ... looks like paper and colored foil."

"That it does," Beeson said, turning the bottle over. "What do you say we have a nip?"

"Maybe just a small one. Or two. But small ... I've got to get that bird back to the compound."

Beeson smiled. He peeled off the silver foil and cracked the seal. Pulled two plastic Solo cups from a half-sleeve of them and poured a finger in each. Handed the red cup to Duncan and noticed the palsy immediately, but said nothing.

Duncan took the cup in two hands and quickly downed the peaty-smelling whiskey.

"Slow down, fly boy," said Beeson with a knowing look in his eyes. "1981 Brora is meant for sipping. Spent twenty-three years in a cask. I'm sure it can stay in your cup for a few minutes. Can't it?"

Duncan said nothing. He placed the cup on the desk and nudged it forward a few inches, universal semaphore for *more please.*

And Beeson obliged. He poured the same amount in the cup, corked the bottle, and put it on the shelf behind him. He raised his cup in a toast and said, "To Cade's safe return."

Duncan reached for his cup, the tremors subsiding noticeably.

Utah Farmhouse

After a twenty-minute dissertation heavy on the pros and cons of raising Alpacas in the high desert, Ray's face lit up like he'd just figured out the answer to the old chicken or the egg conundrum. Brook figured either he'd had a mini stroke or was just plain out of material to talk about. With a grin on his face and the shotgun in hand, he bowed out of the parlor, promising a surprise and telling Brook to sit tight.

In the barn the Kids were getting antsy. With no windows to speak of on the ground level to see what was taking place outside, Wilson was forced to scale a treacherous ladder of simple wood slats nailed horizontal between a pair of vertical support beams. At the rear of the partially full hay loft, which—if he were to believe his own inner compass—faced southwest, he found a pair of sliding doors similar to the ones below. Only these were much smaller, designed to allow bales of hay entry into the loft, not oversized tractors and animals like the doors down below. Still, he couldn't budge these doors. However, he did find a knothole in a slat big enough to allow him to see the portion of the highway perpendicular to where the long drive to the property began its journey up to the house and barn.

The rotters were still filing by. In the five minutes he sat there with one eye pressed to the musty smelling wood, listening to Sasha braying for an update, he got the sense that their numbers were slowly tapering off. The other positive takeaway from his brief stay in the loft: There were no monsters traipsing up the undulating feeder road—that he could see.

Having seen enough to know they were going to be cooped up for a little while longer, Wilson scooted over the edge and, risking life and limb with each step, made it the twenty-five feet to the hay-strewn floor in one piece.

"Well?" Sasha said, even before Wilson could brush the cobwebs and bird crap from his pants.

"Shouldn't be too long," Wilson said. "Assuming the old folks didn't kill Brook and eat her and we're the next course."

Taryn put her arm around Sasha and said, "Don't say stuff like that, Wilson. We've got to stay positive."

He kicked some hay then, looking sheepish, said, "Sorry. Just kidding. I'm sure they're vegans or something."

Worming from Taryn's embrace, Sasha said, "I'm fine," and stalked towards the barn doors to look out at the house.

Letting her go, Taryn said, "How's Chief?"

"Sleeping. I think."

"Seems like he's sick to me."

Wilson said, "Like the flu or something?"

Taryn started walking to the F-650. She said, "Worse ... maybe."

"Like he's been bitten worse? No effin way. He'd have told Brook and she in turn would have told us."

Taryn climbed up on the black truck's running board. Cupping her hands, she peered into the gloom and saw Chief stir and turn away from the window.

Wilson said, "Well?"

Taryn answered, "He's sleeping."

Max padded up and sat next to Taryn and looked up at the truck looming over them both. Then he put one paw on the running board, head cocked, eyes, one blue and one brown, fixed on Taryn's face.

"If only you could talk, Max," she said, unaware how enlightening a gift of that magnitude would be.

"I see someone moving behind the windows," called Sasha, her face pressed firmly to the vertical sliver of light where the barn doors met in the middle.

Schriever AFB

Nash picked the sat-phone off the desk. She turned it over in her small hand and thumbed it on. After the screen came to life, she scrolled to the messages and read the text. With tears forming in the corners of her eyes, she read the text again, mouthing the words. Then, with her throat constricting and hot tears of joy pouring down her face, she plucked her pistol and the half-finished bottle of tequila off the desk blotter. She walked over to the picture of Nadia and her at USC. Took it down off the wall and planted a kiss on the small figures. She put the photo on her desk and turned around again in the small office and made her way to the filing cabinet.

It opened with the usual squeal and she placed the pistol in its holster and tucked it under some papers.

The bottle went in the garbage can with the others. She policed up the broken glass and it went in with the bottles.

Standing in front of the mirror hanging in her closet, she inspected her mess dress blues. Buffed the brass buttons that needed attention with a sleeve. Straightened her collar and tie. Smoothed her skirt and looked at the ceiling reflected off her highly polished shoes.

Methodically, she undressed and stowed everything away in the garment bag. Then she retrieved the crumpled ACUs from the floor and dressed quickly. Bloused the trouser legs and laced up her boots.

Once again comfortable with her place in the world, rank in the Air Force, and her standing with her daughter, Major Freda Nash grabbed a sleeve of Rolaids from her desk drawer, her cover off the desk, and began the short, yet oh-so-long, walk to the Tactical Operations Center.

Chapter 68

Helena's voice carried from the kitchen. "Dinner is ready, Ray." Then, wearing a pair of red-and-white-checked oven mitts, she shuttled a shallow casserole dish from the kitchen and placed it on a coaster on the table. "Come, Brook. Let's eat."

Brook's eyes locked on the dish. The aroma seeping from under its lid was familiar. She'd had whatever it contained before, of that she was certain. Then, with a rattle indicative of a loose pane of glass, she heard a door open and close from somewhere beyond the kitchen, near the back of the house. A beat later Ray called out, "How long until we eat, honey?"

"I just called for you," screeched Helena.

"I was in the shed," Ray hollered as he shuffled through the doorway carrying a paper bag.

There was a rustling and a clunk when he set it on the floor.

Helena brought out another serving dish, the smoky aroma of ham wafting after it. She arranged it near the head of the table, placing a carving knife and fork at its twelve o'clock. Another couple of forays back and forth and Helena had some pumpkin pie filling and cranberry sauce on the table as accompaniments. "Sorry," she said. "I would've made a crust for the pie if I'd have known we were having company for dinner."

"What are you cooking all of this with?" Brook asked.

Helen put a pepper mill and salt shaker next to the casserole. She looked up and said, "Gas," as if she thought the question absurd.

Brook pulled out a chair and sat to the left of the head of the table. *Having company for dinner.* She shook the morbid thought and looked dead ahead at a curio cabinet, all dark wood and glass and filled with dust-catching knick-knacks. She glanced over the spread of food, pausing to watch the cranberry sauce, still in the shape of the can it slid out of, jiggle as she accidently jarred the table. The whole surreal scene was part dinner at her mom's house and part dining in the Twilight Zone. She was surprised Helena hadn't drawn up a placard and provided a fourth place setting for Rod Serling. Shaking her head, Brook asked incredulously, "How can you eat right now with so many of those things out there? And how can you expect me to eat while my friends are out there locked in the barn?"

Ignoring the question, Ray took his seat at the head of the table. Started carving the still steaming and very obviously—based on its perfect symmetry—canned ham. "Helena always cooks special when the surge of deaders shows up. They're back and forth here every couple of days. Means we eat real good at least three days out of the week. But we scrimp the rest of the time," he said. "So you better eat up."

Brook thought: *Like the last supper.* Feeling her stomach growl, she pushed her plate forward and shook her head. She said, "No way. I can't eat with you. Not now. Not in good conscience."

Helena sat down across from Brook. Smoothed her apron and unfolded a linen napkin which went on her lap.

Ray passed the ham and then spooned a fat helping of green bean casserole, complete with onion crisps, atop his slices of ham. "If you're not going to eat," he said, "at least let me indulge you in some *food* for thought."

On the verge of openly salivating, Brook nodded as she watched Helena scoop the creamy green bean goodness—one of Brook's mom's signature dishes—onto what looked to be the elderly couple's best gold-trimmed china.

Between bites, Ray said, "Are you familiar with Friedrich Nietzsche?"

Brook nodded. Said, "German philosopher who said *God is dead.* Even as bad as it's gotten ... I don't subscribe to his thinking."

"Wow," said Helen. "You're the first one who's heard of him ... so far."

Having company for dinner.

Brook squirmed in her seat. Nodded and watched Helena cut into the ham on her plate.

Ray put his knife and fork on his plate. Craned and looked out the picture window. He said, "Whoever fights monsters should see to it that in the process he ... or she ..." He smiled at his display of gender sensitivity and went on, "... does not become a monster. *And if you gaze long enough into the abyss, the abyss also gazes into you.*"

Brook smiled. Nodded again. She wished she had kept her Glock and tucked it in next to the small of her back. Just in case things got any weirder.

Helena glanced out the window and placed her silverware next to her plate. Fork on the left. Knife on the right. The napkin she refolded and arranged neatly at twelve o'clock. She cleared her throat.

Brook noticed the woman's red lipstick was smudged, some of it rubbed off on a front tooth.

Helena said, "To live is to suffer. To survive is to find some meaning in the suffering."

Doing her best not to sound flippant, Brook said, "Nietzsche?"

"Correct," Ray said. He bent over and snatched the sack off the floor. "It's been long enough since the main group of deaders passed to set you and your friends off on your own. But first I want you to have these. Figure given the circumstances ... we'll not be needing them again. I just hope it's what the doctor ordered ... so to speak."

Brook's chair squealed against the hardwood floor as she stood to accept the offering. She unfolded the top and looked inside and her heart skipped a beat. Trailing a shouted, "Thank you," she bolted for the door.

"You'll need these," called Ray.

After skidding on the hall runner and almost falling on her backside, Brook about-faced and rushed back and took the keys to the padlocks from him. Then, still speechless, she turned a one-eighty, straightened the rug, and was out the front door and taking the stairs down two at a time.

Before Brook could begin to doubt her reversal of fortune, she was at the barn with the key turning in the first lock. A beat later both locks were in the dirt and she could hear Wilson rallying the others. With those inside helping, the doors parted effortlessly.

Wilson squinted against the sunlight, his face a mix of emotion.

Brook said, "Chief?"

Wilson answered, "He's sleeping."

"Something is wrong with Max," said Sasha. "He hates Chief all of a sudden. Why do you think that is?"

Brook saw Taryn's features awash in worry. She said, "The Zs are gone, guys." She opened the paper bag, displaying the contents for all to see. "And we can go home now."

Nobody moved. Nor did they acknowledge the good news.

Wilson said, "When were you going to tell us about Chief?"

Brook glanced at her watch. Did a couple of calculations involving mileage and time and estimated airspeed. After a beat she said, "He's not dead yet. So there's still hope. But only if we go right now."

"He died when he got bit," said Sasha. "He did get bit ... right?"

"I think so," conceded Brook. "Just trust me. There's still a chance to bring him back."

Sasha mouthed, "Trust me," to Taryn. She looked at Wilson and, spinning a finger by her ear—the universal sign for *this lady is crazy*—she turned, walked a few paces to the Raptor, and climbed in behind the driver's seat.

Taryn's face suddenly lit up. She grabbed Brook by the elbow and said, "Does this have something to do with the thumb drive I found at Schriever?"

Brook nodded slowly. She said, "Let's go. *Now!*"

Sasha called Max and he came running and jumped into the truck with her.

Chief was snoring when Brook opened the door and climbed in. A good sign, considering the alternative. Plus, at rest, a person's metabolism is much slower. And in theory, so would be the speed in which the virus moved throughout his bloodstream.

She checked the sat-phone. Nothing new there. She thought about hailing the compound but decided once again no news is good news. So she stuck the keys in the ignition and turned the engine over, praying Chief was correct in his assumptions concerning his constitution. Then, with the V10 rumble echoing off the rafters, she amended her prayer, asking that her friend be granted a slow burn against Omega. She wasn't being greedy and asking for the same seven-hour rate of turn the DHS agent named Archie (the first surviving recipient of the Omega antiserum) had been blessed with. On the contrary. She'd only asked her God for another hour. Nothing more. Nothing less.

Chapter 69
Somewhere above Utah

The hollow thunk of the Ghost Hawk disengaging from the refueling tanker jolted Cade awake. Instinctively his hands went for his carbine. A millisecond later he recognized the white noise of the turbines and muffled rotor signature and relaxed. A tick after that he opened his eyes and stretched and noticed the trailing fuel line and fluttering drogue chute tracking slightly above and right of the stealth helo's nose.

Through the port side glass he saw the land below gliding by. From altitude a large swath of ochre desert was crisscrossed by gray stripes of road that merged and ran through a mosaic of circles and rectangles in varied shades of browns and greens. Tiny white and red structures, some with shiny corrugated roofs, rose up here and there. *Farmland going fallow*, he thought. *Nobody left to eat all that food anyway.* He returned his gaze to the blue sky visible through the cockpit glass and watched the gray-blue turboprop, still trailing the refueling boom, gain some altitude. Suddenly there was a flurry of radio chatter in his headset as rounds of beer were promised and then, as absurd as it sounded, considering money had lost all value, an argument broke out over which air crew was buying first. Then there was a whirr and a clunk somewhere fore and below his feet as the refueling boom retracted back into Jedi One-One's fuselage, thus reducing her radar signature by a large degree. *Not that it mattered*, thought Cade. All of the threats to the helo and everyone aboard were below them on the ground. And as long as Ari kept them airborne from here—wherever

371

here was—to the compound and his family, he didn't care if every Z they overflew detected the chopper.

Out of left field the girl named Emily asked, "How can you sleep this close to a dead man?"

Cade answered, "Because he's one of the lucky ones. He's not coming back hungry."

Emily couldn't take her eyes off the form so Cade tried distracting her with conversation. "Where are we?" he asked.

Still staring at the husk that used to be Lasseigne, she said, "I don't know."

But Ari did. And he just so happened to be listening in. He said, "We just finished our third and final refueling of the trip. We'll be setting down in fifteen minutes northwest of Moab."

"Why are we landing?" asked Cade.

"To transfer the girls. They'll go the rest of the way to Schriever in the Osprey."

Cade nodded. Said, "ETA to home?"

"Wait one," said Haynes. "I'm working it up for you."

While Cade waited, he alternated between looking out the port and starboard windows. For as far as he could see the landscape had a reddish-orange hue, made more so by the low westering sun. Smooth wave-looking formations rose up, lending the impression they'd been frozen mid-geological-break. There were spires of wind-eroded sandstone and canyons and arches both formed by eons of hydraulic influence.

Haynes finally came back on and said, "Ninety minutes. Give or take."

Cade fished out the sat-phone, hit a key to wake it up, and saw there were no new messages. Which was a good thing to see. So he tapped out a message to let Brook know approximately when he would be returning to the compound.

The phone went back into his pocket. Then he lolled his head right, closed his eyes, and through his lids still detected a faint residual glow of the sun-splashed landscape flitting by outside the starboard side window.

FOB Bastion

The two-way radio on Beeson's desk emitted an electronic trill. He picked it up, hit the Talk key, and said, "Beeson."

A voice on the other end came out of the speaker and said, "The DHS bird is ready."

Beeson said, "Thank you," though it was more of a grunt than two one-syllable words. He looked a question at Duncan.

Duncan said, "I was out of here two hours ago." He rose from his chair and thanked Beeson for everything.

Beeson said, "A little nip for the road?"

Shaking his head, Duncan said, "Thanks. But, no. I've got a fella who can take the stick now and again ... but I've got to be OK to take off and land that bird."

"Are you ... OK?"

"Thanks to you, I am now." With one hand already on the door knob, Duncan held his other out palm flat to the ground. It was no longer jumping like a live flounder in a frying pan.

Beeson tossed the empty cups in the wastebasket and gave the Vietnam-era aviator a wink and a nod.

***

Daymon rose from the ground, walked from the Black Hawk's shadow and met Duncan a dozen feet from Lev and Jamie, out of earshot. Talking slowly and putting extra emphasis on each word, he asked the older man how he was doing.

"Fine," replied Duncan.

"Fucked up. Insecure. Neurotic. Emotional?"

"Just the latter three," said Duncan. "I'm OK to fly. Raven, on the other hand ... is not doing well." He detailed all that he knew.

Running his hands through his stubby dreads, Daymon asked, "And Cade?"

"No idea," answered Duncan. Pointing at Daymon's hands, which were grease-streaked, complete with dirty fingernails, he asked, "You were helping them with the chopper?"

"Yep. And Jamie and Lev also. We learned a lot and helped shave an hour or two off of our stay here."

"I owe you then," said Duncan. "Stick time on the way home for Urch. Let's mount up."

A handful of minutes later the fully refueled Black Hawk was in the air and the little group of survivors had put FOB Bastion in their metaphorical rearview mirrors.

Utah Farmhouse

At the end of the rutted drive, after enduring the jarring return trip to the smooth asphalt of Highway 16, Brook rolled the F-650 to a crunching halt so Chief could find a more comfortable position for the thirty-minute ride ahead of them.

The second they wheeled out of the barn and the sunlight spilled into the cab she had noticed that his deeply tanned skin had taken on a gray pallor. Now, some five-odd minutes later, he was going white. She saw his eyelids flutter and said, "Chief. Can you hear me?"

Nothing.

Simultaneously, the two-way radio came to life and the sat-phone vibrated in her pocket against her thigh. "What are we waiting for?" asked Wilson in clipped syntax, a hard edge to his voice.

Brook said nothing. She thought: *He's stressed. Hell, who isn't.* She'd had a swarm of butterflies bouncing around inside her gut since the realization Chief was dying finally sunk in.

Pressing, Wilson said, "There's a trickle of rotters coming from the left. Let's go."

Brook said, "Gimme a second, will you, Wilson?" She tossed down the radio. Pulled up the hinged lid and stuck her arm elbow-deep into the center console, searching for something by feel. After stirring the contents and dragging her nails across the very bottom she came up with a handful of heavy duty plastic zip-ties.

Wilson again: *"Better look up now."*

Shooting the radio a dirty look, Brook snatched up her Glock, the suppressor still attached, and peered over her left shoulder. Always amazed by the Zs' tenacity she shook her head and checked the chamber for the glint of brass. Then, cursing under her breath, she punched out of her seatbelt and powered down the window.

There was a guttural groan from the passenger seat. Then, immediately following, a low rasp from the trio of deaders—as Helen and Ray had called them—carried to her window. *Deaders. Has a nice ring to it,* she thought as she squeezed the trigger continuously and the pistol bucked in her two-handed grasp.

"Good shooting," said Wilson over the radio. In the background, Brook heard Sasha up to her usual and hollering at Taryn to drive. With a looming sadness, Brook flicked her eyes to Chief , half-expecting to see he had turned. Instead, his eyes were open and he was smiling. He coughed and whispered, "Good shooting," then his eyes fluttered once and stayed shut.

Spirits suddenly buoyed, Brook shifted her gaze to the three fallen deaders. She let it linger on the child-sized monster with the thoroughly shattered skull and instantly recognized the pink shirt the little girl had been wearing when she turned. Printed on its front were the likenesses of six different Disney princesses: Snow White, Cinderella, Aurora, Ariel, Belle, and Jasmine. In a plastic storage bin under the bed she and Cade had shared in Portland was an identical shirt Raven had grown out of four years ago. Just one of the treasures that had no place in this new world.

With Disneyland's demise and all of the things she used to take for granted running through her mind, Brook secured Chief's wrists with two of the zip-ties. He was unresponsive now and seemed not to notice. Then she leaned across the console and tightened the seat belt around his waist, and with her head near his couldn't help but notice how his shallow breathing had turned ragged and now contained an underlying wet rattle.

Ten minutes seemed like a lifetime sitting in the Raptor with so much horsepower at her disposal and nowhere to go. Fingers knuckle white on the steering wheel, Taryn said, "Do you think Brook is doing what *I* think she's doing?"

"No," said Wilson. "If Chief dies we'll be the first to know. She wasn't lying to us about his condition before. I just think she didn't want to misdiagnose his wounds. With Jenkins gone she probably didn't want to jump the gun and sign Chief's death warrant."

Sasha said, "Lying by omission is still lying, Wilson."

Taryn turned to face Sasha and said, "Me and her have butted heads ... but I still trust her."

"And so do I." proffered Wilson.

Sasha nudged Max aside and leaned over the seat back and stared at Wilson. "Alright, *Amazing Kreskin*," she said, a thick vein of sarcasm in her tone. "Why don't you tell me what she's doing in there *right now.*"

Looking sidelong at his sister, Wilson said, "Cuffing him so he's less of a threat if he does turn."

Knowing there wasn't a valid argument to counter what Wilson said, Sasha growled something unintelligible and slammed back into her seat.

In the F-650 Brook rattled the shifter into *Drive* and steered the big Ford onto the two-lane.

Heading north on 16 with the Raptor on her bumper, Brook divided her attention between the scattered groups of slow moving Zs and watching the road a good distance ahead.

With the navigation unit still on the fritz and her gut telling her Randolph and the junction with 39 was near, she halved her speed from sixty.

Highway 16 jogged to the west and went laser-straight for a short distance with familiar-looking farms passing on the right and the T-shaped tops of power poles and horizontal lines showing through the trees north of them. Brook picked up the radio, keyed to talk, and said, "Stay frosty. I see Woodruff to the right so we're real close now. And if we encounter Zs around the corner I'm going right over top of them and making a thunder run for the junction." She looked at her watch. Thirteen minutes had passed since they left the farmhouse behind.

When Brook finally cut the corner where 16 became Main Street, trees and fencing momentarily blocked her view of the distant intersection. However, she could see the camouflage Blazer listing in the ditch opposite the southbound lane. But what troubled her most was that Jenkins's Tahoe was in the far ditch and the school bus was now perpendicular to 16 with its bashed-in front end facing her. It was immediately obvious the force of the passing horde when they emerged from the narrow highway and spread out at the junction had spun the bus ninety degrees to the north, leaving a fresh arc of yellow paint on the blacktop and the mess of pulped bodies it and the Tahoe had been resting atop exposed and drying in the afternoon sun.

Suddenly Taryn's voice emanated from the radio. Drawing the words out, she said, "We are fucked."

"Don't worry. We have a winch," Brook stated rather pragmatically given the circumstances. She stopped the Ford a dozen yards short of the inches-deep pink and white paste. And to her horror saw movement in there. A hand protruding skyward twitched and the fingers started kneading the air. Elsewhere, tethered by a knot of sinew and trapezius muscle and still receiving nerve impulses, a single left arm pulled along a misshapen head and length of bare spinal column. Reach. Grip. Pull. The disgusting mess moved at a glacial pace. Reach. Grip. Pull. She couldn't believe her eyes, but it was there—crossing the road from left to right.

Brook slapped the transmission into *Park*, grabbed her carbine and Glock, and opened the door. She paused and looked over at Chief and saw the rise and fall of his chest. She also saw the blue veins showing under his skin. Like runners of ivy they seemed to be climbing up his neck and branching out on his parchment white cheek. *Just like Archie.* She hopped down to the road, looked towards the Raptor, and motioned Wilson over.

Once Wilson arrived she gestured at the eighth of a former human being crawling near the centerline and watched with amusement as he flinched at the sight of it and made an instant course correction providing an ample buffer between him and the thing seemingly yanked from his nightmares. He formed up next to Brook, Beretta in hand, and asked, "How in God's name is that thing's arm still working?"

"The brain is still functioning and the still-connected spinal cord is delivering impulses to what's left of it. Simple biology ... or science."

Wilson said, "Or evil."

Brook retraced Wilson's steps and came at the oddity from behind and began raining blows with her M4's collapsed buttstock to its lopsided skull. After the third resonant *thunk* the futile migration across the highway had ceased. But for good measure Brook jumped off the roadway and, with all of her weight in play, delivered a final vicious strike with her rifle that sent a shiver through her forearms and split the skull cleanly in two. As fluid and dribbles of brain matter spilled out onto the blacktop, she faced Wilson and said, "It's done moving. Satisfied?"

Wilson's jaw dropped open. Wide-eyed, he said, "Remind me never to piss you off."

Brushing off the comment, Brook gestured at the open door. "Get in." She pointed out the winch controls; all the while Wilson was eyeing Chief.

"Pay attention," snapped Brook.

"Sorry," he stammered.

"Don't worry, he's not going to turn any time soon," she lied. Then she repeated what she'd said about the winch operation. Asked, "Got it?"

Wilson nodded. Pulled his boonie hat down tight over his ears. "You sure you can haul all that cable?"

"I watched *you* do it all by yourself at the Huntsville blockage."

Wilson made a face. He said, "Good point."

Before setting off, Brook patted the sat-phone in her roomy thigh pocket and then reached over and corralled the 40-channel CB and stowed it alongside. Handed Wilson her Glock and, figuring the horde wasn't too far down the road, told him to hail Taryn on the two-way and have her guard the horn with her life.

This time, freeing the hook from the slot in the F-650's bumper went easier than the first. She disengaged the tension and, holding onto the length of cable two-handed, hauled it over her shoulder and leaned forward in the direction of the bus. Legs pumping, she skirted the pile of formerly human detritus and, beginning to breathe hard, trudged past the bus's yellow roof. With the stubby M4 banging against her back, she curled around the vehicle's less-than-aerodynamic front end and dropped the cumbersome hook and cable to the road. She took a few more paces, propped her rifle against the greasy undercarriage, and slumped to the pavement, winded.

Sitting cross-legged and crying, she pulled out the handheld CB and reached Seth back at the compound. She asked about Raven and listened as Seth told her that the new arrival was a nurse. "Put her on," Brook said.

There was a rustling and then distant voices followed by a metallic clang. She heard footsteps and another rustle as someone picked up the handheld unit.

The lady calling herself Glenda and professing to be a nurse *back in the days before MRIs and CAT scans* said that for the time being Raven was stable but showing no signs of improvement. Brook interrogated Glenda a little by asking her questions about diastolic pressure and O2 levels and then asked to speak to Seth again. When Seth came back on, Brook made sure Glenda had gone and asked him specifically what his gut was telling him. To which he said he was inclined to agree with the woman who, after all, said she was a nurse and, so far, seemed to carry herself as such. Semi-convinced but powerless to do anything to better Raven's situation, Brook powered off the CB and was in the process of putting it away when she heard the scrabbling sound she knew all too well. *Nails on sheet metal,* she thought as she craned around, frantically looking for its source.

Seeing nothing and chalking the noises up to a lone Z trapped inside the bus, she went fishing for the sat-phone. Her fingers brushed the plastic and the sound came again, followed by a scratchy hiss, and before she could react the low hanging sun was blotted out.

The blow to her head nearly knocked her unconscious. She'd heard the sound many times before. Bone on bone. Skull to skull. Instantly stars swirled behind her eyes her head began to ache. Then something sharp was raking her neck and back as she struggled to rise. Her eyes flicked to her carbine and she reached for it. Her fingers brushed the textured fore grip but Murphy intervened and Newton's law was enacted and the rifle slid away from her, the barrel carving an arc in the road grime and clattering to the ground out of reach.

Fighting tooth and nail, Brook got a hand behind her back and, clutching something wet and cold and altogether slimy, yanked on it, using every ounce of strength at her disposal.

Wilson took his eyes off of Chief, whose chest, thankfully, was still rising and falling. He shifted in his seat to see over the large side mirror and craned his head looking for movement or shadow or anything to point to Brook's position in relation to the bus.

The sun was to the left and shining on the bus's undercarriage, so there was no telltale shadow. Moreover, the bus was flat on its side, so seeing her feet moving about was out of the question.

So feeling a tingle worrying the base of his spine, Wilson grabbed the Glock and kicked open the door. In half a beat he was on the ground and running headlong for the bus, oblivious to his own safety.

In the Raptor, Taryn had spent the entire three or four minutes they'd been sitting there on the road trying to keep Sasha calm. The girl was backsliding, and Taryn was growing increasingly tired of her antics. One moment she was praying for a roll of duct tape to apply some over her future sister-in-law's mouth and secure her wrists, and the next she was seeing Wilson out of the truck and sprinting towards the overturned bus.

"Stay here," she barked, and was out the door before Sasha could come up with a snarky reply.

Ignoring anything in his way—blood and guts and bone, it didn't even register in the moment—Wilson rounded the front of the bus, Glock leveled, a solid ten feet of spacing between him and the bumper. As his body cut the plane even with the bus's undercarriage his gaze fell on Brook. She was sitting cross-legged and rocking back and forth with the sat-phone in her gloved hands. As he drew nearer he saw her rifle on the pavement a few feet beyond her. There was a crawler an arm's reach away, its eyes gouged out and the back of its skull nothing but a pulped mess.

With the sun warming the right side of his face, Wilson approached the scene with caution. "Are you OK?" he asked.

Brook said nothing. She finished tapping something out on the keypad then looked up. There were tears in her eyes. She said, "How is Chief?"

Wilson kicked the half-corpse to make sure it was truly dead. And it was. There was no further movement. So he lowered the Glock and finally replied, "He's not looking good."

Brook sighed and said, "It's all my fault, you know. I lied to him. And I lied to you. I lied because I didn't want to lose Raven ... still don't."

"He likes Raven as much as any of us do. Plus ... he volunteered." Wilson helped Brook to her feet. Saw the smudges on her shirt back. Thought it could be oil or blood. Curious, he asked worriedly, "What happened here?"

"The Z fell from above and nearly head-butted me unconscious. Then I snapped out of it and found myself in a life and death struggle."

"And?"

"I'm fine." She powered down the phone and it went into a pocket. "Let me finish what I started."

She scooped up her carbine and handed it to Wilson. She said, "Watch my back."

"How is your back?" he asked.

She said nothing. Instead, she knelt near the exposed front wheels, searching for something sturdy to anchor the cable to.

Below the gore-spattered front bumper she found a hook twice the size of her hand. After closer inspection she determined, based on the way it was positioned and the size of the bolt securing it directly to the frame, that it was put there for exactly the purpose she intended on using it for. She wound the cable around the hook and clipped it to itself. She stood up and pulled it tight and gazed upon her handiwork.

Good to go.

Limping, Brook made her way to the F-650. She climbed in and saw Chief, who appeared to be in roughly the same condition as when she had left him. She retrieved her hat and saw his eyes move behind the closed lids. "Hang in there," she said. "Give me one hour. *Please.*" She started the V10, put the transmission in *Reverse,* and disengaged the e-brake. Applying very little throttle, she inched the rig back until the cable straightened and hummed under tension.

Glock in hand and his head moving as if on a swivel, Wilson backed well away from the taut cable. In case it snapped, the last thing he wanted was to be cut in half and end up looking like the thing Brook had just beaten to a pulp.

Feeling resistance building, Brook pressed on the accelerator and the Ford belched gray exhaust. Ever so slowly the school bus began to move. It wasn't sliding so much as it was pivoting on a point somewhere mid-chassis.

There was a tremendous groan of metal and then a voluminous grating noise as the nose moved a couple of feet. Seeing progress, Brook doubled down on the throttle and held the steering wheel as straight as humanly possible. She saw her efforts pay off when whatever had been creating the pivot point gave way and the bus spun another ninety degrees and started screeching across the blacktop tracking straightaway with the reversing F-650.

Waving both hands groundward as if he were fanning a stubborn campfire, Wilson bellowed, "Stop."

Brook hit the brakes and watched the bus grind to a halt and the tension leave the cable. When she looked over at Wilson he was pointing north down 16 and hoofing it towards the now inert bus.

Taryn saw what Wilson was seeing. Unfortunately so did Sasha, and she started a new and unusually loud bitch session that started Max to growling.

While Taryn stared at the advancing herd of dead that had no doubt been patrolling nearby Woodruff, she tried to calm both the teen and the dog using an even voice and reassuring words.

But that wasn't working so she said, "I'm about to backhand you, Sasha. Then when ... or if ... we get back to the compound I'm

going to kick the crap out of you. And don't think I'm not capable."
She stared into the rearview thinking: *Gauntlet thrown.*

Suddenly Sasha lost all her bluster. She sat back in her seat all
of a sudden silent, her lip quivering rather perceptibly.

Taryn watched as Wilson unhooked the cable and
straightened it out as it was reeling back into the housing somewhere
behind the bumper. Seeing the herd nearing the intersection and even
more undead tottering from the side streets and beyond, she leaned
over the console and popped the door. "Old trick my dad taught
me," she said to herself. She started the engine and got her truck
rolling slowly to the left and hit the brakes hard when Wilson was ten
feet from the passenger door. Equal and opposite reaction was in
play as the brakes grabbed and the well-oiled hinge gave, allowing
Wilson's door to open up right in front of him.

"Convenient," he said as he leaped inside, out of breath.
"Your dad teach you that one?"

"Duh," said Sasha from behind.

In the F-650, Brook could barely tell that Chief was still
breathing. He was, however, twitching, and that was a good a sign as
any. It was an absence of both that she feared the most because then
she figured there would only be a matter of seconds for her to pull
over and uphold her promise to him.

She took a second to call ahead and alert Seth to have the
gate cleared of dead and open on the outside chance Chief survived
the drive there.

Northwest of Moab

With their final aerial refueling of the very long day in the
books and the Herc and her aircrew, who were now owed multiple
rounds of beers, droning away somewhere over the horizon to the
east, the Ghost Hawk and Osprey, their rotors churning lazily, sat
fifty yards apart on an expanse of flat weathered rock in the middle
of nowhere, Utah.

Transferring Emily and Nadia, even with the IV still plugged
into her arm, had gone off smoothly. As Cade watched the dual

rotors pick up speed he wondered how the atmosphere aboard the Osprey was, taking into account that the dozen hard-charging Rangers who had been sitting on their thumbs this whole time had all basically just been given the job of babysitter.

He looked at Lasseigne's still form under the flag and said a prayer for the man. Then he heard the low growl of the turbines change to a manic whine as they spooled up. Gazing out the window, he saw pebbles bouncing on the red rock and sand blowing away in sheets. Finally the rotor blades seemed to lose shape and merge into one solid black overhead disc. Taking advantage of the nearly empty cabin, he stretched his legs out and, though Raven had been on his mind for the last few hours, tried to relax for the rest of the flight—however long that might be.

Then, with timing that couldn't have been better, Ari's voice sounded in his headset saying, "Next stop Huntsville, Utah. Flight time one hour, give or take." Then, a tick later, with timing that couldn't have been worse, the sat-phone vibrated against his thigh. He retrieved it quickly and, hitting a random key, brought it to life. The text message was short but dire. Immediately Cade said, "Can you get me there any faster?"

Ari came back on. "I can shave a few minutes off with the right altitude and a tailwind."

"Not good enough," responded Cade. Then, knowing the bigger bird's capabilities, if not the willingness of the aircrew to accommodate him, he went on, "How about the Osprey?"

"It'll get you there in thirty mikes," Ari said.

"I know it can. But will Ripley agree to take me?"

The Ghost's turbines quieted a little and in turn her rotors began to slow. A tick later Ari said, "I'll ask her. But I can't guarantee you anything."

By now a concerned look was on Lopez's face and he was mouthing, "What's up?"

Head craning forward, Griffin was doing his best to make heads or tails of Cade's unusual request. He pantomimed smelling his pits as if his BO was pushing the Delta boy away.

Cade said nothing to Lopez's query. He was already unbuckled and asking Griffin to hand over the kit containing all of his medical supplies.

Without a word Griffin thumbed the plastic quick release and handed it over.

Cade stuffed the remaining cylinders containing the Omega antiserum inside, zippered the bag, and clipped it around his waist. He patted Lasseigne's leg. Then he looked at one of the few remaining members of SEAL Team 6 and said, "I owe you one, Griff."

Carbine in one hand, rucksack in the other, Cade motioned for Skipper to help him with the door. In the next beat he was on the ground and running full on toward the Osprey and not looking back.

By the time he had drawn to within thirty yards of the black tiltrotor aircraft some kind of a decision must have been made. The rotor wash suddenly seemed less ferocious and the rear ramp on the big bird cracked open and started a merger with the slick red rock. Cade imagined one of two things happening. Either he'd been deemed crazy by his contemporaries in Jedi One-One and would be greeted by a few leveled rifles brandished by confused Rangers waiting with zip-ties to restrain him. Or he'd be welcomed aboard, no questions asked, and might just make it to the compound in time to deliver what he hoped to be life-saving measures.

In the end the latter had been the case. The ramp stopped at full open and the soldiers welcomed him. Within a matter of seconds, the girls, wearing confused looks on their faces, were being led back to the waiting Ghost Hawk by a pair of Rangers.

Cade buckled in and nodded to the loadmaster and then exchanged knowing looks with the remaining ten Rangers of the 75th. The same regiment he'd hailed from so long ago. And like him, they'd been conditioned to expect the unexpected. *Hurry up and wait* should have been the United States Army's mantra. Not: *Be all you can be.*

Chapter 70

Five minutes after negotiating the tight left turn onto State Route 39 West, and with the reverberations of palms slapping the doors a thing of the past, Brook was attacking the road like Danica Patrick—about thirty miles above the posted limit.

As the quarry entrance blazed by on the right, she hit a straightaway and between a break in the trees saw the blue and gold DHS chopper tracking for the compound on a more or less northwest heading.

After another five long minutes of negotiating the twists and turns and rollercoaster-like undulations of 39 at breakneck speed, the clearing and gentle arc of the two-lane near the compound's hidden entrance came into view. And there beside the road was a head-high pile of unmoving Zs and a black Chevy pickup sitting broadside to their approach.

Behind the efforts of a gun-wielding Ichabod-Crane-looking form that could only be Phillip, the gate swung open, allowing both charging vehicles entrance to the feeder road.

Inside the compound, at the security desk, Seth watched the F-650 barreling toward the camera providing the feed gracing the top left corner of the monitor. Like a bull elephant charging through the Serengeti bush, the running boards and mirrors on the lead truck churned the just-turning leaves and thistle and reaching branches of the ground-hugging undergrowth into so much colorful mulch. And hot on the black Ford's tail was the white Raptor, spewing a turbid contrail of like-colored foliage in its wake.

Over his shoulder, Seth hollered, "They're back," and returned his attention to the monitor. But this time he was staring at the panel on the monitor's right lower corner showing the image of the clearing.

In seconds the trucks were past the feeder road's blind spot and bouncing into the clearing. Both trucks came to a juddering halt and in less time than it took for the doors to open, Damon and Lev and Jamie were hustling from the Black Hawk towards the F-650.

Seth watched three of the Raptor's doors spring open and the Kids and Max exit in a flurry of arms and legs and move as one toward the bigger Ford.

Like it had just cruised to a stop in an Indy 500 pit, the F-650 was surrounded by bodies and Chief was hauled out and being carried towards the compound.

In the clearing Brook stopped for a beat and spoke to Duncan, bringing him up to speed on Chief's condition and Cade's impending arrival with the dose of antiserum. To which he said, "Is Raven OK?" She shook the bag's contents and said, "That's where I'm headed right now. When Cade gets here, have him see to Chief *first.*"

Fatigue showing on his face, Duncan nodded and picked up his end of the litter. He looked down on his friend's face and didn't like what he saw. The gray-white pallor and the veins made him look like what he was slowly becoming: a living corpse.

Seth jumped a little from the resonant bang of the compound door blasting open and pranging against the wall. He craned and swiveled his head in time to see Brook, her ponytail bobbing to and fro, take a sharp left towards the Kids' billet where she'd left Raven hours earlier.

Then the two-way came to life on the table in front of him. He took his eyes from the monitor to fetch it. He spoke briefly with Duncan then tossed the radio aside, stood up and pushed his chair under the plywood sheet passing for a desk. He moved his rifle and a couple of other things out of the way in order to make a path wide enough for two men carrying a litter to transit the space. Satisfied there was ample room, he stood with his back pressed to the metal wall and held the lone sixty-watt bulb up and out of the way. A few seconds passed and footfalls echoed in the entry and Lev and Duncan hurried by with the makeshift litter nearly scraping the floor.

In passing, Seth caught a glimpse of Chief, who looked like dog shit warmed over. Suddenly he felt a sudden and uncharacteristic urge to puke. With his jaw trying to lock open and saliva filling his mouth, he sat and put his head between his knees and willed the sensation to pass.

Brook checked her rapid stride at the turn, took a couple of measured paces and stopped and stood in front of the metal door. She breathed deeply, a half-dozen calming breaths, then rapped lightly and took a step back.

Someone from the other side said, "Come in."

Brook tried to place the soothing, motherly voice. Coming up blank, she nudged the door open and cast her gaze around the room's dimly lit confines.

Raven was on the lower bunk right where Brook had left her. A neatly folded washcloth was draped across her forehead, partially concealing her eyes. The person whose voice Brook had heard was sitting, back to the door, on a folding chair and turned as soon as the door hinged open. Seeing the lady up close for the first time, Brook pegged her as late fifties or early sixties. Born when fins on cars were big and families were bigger. The lady nodded and Brook saw a twinkle in her gray-green eyes and a softness to her wrinkled face that instantly set her at ease.

Without bothering to stand or offer her hand, the lady said, "I'm Glenda Gladson. Your daughter has been in good hands. Heidi is wonderful and Tran is no slouch either."

A cold chill coursed Brook's spine. She said, "Where are they?"

"Heidi went to see her boyfriend who arrived a few minutes ago. Guess he's been gone all day."

Brook nodded, confirming the situation. She set the bag on the floor and sat on the bed next to Raven's thigh. She looked Glenda straight in the eyes and asked, "What kind of nursing?"

The lady chuckled. "There weren't as many titles in my day. Don't worry ... I took care of your lovely girl in their stead."

Brook said nothing. She touched the bump on Raven's forehead. Determined the goose egg hadn't gotten any larger. Then she pulled the thin sheet to Raven's knees. Leaning over, she saw on her bare chest angry purple bruising that started low where her back touched the bed and spread upward, encompassing most of her ribcage on the right side.

"We cut her shirt off," said Glenda matter-of-factly.

Brook touched the back of her hand to Raven's forehead. It was cool to the touch. Which was a good thing. *No fever.* But her lips were still tinged blue. Which wasn't. "She has a right side pneumothorax from blunt force trauma," Brook said, all business. "And a couple of broken ribs, I suspect."

"I took a listen. Sounds real bad in there," Glenda said while she removed Brook's stethoscope from around her neck and handed it over. "I heard wheezing too. Does she have asthma or allergies?"

"I've got my suspicions."

"The crash must have been horrible."

"I heard it. It sounded hellacious." Brook shook her head and shot a pained look Glenda's way. "The aftermath looked no better."

"You look a little peaked yourself," said Glenda. "How are you feeling?"

Brook ripped open a foil packet and unfolded an alcohol wipe. "I'm OK to do this."

"I wasn't questioning that," Glenda said. "It's just ... the bandage there on your face. And there's the scratches on your wrist and neck ..."

"I'm *fine*," Brook said. "Has Raven been awake much?"

"Off and on. More off, though. Last time she opened her eyes was about fifteen minutes ago. She asked about you and tried to sit up and then it was lights out again."

Brook grimaced. Looked at Glenda and stated the obvious. "She's in a lot of pain." Then she leaned in close, kissed Raven's cheek. Whispering, she said, "Mommy's here," and though her daughter probably wasn't listening, let alone able to comprehend the fix she was in, Brook went on to explain what had happened and what she was going to do to make it all better.

Raven stirred a little. Her eyes fluttered and opened and seemed to focus. Then she smiled and whispered, "I love you, Mom." A coughing fit came and went and tears streamed from her eyes and wet the pillow.

"I'll get us some gloves. Where are they?"

Brook was about to direct Glenda to the dry storage to get two pair but remembered Chief was in there. Not knowing his state, she decided to chance it. Said, "We'll have to do without."

Shaking her head, Glenda replied, "If you insist."

Ignoring the connotation and inflection in Glenda's voice, Brook pulled a syringe from the bag and ripped off its sterile wrapper with her teeth. Took the safety cap off the large needle.

"We could use a local—"

"We could use a lot of things. These—" Brook motioned to the handful of supplies spread out on the bedspread. "—are for use on animals. But I'm going to have to make an exception and go with what I have."

Glenda said nothing.

Brook took the bottle of sterile solution and drew a few inches of it into the syringe's chamber. She felt Raven's dainty chest, searching for the second and third rib. Traced a line down from the center of her right clavicle to find the second intercostal space. Keeping her finger near the point of insertion, she asked Glenda to restrain Raven. Acting quickly, Brook inserted the needle an inch or so above the chosen rib, looking for a pleural space and the telltale bubbles indicating the needle was in the pleural cavity.

"Bubbles," said Glenda.

Brook pulled the plunger to aspirate the space. Without a catheter or specialized tubing called a stopcock, she had no choice but to evacuate the air a little at a time with only the syringe.

While Raven fought to move under Glenda's weight pressing down on her shoulders, Brook extracted the needle, expelled the air, and repeated the process two more times.

Glenda said, "Wish we could send her to x-ray."

Brook answered, "We're going to have to let time tell the tale." She ripped open another alcohol swab and wiped the puncture site. She kissed Raven again and dabbed some sweat from her brow, smoothed her dark hair back and rose. Said, "I love you, bird."

Glenda looked up at Brook. Saw sweat beading on her brow and upper lip. Passed her the remnants of Raven's T-shirt and said, "Are you sure you're OK?"

Brook turned and covertly swiped away a tear. She nodded and said, "Will you watch her for a little while longer?"

"I'd be honored," answered Glenda. "I'll treat her like my very own granddaughter."

"If my husband, Cade, comes looking for me here. Please send him to the dry storage. If I'm not there, I'll be in our quarters ... resting."

"This place can't be that big. Wouldn't he find you eventually?"

"There's a method to my madness, Glenda," conceded Brook. She looked down on Raven and, though it might just be attributed to wishful thinking, swore that the normal healthy color was returning to her lips.

"Oh yeah," Glenda said. She plucked a plain blue book with gold lettering on the spine off the floor and handed it to Brook.

Brook took the book and asked, "What's this?"

"It's a book I think Duncan is going to find very useful when he returns."

More tears were forming so Brook avoided eye contact with Glenda. She said, "I'll make sure he gets it." When she opened the door a blast of cool air hit her face. When she closed it at her back she felt all alone in the world. She stood there wiping the tears and looking at the book. Read the title: Alcoholics Anonymous. She dried the rest of the tears, tucked the book under her arm, and stalked off towards the entrance.

Once there, she stood in the anteroom in front of the closed door and listened hard. *Nothing.* There was no whining jet turbine. No thumping of rotors carrying up and down the valley. Then the door hinged open and before she could react Heidi entered the gloom and ran head on with her.

All Brook could do to keep from hitting the deck was drop the book and clasp the taller woman's forearm, and then right there in the tight confines they did a clumsy little dance.

A little startled, Heidi said, "Thanks. I guess I was in a little bit of a hurry. How's Raven?"

Brook released her grip and said, "She's stable for now."

"I only left her for a second—"

"No need to apologize." Brook paused for a beat. The sounds of excited voices filtered in through the cracked door. Nothing else, though. She scooped up the book. Then, after a pregnant pause, she said, "I'm the one who owes you an apology for my attitude earlier. Life's too short to sweat the small stuff." She rooted in her cargo pocket and handed over the sample packets of Celexa and pantomimed zipping her lip and tossing the key away.

A little taken aback, Heidi looked at the offering and said, "What's this?"

"Something that might help."

"I've been an asshole ... why?"

"I *know* that wasn't the real you. Besides ... I owe you for watching my girl."

"You and Cade were instrumental in me and Daymon reuniting. And for that I figure I still owe you."

"Cade ... yes. Me? No effin way. I just let him go and do his thing. It's easier that way."

"So if you're back and Glenda is with Raven ..."

"Go," Brook said, pointing at the door. "Be with your man. But wait ... give this to Duncan first thing."

Heidi looked at the book. Turned it on its side and read the spine. She looked up and smiled and stuffed the blister packets in her back pocket, then opened her mouth like she had something more to say. But no words came out. Instead, a tick later, she pursed her lips, did a little pirouette and was out the door.

Brook watched her go and stayed in the foyer until she heard the door open and close again. She turned on her heel and, passing through the security container, she peeled a sheet from the rapidly thinning legal pad and asked Seth for a pencil but got a black Sharpie instead. *You've got one shot at it, Brooklyn. Better not screw it up.* With a steady throbbing starting up behind her eyes, she thanked the man and padded off to the Grayson billet.

Once inside, she closed and locked the door and stood in the inky black listening to her heart beat. She found the hanging string after the second swipe for it and yanked the light on. Pulled over the folding chair and positioned it near her bunk. She placed the sheet from the yellow pad on the seat and emptied her pockets of the sat-phone and two-way radio, the latter two which she put on the bed next to the pillow. Slowly and methodically she stripped off her MOLLE gear and gun belt and placed them along with the Glock on the floor underneath the chair. She sat on the bunk and unlaced her boots and nudged them under the bed. She took a calming breath, pulled out the pen and, using the seat of the chair as a writing surface, jotted down a message and capped the pen.

After a short internal debate she decided to leave the light on. *Safer that way for all concerned.*

Exhausted, hungry, and feeling shaky, she stretched out on top of the sheet. Lying there she realized her hands were trembling and felt a little numb, like she'd been out in the cold for an extended period sans gloves.

She rubbed them together and blew on them a couple of times, then grabbed ahold of the upper bunk supports and shook the bed as hard as she could. Pleased to find it both sturdy in build and stable on the floor with her body weight added, she thrust a hand into her right thigh pocket and came out with a handful of zip-ties. She sat up and fashioned six of them loosely into three identical pairs of handcuffs. She slipped her feet into one pair and cinched them tight. Then she zipped one pair of cuffs around each wrist and tightened them down. Using a couple of the loose ties, she secured both cuffs to the bed's vertical support farthest from the door, bit down on the ends one at a time and yanked them tight, removing as much of the play as she could. Lastly, she thrashed and bucked atop the thin mattress, trying to free herself.

Satisfied she was going nowhere—alive or undead—she slid her left hand close to her right, rolled onto her side facing away from the door, and drew her bound legs up tight against her chest.

As she lay there thinking about Raven and Cade and all of the good times they had shared, a lightning bolt of pure mind-numbing cold coursed through her body, momentarily paralyzing her.

In a matter of seconds she could feel nothing in her hands and feet, and a sensation, like her skin was being slowly peeled away, began creeping up her four limbs.

I'm dying, she thought. *I'm really dying.*

A spasm wracked her body and her fingers and toes curled up tight. As the pounding behind her eyes increased from a heartbeat-like rhythm to a rapid-fire strobe of pure unadulterated white hot pain, the likes which she'd never experienced before, she inadvertently bit down on her tongue and mercifully lost consciousness.

Chapter 71

Thirty minutes after the desert transfer, and with, by Cade's rudimentary calculations, roughly fifty miles yet to cover, the VF-22 Osprey began to descend slowly. And as Cade looked out the window and watched swaths of wide-open desert and the occasional lonely copse of trees blaze by, a woman's voice came over the shipboard comms and all but confirmed what he already knew. "Thirteen mikes to insertion," she said. "Am I putting my bird down or should we kick a fast rope out for Mister Cade Grayson?"

In his side vision Cade saw the loadmaster staring at him. When he turned to face the man, he realized the Rangers were staring at him as well. A long couple of seconds rolled by, then a few half-smiles broke out and some of the men flashed him a thumbs up.

The loadmaster, a fireplug of a man with thick trunks for legs and arms that looked like they belonged to a MMA fighter, approached Cade and leaned real close. Loud enough to be heard over the incessant droning of the twin Rolls-Royce engines, the man said, "Your reputation precedes you. And now I know why Major Ripley signed us all up to ferry you from the middle of nowhere to the middle of Bumfuk Egypt. What's your preference ... rope or wheels down?"

Loudly, Cade said, "Rope."

The loadmaster, whose name tape read *Tanpepper,* flashed a thumbs up and said, "Thanks for your work out of Schriever."

Nodding, Cade said, "Thanks in advance for getting me out of this bird ASAP."

Tanpepper nodded and went about attaching one of the coiled thirty-foot-long fast ropes to an anchor point near the rear ramp.

Some of the Rangers were still casting glances Cade's way, which made him think they were the ones who'd kicked the shit out of Bishop's men a few weeks ago. He wished he knew for certain so he could thank them for doing the heavy lifting that allowed him to roll in unscathed to interrogate the waste of skin. But he didn't have time nor the energy. Getting to the compound was first and foremost on his mind. And rolling around in there trying to break free from where he had stuffed them was the memory of Desantos fighting the good fight against Omega before ultimately succumbing to the indiscriminate little virus. To have gone up against long odds so many times before and come out the other end the better for it and then end up going out the way he had was extremely hard for Cade to wrap his mind around—even after the passage of time and distance.

Over the comms Cade heard: *Five mikes.* He saw Tanpepper prepping the rear ramp for deployment. The loadmaster held up four fingers. Cade thought: *Hang on, Brook.* He checked the sat-phone one last time. Saw no new messages. So he read the last two again. The oldest of which read: *Jenkins is dead. Chief was bitten and doesn't have long to live. My fault.* Then, as if Brook had been fighting some internal battle or contemplating taking her own life to somehow, however misguided the notion was, atone for the perceived transgression, the final message, sent thirty seconds after that first gut punch, consisted of only six possibly life-changing words that read simply: *I was bitten also. Hurry back!*

Tanpepper was now holding two fingers up, like a peace sign, and the ramp had started the slow movement downward.

Cade tightened the nylon lanyard securing the carbine and swung it around his chest until it was behind his right shoulder next to his pack. Made certain his Glock was snug in its drop-leg holster. Tightened the hook and loop straps on both tactical gloves. Then flashed the ruddy-faced Marine loadmaster a thumbs up.

Tanpepper, who was now tethered to the bird with a safety strap, hinged over and grabbed the rope, took a step down the ramp into the eddies created by the prop-driven slipstream, and waited while the aircraft simultaneously pitched up and slowed noticeably.

Cade was tethered as well and had been watching the ground rush up. When the bird pitched back he noticed the gentle curve of the highway drift past, then came the treetops, pointed and seemingly reaching up for the Osprey. Through the canopy he caught snippets of the gravel feeder road now and again. Once all forward movement had ceased and the ground was spinning counter to the bird's clockwise rotation, Tanpepper heaved the coiled rope into space and stepped out of the way.

A veteran of hundreds of insertions such as this, most in the dark, some under fire, Cade grasped the rope and disengaged the safety strap. Though not in uniform, he flashed a crisp salute to the Rangers who were once again staying behind. He bumped fists with the loadmaster before stepping out into the void.

During the five-second slide to the wind-whipped clearing he was bombarded by a dozen different stimuli.

In the first second, painted yellow and orange by the setting sun and looking like an Old West snapshot, he saw the blue and gold Black Hawk at rest near the tree line, its blades already tied down. His eyes flicked to the motor pool where, save for the Police Tahoe and the battered Land Cruiser, all of the vehicles looked to be accounted for. As his body spun around a few degrees clockwise he saw that the solar panels were on their newly constructed frame and facing south.

As seconds two and three rolled by he saw expectant faces staring up at him. Duncan, and Heidi, and Daymon with his shortened dreads whipping about in the rotor wash, were all accounted for. Near the white and black Ford pickups, he saw Taryn and Sasha and Wilson standing in a loose knot, the latter redhead's boonie hat whipping wildly in the down blast. And nearby, prostrate on the ground, its face obscured by a flapping jacket, was a husky male body that by logical deduction had to be Charlie Jenkins's.

During the fourth second Cade's palms and fingers grew hot due to the friction of the fast rope ripping through his gloves.

And finally a wave of sadness hit him as the faces of the recently lost flashed in front of his eyes like a jittery film reel. It sped forward, frame-by-frame, one face at a time until his boots hit earth and he was left with the final indelible image of Desantos staring skyward, eyes open, features frozen in a death grimace.

Praying that he wouldn't be splicing Brook's visage into the feature anytime soon, Cade let go of the rope and, oblivious of everything and everyone, clicked the quick release and let gravity steal his carbine. He leaned into a full sprint towards the compound's entrance and began shedding gear. Legs pumping furiously, he slipped out of his ruck and it bounced and skidded and came to rest on the faux crop circle. He unbuckled his helmet and didn't look back as it fell hard to the dirt airstrip, took a weird bounce, and spun crazily into the long grass, NVGs and comms headset still attached.

Sixty pounds lighter than Cade, Tran failed to heed passage and took an unintentional hockey check near the door that sent him caroming off the metal jam.

"Brook," Cade hollered, his cracking voice preceding him and echoing in the tight corridor.

Startled for the second time in an hour, Seth stood up from his chair and suffered Tran's fate. He went sprawling, his buck-fifty losing out to Cade's bull-in-a-china-shop charge through the space. Flat on his back, Seth bellowed, "She's in the Kids' quarters."

Cade said nothing as he retraced his steps. He didn't stop to help Seth. Just stepped over him. He was on a mission. After a right and a left he barged through the door and into the container without a knock. He saw Raven staring at him wide-eyed. He thought she looked a little pale. Or it could have been the light. But overall she seemed to be OK. "How are you, sweetie," he asked as he went to one knee next to her bunk.

"I'm peachy, Dad," she said in a smarty tone. Then she smiled and Cade's gut told him she'd get by without him for a few minutes. So he shifted his gaze to the woman on the folding chair at the end of the bunk. He had no idea who she was, but seeing how she was alone with his daughter, someone had already vetted her—most likely Brook. He had lots of questions that would have to be levied later. And a very pressing matter just a few footsteps away. So he smoothed Raven's hair and gave her a peck on the forehead and rose, giving her the look he always did upon leaving.

And she took it for what it meant. He always returned when he said he would. Then her face morphed and the smile was replaced with a frown as she looked about the room.

Sensing a question coming, Glenda beat Raven to the punch. "Your mom wasn't feeling well." She shifted her gaze to Cade and said, "She went to lie down. She stressed that you should go see Chief in the dry storage room first. Said he needs your attention ... she didn't elaborate further."

Cade went into the medic pack at his hip and retrieved the antiserum. He exited the Kids' quarters and in seconds had negotiated the underground warren and was banging on the dry storage door. He stood there waiting. Heard some sounds behind the door. Hushed voices. Then a chair's legs screeching against the wood floor. Then there was only the sound of the three aluminum cylinders rattling in his palm as he worked them like a pair of worry beads.

The latch clanked and there was a creak of metal on metal as the door swung inward. Lev was staring out at him, a pained look on his face.

Cade handed Lev a cylinder. Figured after serving in Iraq he'd seen all kinds of medical treatments administered in the field. So he didn't waste words or time. "It's a modified auto-injector on steroids. Goes in the femoral artery." He didn't stick around for a question-and-answer session. He turned and, as he strode down the corridor, he heard Jamie say, "Oh no. Oh no. I'm losing his pulse."

He kept going. Found the door to his billet latched from the inside. So he took a step back—which was all the room there was between walls—and planted a size nine boot next to the spot where he imagined the latch snugged into the stop was tack-welded to the container wall. And he found it. There was a resonant clang—like a mini-gong had been struck. But the stop's weld was stronger than his first kick. So with the return energy still coursing through his bones and chattering his teeth, he took another step back and eyeballed the smudge of mud left behind from his first attempt. He took a deep breath and coiled his muscles and imagined he was kicking through a board at a Tae Kwon Do exhibition. It had been years since he'd set foot in a dojo, but muscle memory made up for the passage of time, and as he started his leg moving forward, for good measure, he pushed off of the wall behind him with both hands.

The weld on the stop must have been big enough to hold a battleship hull together. Because it held again. However, the pivot point where the latch was connected did not. There was a ping and a muffled clatter as metal parts rained down on the plywood floor inside.

Everything slowed and like his descent from the Osprey— when all of his senses had been fine-tuned—the scene inside came to him in little revelatory snippets.

He saw the left wall with articles of clothing held up by hooks welded there. As the door opened further he saw Raven's bunk pushed back against the far wall. *Her own little parent-free oasis.* Then he saw stocking feet and noticed they were trussed. And the ties binding them were secured to the bed rail by more of the sturdy ties. His eye traced right and saw Brook on the bed, her back to him. He was a step into the room and the door was coming back at him—fast. *Equal and opposite reaction.* He stepped left and the door missed him by an inch on its return travel.

He slid on his knees and saw the chair by the bed and his mind registered the bold black writing against yellow that said: *I love you both. Take care of my baby bird.* His eyes flicked back to her and saw that her small frame was trembling. Sharp tremors interspersed by a kind of nonstop judder. Then the bed moved half a foot as his pelvis hit the lower rail.

With one hand on her shoulder he tried to roll her towards him. Simultaneously he was biting the cap of the cylinder clutched in his left hand.

Realizing her hands were also secured to the bed corner and her body wouldn't move very far without them being cut through, he readied the injection and climbed on the bed and straddled her body.

Her skin was hot to the touch but there was a pulse, however faint. And like Desantos when Cade had carried him from the Ghost Hawk towards the infirmary at Schriever so many weeks ago, Brook was in the danger zone.

Cade removed the plastic cap with his mouth, exposing the needle, and spit the cap onto the floor. Without a nanosecond's hesitation he ignored her thigh and instead plunged the needle into her neck where her snaking carotid bulged just under her ashen skin. The antiserum transferred into her bloodstream with no noticeable effect. And like Lasseigne's plight many hours before, only time would tell.

Cade drew his Gerber from its sheath and started to carefully saw through the ties binding his dying wife. With each swipe of the blade he said a prayer. And during the entire process there was an overwhelming feeling of gratefulness that the blade was only cutting through thin strips of hardened nylon.

Once her feet and hands were freed, Cade stretched out on the bed next to her and, without concern for his own well-being, wrapped her in a bear hug from behind and clasped his hands below her sternum, locking his fingers.

As he nuzzled her neck and basked in her scent, he whispered into her ear, "Fight it, Brooklyn Grayson. For Raven. For me. There's no room in our lives for another ghost."

Thanks for reading *Ghosts*. Look for a new novel in the *Surviving the Zombie Apocalypse* series in 2015. Please feel free to Friend Shawn Chesser on Facebook. To receive the latest information on upcoming releases first, please join my mailing list at ShawnChesser.com.

ABOUT THE AUTHOR

Shawn Chesser, a practicing father, has been a zombie fanatic for decades. He likes his creatures shambling, trudging and moaning. As for fast, agile, screaming specimens... not so much. He lives in Portland, Oregon, with his wife, two kids and three fish. This is his eighth novel.

CUSTOMERS ALSO PURCHASED:

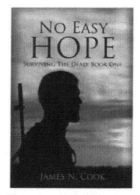

JOHN O'BRIEN
NEW WORLD SERIES

JAMES N. COOK
SURVIVING THE DEAD SERIES

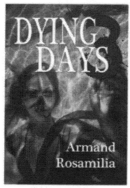

MARK TUFO
ZOMBIE FALLOUT SERIES

ARMAND ROSAMILLIA
DYING DAYS SERIES

HEATH STALLCUP
THE MONSTER SQUAD